JACK OF SPADES AND AMBUSH ON THE MESA

Two Full Length Western Novels

GORDON D. SHIRREFFS

WOLFPACK
PUBLISHING
— EST 2013 —

Jack of Spades and Ambush on the Mesa
Paperback Edition
© Copyright 2021 (As Revised) Gordon D. Shirreffs

Wolfpack Publishing
5130 S. Fort Apache Rd. 215-380
Las Vegas, NV 89148

wolfpackpublishing.com

Paperback ISBN 978-1-63977-090-8
eBook ISBN 978-1-63977-069-4

JACK OF SPADES AND AMBUSH ON THE MESA

JACK OF SPADES

CHAPTER ONE

A coyote howled through the soft velvety darkness. A spur chimed faintly like a cracked silver bell behind and below Jack Spade. He did not need to turn his head to look down the slope behind him to know that it was Burt Lasser. Burt stopped just below Jack. The sweetish odor of a Mexican cigarette drifted to Jack. He turned his head a little and spoke out of the side of his mouth. "Get rid of that smoke," he ordered. "Those soldiers down at the springs might see the glow of it."

Burt laughed softly. "Them nigger troopers can't see this far," he said.

Jack shifted a little on his belly. "Don't bet on it," he said dryly.

The spurs chimed faintly. Burt squatted beside Jack and looked down at him. "You ain't got your heart in this thing, have you, Jack? I've been feeling it for the last two days." There was a faint challenge in his low voice, but then of late that challenge in his tone was always there.

"It's a Federal offense," reminded Jack.

"Christ! You talk like a lawyer! That paymaster down there has at least thirty to forty thousand dollars in his moneybags and maybe only a couple of squads of nigger troopers to guard it. We can jump the camp just before dawnlight, get the loot, and be over the border into Sonora by midnight tonight. You know them buffalo soldiers down there won't fight."

"You could be wrong," said Jack. "Don't underestimate them. Besides, we're outnumbered. There are only six of us against maybe twelve to fifteen of them."

Burt took his cigarette from his mouth and eyed it as though he had never seen one before. "You afraid of the odds, *amigo?* You don't sound like yourself these days."

Jack raised his head and turned it to look at the shadowed face of Burt. "I'm not afraid of the Devil himself," he said softy. "You know it. Don't talk to me like that again— ever! *¿Comprende?*"

Burt placed the cigarette between his lips and drew in on it. The glowing of the tip lighted up the lean planes of his face and those curious, staring light-gray eyes of his that blinked about half the number of times of the average person's eyes. "It ain't the odds that are bothering you, Jack," he insinuated.

"So?"

Burt ground out the cigarette. "It's because it's a Federal offense, ain't it?"

There was more to his question, but it was left unsaid, and yet Jack knew what he was driving at, as he always did when Burt wanted to rile him.

"Just because you want to stay on the right side of the United States. That's it, isn't it?" continued Burt.

"You're doing the talking," said Jack.

"You're in trouble on both sides of the border. What difference does it make now?"

Jack bellied up the slope and peered between two rocks down the long slope to the springs. The wind fanned a fire into momentary life. The embers peeped through the thick bed of ashes like rubies lying on dark velvet. It was very quiet except for the faint husking sound as the wind rustled the dry brush on the slopes.

"Look! Dammit!" snapped Burt. "You've got to make a choice, Jack! You're either Jack Spade, an American whose mother was Mexican, or Juan Espada, a Mexican whose father was a *Yanqui*."

"The choice is not yours," said Jack over his shoulder.

"Maybe it's ours," replied Burt quietly. He jerked his head backward, indicating the long, dark slope behind him whose bottom held a bowl in the rock within which was the faint light of a fire.

Jack looked down the slope. Figures moved about the fire. They were all there—Toribio Vasquez, Mooney Dade, Josh Burson, and Lupo Zamacona. There was yet another. Estela laughed even as Jack thought of her. The laugh echoed from the slope and died away. "They're making too much noise," said Jack.

"I said: Maybe the choice is ours," repeated Burt.

Jack spat leisurely. He wiped his mouth with the back of his hand and shook his head. "No, Burt," he said.

"You got to crap or get off the pot, Jack," insisted Burt. "You're a Mex or you're a Yankee." He felt within his shirt pocket and withdrew the makings. He began to shape a cigarette. "If it was me, which it ain't, because I'm pure Yankee on both sides, and no offense to you, Jack, I'd take the Sonoran side of the border."

"Why?" asked Jack. He would know the answer well enough.

Burt slid down the slope and thumb-snapped a lucifer into a spot of flickering flame. He held it to the tip of the cigarette and looked at Jack with those curious, gray, staring eyes of his through the light drift of smoke. "Over in Sonora you're accepted for what you are, *amigo*. Your mother was a de Las Casas, and that still means something in the Valley of the Rio Nevome. Your father was a Texan who fought for the Confederacy and couldn't stand to take the oath of allegiance like the rest of them whipped Rebels."

Jack slowly closed one big hand into a fist.

"What is it they call them kind'a Rebels?" asked Burt.

Jack did not look at him. "You know," he said.

"Unreconstructed," said Burt. He fanned out the match. "Which means you ain't really an American at all, mister."

"Sometimes you talk too much," murmured Jack.

"Sometimes I don't talk enough! The boys are getting fed up! I'm getting fed up! We haven't made a good hit in months! Now we've got this chance to fill our saddlebags with maybe thirty-five to forty thousand dollars' worth of good United States currency and you're straddling the fence! By God, Espada! It ain't the odds at all! You still got it in the back of that thick skull of yours that some day they'll accept you on this side of the border. Well, they won't! You know what you are to these people! You're a spic! A greaser! The name John Spade don't mean a Gawddamned thing to these people! To them you're Juan Espada——a Gawddamned spic!"

Jack sat up. He got slowly to his feet. "You sound like maybe you think that way too," he said coldly.

"You know better'n that! Look, Jack! We get down there before dawn and get that loot. We split ass for the border and get there by midnight. Once we're over the border we're in the clear. The Rurales couldn't care less what we took from this side of the line. We can live like kings in the Rio Nevome country."

"On maybe five thousand dollars apiece?" asked Jack.

"To them greasers down there that's a fortune!"

"Greasers?" said Jack.

"There you go again! Listen, Jack! You and me are the brains in this *corrida*. We figure out the plans. We take the most risk. Maybe we should take the most loot."

Jack laughed softly. "Tell Lupo Zamacona that, or Mooney Dade, or Estela." His brown face split into a wide grin. "Yeh," he quietly added. "You tell Estela that, Burt."

"She's your woman, ain't she?"

Jack looked down the slope. The fire was very low. The faint aura of strong coffee came drifting up the slope with the night wind. It would dissipate before it could reach the sleeping troopers on the far side of the ridge. "She's no one's woman but her own," said Jack.

"Not even her own brother, Lupo the Wolf, can handle her."

"You in, or are you out?" demanded Burt.

"Don't push me," warned Jack.

"I got four men down there who agree with me," suggested Burt.

Jack looked sideways. "You just might be calling me with a lousy hand," he said.

"It'll be dawn in an hour," warned Burt. "I ain't about to be caught in these hills. You know there might be a helluva big posse to the north of us. We've lost enough time as it is."

"You're running the *corrida* now?" asked Jack.

"Somebody has to," replied Burt evenly. "*You* ain't."

Jack spat down the slope. "You haven't got the brains, Burt," he said calmly. He waited for Burt to make his move. Maybe that would be the best way out at that.

Burt flushed. His thin-lipped mouth worked a little under the blonde Mexican dandy mustache he affected. His icy, killing temper was beginning to show.

Boots grated on the rocky slope and a conical Mexican sombrero seemed to float up into view from a pool of black water. "The dawn is not far off," warned Toribio Vasquez.

"Sonora by midnight with thirty to forty thousand dollars," reminded Burt.

"Maybe six thousand apiece," said Jack.

"A nice haul," agreed Toribio. He smiled, revealing his strong white teeth. "In Arizona, not so much; in Sonora, a fortune, my friends."

"If the Rurales don't get us on the way south," said Jack.

Toribio shrugged. "What do they care about the money of this country?"

Jack looked down the slope. A man laughed beside the dying fire. "There isn't one of us the Rurales wouldn't like to net," he said.

"Perhaps," said Toribio. "We must risk it, Juan. We are on the run here."

Jack shook his head. "It isn't worth it," he said.

Toribio thrust his head toward Jack. He spat fiercely. "Have you lost your guts, Juan Espada? The Jack of Spades talks like a woman!"

Jack stepped in close and backhanded Toribio so viciously

that his hat flew off and he staggered back down the slope. Toribio dropped his hand to his pistol butt and almost drew, but love of life stopped his impulse. Jack Spade had moved so swiftly that even Burt Lasser was surprised. A knife had appeared in Jack's right hand ready for a killing throw. The softly cursing Mexican wanted to draw—Christ how he wanted to draw! Jack's eyes seemed fixed in his head as he waited for Toribio to make the decision between retaliation and living to see Sonora once again. Slowly, ever so slowly, Toribio raised his gun hand, never taking his eyes from those of Jack Spade. Toribio should have known better. There was only one other accusation that would put Jack into a killing mood—pointed mention that he might have Indian blood in his veins—and it was something that Toribio had never said, nor would ever say unless he lost his mind or reason.

"Forgive me, Juano," he said softly with an ingratiating smile. "The nerves are tight like the springs. The dawn is close. You understand?"

Jack slowly sheathed the knife. "I want no part of it," he said.

Burt Lasser jerked his head toward the dying fire. "Go get the others," he said.

Toribio looked hesitantly from Burt to Jack and then at Burt again; finally he settled his eyes on Jack. Jack walked up the slope and looked down toward the springs. There was no sign of life down there, although there must be a sentry on duty. Jack walked back past Burt and Toribio. Without a word he seemed to vanish into the pool of darkness. Toribio looked at Burt. He was about to say something and then thought better of it. He knew too well of Burt's hair-trigger temper, whose sear slipped so easily into a coldblooded killing rage. Toribio turned and walked after Jack. Burt Lasser stood there staring fixedly down toward the fire. A horse whinnied down at the springs. The wind soughed dryly through the Grindstone Hills. Burt walked down the slope accompanied by the soft, silvery chiming of his Chihuahua spurs.

Mooney Dade looked up from the dying fire. "Christ-amighty!" he blurted out. "What the hell we waitin' for? Them niggers will be rollin' out of them blankets in less'n an hour, Jack."

Gray-haired Lupo Zamacona was shaping a cigarette with his long, brown hands. "We still have time to get into the hills south of here before full daylight. The horses are fresh and we can take mounts from the soldiers. We can ride them until we wear them out and then shift to our own horses. Eh, Juano? Is that not a good idea?"

"Jack thinks it's too big a risk," said Burt from the slope just above Jack.

Josh Burson glanced up at Jack. His eyes were a little too bright. He had a bottle somewhere. He *always* had a bottle somewhere. "Maybe Jack is right," he suggested.

"Shit!" snapped Mooney Dade. "That loot is right over this ridge! All we got to do is cash in our six-shooters and get to hell over the border. What risk is that?"

Jack spat to one side. "If you don't know, Mooney," he said quietly, "there's no use in explaining it to you."

Jack squatted by the fire and poured the last of the coffee into a tin cup. "Where is she?" he asked.

Lupo jerked a thumb toward a heap of blankets. "She's smarter than we are," he said. "She fills her belly and gets her sleep while we sit around arguing about making a hit."

"And we do the work and she gets paid just the same," said Mooney.

"She's supposed to be the cook," said Josh. He grinned loosely. He slanted his eyes toward Jack. "How's the coffee, Jack?"

"Lousy," replied Jack.

"She made it," said Josh. He grinned again.

"Jack thinks it's too big a risk," repeated Burt.

"Everything in life is a risk," said Lupo philosophically. "Look at me. My mother risked making love to a priest and got me."

Jack slanted his eyes sideways at Lupo. "Maybe she

thought she'd get another Christ," suggested Jack. "She made one helluva mistake there, Lupo the Wolf."

Lupo slapped his thigh. "You bring the tears to my eyes, Juano."

"Let's get on with it," rasped Toribio. He had not forgotten the backhanded blow to his face and the worse blow to his pride as a man.

Jack sipped the rank coffee. They could carry it off. It wasn't really the odds that bothered him. The *corrida* was composed of professionals, each an expert in one thing or another and all of them experts with gun and knife and sudden killing. Maybe it was really the killing he dreaded. It was one major difference between him and Burt Lasser. Burt *liked* to kill.

"Maybe Jack thinks they might make him a good United States citizen if he keeps us from taking that Government money," suggested Mooney. "Hell! It never worked for *me!*"

The wind shifted and died away as it always did before the coming of the false dawn.

"You lead us, Jack, or we go on our own," said Burt Lasser.

"Crap or get off the pot," said Mooney Dade, "but do it now, *hombre.*"

"Go on then," said Jack. "I wash my hands of it."

"Like Pontius Pilate?" suggested Lupo. "You think maybe it is *that* easy, Juano?"

Jack looked across the dying fire into the eyes of the Mexican. "Don't get in my way, Lupo," he warned.

"*¡Es el día!*" cried Josh Burson in his cow-pen Spanish. He jerked a thumb toward the eastern sky, which now showed a faint wash of pewter light against the darkness. "Gawd-dammit! They'll be up and around in half an hour!"

The heap of blankets moved. A smooth, brown arm slid out and stretched itself like a creature seeking the warmth of the coming sun. A dark head protruded. Estela's eyes were full of sleep and she yawned like a cat, revealing her even white teeth. "Bring me coffee, Juano," she requested. It was almost an order.

Jack did not move. He knew the others were covertly watching him.

"Juano, my heart!" she said. She held out a slim hand for her coffee cup.

Jack stood up and emptied the dregs of the cup into the bed of ashes, raising a quick spurt of acrid steam. He reached out with a boot toe and tipped the battered coffee pot on its side to let it drain.

Lupo got to his feet and sauntered over to his half-sister. "Get up," he said. "We're moving out."

"Not until I get my coffee," she insisted.

Lupo grinned. He dragged the blankets from her. The fire flared up and the light touched her naked, brown-budded, full breasts and brought out the warmth of her skin. Lupo quickly rolled the blankets and tossed the roll to one side.

"You're sure then?" Burt asked Jack.

"I say we forget it," replied Jack. He looked from one to the other of them, three Americans and two Mexicans. It was the moment of truth. Either they listened to him, their leader, and forgot about the raid on the paymaster's party at the springs, or they threw in with Burt Lasser and hit the paymaster's till for thirty to forty thousand dollars. In any case, their decision would decide who was to lead the *corrida* from then on.

Josh Burson looked away from the hard, searching blue eyes of Jack Spade. He hawked and spit. Mooney Dade tried to hold those eyes with his, but it was no use. He, too, looked away from Jack Spade. There was no question about Toribio Vasquez. He hated Jack's guts with a passion. Lupo was simple enough—his allegiance was to the one who would get him the most loot.

Estela stood and pulled down her split skirt about her long, brown legs. She pulled on her half boots of figured leather with her naked breasts swinging freely as she moved. She quickly combed her thick, lustrous hair and then, only then, did she slip on her shirt over her naked upper body. She shrugged into her leather jacket and hung her wide-brimmed hat about her slim throat by its braided *barbequejo* strap. She walked to the dying fire. "Bastards," she said as she saw the fallen coffee pot. She looked up at Jack. "I need a drink, Juano, my heart."

"The brandy is with the horses," said Jack.

"You in, or you out?" demanded Burt.

Estela yawned again and came close to Jack. "Thirty to forty thousand dollars," she said softly. Her great, dark eyes held his. She cupped a cool hand against the side of his face. "Juano?" she pleaded.

"Jack?" said Burt.

Jack looked at the tall man. "No," he said.

"All right then," agreed Burt. He shifted a little on his feet and his spurs chimed. He looked directly at Jack. "If you change your mind and want in, you follow *my* orders."

Jack smiled easily. "That cinches it then," he said.

"*¡Bueno!* You'll come with us then!" cried Estela.

Jack threw back his head and laughed. "Led by Burt Lasser? Christ's blood, *amigos!* He'll lead you into nothing but a hanging! Take my word for it!"

She tried to rake her nails across his face, but he gripped her wrist and forced her arm down so hard that she winced in pain, but she did not cry out. "Lupo!" she called.

Lupo the Wolf looked up from the fire. "He is your man," he said quietly.

Jack turned to walk toward the horses, turning his back on Burt Lasser. Lasser took three short, plunging strides, whipping out his six-gun as he did so. He swung it full-arm so that the long barrel struck Jack just above the right ear. Jack went down like an ox felled in an abattoir, and he did not move. A slow, red worm of blood ran down the side of his face into the corner of his mouth.

Lasser stood there with unblinking eyes. His chest rose and fell. He stepped forward and hooked a boot under Jack and threw him violently over on his back. He raised the boot with its Chihuahua spur armed with three-inch needle rowels.

"That's enough, Burt," said Josh Burson.

The staring eyes slanted toward the little man. "You want some of it too, you drunken little bastard?" asked Burt.

Josh wet his dry lips. "No, but it ain't goin' to do any good at all, Burt."

Burt laughed, but there was no mirth in his eyes. "I wasn't figurin' on doing him *good*, Josh." He looked at the others for some confirmation. "I say we ought to get rid of him right now."

Toribio reached for his knife. Lupo clamped a hand on Toribio's wrist. "Wait," he said.

"I didn't know you was a great *amigo* of his," said Mooney.

Lupo shook his head. "You're right. It isn't that, my friends." He jerked his head toward Jack. "Remember his mother was a de Las Casas and that is a big name, very big in the Rio Nevome country. We'll have trouble enough with the Rurales without arousing the de Las Casas up against us. Besides, every *campesino* in Sonora knows and admires the Jack of Spades." He laughed shortly. "That is more than any of us can say, and *I*, myself, am a *Zamacona.*"

"Shit," said Toribio Vasquez.

"Lookit the Gawddamned sky!" rasped Josh Burson. "Let him he! He was a good leader, *amigos!* We got to allow him that anyway!"

"There is salt in that," agreed Lupo.

"Come on then!" snapped Burt. He kicked Jack in the side and strode down the brushy slope toward the horses. He grinned to himself. Let the bastard he there, he thought. Maybe the soldiers or the lawmen would pick him up, but they wouldn't believe any story he told them even if it was true. He was the Jack of Spades. That would be enough to condemn him. "Think your way out'a *that* one, *hombre,*" he said.

The others came through the rustling brush. The last one was the woman. Now and again she looked back toward the unconscious man.

"Forget him!" Burt called back. "I'm more of a man than he ever was!"

Her dark eyes steadied on him. "Shit," she said in precise English.

They unpicketed the horses. Burt mounted and reached for the reins of Jack's roan.

"No," said Estela.

Burt eyed her. "I'm running this *corrida* now," he reminded her.

"Not *me,*" she said.

He pulled at the reins.

She slid a hand inside her left sleeve and withdrew a silver-mounted double-barreled derringer. She thumbed back both hammers. The little gun with the big bite was steady in her slim, brown hand. For a moment they faced each other, and then Burt let the reins fall to the ground.

"Come on," he ordered in a hard voice.

The horses' hoofs clattered on the hard ground and loose rock. The roan raised his head and sniffed the cool dawn air. Slowly he walked back toward the fire and stopped beside his master.

CHAPTER TWO

The echoing reports of the large-calibered rifles slammed back and forth in the defiles, sounding like the irregular ripping of heavy canvas. A man screamed like a wounded mare. Hoofs thudded on the hard ground beyond the ridge. Jack Spade opened his eyes to the gray light of the dawn. He sat up, wincing at the stab of intense pain through the side of his head. The right side of his head seemed to be protruding beyond his ear. The roan whinnied softly. Jack gripped a stirrup leather and pulled himself up to his feet to lean against the roan. Jack fumbled with the straps of a saddlebag and then withdrew a bottle of *bacanora*. He pulled the cork out with his teeth and then spat it out. He upended the bottle and drank deeply. For a moment his stomach became queasy and he almost threw up the raw liquor, but then he steadied himself. He slowly wiped his mouth with the back of his hand and slanted his eyes toward the ridge top. The shooting was still going on.

He emptied the last of the booze and hurled the dead soldier far into the brush. It smashed and tinkled on the harsh ground. A man shouted beyond the ridge. Another laughed. A pistol shot punctuated the sudden quietness. Then it was quiet again except for the rustling of the rising dawn wind through the dry brush. Moments ticked past and then the wind brought the intermingled sound of many hoofs on the hard ground, and then in a little while that too died away.

Jack felt in the saddlebag for the other bottle. A feeling of relief came through him as he felt its roundness in the bottom of the bag. It was full. He'd need all of it that day. He led the roan along the northern side of the ridge and passed through the place where they had picketed the horses. There was nothing there but piles of wet manure.

He rounded the eastern end of the ridge and led the roan down the sloping valley floor toward the springs. The roan's hoofs rang like cracked bells on the harsh, rocky soil. A wraith of pungent smoke hung over the silent camp beside the springs. It shifted and whirled upward with the rising wind. By the time the sun was fully up that smoke could be seen for miles. There was another odor with that of the acrid-smelling smoke—a sickening, sweetish odor. He saw the first of the bodies sprawled half in and half out of a tangle of gray, bloodstained issue blankets. The rising sun shone on the black face and the even white teeth revealed by the thick, drawn-back lips of the dead trooper. The staring eyes looked accusingly at Jack.

Jack led the shying, blowing roan into the center of the carnage. Two troopers lay tangled together in a heap beside the paymaster's Dougherty wagonette. Another trooper lay sprawled on his belly. The back of his head had been smashed by soft bullets at close range. Already the first of the flies to come was buzzing sleepily about the red mess. A trooper lay with his head and shoulders in the spring nearest the wagonette. The bloodstained waters were spreading across the clear sheet of pool water. Smoke arose from the thick woolen shirt of a huge trooper who lay across the embers of a fire. His flesh was already searing. Jack pulled him from the fire and threw water on the smoldering shirt. His guts turned queasy at the sweetish stench of the scorched body. Jack raised his eyes. Beyond the springs he saw a pair of pinkish heels protruding from under a low creosote bush. There was no use in investigating that body.

The *caliche* soil near it was stained black with blood that had soaked quickly into it. No man could lose that much blood and still be alive.

The flies were gathering. Jack shaped and lighted a cigarette to get the burning stench out of his nostrils. All of the troopers' horses and the pair of mules that had hauled the Dougherty wagonette were gone. Trust Burt to think of that. "Make it look like Apaches," said Jack aloud. "Damned fool," he added. Burt had left the issue .45/70 single-shot trap-door Springfield carbines lying about the camp and at least several issue Colts. That was something no right-minded Chiricahua or Tonto would have done. Money meant nothing to them. Horses, mules, and good weapons meant everything: the horses for riding, the mules for eating, the weapons to kill more White-Eyes.

Seven dead troopers and not a stripe showing on the shirt sleeves of any of them, thought Jack. He walked over toward the Dougherty wagonette, and as he did so the powerful smell of spirits came to him on the shifting wind. He opened the rear door of the wagonette and looked right into the gray, flaccid face of a bearded white man whose wig had tilted rakishly down over one closed eye. A blouse with captain's bars on the epaulets hung from a hook at the side of the wagonette interior. The odor of booze hung in the wagonette. A smashed bottle lay beside the murdered paymaster. At his feet was an empty whiskey case. Jack wondered how many of those bottles had been taken away by the raiders. Josh Burson would have a field day.

He let the door drive shut in the wind. There was no use in looking for any of the money. Burt Lasser would have the full sum of it with him on his horse. Jack walked to the roan and led him to the pool farthest from the one where the dead trooper was staining the water. Something was missing. Jack leaned against the roan as he drank, shaping a cigarette and studying the camp. He had figured on perhaps two squads of troopers, say twelve to fifteen men, with a corporal and perhaps a sergeant in command. That was the usual routine. The raiders hadn't taken any of the bodies with them, therefore all of them must lie dead in the camp, but not one wide set of corporal's or sergeant's yellow chevrons showed on the blue shirts of the dead troopers. "Loco," said Jack. He lighted up.

"Doan you move, white man," said a voice from the brush beyond the spring.

Jack distinctly heard the double cluck-cluck of a rifle hammer being thumbed back. He slowly turned his head. His eyes widened. One of the biggest black men he had ever seen stood facing him across the pool. An issue carbine was held at waist level, aimed right at Jack's gut. Jack moved away from the horse. The Negro's eyes moved nervously back and forth.

"Stay right wheah yuh are, white man," he warned. "I kin kill yuh befoah yuh move anotheh step."

He was big, thought Jack. Jesus, but he was big! His shoulders and great chest strained at the fabric of his blue shirt. His great thighs thrust themselves against the light blue of his trousers. Cool as it was his broad, purely black face ran with sweat. Jack saw the wide double chevrons of a corporal on the shirt sleeves. "They're all dead," he said. It was a stupid thing to say.

"Yeh! But you didn't get away!"

"I wasn't with them," said Jack. That sounded even more stupid. "How'd you get away?"

The Negro looked quickly over a broad shoulder.

"I asked you how you got away?" repeated Jack.

The Negro quickly looked back at Jack. "They didn' see me," he replied.

"You're lying," said Jack evenly.

"You watch whut yuh say!" snapped the black. He came around the side of the pool, moving with surprising grace for all his size, like a great, black hunting panther. "I'm takin' that hoss," he said.

"Where?" asked Jack casually.

"I got to report this killin'," replied the corporal.

Jack nodded. He took his cigarette from his mouth and

looked at it. "How are you going to explain where you were when all this was going on?" he asked.

"Whut you mean?" demanded the Negro.

Jack shrugged. "Strange that everyone in the camp got killed except you, mister. You haven't even got a scratch on you."

"I fell and bumped my haid," explained the trooper. "When I come to, they was all gone and the money too."

"Bullshit!" said Jack. He leaned his head forward. "You ran away, you black bastard!"

"Doan yuh say that! Doan yuh ever say that again!"

Jack's eyes held the trooper's, and at last the trooper looked away. "I was up all night on guard," said the Negro. "I fell asleep in the brush ovah theah. The first shot wuk me up. It was all ovah befoah I cud do anything. I lay hid until I heard yuh comin'."

"You were up all night on guard?" asked Jack curiously. "You? A *corporal?*"

The dark eyes looked at Jack. "I jest got these stripes a week ago," he said. "I wasn't sure the boys would stay awake on guard, mistah, so I done it myself."

"That was brilliant," said Jack dryly.

"It tuk me ten yeahs to git these stripes, mistah!" yelled the trooper. "Yuh know whut that means to a man? No, yuh don't, 'cause yuh ain't no soldier like me! *Me!* Corporal Henry Cabell, Company C, Tenth United States Cavalry! Tha's who! They cain't call me *Hunk* no moah! They got to call me *Corporal* Cabell now!"

Jack spat to one side. "Past tense," he said dryly.

"Whut that mean?" demanded Cabell suspiciously.

"You *were* a corporal," explained Jack. "You go on back and report, black man, and when you tell them the truth, how you fell asleep on guard because you couldn't handle your squad enough to make them stand guard awake, you know how long you'll be a corporal? First, they'll rip those fresh, new stripes off of your sleeves and then they'll court martial you."

"Why?"

Jack looked about them. "I hope I don't have to explain that," he said quietly. "God's blood, mister! You fouled up your first real responsibility to a fare-thee-well!"

The dark eyes had a haunted look in them. Cabell looked away from Jack. "I got to have that hoss, mistah," he said. "Git away from him! Drop that pistol!"

Jack unsheathed his Colt and dropped it on the ground.

"Git back!" warned the trooper.

Jack eyed him. "You going to let your comrades lie here like this?" he asked. "The flies are already gathering. The sun will heat the bodies and make them swell. By midafternoon you wouldn't even recognize your own brother if he was lying here. By dusk the stink will start when the body gas escapes, and the stench will carry on the wind for half a mile. Tomorrow the buzzards will gather. They'll find the bodies all right. You ever see them at work, mister? Ripping and gouging out the soft parts first."

"Shut up!" yelled Hunk Cabell. He darted his eyes this way and that as though looking for a means of escape.

Jack moved quickly toward the big trooper. "They're still your responsibility even if they are dead," he said.

Hunk stared at the body lying near the fire.

"You can drop that carbine now," quietly suggested Jack.

Hunk whirled. He looked right into the twin muzzles of a double-barreled derringer. "Where'd yuh git that?" he demanded.

Jack smiled easily. "Trade secret," he replied.

"I can shoot too," warned Cabell.

"Don't try it," said Jack.

They stood there as the sun rose, warming their backs and glinting from the quiet waters of the springs. "Give me the hoss," pleaded Hunk.

Jack shook his head. "Drop the carbine," he repeated.

The Springfield thudded on the hard ground.

"Get back," ordered Jack.

Cabell walked slowly backward.

Jack knelt on one knee and filled both of his canteens. He hooked them to his saddle. He mounted the roan and replaced the derringer with his Colt. "There's a telegraph way station at Dutchman's Crossing," he said. "That's ten miles from here. Due west. Take water with you," he added.

Cabell pleaded with his eyes but knew it was no use. He picked up a canteen and hooked it to his cartridge belt. He walked past the fireplace and the Dougherty wagonette toward the rutted road. Once he turned and looked back. The stranger was gone.

The sun was fully up when Jack reined in the roan on a saddle-backed ridge two miles from the springs. He uncased his good German field glasses and focused them on the road. He picked out a tiny figure moving slowly to the west. As he lowered the glasses his eyes caught a movement of dust beyond the ridge to the north of the springs. Many riders, he thought. The words of Burt Lasser came back to him: "I ain't about to be caught in these hills. You know there might be a helluva big posse to the north of us. We've lost enough time as it is."

He cased the glasses and rode down the slope of the ridge. He did not look to the north again. There wasn't time for that. By keeping to the eastern hills and then to the Chiricahua Mountains he might be able to make the Mexican border in three days, and he could get past the Chiricahua Apaches.

CHAPTER THREE

Spade was turned back from the approaches to the Chiricahuas although the posse never saw him. Twice he tried to get back into those hostile and yet sheltering mountains, and each time he was forced further south and west. He got through the Swiss-helms without being seen and managed to cross the Whitewater River as he headed for the dangerous Valley of the San Pedro. He rode out the roan and transferred his saddle to a gray he stole from an isolated ranch in the hills. The gray went down at last, and he switched his saddle back to the partially rested roan. All the time he rode he seemed to feel an invisible net slowly and inexorably closing in on him, and he wondered time and time again if Burt Lasser and the boys had made it to the border.

He made it to the Babocomari and was forced south again when he was seen. A single rifle shot warned him that a posse was behind him and gaining ground on their fresher horses. The border was still thirty miles away and he knew he'd never make it on a straight line. He turned toward the Canelo Hills, softly rounded and shadowed on their eastern slopes as the sun went down behind him. "Jim Tolleson," Jack said aloud. It was his last bet—the last cast of the dice on his break for the Sonoran border. "With the Rurales forming a welcoming committee," he said. His sentence was punctuated by another rifle shot.

"Go to Hell!" he shouted defiantly over his shoulder.

He slowly gained ground, but he knew it would not last. He rode as though he was part of the lathered roan, climbing out of a dry valley, topping a ridge crest, plunging down the far side, and hammering down the center of a rutted road with the yellowed flecks of foam that were flung back from the roan's mouth drying on his face.

The roan went down at last with no warning. Jack cleared sweated leather and hit the hard ground spraddle-legged, jerking his six-shooter free from the scabbard as he did so. He whirled to see the roan crash down beside the road and he knew it was dead. He jerked at the butt of his scabbarded Winchester, but it was pinned beneath the dead horse and there was no time to waste on the rifle. He sprinted across the road and plowed into a tangle of tornillo brush, stamping hard on the ground to make clear tracks. Two hundred yards from the road he reached a shield of naked rock that overlay the soft ground. He turned hard right and raced at full speed across the sloping rock shield and then dropped behind a ledge at the southern edge of the shield. He ripped off his worn boots and dropped into a dry wash cursing savagely in eloquent Spanish as he felt the sharp-edged stones cutting into his dirty socks, lacerating his soles.

He reached the road and leaped across it like a mountain goat, and then plunged into the thorny brush on the far side of it. He legged it like a chaparral cock through the brush as the thorns ripped pitilessly through his clothing and hooked their tiny barbs into his sweating flesh. He flung himself belly down on the first naked hill spur. He had been running for an hour through the brush in the thick darkness before the coming of the moon. He rested his head on a rock and felt the tom-tom thudding of his heart against his ribs and the hot, stinging sweat running in rivulets down his body. His breathing was brassy dry and harsh in his throat. His head swam and his eyes burned. The moon slowly arose and found him still there.

Far down the slope he could see mounted men casting back and forth on both sides of the road. Even as he watched them he heard the staccato sound of three closely spaced rifle shots. He grinned weakly. They had found his tracks on the *other* side of the road—the east side. He rolled over on his back and yanked his hot boots on over his burning, bleeding feet. He crawled down from the spur and into a defile as yet unlighted by the rising moon. His last chance was to reach Tolleson's ranch and get a horse, saddle, and rifle for his last try to reach the border.

The moon was fully up when at last he threaded his way through a *bosquecillo* of dusty willows and cottonwoods that bordered the dry stream bed. He passed like a ghost in and out of the soft patches of moonlight that filtered down through the ragged openings in the leafy roof over his head. Now and then he would stop to listen and to look back over a shoulder, and the moonlight would reveal his hard-hewn face, flecked with blackish patches of dried blood from thorn wounds and stippled with the dried, yellowish foam from the roan's mouth. Now and then he'd pass a dirty hand across his dry mouth. Twenty miles at least to the border. There was yet a good chance, or a good try, depending on how one felt about it.

He paused at the edge of the *bosquecillo* and looked toward the cluster of adobes and jacales that marked Jim Tolleson's rancho. A man who has been pretty much on the run from the law for some years will work through his relatives and friends until at last none of them will have anything to do with him; but somehow, somewhere, there is always *one* left to extend a helping hand. Such a one was Jim Tolleson.

Jack walked cat-footed toward the lightless and silent group of moonlighted buildings. Now and then he stopped to listen. No dog barked. No mule brayed. No horse whinnied. It was quiet—it was too damned quiet. The hackles rose a little on Jack Spade's neck. He rested his hand on the butt of his Colt and wet his dry lips with the tip of his tongue. In Jack's mind a mental picture formed of a bottle of Jim's home-brewed beer, dewed with cold sweat, fresh from the spring-house in the hollow behind the ranch buildings.

He swung his dusty head back and forth like a questing hound. There was nothing living to be seen. The wind whispered faintly, rustling the leaves of the trees and swaying the dry brush. Jack padded on a few feet closer to the silent buildings and again he stopped. He looked behind him. He felt as though he was being watched. Once Jim had said: "It don't pay an owl hooter to have an imagination. Such a man has got to live with himself, and when he starts to thinking about what he's done and what he is, it don't make an easy pillow for him to rest his head on at night."

Jack stopped behind a sagging jacal. The old man always talked a lot. He liked *man* talk. That was the hell of it, for he was a widower with three daughters.

The quietness seemed to *grow,* if such a thing was possible. Jack touched the butt of his pistol. Maybe the old man had finally pulled out, lock, stock, and barrel, as he had often threatened to do in the past, to go live in the house he had bought in Bisbee on Quality Hill, but somehow he had always been there at his *estancia* when Jack would stop by on one of his usually hurried visits. Amy would be well grown by now. She wasn't the prettiest. Sue and young Lucy were prettier by far, but Amy was the smart one and she had a certain way of looking at Jack.

Jack stood in the shadow of the jacal. The place didn't seem as though it was abandoned. Time was a nagging spur in Jack's tired mind. He knew better than to rush things, but it was only a matter of time before the posse would realize he had tricked them and then would ride through the pass he had just walked through. He looked back at the serrated hills through which he had just passed. There was no telltale thread of dust rising in the pale moonlight. Maybe they had turned south again instead of west and were waiting for him closer to the border.

He walked softly toward the corral. The corral was

empty and the bars were down. An icy feeling came through Jack. He would never make it on foot to the border and there wasn't another *estancia* south of Tolleson's where he could buy, beg, or steal a horse. His only other alternative would be to hide in the hills, but eventually they'd flush him out. Where in the name of God were the Tollesons and Jim's beloved horses?

The wind rose and shifted and the windmill began to grind around to face it. It whirred steadily as the big vanes felt the wind pressure. Jack crossed to the rear of the low adobe house and stepped up on the warped boards of the back porch. He pressed an ear against the kitchen door and it opened silently. A cool draft played about his heated face.

"Jim?" called out Jack. There was no answer. "Amy? Sue? Lucy?" he called. No one answered. Jack looked over his shoulder toward the barn. The door hung open, and as he watched the wind caught the door and slammed it shut. The echo died away in the hills behind the *estancia*.

An eerie feeling crept through Jack. It was as though no one had lived on the isolated *estancia* for years, and yet he knew it could not be so. The signs of recent occupancy were many. A good McClellan saddle had been placed on a top corral rail. A trash box on the porch held a number of emptied tin cans whose metal was still bright. No windows were broken. No tumbleweeds had piled up against the fences. The place actually *felt* as though it had recently been occupied.

Jack stepped into the kitchen. Something rolled beneath his left boot. He picked up an empty tin can and held it so that the moonlight streaming in through the door shone on the label.

"Tomatoes," he said. "Someone likely missed the trash can and didn't pick it up. Maybe the old man is batching while the girls are in town." He shook his head. Jim had spent three hitches in the Regular Cavalry and had retired as a squadron sergeant-major. Jim was neater around a house, or quarters, than many women would be.

Jack thumb-snapped a Lucifer into life and looked about

the big kitchen. The table was littered with dirty dishes, empty tin cans and bottles, as well as scraps of food. A mouse leaped from the table and scuttled for cover. Jack walked to the big range and placed a hand on it. It was still faintly warm.

"Jim! Jim Tolleson!" cried Jack. The door creaked shut in the rising wind.

Jack took a candle from a cupboard and lighted it. Glass crushed under his right bootheel. He picked up a piece of bottle held together by the label, and the strong fruity odor of booze came to him. Jim must have had recent company —*drinking* company, for the old man was almost a teetotaler.

"Maybe the girls took up drinking," said Jack. He grinned at his own stupid joke. The grin faded. There was something very odd about the dark and silent house.

Jack walked into the long hallway that led to the front of the house past four bedroom doors. Once he thought he heard a faint sound behind one of the doors. He turned but heard nothing further. The place was alive with mice, he thought.

He paused at the doorway into the living room. The faint odor of spirits and something else came to him. He walked around the old horsehair-stuffed couch and stopped short. The flickering light of the candle revealed Jim Tolleson lying flat on his back with his long arms flung wide. His head was turned a little to one side and it seemed oddly misshapen. His eyes stared unseeingly up at the low ceiling. His mouth gaped opened revealing his yellowish tobacco-stained teeth. His beard stuck straight out from his chin as though it had been stuck on a death mask as an afterthought. The faded carpet had been dyed darkly in an irregular halo that spread out about the dead man's head. A steady buzzing sound arose from the head area and Jack saw the flies crawling through the old man's thin gray hair to get at the coagulated blood.

"Jesus God," breathed Jack. He got down on one knee and rolled the old man over onto his lean belly. Jack's guts turned over and he looked quickly away. The whole back of the narrow skull was a shattered mess of blood and hair with bits of whitish, bloodstained bone showing through it.

Jack stood up. The icy horror crept again through Jack. " *'Paches,*" he said softly. The smashed skull was their trademark on those they killed, for it kept the spirit of the dead from following them for vengeance.

There was nothing he could do now for the old man. It was the girls that now concerned Jack. There would be nothing to fear from the Apaches now. They would not return to that place of death for fear of hearing the voice of the dead man coming from Bu, the Owl, who would haunt that place for several days.

Jack opened the front door. He knew now why the horses and mules were no longer there. The bright moonlight silvered the dusty leaves of the trees and laid a soft wash of light on the hard ground. The windmill turned slowly and then ground to a halt as the wind died away. Water overflowed from the stock tank onto the hard ground, and the spreading pool reflected the light of the moon.

Jack walked softly back through the living room. The flies had settled again on the head of the dead man, buzzing a soft and sickening requiem for the dead. Jack shooed them away and placed an antimacassar over Jim's head. He paused at the entrance to the hallway.

"Amy? Sue? Lucy?" he called out. The kitchen faintly echoed his voice. "Amy? Sue? Lucy?"

It became graveyard quiet in the big house. The *broncos* must have caught Jim flat-footed. His big Sharps rifle was still resting on its pegs above the big field-rock fireplace in the living room.

"What about the girls? Eh, Jack? *What about the girls?*" The mind voice nagged him into walking into the dark hallway. He opened the first bedroom door and thrust in the candle. It was Jim's room. The bed was neatly made and his worn carpet slippers were placed side by side on the thick shag rug beside the bed. The faint odor of stale tobacco smoke hung in the room.

He closed the door behind him. Once again he thought he heard a faint sound, but he wasn't sure. He wasn't sure of anything anymore. The next room was Amy's, the oldest of the three pretty Tolleson girls. The room was empty of life. The four-poster bed was neatly made; the room itself, in perfect order. The lingering odor of lilac hung in the dead air. Jack crossed to the big wooden wardrobe and opened the doors. The lingering feminine aura came to him although there were only a few cotton house dresses hanging in it. "Beats the hell out of me," murmured Jack.

He closed the door. The faint sound came again. This time he was sure of it. An eerie feeling came over him. It sounded like the whimpering of a child, and yet there were no children in Tolleson's house. Lucy, the youngest and prettiest of the three sisters, had been twelve years old the last time Jack had stopped by. He had given her a coin silver bracelet for her birthday, but he hadn't told her where he had gotten it. It had been part of the haul from the Hermosillo stagecoach down in Sonora that he had held up just ten days before he had crossed the border into Arizona Territory two spits and a long jump ahead of the Rurales.

Jack padded softly to the last door on the left side of the hallway. He eased open the door. The candle guttered in the draft. A frightened sob was suddenly cut off.

"Sue? Lucy?" he said. It was Sue's bedroom he thought. Faintly in the dim light he saw something white in a corner. It was a face that seemed like a mask, so fixed was it, with great, staring eyes that seemed to drive a knife into his flesh. He walked closer, holding out the candle. It was a face he could not recognize, and yet he knew that it was someone he should recognize. The eyes were like shallow, sun-lighted blue pools in the light of the candle.

"Sue," he said uncertainly. It *must* be her!

She moved slowly, pulling up a wrinkled bedspread up about her neck. There were bloodstains on the spread. He looked quickly sideways. The floor was littered with shreds and scraps of clothing as though they were feathers after a chicken plucking. The scraps and shreds were women's clothing, and underclothing. He looked down at her again. Her slim naked legs were thrust out from beneath the coverlet. Her unreasoning eyes stared at him for a moment, and then her mouth squared and fear grew like a poisonous cloud in her eyes. She shrieked in a tone that cut into his senses like a rusty knife blade. He jumped back and caught a heel in an article of clothing. It was a pair of young woman's underdrawers, or what was left of them. Jesus, he thought, they didn't waste any time on her! "Where's Amy?" he asked.

She stared at him with unblinking eyes.

"Where's Amy?" he asked. "Where's little Lucy, girl?"

There was no answer from her. He turned on his heel and went into the hallway. He pushed open the door of the next bedroom and thrust the candle in ahead of him, as though the flame would cleanse the horror he expected yet did not want to see. In a moment he saw what he had dreaded. He slammed the door shut and felt the green bile rise up in his throat. He ran into the kitchen and snatched a bottle from the table in passing. As he reached the porch he jerked the cork from the bottle with his teeth and spat it to one side. He upended the bottle and drank deeply. It was rye—good, solid, hard-hitting rye whiskey.

Jack looked up at the empty moonlighted hills. "Amy," he said. Maybe it would have been better for her if she had died as her father and Lucy had died, or if she too had reached the mindlessness of sixteen-year-old Sue. If they had taken her into the hills with them. . . He forced the thought from his mind.

He looked back over his shoulder into the dark house. He could not go back in there, and yet he knew he had to. By now he should be striking out on foot for Sonora, on his hands and knees if need be. But he couldn't leave that girl alone in the house. She couldn't take care of herself. The next *estancia* was at least fifteen miles to the north, and that was in the opposite direction from the border.

He drank deeply, but the rye seemed to have little effect on him. The wind shifted, gained strength, and began to spin until it reached a steady whirring pitch, and more water was pumped up to overflow from the tank into the ever-widening pool on the ground. All the water that could be pumped out of the well could never erase the bloodstains from the *casa* of Jim Tolleson—not *ever*.

He forced himself to go back into the kitchen. He placed the half-empty bottle on the littered table. The *broncos* had evidently eaten well in their usual way, everything and anything, cramming down peaches in thick syrup, canned tomatoes, preserves, embalmed beef, crackers, and sardines and not worrying about the order of their going. Food was just food to an Apache. He was surprised they had left the bottle of rye. They drank like they ate. He had a momentary vision of Amy, stripped to the skin, lying helpless somewhere in those moonlighted hills with perhaps a dozen rutting bucks taking turns on her.

He walked into Sue's room. She still sat there staring straight ahead. "Can you understand me, girl?" he asked.

She did not answer. Her even white teeth bit into her lower lip to suppress a sob.

"You've got to understand me," he said.

It was no use. He got down on his knees. "You're all right now," he said,

"Lucy," she said.

He nodded. "I know."

He reached out a hand to soothe her. She screamed like a wounded cougar and the sound tore through him and echoed in the hallway. "For God's sake, child," he pleaded.

She screamed again and snapped at his extended hand like a mad dog. She gripped his arm with surprising strength and dragged him toward her. He lost his balance and fell over her as the coverlet slid to the floor, and he saw her young breasts dewed with cold sweat and raked with ragged fingernail gouges. She snapped at his face. He threw himself to one side and she rumbled over him. They rolled over and over on the shag rug amidst the litter of her clothing with the sweat of her splashing into his face while she screamed and screamed insensately. He broke free at last and staggered toward the door. "For the love of God, child!" he shouted. He turned toward the door.

A man stood there with his low-pulled hat over his eyes. The man looked down at the naked, screaming girl, as she groveled on the bloodstained clothing and rug. The candle-light reflected from the polished star the man wore on his vest. His Winchester came up butt first. "You—dirty—spic —sonofabitch!" he yelled.

The metal-shod butt struck Jack cruelly over the left temple and he fell backward over the screaming girl. He tried to get up. The man jumped up from the floor and kicked out with his right leg. The spurred bootheel struck Jack alongside the jaw and that was the last he knew.

CHAPTER FOUR

"He's Juan Espada," the hard voice said.

"John Spade," said Jack, even before he opened his eyes. He lay on the floor in the living room with his shirt and jacket wadded up about his upper body. He had been dragged by the heels into the living room. His gunbelt was gone. His head throbbed and his mouth had leaked blood when he spoke his name.

"I said *Juan Espada*, greaser," the hard voice said again.

Jack blinked his eyes in the bright lamplight. Five men stood in the room looking down at him. Jim Tolleson's body had been covered with a Navajo blanket. His long, narrow feet stuck up from under its lower edge. The lamplight shone dully on the stars worn by the five men. A green-eyed man stood closest to Jack. He held a Winchester rifle by the barrel with his hand just under the front sight. He was the one who had bootheeled Jack in Sue's bedroom, and he was the one who had called Jack "Juan Espada." Jack heard voices outside. A horse blew hard.

"You don't look as pretty as your picture on the Wanted posters, Espada," said one of the men. He bit off the end of a cigar and dragged a match across the polished top of the table to light it. Between puffs as he lighted it, he looked down at Jack. "Maybe Fos changed your face at that," he said. He grinned around the cigar. "Fos is a good man with a fist and bootheel, greaser."

Jack looked at the tall, green-eyed man. Fos—he'd remember that name. Maybe some dark night when he caught Fos alone they could decide, man to man, who'd get the final booting.

Boots thudded on the front porch and a broad-shouldered, gray-haired man came into the living room. He took off his hat as he saw the covered form of Jim Tolleson.

"He likely died quick, Sheriff Henderson," volunteered one of the deputies.

"How, Charley?" asked the sheriff.

"Whole back of his head blowed off, Sheriff."

The sheriff's gray eyes studied Jack. "You've sunk a little lower, eh, Spade?" he asked.

Jack raised his head and wiped the blood from his mouth. "It wasn't me, Sheriff Henderson," he mumbled through the blood.

"Listen to him!" jeered Fos. "We found him in the girl's bedroom, tusslin' with her on the floor and she was as naked as a jaybird, with him stinkin' of redeye and her with her own father and sister dead in the same house."

Henderson took out a cigar case and selected a cigar. He bit off the end and thrust it into his mouth. "Something new for you, isn't it, Spade? What was it? The booze?"

"It wasn't me," insisted Jack mechanically.

Henderson thrust the tip of the cigar over a lamp cylinder and drew in on the weed. He withdrew the lighted cigar from the cylinder and looked sideways at Jack through the rifting smoke. "I thought Jim Tolleson was your last friend on this side of the line," he said.

"He is. *Was*," replied Jack. "And all the time you're standing around here those *broncos* have Amy Tolleson somewhere in the hills. You saw what they did to the two younger girls."

"Listen to him," said Fos again.

Henderson blew out a puff of smoke. "They haven't got Amy, Spade. Whoever *they* are. She's been living in Jim's house in Bisbee while she's teaching school there." He eyed Jack again. "Jesus, but you must have been drunk."

"Sobered up fast enough," said Charley.

Jack sat up. His head reeled. "You don't really believe I did all this, do you?" he asked.

Fos moved a little. One of his spurs jingled. He gripped the Winchester so hard the knuckles shone whitely through the brown skin of his hand. "Let me work a confession out of him, Sheriff," he pleaded.

"Damned near broke his jaw as it is," said Henderson. "No, Fos. We've got him now. Funny thing though, he could have made it to the border if he hadn't stopped here. That other posse was heading toward Palominas when my messenger caught up with them."

"It was *bronco* Apaches," insisted Jack. But now there was no certainty in his voice.

"*Broncos,* shit!" snapped Fos. "You come here looking for a horse and money, The old man refused you. You killed him, got drunk on his booze, and then went after the girls. Good thing I figured you'd be headin' this way, or you might have killed the other girl."

"I sent you here, Fos," said Henderson.

"Yeh! Yeh! Well, anyway, we nailed him in the act, Sheriff."

Henderson nodded. "I had a hunch he'd stop here. Jim was the last friend he had in Arizona Territory. You must have been loco with booze to do what you did."

Jack looked up at him. "All right," he said quietly. "If it was me that did all this, where are Jim's horses and mules? He usually had at least two dozen good horses here and maybe half a dozen mules. There isn't even a lame burro around here! Sheriff, I tell you it was someone else that did it! *Broncos!*"

Henderson hesitated. Finally, he shook his head. "Nothing doing, Spade," he said. "I'll accept the fact that someone else might have run off the horses, but nothing you can say will convince me that it wasn't you who killed the old man to get at his booze and his daughters." He reached down and dragged Jack to his feet. He shoved Jack toward the hallway. Jack could hear Sue whimpering in her room. Jack walked through to the kitchen. An oil lamp had been lighted, but the wick had not been trimmed and the oily smoke hung under the low ceiling.

Henderson poked about in the table litter. "You still insist it was Apaches, Spade?" he asked.

"Yes," replied Jack.

"Smell this then." Henderson shoved a flat, empty tin can under Jack's pose. It was a sardine tin. Jack raised his eyes and looked into those of the sheriff. There was an icy, sickly feeling in Jack's gut. He knew and the sheriff knew that Apaches never ate fish of any kind. It was a taboo so ancient that an Apache himself couldn't tell you why. "There are five empty sardine cans here on the table," said Henderson quietly.

"Espada must have had one helluva appetite," said Charley.

"And a thirst," said another deputy.

"Before God," said Jack. His voice died away.

"Kelly," said the sheriff, "you got a girl about Sue's age. You go get Sue and dress her up. Bring her in here."

No one spoke while Kelly dressed the whimpering girl. Jack slanted his eyes toward the open door, but he knew better than to make a try for it. Any man in that room could hit him between the shoulder blades with a slug before his feet could hit the dirt beyond the porch.

Kelly led the girl into the kitchen. Henderson took the cigar from his mouth. "Miss Tolleson," he said in a kindly tone. "I know what you've been through and what a grievous loss you have suffered, but we must have you identify the man who committed the crimes against you and your family."

Sue's vacant eyes looked beyond the sheriff to the other men and then at Jack. Cold sweat worked down his sides.

"Is this the man, Miss Tolleson?" asked Henderson as he pointed to Jack.

"She can't talk, Sheriff," said Jack desperately. "Her mind is gone. Can't you see that?"

"Miss Tolleson?" asked the sheriff.

She slowly raised an arm and pointed a finger at Jack. "It was him," she said in a low voice. "Oh, God! I remember now! He had me on the floor with him! It was *him!*" She ran from the kitchen with Kelly after her.

"No use lying anymore, Espada," said Fos.

"My name is John Spade," said Jack.

"That's not what they call you along the border," said Charley.

"My father was a Texan," said Jack.

Fos grinned. "And your mother was a spic."

"She was a Mexican," said Jack.

"Likely half nigger or Indian at that," jeered Fos.

Jack moved so swiftly that he could not be stopped. His left sank into Fos' lean gut just above the big gun-belt buckle and his right clipped the tall man's jaw, driving him back against the wall. Fancy display dishes crashed to the floor from a wall rack. Fos sagged to one side and Jack hit him with everything he had. As Fos' head dropped forward Jack brought up a knee against his face and something cracked.

Two men dragged Jack back from the raging deputy who was clawing for his gun. They shoved Jack out onto the porch. He decked one of them and had the other by the throat out on the moonlit ground when Henderson plunged from the house with his drawn Colt. He laid the long barrel neatly over Jack's left ear and Jack went down for the long count. Henderson sheathed his Colt. "I hated to do that," he said.

"You should have finished the job," said the man whom Jack had been trying to strangle.

"My job is to bring him to justice," said the sheriff.

"You'll have the hell of a job keepin' the Bisbee mob away from him," ventured Charley as he got up from the porch and rubbed his jaw.

"I can do that," asserted Henderson. He looked down at the bloody face of Jack Spade. "He's a real man," he said quietly. "Too damned bad he took the wrong trail. Well, it won't matter in a couple of months."

Somewhere in the moonlighted hills a coyote howled, as though trying to reach his brother, but his brother lay still on the hard ground with his blood dripping slowly onto the thirsty *caliche*.

CHAPTER FIVE

T he hot sun of early October slanted through the barred cell window on the second floor of the Bisbee Jail. Flies buzzed lazily in and out, swerving suddenly to avoid the layered drifts of tobacco smoke from the Lobo Negro cigarettes that John Spade smoked one after another. The faint voices of men sounded from outside, intermingled with the thudding of a sledge or hammer and the occasional whining of a saw. Jack didn't have to look from the window to see what was going on. He had seen the start of the construction several days past. It was a scaffold, but it wasn't for him— not yet anyway. Likely the county could save time and money by keeping the scaffold for him, but he had not as yet been brought to trial.

"You have the cigarettes? No?" asked Augustin Chacon from the next cell.

"I have the cigarettes. Yes," replied Jack. He sat up and placed a limp pack of Lobo Negros between two fingers. He thrust the pack between the end bar and the wall and felt the Mexican take it. "I will repay you, *chico*," promised Augustin.

"Forget it, *amigo*," said Jack. "How long will it be, Augustin?"

He heard Augustin's feet shuffle on the dirty floor of the

cell. "They do well," replied Augustin from the window of his cell. "These *Yanquis* always work so hard and fast."

Jack spat on the floor. "Especially when they're going to hang a Mexican," he said dryly.

"A *greaser*," corrected Augustin.

Jack sat up and looked out the window. "Who was your father?" he asked idly.

Augustin laughed. "I wish I knew! It is said he wooed and won my mother in one night, and in that same night, I, Augustin Federico Donaciano Gaspar Hernan Chacon, was conceived. It was a night to be remembered, my friend. It is said that the stars in their courses stopped high over the Sierra del Humo and looked down smiling upon Los Molinos, where a boy child had been conceived. Was that not a miracle, my friend?"

"And nine months later three Wise Men came across the Sierra del Humo riding on jackasses to look for that same boy child," added Jack dryly.

"I was a seven months' babe, born with a caul over my head," said Augustin.

"Your father must be proud of you now."

Augustin spat between the bars. "The *cabrón* left my mother before dawnlight on the same night I was conceived. She never saw him again."

"He should come back to see your performance on that scaffold down there, *chico*."

"It was an honest killing, Juan Espada," said Augustin. "These gringos do not have the finesse, the fine points of honor of we Mexicans."

"It is said that you shot that Tucson storekeeper in the back, *chico*."

"He would have killed me had I not killed him."

"It is also said that he did not have a gun."

"Was that *my* fault!" cried Augustin.

Jack shook his head.

"And you, Juano? Does not your conscience bother you and keep you awake at night because of your killings?" asked the Mexican.

"I did not kill those people," he said.

"Perhaps not, but it is said that you also killed many Negro troopers at Granite Tanks, as well as an Army paymaster."

"No," said Jack. "That is not true!"

"Well, it does not matter. One killing is enough to have a man hanged. My case is a good example. My trial was fair enough, I must admit. One must be fair in such matters. Also, it is well to go to one's Maker in the Heavens with a clear conscience."

"What makes you think you're going *that* way?" asked Jack with a grin.

"One can dream, *amigo,*" quietly replied Augustin.

Jack dropped back on his bunk and covered his eyes with an arm. Even if he was cleared of the Tolleson killings he was still a suspect in the massacre of the troopers at Granite Tanks. The Negro trooper who had survived the massacre had accurately described Jack, and the *corrida* had been seen on their flight south and recognized as being the one once led by Jack Spade, or Juan Espada, as the case may be. If he was not condemned to death he'd end up at Yuma Pen, and the thought of that place was enough to turn his guts to mush. Hell on the Colorado! The bulls there had no use for any con, and their treatment of Mexican nationals made their lives there a living horror for any poor spic who had run afoul of Arizona Territory's gringo-slanted laws and lawmakers and enforcers. Maybe Augustin was better off at that. If he was sent to Yuma Pen he'd curse the woman who had given him birth, on the seven months' plan, before he died insane, or broken and diseased in the infamous Snake Den.

Footsteps sounded on the wooden stairs and along the corridor between the rows of cells. They stopped outside Jack's cell.

"Spade," said Sheriff Henderson. Jack withdrew his arm from across his eyes and looked right into the lovely eyes of Amy Tolleson. "Visitor," said Henderson. He looked at her. "You want to see him alone, ma'am?"

"If you please," she replied.

He walked heavily to the stairs and down them, and when the sound of his footsteps had died away she spoke. "I don't believe you did it," she said.

He stood up. "Thank God for that," he said. "How is Sue?"

"She is with me here in Bisbee, Jack. She hasn't improved. She doesn't speak at all now."

"She's told you nothing?"

"Nothing," said Amy. She studied him. "My sisters always liked you, Jack."

"And you?" he asked. He knew what *her* answer would be.

She shrugged. "I like you too, Jack."

"Nothing more?"

"Why should I? You are a child of the moonlight. Here today and gone tomorrow. Wanted on both sides of the border. We never knew where you were or what you were doing except through rumors, and none of those rumors did your reputation any good. What kind of a life is that?"

"They sing such songs about him in the *cantinas* and *pulquerias* of Sonora, *señorita*," said Augustin. "*¡Mucho hombre! La Corrida de Juan Espada! ¡Ah, Chihuahua!* I could sing it for you, *señorita*."

"You do and I'll break your neck, *chico*," promised Jack.

Augustin laughed. "Too late! I am promised to another!"

He studied her. "Why have you come to see me?" he asked.

"I know you did not kill my father and sister. Dad was like a father to you."

"I wish he had been my father," said Jack.

"Then she would be your sister," said Augustin. "Such a fate would be too cruel!"

Jack gripped the bars with his strong brown hands. "Keep out of this, Augustin," he warned. The timbre of his tone was enough even for Augustin. There would be no further remarks out of him.

"How can I clear myself?" asked Jack. "I've got to get out

of here to find the man who came to your *estancia* and killed like a wild animal."

"You should hear the talk about you in the streets. If you're caught outside of the jail you'll be lynched in the street. The troopers at Fort Bowie are forbidden to come to Bisbee. Dad's old squadron is there." Her meaning was plain enough.

Jack could hear the steady ringing sound from a big nail being driven well and truly into sound wood.

"I don't think Sheriff Henderson thinks you're guilty," she continued.

"That won't save my neck."

She looked down the corridor toward the stairs. Quickly she passed something to him. It was a coil of light, strong rope. He quickly thrust it under his mattress. He looked deep into her lovely eyes.

"After dark," she whispered, "when the workmen quit for the night, lower the rope to the ground." She stepped back. "Goodbye, Jack," she said, and walked quickly to the stairway.

Shadows had gathered on the east side of the building where the scaffold was being built. The sound of saws and hammers ceased. The workmen left the area and it was very quiet in the empty lot. It grew darker and darker and the streetlamps were lighted, but none of them threw light onto the empty lot and the gaunt structure that was taking shape there day by day.

Jack cat-footed to the window and tied a piece of wood to the end of the rope to give it weight. He let it out inch by inch until he felt it strike the ground. He waited, hungering for a cigarette, but not daring to light one.

"You are very quiet, *amigo*," called out Augustin.

Jack did not answer. The man had ears like a Yaqui.

"You know, *amigo*," said Augustin. "I wish the cell windows looked toward the south."

"Why so?" asked Jack.

"One could perhaps see Sonora," said Augustin.

"Twelve miles away?" asked Jack.

"One might perhaps see the sun on the mountains."

"I'd like to be down there seeing the sun on the mountains on this side of the border," said Jack.

"They are looking for you down there too, *chico.*"

"But not with a murder charge," said Jack.

The rope was gently tugged. Slowly, ever so slowly, Jack eased up the rope. Something hung from the end of it. Once it struck the side of the building, and Jack stopped hauling it up. Minutes ticked past, and he began hauling again. Yellow eyes of lamplight came open in the buildings within sight of the cell. Chimneys began to breathe forth the smoke of cooking fires that rose to mingle with the acrid sulphur smoke belching from the smelter chimneys and lying low over the hills about Bisbee.

Footsteps sounded on the stairs. Jack quickly pulled in the rope. A cloth-wrapped bundle had been tied to the end of it. He untied it from the rope and slid it under his mattress. He coiled the rope, dropped it on his bunk and covered it with his blanket, and then he sat down on the blanket.

A deputy lowered and lighted the corridor lamp and then hauled it up again. The yellow light streamed into Jack's cell. The deputy looked in at Jack. "Thinking about your crimes in the dark, Espada?" he asked.

"Spade," corrected Jack.

"Espada, Spade, and *shit*, they're all the same," said the deputy. "A killer don't smell no better by *any* name." He walked back down the stairs.

"You have any friends in Bisbee who might help you?" asked Augustin.

"None," replied Jack. "And you?"

"Only whores, pimps, and gamblers," replied Augustin.

"You move in lovely society," murmured Jack.

"They understand the soul of a poet, *amigo.*"

Jack heard the creaking of Augustin's bunk as the Mexican lay down. Jack swiftly untied the cloth-wrapped bundle. There were two good files in it and a hacksaw blade. There was also a piece of paper with a number written on it, which puzzled him until he realized it was the number of the Tolleson house on Quality Hill.

Footsteps sounded on the stairs again. Jack slid the files and the hacksaw blade under the mattress. He stood up when Sheriff Henderson stopped outside Augustin's cell with a plate of food in his left hand and a cup of coffee in his right. The sheriff handed them through the opening in the bars to the Mexican.

"What about me?" asked Jack.

Henderson unlocked Jack's cell door. "You come on downstairs and eat with me," he said.

"Favoritism!" cried Augustin.

Henderson looked sideways at Jack. "Don't try anything funny, Spade," he warned.

Jack shook his head.

"You make a break from this *encarcelar*, Spade, and within fifteen minutes they'll be stringing you up. *¿Comprende?*"

"*Yo comprendo*," replied Jack. He followed the big sheriff down the stairs and into his office.

Henderson drew the window blind. He jerked a thumb toward a filled plate flanked by a coffee cup and a dish with a slab of pie on it. "Eat," he invited. "I want to talk with you."

"*Gracias*," said Jack.

"*For nada*," countered Henderson. He bit the end from a cigar and spat out the tip. He lighted it and eyed Jack through the smoke. "The pie is mince. Mother makes a good mince pie."

Jack began to eat and all the time he ate he knew Henderson was watching him and weighing him for some purpose of his own. Jack finished the stew and ate the pie. He looked up. "You're right about the pie," he said.

"I know that. What bothers me is whether I'm right about you or not."

Jack narrowed his eyes. Henderson shoved a cigar box toward Jack. Jack selected a long nine and lighted it from the lamp cylinder.

"You didn't kill those people," said Henderson.

Jack stared at him. "You believe me then?"

Henderson nodded. "What about the Granite Tanks thing?"

"I was there, but I wasn't mixed up in it."

"I know. The Nigger trooper said he hadn't seen you with the others. Besides, it wasn't your way of dong things."

"Gracias," said Jack.

"But, my sayso isn't going to clear you, Spade."

Jack nodded. "I know." He puffed at his cigar. "Get to the point," he suggested.

"You've got plenty of time," said Henderson. "Wait until the neighborhood is asleep."

Jack slowly took the cigar from his mouth.

Henderson waved a hand. "It was my idea," he said. He leaned forward. "Now you and I both know it wasn't Apaches at Jim's place. The Apaches knew Jim of old. They wouldn't bother him."

"It's hard to believe a white man would do things like that," said Jack.

"There was more than one of them," said Henderson. "There were three or more of them. Possibly several Mexicans."

"Go on!" said Jack. "You know something, Henderson! *By God, you know something!*"

"Whoever it was got over the border," continued Henderson. "I let the boys take you here from Tolleson's place and I went south on my own. I picked up the trail of fifteen to twenty horses and mules being driven south in a helluva rush. I found a broken-legged mare with Jim's Slash-Bar-T brand on her lovely flank. They hadn't even waited to put a bullet into her head. I found something at the West Fork of the San Pedro." He opened a drawer and tossed a spur across the desk.

The lamplight glittered on the silver chasing. Jack stared at it. He would not touch it.

"You know whose it is?" asked the sheriff.

Jack dumbly nodded.

"It's Burt Lasser's, isn't it?"

"Yes."

"You know who was with him?"

Jack nodded. "Probably Mooney Dade, Josh Burson, Lupo Zamacona, Toribio Vasquez, and Estela Zamacona."

"A woman? A woman was there when that filth was going on?"

"You don't know that woman," said Jack dryly.

A moth fluttered against the lamp shade. A man shouted in the street.

Jack looked up. "I'm getting over the sickness of it," he said quietly. "I want only to kill now."

"That's not up to you."

Jack smiled a little crookedly. "No? Then who is it up to, Henderson? They're over the border by now with maybe forty thousand dollars from that payroll money, a *remuda* of some of the best blood horses in the Southwest, and the blood of ten people on their hands. What can *you* do about it? Not a Goddamned thing!"

Henderson nodded. "We have no extradition with Mexico at this time." He leaned back in his chair and took a bottle and two glasses from a cupboard. He filled the glasses and handed one to Jack. "Now you know why Amy risked arrest to get those tools to you. She believes in you, Jack. She was the one who finally convinced me to risk letting you escape to go after Lasser and his *corrida*."

"You know I'm wanted in Sonora," said Jack.

"Not as bad as you're wanted here. There's not a chance of clearing you, Jack, unless you bring back Lasser or one of the others to testify that you weren't mixed up in this filthy killing business."

"You're not giving me much," said Jack dryly.

"It's better than nothing."

Jack drained the glass. "What's in it for me?" he asked.

"You get across the border and round up Lasser and as many of his *corrida* as you can. You also try to get back that payroll money. You bring your prisoners and that money to me, and I'll see that you're cleared."

"As easy as that," said Jack.

Henderson refilled the glasses. "God knows, Jack, it's a

slim chance, as slim a chance as I've ever seen in a lifetime. But you know the owl-hoot trails from here to Sonora and clear down to Sinaloa. You know those people, and the *campesinos* think of you as a sort of Robin Hood. That's some advantage."

"Yeh," agreed Jack. "I was just thinking of Lasser and his bunch. It's mean enough to bring one of them in without trying for the whole *corrida.*"

"They'll likely be together," said Henderson.

Jack drained his glass and looked into it. "Do I have to bring them *all* back?" he asked at last. His meaning was plain.

Henderson suddenly felt chilled. He stood up. "I'm here alone tonight. There was chloral hydrate in Chacon's coffee, so he'll be sleeping long and late and waking up with one helluva headache, the spic sonofabitch!"

"I'm to go to Tolleson's place on Quality Hill then?"

"Yes. It'll be the last place anyone will think of looking for you. She'll have guns and money for you."

"What about Sue? Supposing she sees me?"

"She probably won't, but if she does it's a risk you'll have to take. You'll be taking risks every day from now on, Jack. I don't have to tell you what will happen if you're seen before you reach the San Pedro. If I'm not here to save your neck you'll be swinging from a lamppost in Brewery Gulch. *¿Comprende?*"

"*Yo comprendo,*" replied Jack. He held out a hand.

"Thanks for the break and the hot mince pie, Sheriff."

"*For nada, amigo,*" replied Henderson. He followed Jack up the stairs and locked him into his cell. For a moment he looked at Jack. "*Vaya con Dios,*" he said, and then he was gone.

CHAPTER SIX

Somewhere in town a clock struck ten. The dry night wind scrabbled softly at the walls of the Bisbee Jail. The sound overlaid that of the steady *wheet-wheet-wheet* of the good file as it bit deeper and deeper into the iron bar. Jack laid aside the file and took the hacksaw blade. He cocked his head and listened to the night sounds. There was no sound from the cell of Augustin Chacon. He worked steadily. Blood ran from his abraded fingertips, but he kept on. Sweat dripped from his face and ran down his sides. The bar was cut through at half past ten.

The clock struck eleven. A man laughed somewhere in front of the jail. Jack stopped filing. He waited a little while. By half past eleven he had removed one bar. He tried squeezing through the gap, but it was no use. His hands were raw by now and blisters raised, broke, and then exposed the fresh, wet skin beneath. A few minutes after the clock struck twelve, he had removed the second bar. He thrust out his head and looked down at the lot. He could see the faint light from the shaded window of Henderson's office. The light touched some of the shavings and sawdust from the wood used to build the scaffold.

Jack fashioned a knot about the two remaining bars and

cut through one section of it in such a way that all he had to do once he reached the ground was to flip the rope hard enough and the knot would loosen so that he could retrieve the rope. It wouldn't do to let it hang there to be seen in the morning light. He'd have to trust Henderson to not sound an alarm until the last possible moment.

Jack thrust a leg out of the window.

"Do not leave me here alone to die with the harsh rope about my neck," said the low voice from the next cell.

Jack hesitated. This was something he had not figured on.

"The coffee was lousy enough without the dope in it," said Augustin.

"You're slick," said Jack.

"I agree. Now pass me the file and the saw, *chico*. I won't take long."

"You'll shit too!" snapped Jack.

"Look, *amigo*," said Augustin patiently, as though he was addressing a child. "I mean to get out of here. Now, pass the file and the saw!"

"Up your ass, *chico*," retorted Jack.

Augustin laughed softly. "I have the ace up my sleeve, Juano. You climb out of that window and I will sing like a Missouri canary. You'll hear me braying all the way to Tintown. How far do you think you will get then? The saloons are full of drunken men who hate your Mexican guts! They need something to top off a boring night. You know what I mean, eh, *chico*?"

"I haven't got time to wait for you," warned Jack.

"You'll wait all night if you have to," retorted the Mexican.

There wasn't a damned thing Jack could do about it. The Mexican had him by the short hairs. This was something Henderson hadn't figured on—Augustin certainly knew that Jack's escape had been engineered by Henderson and Amy Tolleson. He passed the files and the saw through the bars at the front of the cell and then sat down on his bunk.

The clock struck one. "Well timed," said Augustin. "That's the first bar."

"Keep cutting, you bastard!" snapped Jack.

It seemed hours later, although it was only a little after two when Augustin finished with the second bar. Jack let himself out of the window and slid down the rope to the ground. He flipped the rope and it came loose from the bars and coiled down about his shoulders. He stepped back, coiled the line, and then cast it upward. Augustin caught it on the first cast. He made it fast to the bars and came down hand over hand. He stepped back, flipped it, and caught the rope as it came down. The Mexican had been around, thought Jack. *"Vaya con Dios, chico,"* he said.

Augustin grinned evilly. "Not on your tintype, *amigo,*" he replied. "We stick together. We need each other."

Jack raised a hard fist. Augustin shook his head. "I said I can bray like a jackass," he threatened.

Jack led the way toward the street. Hoofbeats sounded at the corner. The two fugitives faded into the darkness between two buildings and into an alleyway. The hoofbeats passed by in the street. They made their way through the reeking alley. Once Jack glanced sideways at the Mexican.

"I won't make any noise if I live," said the Mexican. "But I will not die quietly, *chico.*"

They reached the foot of Clawson Street. Jack drew Augustin into a doorway. "I'm going into Miss Tolleson's house," he said quietly. "It's the one where she lives now with her young sister who has lost her reason. Look you, *hombre!* I'm taking you in there with me, not because I want to, you understand, but because I have no choice. By daybreak this town and the hills nearby will be full of men and dogs hunting for the both of us. We'll have to lie low in the house until we can make a break for the border. You understand, eh?"

"Clearly," replied Augustin.

A big hand gripped the front of Augustin's shabby *charro* jacket and twisted it into a tight ball that constricted the

Mexican's breathing. The cold blue eyes seemed to bore into Augustin's dark eyes. "I can kill very quickly, *hombre,*" warned Jack. "Remember that I want no trouble from you in that house. I want no trouble from you—*ever.*"

Augustin swallowed hard. "By the bones of my sainted mother, I will not betray you. You must trust me, dear friend."

Jack led the way up the slope of the dark street. Here and there below them in the town yellowed lights showed. The town was quiet enough—for Bisbee on a Saturday night.

Jack rolled over the rear fence of the Tolleson place. A dog barked somewhere down the hill. Augustin quickly followed Jack. Jack cat-footed to the rear porch. He tapped gently on the door. He heard soft footsteps.

"Who is it?" asked Amy.

"Jack," he replied.

"Thank God!"

"I'm not alone," he warned.

"What do you mean?"

"It's all right. Let us in!"

Jack whistled softly for Augustin. The Mexican came silently through the darkness as the door swung open. Jack walked in followed by the Mexican. Amy closed and bolted the door. She lighted a candle and saw the dark, grinning face of the Mexican. Her head jerked backward in surprise and fright. "My God!" she cried. *"Him!"*

"I had no choice," said Jack.

"I feel so welcome here," murmured Augustin. He eyed her wrapper-clad figure.

"Where is Sue?" asked Jack.

"Asleep, under a sedative," said Amy. "There is a room in the cellar for you. This town will be alive with men hunting for you by daylight."

"That is the story of my life," said Augustin.

Amy led the way into a back bedroom. She pulled aside a shag rug and revealed a trapdoor cut into the floor. Jack pulled up the trapdoor. A ladder led down into the darkness.

"There is another way out of there?" asked Augustin.

"No," she replied. She drew her wrapper closely about her.

"This, I do not like," he said.

"You have no choice," she said. "Remember, these people know what you did to that storekeeper in Tucson."

Jack walked to a window and let up the shade. He parted the curtains. "I have to agree with him," he said over his shoulder. "I'm not going to be caught alive, Amy."

Augustin nodded. "You have guns?" he asked Amy.

Jack pulled down the shade. "Not for you, *hombre*."

"I had more freedom in the jail," said Augustin.

"You can always go back," suggested Jack.

Amy left the room. Jack walked to the door and looked back at Augustin. "Get some sleep," he said. "We might have to leave before dawn, risky as it is."

She waited for him in the living room, sitting in the darkness. "Can you trust him?" she asked.

He closed the door behind him. "Only until we get out of Bisbee," he answered. "He knows what will happen to him here."

"And you?" she asked.

He shrugged. "I won't be taken alive."

"I can't give you the guns then," she said.

"You know what you are asking?"

She nodded. "You can't use those guns against those people, Jack."

"All right," he agreed. She was right. He shook his head. "God help me."

She stood up and walked to a window to look down on the town below the slopes of Quality Hill. He came and stood close behind her. She turned her head to look up into his shadowed face. "You really haven't a chance, have you?" she quietly asked.

"I'm alive," he said. "They haven't caught me yet."

"But those others—the men who came to my father's house. How can you fight all of them?"

He smiled. "One at a time," he replied.

"You can't get all of them."

"I may not try very hard to get all of them—to bring them back, that is."

"Killing them is not the answer for you."

"It is if they want to kill me first."

"It doesn't make sense."

"It's very practical, Amy."

She turned to face him and touched his face with a cool hand, and the sudden and hot memory of Estela doing that very thing came surging through him. He placed his big hands on each side of her slim waist. It was the first time he had ever touched her. It was very quiet in the darkened house.

"You'll come back?" she asked huskily.

He drew her close and she tilted back her head. He kissed her hard and then tenderly. She slid her arms about his neck and held onto him with surprising strength. A soft whimpering sound came to them from beyond the closed hallway door. She drew back a little, but Jack held her close to him. He drew her to the couch and passed a rough hand across her face. "Don't speak," he said softly. He could feel the warm wetness of her tears.

"Will you come back?" she asked.

He nodded as he drew her close. Forgotten was his utter danger and the crimes of which he had been unjustly accused. She was clinging to him because she wanted him and because she seemed to know that he would not return. There was a deceptiveness about her body, for it had never seemed so full to him before.

She struggled a little at first and then responded eagerly and then passionately, until he found she was a delight despite her absolute lack of experience in such matters, for she seemed to know intuitively what to do and how to please him. At the last moment she would not free him and he let himself go fully. They clung together after the heat and passion of the act and did not speak.

A dog barked sharply down the hill. Jack raised his head.

She cupped her hands about his face and drew him to her full hot lips.

"Wait," he said. He raised his head again.

"Amy," Sue said from the darkness of the doorway. She came forward softly toward the couch through the darkness as they lay there in their warm nakedness.

"Oh God," breathed Amy. "No! No!"

"Is that you, Amy?" she asked. She looked about uncertainly.

Jack slid from the couch and stood close beside a wall cabinet, softly cursing in his mind.

Somewhere down in the town a bell began to ring. Jack slanted his eyes sideways to look toward an unshaded window. There was no glowing of a fire within his scope of vision, and yet the bell rang steadily, echoing back from the dark hills that encircled the town.

"Go back to bed, Sue," said Amy.

Jack could hear her as she tried to dress in the darkness.

"Are you alone, sis?" asked Sue.

"Of course! I laid down here to rest. Now go to bed!"

Jack could see her as she came close to the couch. She was so close he could almost touch her, and he caught her faint feminine fragrance. It seemed to him she could hardly miss scenting the passion sweat that still dewed his body.

"Why is the bell ringing?" asked Sue.

Amy stood up. "Come," she said. She led her sister to the hallway and closed the door behind her.

Jack fumbled into his clothing. He ran to the window and looked down toward the town. Lights were coming to life behind dusty windows. The bell did not stop its harsh clangor. That was no church bell, he thought.

"Juano?" asked Augustin hoarsely from the hall doorway.

Damn him! He walked like a cat. How long had he been there in the hallway? How much did he know?

Augustin cat-footed across the room. "It is not a fire," he said.

"No."

"The alarm then?"

"Yes. I think so."

"We stay here?"

The fear of being hunted down came over Jack. He felt the cold sweat of the pursued running from his pores to join the hot sweat of recent passion. "I can't," said Jack.

"Nor I, Juano," agreed the Mexican.

She closed the door behind her and came quickly across the room. "You must hide," she said.

"No, Amy," said Jack. "I can't wait for them down in that cursed hole."

"You won't have a chance in the streets."

"We might have if we leave now. Where are the guns?"

"You won't use them against these people?"

"Dammit!" he barked. "Get the damned guns! *Now!*"

She brought them to him. A Winchester saddle-ring carbine and a gunbelted Colt. The belt loops were filled with cartridges. "They are both .44s," she explained.

He swung the gunbelt about his lean waist with practiced ease and settled it about his hips. He dropped his hand for a draw and the cutter slipped from the shaped leather almost as though it was spring-impelled as from a half-breed shoulder holster. He took the Winchester from her hands.

"The magazine is full," she said. She handed him a wad of bills.

He drew her close. "We'll have to leave now," he said.

They walked through the darkened hallway with Augustin padding along behind them. Jack paused at the kitchen door. Augustin reached across a side table and neatly removed a knife from a wall rack. He surreptitiously slid it down inside his right boot.

"I'll go ahead, Juano," he volunteered. He passed them and went out into the darkness of the yard.

He drew her close. "I'll be back," he said. She rested her head against his chest after he kissed her. She was sure he'd never come back, perhaps he might never leave Bisbee. "I'll be back," he said again. He raised her head by lifting her chin and looked into the tear-wet dimness of her face. He kissed her again and walked out onto the porch.

"Jack," she said suddenly. He turned. "Even if you don't return," she said, "there will always be a part of you with me."

He was gone across the wide darkness of the yard like a hunting cougar.

CHAPTER SEVEN

Their pounding boots splashed through the wet filth of a rutted alleyway. The ringing of the bell seemed to be pursuing them. Hoofs thudded on the street ahead of them, and they went to earth as a knot of horsemen galloped past not fifty feet away.

Jack sprinted across the street into the next alleyway with Augustin close behind him. "Head south, *chico*," gasped Augustin.

"West," said Jack.

"Are you loco? South is Sonora!"

"West is freedom," said Jack. He ran down the alleyway. A dog lunged from the shadows, growling deep in his throat. The metal-shod butt of the Winchester crushed in his skull, but Jack Spade didn't lose stride in the killing process. Henderson had said: "I don't have to tell you what will happen if you're seen before you reach the San Pedro."

Jack forced his tiring legs up a steep street, past flights of wooden and stone steps that led up to houses perched tier upon tier up a narrow canyon. He glanced back past the sweating face of the Mexican to see a swinging lantern making a pale wash of light at the foot of the street.

A light went on in a house. Jack cut hard to the left and plunged through a gully that was littered with trash. Tin cans were kicked aside as the two fugitives cut through the gully. A house door was flung open and the light that streamed from it caught the two men in mid-stride like flies caught in amber, and then they were gone into the darkness. A man shouted from the street.

Jack climbed the side of a bare ridge and threw himself belly-flat at the top of it. Lights were winking on all over the town, which lay below them. Behind them the hills were dark and empty of life.

"Give me a gun, *chico,*" demanded Augustin.

"No shooting," said Jack.

"They will not catch me alive," said Augustin.

"You talk like a Gawddamned hero," said Jack dryly.

Augustin wiped the sweat from his face. "Would you shoot if they closed in on us?" he asked.

"Wait and see," suggested Jack.

"Mother of the Devil! I am escaping with a madman!"

"Come on," ordered Jack. He walked down the western slope of the hill with the panting Mexican close behind him. Augustin had spent too many months in jail, but fear was the goad this night, and if he had lost the use of his legs he would have walked on his hands.

Jack stopped short. A shack stood at the bottom of the hill, and a horse whinnied from the darkness behind it. "Wait here," said Jack.

He padded to the shack. There was no sound from within. He eased open the door and slipped inside, thumb-snapping a light from a match. The one room of the shack was unoccupied; likely it was a miner's shack and he was on shift that night, or more likely getting drunk down in Tintown. Jack opened a cupboard. There was plenty of canned food, but he didn't want to risk suspicion that anyone had been in the shack. He took a drink from a full bottle of rye and filled an empty tin can for Augustin. He whistled.

Augustin limped into the shack. "There is food for the belly?" he asked.

Jack handed him the tin can. "Here is food for the soul,"

he said.

Augustin emptied the can and wiped his mouth. "There is a horse in the corral," he said.

Jack left the shack and walked toward the corral, talking horse talk deep in his throat. "Hoh-hoh-hoh-hoh," he grunted. The horse came to him and he stroked its nose.

"You have a way with the *caballos,*" said Augustin.

"Why not?" asked Jack. "She is a mare."

"That is so. I know how you made out back at the house."

Jack turned slowly and Augustin stepped quickly back. "Break down that fence as though a horse had kicked it down," said Jack.

Jack found a bit and bridle hanging at the back of the shack, but there was no saddle. He mounted and waited for Augustin to get up behind him. They rode to the west. After an hour they took turns, riding and walking, walking and riding.

Jack plodded along behind the mare. Augustin turned. "Look," he said. *"¡Es el día!"*

The eastern sky had the faintest tinge of light gray to it. They crossed the San Pedro in the full gray light of the dawn with a cold wind rattling the gravel on the banks of the river and rustling the dry brush. An hour later the mare went down and could not get up again. Jack stripped the bit and bridle from her and lifted a rock. He dropped the rock atop the gear and looked down at the mare.

"A typical woman," observed Augustin. "Pretty, but weak."

"She did well enough," said Jack.

They let her lie there. Jack set the pace, driving on and on with a tireless leg-swinging stride. The sun hit their backs through the windless air and behind them the heat waves shimmered up from the wide Valley of the San Pedro. They did not try for the water holes for fear they might be watched. Their thirst grew and grew and became a living thing that tried to destroy them.

When the late-afternoon sun was slanting against their

dusty faces, they were high on the slopes far west of the San Pedro. They dropped at last to rest. A faint scarf of dust seemed to boil up from the west bank of the river.

"A posse," said Augustin.

"Dust devil," corrected Jack. He dropped flat on his back and flung an arm over his burning eyes.

Something brushed Jack's side, and before he could move Augustin had the Colt in his hand. Jack looked into the dark eyes of the Mexican.

"Don't move," suggested Augustin.

Jack smiled. "What do you plan to do?" he asked.

Augustin sucked at a tooth. "I don't really know, *chico*. It just bothered me to see you carrying all the artillery. You must be tired."

"Not *that* tired," said Jack.

"Do not try to get the Winchester," warned Augustin.

"You plan to go on by yourself?"

Augustin shrugged. "We were almost cellmates. We have come a long way together. On the other hand, I am not wanted at this time in Sonora, and if I am seen with you, perhaps they will judge me with you. The Law of the Roped Ones." He held up his free hand just behind his ear and jerked it upward, at the same time tilting his head forward and to one side and thrusting out his tongue.

"God will sort the souls," said Jack piously. "He will know of your innocence, *chico*."

Augustin grinned. "I would not face my Maker with lies upon my lips."

"Then you *are* perhaps wanted by the Rurales?"

"They *love* me in Sonora," said Augustin. "They do not understand me, *amigo,* but they love me just the same."

"Can you keep on? There's a little-used water hole in the Huachucas—Dripping Springs. It's perhaps a five-mile stroll from there to Sonora."

Augustin stood up. "I can keep on, *amigo*. But first give me the gunbelt, if you please."

Jack unbuckled the belt and handed it to the Mexican. Augustin buckled it about his lean waist and slid the Colt into its sheath. He stood there a moment and then darted his hand down for a draw. Jack had no expression on his face. The man was *fast!* Jack picked up the Winchester and led the way through the shadowed brush that clothed the broken slopes. A cool dusk breeze had begun to sweep down the slopes. It dried the sweat on his face. His throat seemed like a tube of corroded brass. He thought of the overflowing stock tank at the Tolleson place and wondered if anyone had locked the windmill to keep it from pumping up useless water. They were closer to the Tolleson *estancia* than to the water hole, but Jack could not bring himself to go back to that haunted place of horror.

The darkness covered the Huachucas in a velvety, dark-bluish shroud. Now and then a coyote broke the quiet. The night wind shifted a little and rustled the brush and the scrub trees. There was a faint trace of moonlight in the eastern sky.

Jack walked softly on. A horse whinnied suddenly from the darkness ahead of him and he stopped short.

"Before God!" hissed Augustin. "A horse! Maybe we are in luck!"

"It might be the law," whispered Jack over his shoulder.

"How would they know to get ahead of us?"

"The telegraph," replied Jack. He went to earth and bellied down the long, dark slope. Somewhere ahead of him on the far side of the shallow canyon he heard the splashing of water, and his throat seemed to close up at the sound. The faint sound of hoofs striking the hard, echoing ground came to him. Jack rested his chin on his crossed forearms. The telegraph wires could have been running hot all that day. There was an operator at Fort Huachuca, and the fort was not more than fifteen miles north of the water hole.

A horse whinnied and another blew hard, almost like an echo. *"Two* horses!" hissed Augustin.

"Yeh," said Jack in a low voice, "but who's with them?"

There was a quick spurt of light near the water hole. A match had flared up to light a cigar or cigarette. The match arched through the air. The faint glowing of the tip of the cigar or cigarette moved slowly about the water hole. Maybe one man and two horses. The man stopped beside the water hole. A shadowy form moved near him, and then another, and from the other side of the water hole another horse whinnied.

"Mother of God!" hissed Augustin. *"Three* horses!" He wiggled on the ground like a girl getting her first real feel. "Let's get them!" he said.

"Wait! Damn you!" snapped Jack.

The moon rose higher and cast its silvered light down into the Valley of the San Pedro and onto the rising eastern slopes of the Huachucas. A coyote gave melancholy tongue up the canyon to greet the new moon.

The man moved about. The clearly recognizable sound of a saddle being flung onto the back of a horse came to the two watchers in the shadows.

"Come on," whispered Jack. He bellied down the slope heedless of the sharp-edged stones. He stopped twenty yards downwind of the water hole. A horse voided and the acrid odor of the urine drifted down on the wind. Jack raised his head. The man was on his knees beside the pool filling a canteen.

Jack drew Augustin's head close to his mouth. "I'll ease up behind the water hole. I can cover him from up there. You move in on him and get the drop on him. For God's sake! No shooting!"

"I might only kill him a little," whispered Augustin.

Jack worked his way through the brush and tumbled rock to a ledge that overhung the water hole. The man was fastening his canteen to his saddle. He was big and dressed in dark clothing. Augustin came out of the darkness like a hunting cat. His hand was poised over his six-gun. The man whirled. Augustin dropped his hand for a draw, but the big man was too fast. He drew and extended his pistol. "Stay wheah yuh are, man," he warned.

He was fast! Faster than Augustin, thought Jack. Jack stood up. "Drop that gun, mister," he said as he levered a round into the chamber.

The man turned and the moonlight struck his face. His face was as black as a polished boot. He held the gun in his hand.

"Drop it!" snapped Jack. The pistol struck the hard ground.

Augustin moved forward. *"Soldado negro,"* he said with a sneer.

Jack slid down the slope. "Drink, *chico,*" he said. "We haven't got much time."

"I know you," said the big trooper. "You was at Granite Tanks."

"Corporal Cabell," said Jack with a slight bow. "A real pleasure to meet you again. You came in handy, mister."

"Private Cabell," corrected the trooper.

"We'll need two of those horses," said Jack.

"Befoah yuh take 'em, mistah, yuh better look at the brands," said the Negro.

Augustin raised his head and wiped his dripping mouth. "Jesus Christ!" he cried. "They have the U.S. brand!"

Jack knelt on one knee. "Get back, Cabell," he ordered. He drank while Augustin covered the trooper. Jack raised his head. "Fort Huachuca?" he asked.

Cabell nodded. "I'm out huntin' strays. Found two of them, as yuh kin see. I was headin' back to the fort after moonrise."

Jack walked to the saddled horse. It had cantle and pommel packs, a scabbarded .45/70 trap-door carbine, and a full forage bag of oats. Forage bags hung over the backs of both of the other horses. All three horses were sorrels, which indicated to Jack that they must be from the same cavalry company. "You planned a long hunt for those strays, soldier," he said over his shoulder.

"Company commander tole me not to come back lest I found them," Cabell said easily.

"He's lying," said Augustin. "He's a deserter cutting south for the border."

Jack eyed the chevronless blue shirt sleeves. "Busted you for that mess at Granite Tanks, eh?" he asked.

"Nope—for fighting," replied Cabell.

"And they let you alone off the post with three good horses, cantle and pommel packs, issue pistol and carbine, full saddlebags, and only fifteen miles from the border?"

Cabell shrugged. "You doan have to believe me, white man. Besides, it ain't none of your business."

Somewhere in the hills a coyote howled. A thin thread of sweat worked down from under Cabell's forage cap and glistened on his dark skin.

"It's getting late," put in Augustin impatiently.

"Yuh kill a soldier," said Cabell, "and yuh'll find out it's a lot later than yuh think."

"Listen to him!" jeered Augustin.

Jack drank from the water hole. The big black man bothered him. Jack and Augustin had the horses they had wanted so desperately. They could leave Cabell at the water hole.

"Los muertos no hablan," said Augustin quickly.

Jack shook his head. *The dead do not talk.* He would not let the Mexican kill the big trooper to keep his mouth shut, and yet it was a problem having him on their hands. Why was he there alone in the night prepared for a long ride?

"¡Andale! ¡Andale!" cried Augustin impatiently.

"I know what he wants," said Hunk. "Killin' me ain't the answer, mistah."

"You speak Spanish?" asked Jack.

Cabell nodded. "I get by," he said.

"Listen!" cried Augustin.

The shifting wind had brought the sound of hoof-beats to them. Jack turned quickly. Horsemen had appeared on a moonlighted hilltop. One of them shouted when the men were seen at the water hole.

"Soldiers!" said Augustin.

"They're after me, not you," said Cabell with a wry grin. "Maybe they *are* after you, too, at that. Yuh doan look like no tourists to me."

"You're a deserter?" asked Jack.

Cabell looked down at his huge, pink-palmed hands. "More than that," he quietly replied. "I bruk the jaw of the

officer that busted me. It'll be Leanvenworth on the rock
pile for the rest of my days if they catch me, mistah."

"Get out of the way!" snapped Jack. He mounted the
saddled sorrel as Augustin swung up onto the back of one of
the extra horses. "Move out!" yelled Jack at the trooper.

A carbine cracked flatly from the hill slope and echoed
through the canyon. The big sorrel ran easily. Jack glanced
behind him to see the sweat-glistening face of Hunk Cabell.
They could leave him once they crossed the border.

The moonlight shone through the rising dust as the
three horsemen headed south toward the border. Now and
again a carbine flatted off behind them, but the three sorrels
were gaining ground by the yard. Cabell had picked his
horses well.

"How far, mistah?" yelled Hunk.

"Half a mile, soldier!" Jack flung back over his shoulder.

They passed a lion's paw-shaped hill, and beyond it was
a ruined adobe. Jack slapped the dusty rump of the sorrel
with the buttstock of the Winchester. He let the big horse
run freely. In twenty minutes he drew in the sorrel and
looked back. The heaving sorrel went on as a carbine
cracked once more, far behind the three fugitives. Jack
grinned back at Cabell. The moonlight shone on his even
white teeth. "Welcome to Sonora, mister," he said to
Cabell.

Another mile passed beneath the hoofs. Augustin drew
rein. He turned toward the Negro with a cocked Colt in his
hand. "Get down, you," he ordered.

Cabell looked at Jack. "I doan know this country," he
said. "I cain't go back theah. I figured maybe I cud sell off
two of these hosses for livin' money and get far enough
south so's I cud work in the mines, or mebbe become a
vaquero on a ranch somewheres."

"Get down!" snapped Augustin.

Cabell slid to the ground and eased his crotch. "Kin I
have a canteen watah, at least?" he pleaded.

"You won't get fifteen miles after the sun comes up," said
Jack. "It's still hot as hell around here even for this time of

the year. There isn't any water for forty miles on this side of the border."

Augustin looked quickly at Jack, opened and then closed his mouth. He kneed his sorrel over to pick up the reins of the horse Cabell had been riding. Jack looked beyond the trooper toward the west. Thin dust was rising in the moonlight. There was a cased pair of field glasses hanging from the saddle of his horse. He uncased them and focused them through the moonlight, which was about as bright as daylight. He made out at least twenty horsemen. They wore dark clothing and tall sombreros. *¡Ojalá!*" he said. "Rurales!"

Augustin wasted no time. He dropped the reins of the trooper's sorrel and kicked his mount viciously in the sides. He galloped toward the distant hills to the south.

Jack grinned. "I had a feeling they'd have a welcoming committee for him," he said. "Come on, soldier! Those damned Rurales just might turn you over to the troopers! *¡Andale!*"

Cabell was up onto the back of the sorrel like a Cossack. They raced after the Mexican. "*¡Gracias!*" yelled Cabell.

"*Por nada!*" Jack yelled back. "I wouldn't leave the Devil himself out here without a horse!"

The hoofs drummed on the hard, echoing earth. Now and again, Jack would look back. The Rurales had spread out into a wide crescent-shaped line. He knew their tactics. The horns of the crescent would turn the fugitive back if he tried to break east or west. He would be forced to ride south with the horns ever pressing him one at a time, keeping him at a gallop, until at last the center of the crescent would close in on his tiring horse. The swift-running Tarahumare Indians of Mexico ran down rabbits that way.

"They won't catch these mounts!" yelled Cabell.

"They are great riders on fine horses," Jack yelled back.

"But their horses are tired," shouted Cabell. "They are losing ground, *amigo!*"

It was so. Jack and Hunk reached the base of the moonlit hills and looked back. The Rurales had given up the chase.

CHAPTER EIGHT

The moon began to wane as they rode south. A cool wind blew across the empty hills. Jack rode up alongside Augustin. "Where to?" he asked.

Augustin began to shape a cigarette as he rode. He lighted it and tossed the makings to Jack. "There is water ten miles from here, *chico,*" he said.

"A *tinaja?*" asked Jack.

Augustin shook his head. "The rock pans are all dry at this time of the year. The fall rains have not filled them."

"What then?" asked Jack as he lighted up.

"San Luis Viejo," replied Augustin.

Jack looked back at Hunk. He tossed the makings to him and saw a scowl pass over Augustin's dark face. "There's nothing there," said Jack.

"No people, no town, and no hope," replied Augustin. "But there is water there. No one goes there anymore, not even the Rurales."

"Why?" asked Hunk as he lighted up.

Augustin looked back at him. "Because it is haunted, black man."

Hunk laughed. "I doan believe in no ghosts," he said.

"I did not say it was haunted by ghosts," said Augustin.

"What then?" asked Hunk.

"Maybe you'll see," replied Augustin.

The moon was almost gone when they reined in on a ridge overlooking a shallow valley through which a dry watercourse wound its way. On the eastern side of the watercourse, huddled about a tumble-down bridge, lay an ancient *poblado*. Not a light showed. Nothing moved in the narrow streets. Not a sound came from the settlement. Beyond the ridge and up a slope, almost backed against a huge rock outcropping that thrust its bald head through a thin covering of soil and dry grass, stood the ruins of an ancient mission church.

"San Luis Viejo," announced Augustin.

The last of the moonlight glinted from a pool of water beside and to the rear of the church. The valley was tomb quiet except for the sepulchral whispering of the wind.

"As you see," said Augustin, "there is no one here."

"I've heard of this place," said Jack. "It's very old. I didn't know there was much of anything left here anymore."

Augustin laughed. "My mother is buried there in the *campo santo* beyond the church, *chico*."

"She lived here?" asked Jack.

Augustin shook his head. "She *died* here. That was twenty years ago, and even then the place had been long abandoned. We were traveling to Santa Cruz. The Apaches attacked at dawn. They killed everyone. Blood ran into the pool of water and turned it red. The blood soaked the floor of the church and splattered the walls. They were like Devils from Hell." Augustin's voice died away.

"You said *we*," said Jack. "You were here then?"

Augustin began to shape a cigarette. "I was only a child. I saw my mother raped and slain. The Apaches— they were Chiricahuas—took me with them. The last thing I saw was the smoke and flame rising from the church in which the body of my mother lay."

No one spoke. Jack studied Augustin out of the corners of his eyes. This was a new side to Augustin Chacon.

"You escaped?" asked Hunk.

Augustin shook his head. "I lived with them for two

years, learning how to be a warrior. In the end I was freed when the soldiers surprised the band in which I was captive. When I returned to this place it was as empty of life as it had been when I had last seen it. The victims had been buried over there in the *campo santo.*" He lighted the cigarette and slowly waved out the flame of the match, but his eyes never left the ancient ruin across the dry river. "I had no place to go. I had no family. No one wanted me. I learned to live by my wits."

"But you got away from the Apaches," said Jack.

Augustin looked slowly at Jack. "It was not a bad life," he said quietly. "I learned many things." He touched his sorrel with his heels and rode down the slope toward the *poblado.*

"He said it wasn't haunted by ghosts," said Hunk. "Whut did he mean, mistah?"

Jack shrugged. "Memories, maybe. *¿Quien sabe?*" He rode down the slope after the Mexican.

"Wait," said Jack as Augustin reached the edge of the settlement. He slid from the saddle and handed the trap-door carbine to the Mexican. "Cover me," he said. He took his Winchester and walked into the town and through a narrow street where the empty windows of the houses seemed to stare unseeingly at him like the eye sockets of long-dried skulls. His light footfalls echoed faintly from the houses. He stopped at the edge of the little plaza. The wind played with the dust and the scattered leaves from a few dying trees.

Jack crossed the dry riverbed beside the ruined bridge and paused at the western bank to eye the church. The front facade was in shadows but the moonlight still rested on the domed roof in a clear silvery wash of light that softened the ruins.

Augustin spoke from the eastern bank. "There is no one there, *chico,*" he said. "Go on." He laughed softly. "Not even the Apaches come here anymore."

As Jack walked up the slightly sloping ground toward the ruins, Hunk spoke to Augustin. "Cautious, ain't he?" he asked.

"That's why he's still alive," said Augustin.

The front doors of the church gaped open and one of them hung askew on its rusted hinges. Jack padded inside and stopped opposite the door of the baptistry. The nave and the sanctuary were dark except for the faint, filtered moonlight that came through gaps in the roof and the rear wall of the church behind the sanctuary. Jack lighted a match and scooped up a handful of dried stalks from the floor. He bound them together with a scrap of cloth and then lighted the end of the improvised torch. The guttering light revealed the scabbing wall paintings streaked with ugly stains like blood that had been long dry. The stations of the cross were empty. His boots kicked through loose piles of dirt and plaster as he walked toward the sanctuary.

The sanctuary had holes dug into the floor and behind the remains of the altar. Jack grinned. There were always treasure hunters in these long-abandoned places. "Sacrilegious bastards," he said. He walked down the few steps that led from the sanctuary into the sacristy and stumbled over a pile of rusted tin cans. The faint odor of old fecal matter and dried urine hung in the dead air. "Bastards," said Jack again. He passed from the sacristy through a narrow, crumbling doorway to the rear of the church. The last of the moonlight gleamed dully on a pool of water that had been neatly surrounded by paving. A narrow trough crossed the paving and met the foot of the huge rock outcropping. Jack walked to it. Water ran a quarter of an inch deep over the stones and into the pool. He tasted it. "Sweet," he said.

He walked to the crumbling wall of the burial ground, the ancient *campo santo,* and looked at the long-forgotten memorials to the long-forgotten dead. Somewhere in there were the violated bones of Augustin's mother. He walked back to the church and along the side of it to the front of the empty building. He waved the others on. He felt for his makings as they led the horses up the slope. "We can stay here until before the dawn," he said as he lighted up. "Those Rurales might still be tailing us. We're still too close to the border to suit me, *amigos.*"

"And me," agreed Augustin.

"I thought you once said you had no troubles in Sonora," reminded Jack.

"There was a little matter that had slipped my mind," replied Augustin. "One easily forgets such things."

"Like a killing," said Hunk.

"Screw you, black man," said Augustin in good, pithy Anglo-Saxon.

"I'll take care of the horses," volunteered Hunk.

"Don't try to get out of sight," warned Augustin.

Hunk shrugged. "I got no place to go," he said.

Augustin watched Hunk lead the tired horses to the spring. "We should have gotten rid of him," said the Mexican.

"Why? He hasn't harmed us. In fact, if it hadn't been for him, we'd likely be on our way to a necktie party in Bisbee."

"His help was not intentional."

"Split hairs!" snapped Jack. "We can keep two of the horses and let him go his own way."

Augustin took the makings from Jack's shirt pocket. "He doesn't know this country. He could easily get lost. He might be picked up by the Rurales, or caught by the Apaches, or have his black throat cut by bandits."

"That's his concern," said Jack.

"Why waste a good horse?" Augustin lighted up. "Besides, I want to keep this carbine."

Jack spat to one side. "Go tell him that, *hombre.*" He looked sideways at the Mexican. "He isn't armed. You have two guns. You go and *explain* it to him."

"Up your ass," said Augustin.

Jack was still laughing as he walked to join the trooper. "Cabell," said Jack. "I want to talk with you."

"Call me *Hunk,*" said the trooper.

"Because you are a hunk of man, eh, *amigo?*"

"Talk spic," suggested Hunk. "I got to get practice. I wisht I had more brains than hunk, mistah."

"They call me Juan, or Juano on this side of the border,"

said Jack. "You had enough brains to get out of the Army, Hunk."

Hunk tasted the sweet water. He looked up at Jack. "It was a home to me, Juano. Never knew my paw and maw—died of fever when I was a boy. I got raised from heah to theah and back agin and fed by gettin' a crust heah and a bone theah, beggin' and stealin' until I was fifteen."

Jack handed him the makings. "What then?" he encouraged.

" 'Listed in the Army. The Army figgered I was a grown man."

"I can see why," dryly observed Jack.

"That was ten years ago," continued Hunk. He looked down at his reflection in the pool as he slowly fashioned a smoke. "I figgered on servin' out my time." He closed a big black fist. "This ol' hand give me my discharge mebbe twenty years ahead of my time, and I cain't never re-enlist, white man."

"Juano," said Jack. He snapped a match into fire and held it to the tip of the cigarette.

"You saved my life back theah," said Hunk around the cigarette. "That Augustin, he'd have shot me down if it wasn't for you. Twict, that was. At the springs and just acrost the border."

Por nada," said Jack. "He talks much and says little."

"No! He meant it! I know men, mistah. Ten yeahs in the Army taught me that, if nothin' else. White men and black men, and spics like him especially, they all the same when it comes to the killin' mood. That spic back theah, he got *killin'* blood."

"My mother was Mexican," said Jack quietly.

"Shit! You're a *white* man, mistah. You look like a spic except for them damned blue eyes of your'n, and you talk spic like yuh was born to it, but yuh also talk good American, like our officers. You're different. Back on the Arizona side I cud have sworn yuh was a Yankee white man and now I ain't so sure. Yuh changed oncet we crossed the border. Why?"

"It's just an act," replied Jack. He grinned. "A professional trick."

"Anyways, I wouldn't turn my back on *him,* but I know I kin trust *you.*"

"I have a heart of gold," said Jack dryly. He took off his hat and let the night breeze cool his forehead. "Anyway, after tomorrow it won't matter. You go your way and I'll go mine. I'll see to it that he doesn't give you any trouble."

Hunk grinned. "Him? Long's he don't get behind me with a gun or knife I ain't worried."

"You got grub in those saddlebags?" asked Jack.

"Sure." Hunk stood up. "I'll take over for *cocinero* of this *corrida.*"

Jack laughed. "Except for the brunette color, *amigo,* I could swear you were a real *campesino.*"

Hunk unsaddled the sorrel Jack had been riding. He looked about. "Where do I cook?" he asked.

Jack jerked a thumb over his shoulder. "In the church," he said laconically.

Hunk hesitated. "Is that right?" he asked.

Jack took the reins of the horses and led them away from the water. "That church hasn't been used for maybe a hundred years. Hunk."

"That don't make it any different."

Jack stopped. He eyed the big man. "You a Catholic?" he asked.

"Baptist—I think," replied Hunk.

"Then it doesn't make any difference, does it?"

"It's still a church," said Hunk defensively.

"A man has to eat," said Jack. "Surely God wouldn't hold that against him." He led the horses to a patch of dry grass. He walked back to the saddle. Hunk was gone. Hunk had had the foresight to include three picket lines and three picket pins in his gear. "Strays," said Jack aloud. He grinned. "I'll be Gawddamned!" He walked back to the horses and picketed them. The moon was gone by the time he walked back to the church.

Hunk had made a fire in a corner of the nave, as far away

from the sanctuary as he could have placed it. He looked up from his fire. The sweat glistened on his face. Issue bacon was frying in a metal spider. Issue hardtack had been neatly laid out on a square of clean cloth. Beans bubbled in a pot. A coffee pot was beginning to steam, filling the air with its strong aroma.

"Courtesy of the United States Government," said Jack dryly. He grinned. "You thought of everything. Now how about thinking up a story for the Mexican authorities?"

"There ain't no 'tradition between Mexico and the United States at this time," said Hunk.

"Extradition," said Jack. He knelt and stirred the beans. "You might run into some *bandidos* first."

"I got seven handy rounds to take care of that," replied the trooper.

"Past tense," said Jack. "Augustin has your Colt and carbine."

"Doan I git 'em back?" asked the Negro.

Jack shrugged. He looked up. Augustin came out of the sacristy buttoning his trouser fly. "Ask him," he suggested.

"He wouldn't give me *shit*," said Hunk.

"He will if I tell him to," said Jack. "You really want them though?"

Hunk laughed. "I meant the carbine at least."

Augustin eyed the food. "How soon do we eat?" he asked.

"Coupl'a minutes," replied Hunk.

Jack looked up at Augustin. "Give him his carbine," he said.

Augustin's eyes narrowed. "I need it, *chico*."

"Give it to him," said Jack. He stood up.

"It's mine now," said the Mexican.

"Give it to him," said Jack.

Augustin gave Jack look for look. There was something in Jack's cold blue eyes that made him look away. He walked into the baptistry and came out with the single-shot carbine. He leaned it against the wall near the fire.

"Eat and go stand guard," said Jack to Augustin.

"I have no rifle now," said Augustin.

"Take my Winchester and keep to hell away from the horses," ordered Jack.

Augustin opened and closed his mouth. Hunk filled a tin plate with bacon, beans, and hardtack and handed it to the Mexican. Augustin squatted back against the wall as he ate, but his eyes darted toward Jack every time Jack looked away from him. Augustin emptied his plate and placed it on the floor. He fashioned a cigarette and lighted it. Casually, with seeming unconcern, he walked to the Winchester and picked it up. He looked at Jack's back. "There's a cartridge in the chamber," said Jack without turning.

Augustin walked out into the darkness.

Hunk handed a plate to Jack. "He hates your guts," he suggested.

Jack shrugged. "He knows who's running this *corrida.*"

"That mean me, too?"

"You want in the *corrida?*" asked Jack.

"I'd like to be."

Jack nodded. "You are." He began to eat.

Hunk filled a plate for himself. "Ain't you the one they call 'Jack of Spades'?" he asked.

Jack nodded shortly. "You know I am.

"Sometimes they call yuh Jack Spade and sometimes Juan Espada, don't they?"

"Sometimes," admitted Jack.

"How come?"

Jack emptied his plate. "Prime grub," he said.

"That's Yankee talk," said Hunk.

Jack sat down with his back against the wall. He took a cup of coffee from Hunk's big hand. "What's bothering you?" he asked. He sipped the coffee. "My father was a Texan. Fought all through the Civil War with Hood's Division. He wouldn't take the oath of allegiance to the United States and came down here to the Rio Nevome country. Married a Mexican woman, name of de Las Casas. She was my mother. He ran a ranch until he died." Jack began to shape a cigarette. "He never forgot Texas and the United States," he quietly added.

"And he wouldn't go back?"

Jack shook his head.

"So you're not an American then?"

Jack lighted up and looked at Hunk through the smoke. "*I* think I am," he said.

"But you're whut they call a Mexican national, ain't you?"

Jack nodded. "But my father was an American."

"But he wasn't a citizen no more."

The cold blue eyes fixed themselves on Hunk, but the big man did not look away. "My father was an American," repeated Jack.

"He didn't take no oath of allegiance aftah the wah," persisted Hunk.

Jack leaned forward. "Listen, you! He was an American! I'm an American! I'm also a Mexican! I've got dual citizenship! Is that clear?"

"I doan mean to rile yuh," said Hunk as he filled a plate for himself. "I'm jest curious about yuh, Juano. If'n yuh want to be an American so bad, how come yuh get into all kinds'a trouble up theah?"

"Who thinks I want to be an American?" demanded Jack.

"*You* do," quietly replied Hunk.

Jack leaned back against the wall. "Just how much do you know?" he asked.

Hunk slanted his dark eyes at Jack. "I knowed yuh didn't have nothin' to do with them killin's at Granite Tanks. It ain't that, mistah. Yuh know we got a telegraph way station at Fort Huachuca."

"What did you learn from that?" asked Jack.

"Nothin' much."

"You're a damned liar! Out with it!"

"All right then! Yuh ast me! I learnt yuh was wanted for them horrible Tolleson killin's. I knowed yuh escaped from the Bisbee Jail. I knowed they got a three-thousand-dollar reward out for yuh, dead or alive. Your description is spread all over Arizona Territory by now: White man. Looks, talks, and acts like an American born but can slip easily into the character of a Mexican national. Speaks Spanish and English without a trace of accent in either language. Five feet and eleven inches tall, or thereabouts. Broad shoulders and powerful build. Black hair and mustache and light blue eyes. Faint knife scar on left cheekbone. Known in both Arizona Territory and the State of Sonora by the name of Juan Espada, but when in Arizona uses the name John Spade. Known on both sides of the border as the Jack of Spades. Wanted for the murders of James and Lucy Tolleson and for possible involvement in the paymaster holdup and murders at Granite Tanks, in which forty thousand dollars was stolen. Spade, or Espada, escaped from the Bisbee Jail with one Augustin Chacon, a Mexican national under sentence of death for the murder of a Tucson storekeeper. There is a five-hundred-dollar reward for Chacon. Both men are thought to be armed. Both are dangerous and may be considered as homicidal murderers."

There was a long pause. A stick snapped in the fire. Jack looked up. "You've got a first-class memory, soldier," he said at last, "and you've even lost that accent of yours in the telling."

"I got to have a memory like that," replied Hunk. "Yuh see, I cain't read."

There was a faint scuffling noise near the door. Jack cat-footed toward it. He saw the dim shape of the Mexican standing twenty feet away, intent on lighting a cigarette. "Put that damned thing out!" snapped Jack. "It can be seen for a mile at least!" He walked back to the fire. "He'd sell his own grandmother out to be a whore," he said.

"He ain't exactly in any good position hisself, Juano."

Jack spat into the fire. "For three thousand dollars he'd find a way all right." He grinned. "It must gripe his ass that they're offering only five hundred for him."

Hunk laughed. "Such conceit," he said.

Jack studied him. "Aren't you afraid to be here with two homicidal maniacs?" he asked.

"Hell no! Not as long as I don't let him get around behind me."

"And what about me?"

Hunk looked up. "You ain't no homicidal maniac! Yuh weren't mixed up in the massacre at Granite Tanks and yuh didn't kill them Tollesons neither. I know!"

"*Gracias,*" grunted Jack. "Someone believes in me."

"*Por nada,*" responded Hunk. "I got to believe in you, Juano, 'cause I ain't got no one else to believe in outside of God."

Jack raised his head. One of the sorrels had whinnied sharply. "Put out that fire!" he snapped. He snatched up Hunk's carbine and ran to the door. He stepped outside and stayed in the deep shadow of the doorway. "What is it, *chico?*" he softly called out.

"Five horsemen! They are crossing the river!"

The fire was out but the pungent aroma of food and the acrid odor of the smoke drifted through the doorway.

"*¡Hola,* the church!" a whiskey-hoarsened voice shouted.

"*¿Quien es?*" responded Augustin.

"We are friends! We need water, *amigos!*"

"Come back at dawn," said Augustin.

"Your voice sounds familiar," yelled whiskey voice. "Is that Augustin Chacon?"

"The same, and you are my cousin Santiago Galeras!" Hoofs thudded on the slope.

"Stay where you are!" yelled Jack. Augustin came quickly to him. "What have we to fear?" he asked. "He is my cousin. At least I *think* he is my cousin. One is not always sure of such matters in a family as large as mine."

"One is not sure of anything in this country."

"They are positively not Rurales," said Augustin.

"I think I've heard of him," said Jack.

"A Child of the Moonlight," said Augustin. "We had better let them come on. We want no trouble with them."

"Do we sit our horses here all night?" yelled Galeras.

"We are a little careful, Santiago," called out Augustin. "The Rurales may not be far away."

"They have gone east to La Zarza, and with good reason."

"Why so?" said Augustin.

Galeras laughed. "They think *we* have gone there!"

"Let them come on," said Jack. "Keep your guns handy and a wall at your back. There are three of us, well armed. They probably won't take chances with us."

"*Three* of us?" asked Hunk from the darkness behind Jack.

"You can count," replied Jack. "You wanted me to deal you a hand. You've got it. Go start up the fire."

Hoofs thudded on the hard ground. The growing fire-light came through the half-opened doorway and flickered on the first horseman. He was a huge, squat man sitting a powerful dun. His face was hard and set as agate, and even when he smiled, as he now did at Jack, his black eyes did not follow suit. He dismounted heavily. "I smell food," he said.

Two Mexicans dismounted from tired, dust-stained horses. The fourth man sat his mount well back, just beyond the scope of the light. The fire flared up as Hunk fed it and the light struck the face of the fourth horseman. "Hello, Jack," he said.

Jack looked up. "You're a long way from Granite Tanks, Josh," he said.

He looked beyond Josh to the fifth and last rider. It was a slim figure who dismounted and came forward with a little bit of a swagger. "You have brandy, Juano?" asked Estela Zamacona.

Jack shook his head. "Where are the others?" he asked.

Josh dismounted. He jerked a thumb toward the south. "*Mas alia,*" he said shortly.

"How much farther on?" asked Jack.

"We'd like to know," said Estela. She reached into Jack's shirt pocket and withdrew the makings. Josh moved so that his horse was between him and Jack. "They didn't bother to tell us," said Josh.

"Pulled foot on you, eh? Where's the loot?"

"We don't have a Gawddamned peso," said Estela. She

expertly fashioned a cigarette and leaned forward for Jack to light it. The intermingled scent of cheap perfume and stale sweat came to Jack. Jack snapped light to a match and held it to the tip of her cigarette. "How'd your beloved brother leave you, his dearly beloved sister, behind?" he asked.

She sucked fire into the cigarette. "That sonofabitch!" she said around the cigarette.

"Water the horses, Hernan," said Galeras to one of his men. He walked past Jack into the church, and Estela followed him. Jack put an arm across Josh Burson's chest as the little man headed for the doorway. "Wait," he said quietly.

Josh looked up into Jack's eyes. "They screwed me out of it, Jack," he said.

Jack jerked his head back toward the church. "What about her?"

Josh shrugged. "She wouldn't play footsie with Burt and still wanted a share of the loot. Said she was entitled to your share because you were her man and she was your woman and you walked out on her."

Jack waited until the two Mexicans were gone. "Is that all?" he asked. "You wouldn't lie to me, eh, Josh?"

"No," replied the little man.

"When did you part company with them?"

Josh wet his dry lips. "Right after we hit them niggers at Granite Tanks," he said.

Jack nodded. He dropped his arm. "Go get some grub," he said. He watched the little man walk bow-legged into the church. There had been a lingering, sickening fear in Josh's washed-out blue eyes, something more than lack of booze and being left out of the spoils from the Granite Tanks raid. There was something much, much more behind his look of fear.

CHAPTER NINE

Santiago Galeras dislodged a stubborn bit of bacon from between his prominent white teeth, worrying it loose by the expert manipulation of a dirty fingernail. He looked sideways at Jack. "Juan Espada," he said thoughtfully. "I have heard much of you."

"And I of you," said Jack politely.

Galeras grinned widely. "It is said that the Rurales have more interest in you than they have in me."

"That is hardly possible," murmured Jack modestly.

"We both have our reputations, eh, Juan Espada?" His dark eyes flicked toward Hunk who squatted beside the wall with a cigarette hanging from his thick lips. "It is strange to see a *soldado negro,* still in the uniform of the United States, here in our beautiful Sonoran countryside. And those horses! ¡*Chihuahua!* With the U.S. brand on their flanks."

Hernan nodded. "Clearly to be seen, Santiago," he added.

"I. & C," said Hunk. He studied Galeras. "That means Inspected and Condemned, mistah."

"So they do not, then, belong to the U.S. Government?" asked Galeras pointedly.

"They're mine," replied Hunk. "I bought them at auction when I got my discharge."

"So I see," said Galeras.

"Those horses do not look condemned, Santiago," said Hernan.

"None of us look condemned, yet we are condemned in the eyes of the Rurales," put in Jack.

Santiago nodded. "A good point! And the fine carbine there, leaning against the wall. That too is condemned, eh?" He studied Hunk. "You bought that too at auction?"

Hunk looked easily at the burly Mexican. "Them guns you carry, mistah. You bought *them?*"

"That is my business!" said Galeras.

"Even up then," said Hunk. He flipped his cigarette into the fire.

Estela got up and smoothed out her split skirt. She swayed past the studied looks of the men about the fire and gave Jack the come-on, then walked toward the dim sanctuary. She turned into the sacristy.

"Which way you headin', Jack?" asked Josh.

"South," replied Jack.

"Rio Bavispe country?"

"Maybe," said Jack.

"After Burt Lasser?" persisted Josh.

Jack shrugged. "Why?"

"Yuh forget he buffaloed yuh at Granite Tanks?"

"No, but that's no reason to chase him all over Sonora is it?"

"No," replied Josh. "But he's still got all that money, *amigo*. They cut me and the gal out, Jack. I don't give a shit about that connivin' bitch, but I got a right to my split, ain't I?"

"Figure it out for yourself," said Jack. "You aim to go after those hard cases all alone?" He grinned. "You aren't big enough to hunt grizzly bears with a willow switch, Josh."

"I'll ram my Gawddamned navel down into the Gawddamned sand atryin'!" snapped Josh. "Besides, Santiago here and his boys agreed to go along with me on a fifty/fifty split. I get fifty percent and them three can divide up the other fifty."

Jack glanced at the impassive faces of Santiago, Hernan, and Antonio. Christ yes, he thought, they'll split fifty/fifty with you. "What about Estela?" he asked.

Santiago spat loosely into the fire. "She is only a woman, Espada."

"Not quite," said Jack dryly.

"With you to lead us," put in Josh, "we can take care of Lasser and his boys."

Santiago looked slowly at Josh. "It is I who leads," he said coldly.

"There's your answer, Josh," said Jack. He stood up. "Anyway, without me, you'll make a better profit." He walked out of the church and rounded the front of it.

Augustin stood near the water pool, watching Estela as she washed herself in the overflow basin. Jack fashioned a cigarette as he neared the two of them. "Those horses could stray from here to the Rio Bavispe, *chico,*" he said.

"You told me to stay away from them," replied Augustin.

"Not *that* far away," said Jack. He looked toward the church. "Your cousin has an eye on the three sorrels, *chico,* as you have an eye on the woman."

Augustin nodded. He looked sideways at Jack. "This one, too, is your woman?"

Jack shook his head. Augustin shrugged. "That is what she said."

Jack lighted the cigarette and thrust it between Augustin's lips. "She belongs only to the man who can pay her well, *amigo.*"

"How much is that?" asked Augustin.

Jack grinned. "You ask *her, amigo.*"

Jack walked over to Estela. She was brushing her thick, luxuriant hair. "You took your time," she said.

"Josh was trying to talk me into going along with you and Galeras," said Jack.

"Well?" she asked.

"You know what will happen. I doubt if they'll ever catch up with Burt and his boys, and even if they did, they haven't got much chance of taking that loot away from the Lasser, Vasquez, Dade, and Zamacona Company."

"I know that," she said.

"How'd you get mixed up with that lovely bunch in there?" he asked.

She shrugged. "I had no one to ride with but Josh. He got drunk in a *cantina* and shot off his mouth in front of Galeras and his boys. Right away they latched onto him, as the *Yanquis* say. What else could I do?"

"Your social status has slipped a little, eh, Estela? From me to Lasser to Josh and eventually Galeras." He jerked back his head to avoid the full-arm sweep of her open hand against his face. He caught her as she went off balance and felt the pressure of her full breasts against his chest. She tried to claw at his face, but there wasn't much heart in the effort. Her arms crept about his neck. She looked up into his face and for a fraction of a second he almost thought he was back in the dark living room of the house on Clawson Street in Bisbee. Her lips sought his and her hands passed up and down the back of his head and neck while she thrust herself at him. There was a deep distaste in him for her, but he had to play her game.

At last she stepped back and touched her hair here and there as she studied his face to see the effect her unspoken promises had had on him. "Forget Josh," she said in a low voice. "Ride with me, Juano. I know where Burt is going."

"Tell me," he said.

She shook her head. "Not now. I'll guide you well enough, Juano. Will you take me with you?"

"Of course I will, only to keep Galeras from bedding you on the bare ground, *chiquita.*"

She spat to one side. *"Him?* A pig would make a better lover!"

"Tell me, *chiquita,*" he said quietly. "Where did you part company with Burt and the boys?"

"After Granite Tanks," she replied. She felt in his shirt pocket for the makings.

"You are sure of that?"

She began to shape a cigarette. "Yes. Why do you ask?"

"You stopped nowhere else?" he asked.

She placed the cigarette between her full lips. He thumb-snapped a match and held it to the end of the cigarette, and when he looked over the flare of the match into her great, dark eyes he knew she was lying. "You tell me the truth," he said softly, "or I leave you here with the pigs."

She looked away from him. "I don't remember," she said evasively.

"When Galeras takes you," he warned, "it won't be in a bed but probably out in the brush with the gravel scraping your bare butt."

"It was at a ranch," she said at last.

"Tolleson's?"

"Yes."

"You saw what happened there?"

"Mother of God! Yes, I saw the beginning of it! I heard the rest of it! I ran from that house as though the Devil himself was after me! You believe me, Juano? I knew he was your great friend." She turned her head aside. "Those young girls! It was awful! I wanted to run away, but there was no place to go and I was afraid to go alone."

"They were all in on it?"

She nodded. "All."

"That includes Josh?"

She looked past Jack toward the church. "He was drunk, Juano. He was so drunk he went after the girls like an animal. After they were done they drank more and ate like the pigs they are. I would not go with them. I hid in the *bosquecillo* until they drove the horses and mules past it. When I went into the house. . ." Her voice died away. She dropped the cigarette and covered her face with her hands.

Jack knew that it was not an act. He knew her well enough for that. "Go on," he urged.

She looked up at him. "Josh was lying drunk in the kitchen. I sobered him up enough to get him out of there. They didn't care for me, and less for him— they had left him to take the blame for what had happened. I got him out of there and away from the *estancia*. The rest you know."

He fashioned a cigarette. Augustin was near the front of the church. No wonder Josh still held that lingering, sickening fear in his eyes when he looked at Jack. He knew what the Tollesons had meant to Jack. It was bad enough what he had done there, but the worst of it, to an alcoholic like Josh Burson, was that he probably could not even remember the evil that he had done.

Augustin came padding through the darkness. "There is trouble," he said in a low voice. "My cousin and the black man have the disagreement."

Jack walked quickly toward the church. He slipped into the sacristy and stopped at the stairs that led up into the sanctuary. He looked around the corner of the wide doorway. Hunk stood with his back to the wall and his big hands on his slim, horseman's hips eyeing the burly Galeras. "I tole yuh twict," he said evenly, "that this grub is for me and my two partners."

"And the horses too, eh?" asked Galeras.

"You're slowly gettin' the idea, mistah," replied Hunk.

"There is enough food for all of us," insisted Galeras. He walked over toward the saddlebags and lifted a flap with the toe of a boot. Antonio and Hernan stood behind the fire on either side of the big black man watching him closely. Josh squatted on his heels, teetering back and forth a little. He looked uncertainly from Galeras to Hunk and back again.

"That's enough, mister," warned Hunk.

Galeras seemed to casually move a hand, but when he raised it, it held the short, hooked blade of a *sacatrapos*. "So, you wish to die so young?" asked Galeras solicitously. He smiled. "Get back, black man."

Hunk did not move. The blade flicked out toward him. Hunk swayed back a little. The blade followed him and the tip of it touched the front of his shirt. Hunk's left hand cut hard sideways to drive the knife arm outward. The knife tip raked across his shirt, slitting the taut fabric. Hunk stepped in close and clamped a murderous double wristlock on

Galeras' right arm, and at the same time he brought up a knee into the Mexican's crotch. The knife tinkled on the paved floor. Galeras gasped with the pain and shock of the wristlock and the knee in his privates. He jumped backward and clawed for his pistol. "Antonio!" he yelled.

Antonio jumped toward Hunk. Hunk went low and came up, pile driving a left into Antonio's belly and smashing against his jaw with a right cross that dumped him right into the fire. He shrieked as his butt felt the searing pain of the thick bed of embers.

Hernan drew his pistol. "Behind you, Hunk!" yelled Jack. He ran through the echoing nave toward the group of cursing men. Hernan fired right across the fire toward Jack and missed. Jack fired his Winchester. Hernan spun sideways and fell over Josh, who was scuttling for cover on his hands and knees. Antonio rolled away from the fire and freed his pistol. He raised it to fire at Hunk. Hunk kicked out and caught the Mexican on the point of the jaw and his head snapped backward, his neck cleanly broken. He fell back into the fire again.

Galeras crouched and thrust forward his pistol to fire, but Hunk had snatched up his carbine. He fired at hip level and the muzzle almost touched Galeras' chest. The shock of the soft-nosed .45/70 slug dumped Galeras onto his rump and his head snapped backward and struck the pavement.

Josh fired across Galeras at Jack. Hunk whirled and stabbed the butt of the carbine toward Josh's contorted face. Josh whirled toward him to fire. Jack fired twice. Josh slammed back against the wall. His Colt fell from nerveless fingers. He looked strangely at Jack. "You've done it, Espada," he said in a low voice. "You've killed me." He fell sideways.

Jack ran through the swirling gunsmoke. He knelt beside Josh. Josh looked up at him. "I should'a knowed better," he whispered. Blood leaked from the side of his mouth. "I knowed all the time you'd kill me."

"How so?" asked Jack.

"I was there at Tolleson's place. Believe me, Jack, it was

the booze. I don't remember. It was the woman told me about it." He closed his eyes.

"Where was Burt heading?" asked Jack.

"Tres Alamos," mouthed Josh.

"Josh?" asked Jack.

Hunk dragged Antonio from the fire. "The little man is dead, Jack," he said quietly.

"*¡Jesus Cristo!*" cried Augustin from the doorway. "What a bloodletting!"

The woman came softly from the sacristy. She looked impassively at the dead. "He looks more like a pig than ever," she said, looking at the gape-mouthed Galeras.

"I think he loved you," said Jack dryly.

"Mother of God!" she cried.

Augustin cat-footed into the church. "They have relatives in this country," he said. "If they find out. . ."

"We kin blame it on the 'Paches," suggested Hunk.

"No," said Augustin. "Everyone knows they do not come here."

The powder smoke drifted slowly out of the open door mingled with the smoke from Antonio's smoldering clothing. "There is a vault beneath the sacristy," suggested Augustin. "Few people know of it."

They all looked at each other. "Find the door and open it," said Jack to Augustin. He looked at Estela. "Scrape dirt over the bloodstains." He picked up Hernan and placed him across his shoulders. "Hunk, you bring the pig." They carried the bodies into the sacristy while Augustin uncovered the trapdoor. They dumped the bodies into the vault.

"Rest in peace," said Augustin.

"Our loss is Heaven's gain," added Jack.

Hunk stared at them. "We jest kilt four men," he said.

"They would have killed us," said Jack. "Not Augustin, of course. He stayed out of the way until he was sure which way the fight would go."

"I am a cautious man," confessed Augustin.

They closed the trapdoor and kicked dirt over it.

Augustin replaced the thick litter that had covered it. "We can burn the church down on it," he suggested.

"The smoke could be seen for miles," reminded Hunk.

They returned to the nave. Estela sat by the fire smoking a cigarette. "What now?" she asked Jack.

"We'll leave now," said Jack. "I don't want to spend any more time around here than I have to."

They gathered their gear and carried it out to the horses. Augustin kicked out the fire and poured water over it.

They rode south in the windless darkness, driving the four extra horses ahead of them. At first dawnlight they rode down into a *malpais*, a country of shallow, crisscrossing canyons and deeply eroded arroyos. When the sun arose they found a deep cleft beneath a beetling cliff and into it they threw the extra gear they did not need. Hunk climbed partway up the slope and kicked down loose earth to fill the cleft. "We can turn loose the extra hosses in heah," he said.

Jack shook his head. "No. We can't take a chance on them being found. We've got to kill them."

"I doan like that," said Hunk.

"The sorrels have to go," said Augustin.

Hunk stared at him in horror. "No yuh don't!" he yelled. "It's bad enough for them other hosses!"

"He's right," said Jack. "Those U.S. brands are nothing but future trouble for us."

"Mebbe these Mex horses will be too," said Hunk. "Someone might know where they come from, Jack."

"Stolen, most likely," put in Augustin. "Do not fear. I have a cousin in San Juan de la Paz who will trade with us."

Hunk looked from one to the other of them for support, but it was no use. He unsaddled his sorrel and placed the saddle on a big gray. He did not look as Augustin and Jack led the three sorrels and a limping roan around the shoulder of a cliff. Four pistol shots ripped out to break the brooding quiet and the echoes chased each other down the canyon until they died away.

Hunk sat his horse as they returned. "Poor bastards," he

said quietly. "They never did no one no harm." He touched the gray with his spurs and rode up the slope to the south.

Estela watched him ride. She looked sideways at Jack. "Maybe you should get rid of him too," she suggested. "He's got U.S. on his flank too."

"She has a point," agreed Augustin. "I have suggested that before this time."

Jack looked at him. "You talk too much and say too little," he said coldly. He rode up the slope after the big trooper.

Estela shaped a cigarette as she sat there watching Jack ride up the slope. Augustin eyed her full breasts and rounded hips. "You know where this Burt Lasser has gone," he said quietly. "Juano has little use for you, *chiquita*. Maybe we should form a partnership and go after Lasser ourselves."

"And what of them?" she asked, jerking a thumb after Hunk and Jack.

He smiled. "Maybe the both of them have the U.S. brand on their flanks." His meaning was clear enough.

She lighted the cigarette and looked at him over the flare of the match. "Galeras was a pig and you, you sonofabitch, you are a slinking coyote!" She touched the flanks of her horse with her heels and rode after the other two.

Augustin shrugged. He held out his hands palms upward. "Now what did I say wrong?" he said to himself.

"Four to go," said Jack as he closed up beside Hunk.

Hunk looked at him curiously. "I doan get it," he said.

"Just talking to myself," said Jack. He placed a hand on the cantle and looked back toward the other two riders, but he was looking far beyond them in reality. Josh Burson had been at the Tolleson place, but somehow he was almost incidental, as would be Mooney Dade, Toribio Vasquez, and Lupo Zamacona. Burt Lasser was not incidental. All of Jack's smoldering hatred had settled on that damned, unblinking killer. If the others stood in Jack's way to find Lasser, they would die as Josh Burson had died, with a bullet in his guts, and be buried in an unmarked grave with no one to mourn over it.

CHAPTER TEN

"Tres Alamos," said Augustin Chacon. He reined in his horse and pointed down the long slope furred with yellowed grass that moved gently in the shifting late-afternoon wind like the wavelets on a lake.

Jack looked across the wide, shallow valley toward the distant town. Tres Alamos had been the last words Josh had said. Did a dying man always speak the truth?

"They said at San Juan de la Paz that no such men had been seen there," said Estela. "That was on the road to Tres Alamos. No one has said they saw them on the road."

"Maybe they lied," said Augustin. "It is easy enough to do."

"You should know," said Jack.

Augustin touched his horse with his spurs and rode down the slope beside Hunk.

Estela held out her hand for the cigarette Jack was fashioning. "Tres Alamos?" she questioned. "Why come here?"

Jack placed the cigarette between her lips and lighted it. "Where else?" he asked.

She shrugged. "I said I knew where they were going. It was not to Tres Alamos."

"We are almost there now, *chiquita*," said Jack.

She studied him through the smoke of the cigarette. "Don't you trust me, my heart?"

"Of course! But you will not tell me where Lasser has gone. Therefore, my heart, *you* don't trust *me.*"

Jack rode down the slope after the others.

Her great dark eyes studied his broad back. "Son of a pig!" she snapped. "My father was a Texan," called back Jack.

"It is the same thing! Is it not true?" she cried.

Jack laughed. He spurred his horse and caught up with the others. "We'll need supplies," he said.

"Do you think they are here?" asked Augustin.

Jack shook his head. "It's hardly likely. They're moving too fast."

It was after dusk when the four of them rode into the one long, winding street that followed the dry watercourse of Tres Alamos Creek. The mingled odors of burning resinous wood and rich, greasy food came to them mingled with the pungent and acrid odor of fresh horse and mule droppings.

"¡Parada!" ordered Jack. He slid from his saddle and led his tired bay in between two adobes.

"What is it, Jack?" asked Hunk as he led his horse in beside Jack.

"A horseman with two loaded burros," replied Jack.

Estela and Augustin led their horses past Hunk and Jack. Jack handed the reins to Hunk and cat-footed back to the street.

"By God!" he said over his shoulder. "It's Toribio Vasquez!"

"Then they must all be here," said Augustin.

"I wonder," mused Jack. "He's alone now. He's got two loaded burros."

"Let me find out," suggested Augustin. "I am not known here in Tres Alamos and Vasquez does not know me as he would know you." He walked into the street toward Vasquez, who was checking a lashing of one of the *aparejo* packs on the back of a burro.

"You trust that spic?" Hunk asked Jack.

"Up to a point, Hunk," admitted Jack.

"Mebbe yuh ain't too bright in the haid," suggested the trooper. "He knows what you're after all right."

"He'd be an idiot if he didn't know."

"He's no idiot," said Estela from behind them. "Crooked yes, but an idiot—no!"

Hunk slanted his eyes toward Jack. "You're really hot after that paymaster money, ain't yuh?"

"It's a fortune down here," said Jack. "You give me a hand and you'll get your fingers into that loot, Hunk."

"Yeh," said Hunk quietly.

Jack looked quickly at him but his black face was enigmatical. "I'll go along," promised Hunk.

"We can get rid of the coyote later on," said Estela.

Augustin came quickly to them. "He is alone. He is unknown here. He bought food and much liquor, perhaps for four or five men. He is riding south and west they think."

"You found all this out in such a short time?" asked Jack.

Augustin grinned. "I found a second cousin here."

"Christ!" said Jack. "Your family must be littered all over Sonora."

Augustin proudly waggled his head. "We Chacons," he modestly admitted.

Vasquez rode south on the dark street leading his two heavily laden burros. "He'll lead us to them," said Jack. "They can't be too far away."

"We need supplies too," reminded Hunk.

"There isn't time for all of us to stay here and get them," said Jack. He looked at Augustin. "You," he added.

"Why me?" demanded Augustin. "Sure! You take off after him and find his friends and get the loot, and I stand here in the street of Tres Alamos like a damned fool with a burro load of supplies!"

"The woman will stay with you," said Jack.

"Not on your tintype!" she snapped.

"All right," agreed Jack. He gripped Augustin by the front of his jacket and drew him close so that Augustin could see Jack's cold blue eyes. "Now listen, *chico,*" he said in a low voice. "You stay here and get the supplies. I am going after Vasquez. Hunk will meet you on the road to show you which way I have gone. Get it?"

"And I am here in Tres Alamos with the empty hands!" cried Augustin.

Jack backhanded him so that his head struck the wall behind him. "Who said you were in on the deal in the first place! You owe your miserable life to me, you goat!"

"But I'll end up with nothing," yelped Augustin.

Jack grinned crookedly. "The laborer is worthy of his hire," he said.

The dark eyes searched Jack's face. "How do I find you?" he asked.

Jack grinned again. *"We* find *you, chico."* He shoved Augustin toward the street. Hunk handed Augustin the reins of his horse. Augustin scuttled down the street.

"He'll try to kill you some day," said Estela quietly.

"Not as long as I can face him," said Jack.

"He'll wait his chance," she warned.

"She's right," agreed Hunk.

They led the horses into the street. It was in darkness now, except that the darkness was broken here and there by streaks and patches of soft light from under doors and through chinks in the shuttered windows. They passed the last adobe. They rode steadily but not too fast so as to keep the sound of their hoofs from reaching the ears of Toribio Vasquez. The wind was blowing in their faces, which would help conceal the thudding of the hoofs from the Mexican.

Hunk reined in. "Listen," he said.

The faint, hollow sound of hoofs striking the hard, rutted road came back to them on the wind. They rode on, and in two miles they could no longer hear the sound of the hoofs. It was Hunk who spotted the pinpoint of light that came and went almost like the blinking of an eyelid. "West," said Hunk. "It's dark as the inside of a boot ovah theah."

"There will be a moon," said Jack. He shoved back his hat and let the dry breeze cool his forehead. To the west rose the dark, humped shapes of hills. "He's heading for those hills, Hunk."

"Yuh know this country?"

"I think so. I'm getting closer to home." Jack pointed in a southwest direction. "There's a pass there. It isn't much traveled."

"Yaqui country," said Estela.

"Ride back and find Augustin, Hunk," ordered Jack. "We'll ride after Vasquez. When we reach the hills I'll leave Estela behind to guide you on."

She slanted her dark eyes at him. "Sure, Juano," she agreed.

Hunk hesitated. "Mebbe I ought'a stick with yuh," he suggested. "The lady heah cud go back for Augustin."

"Not me!" she said. "I'm sticking close to Juano."

"You're getting like Augustin now," said Jack to Hunk.

"It ain't that! Supposin' Vasquez has his *companeros* waitin' for yuh in them hills!"

"I've got Estela," replied Jack. He grinned. "Your solicitude grips my heart, soldier."

Hunk kneed his horse away from them. "Mistah," he said quietly. "I ain't even sure yuh got a heart." He rode off into the darkness.

The light flicked again, this time farther to the southwest. As Jack had predicted, Toribio was heading for the pass. He rode on, and Estela spurred until she caught up with him. "Why does the black man ride with us, Juano?" she asked.

Jack shrugged. "He has no place to go. Big as he is, he'd be like a lamb being led to the slaughter if he came into this country alone. He'd be shot in the back or have his throat cut while he slept, by Yaquis or maybe bandits."

"Since when have you become so charitable?" she asked.

"I'm aging," he replied.

"Crap!" she said. "He's after something, that black man. He's not as obvious as Augustin, that son of a she goat. But he's after something, Juano."

"We all are," said Jack. "Even you, my heart."

An uneasy feeling came through Jack. This was the border of the Yaqui country, of the fierce, predatory Indians who did not give nor ask quarter. Most of the *poblados* and ranches in that country held their homes, women, and horses only as far as the range of their rifles.

There came a faint wash of pewter light in the dark eastern sky. The moon was rising. It would not do to be caught out on the open plain in the moonlight.

There was no sign of Toribio Vasquez and his two animals when the silvery light flooded out beyond the mountains to the east to illuminate the rolling, grassy western plains. The notch of the pass showed clearly as Jack and Estela rode behind a low ridge that was still shadowed from the moonlight.

"He's gone into the pass," said Jack. He dismounted and led on his horses until at last he stood within the shadow of a towering pinnacle of rock with the mouth of the pass just beyond it. There was no sign of life in the mouth of the pass.

"Stay here," said Jack to the woman. "You'll be all right."

"Will you?" she asked. "Maybe he knows he's being followed. Be careful, Juano. I would die of a broken heart if anything happened to you."

Jack nodded. "You could always take the veil," he suggested.

"You coldhearted bastard!" she snapped.

He grinned back at her as he led on the bay. Partway into the mouth of the pass he withdrew his Winchester from its saddle scabbard and levered a round into the chamber. The walls of the pass closed in as he went on, and soon he was in darkness untouched by the moonlight. The walls spread apart in time, and he paused to look out on a jumble of broken rock stippled with thorned brush and scrub trees. The trail twisted and turned through it, sometimes almost doubling back on itself. Fifty yards into the tangle he found a few fresh hoofprints and a crushed cigarette butt that was still fresh. Now and then he would stop to listen, but all he heard was the dry voice of the night wind.

Jack stopped midway through the open area. Beyond it the walls of the pass again closed in, showing a dark slot as yet unlighted by the moon. He looked back the way he had come. A rifle cracked flatly. Jack hit the ground. The bay was down with his head flung back in sudden agony and dark blood running from its gaping mouth. The echo of the shot chased back and forth between the pass walls and then died away. The faint stink of powder smoke drifted down into the bottom of the pass.

Jack scanned the southern side of the pass. He figured it had not been a Yaqui. No Yaqui in his right mind would have killed such a fine horse. The faint sound of a burro bray came down to Jack. He left his Winchester in the trail and vanished into the thick jungle of sharp-edged stones and tangled brush. It must have been Vasquez who had fired down on Jack's horse. Jack wondered if Toribio had known it was Jack in the pass bottom.

He wormed his way up the treacherous slope. Somewhere above him he heard a faint sound. He bellied farther up the slope. A man coughed softly. The sound came from *below* Jack.

Minutes ticked past. Something kicked a stone loose from above Jack. It bounded down the slope, clicking sharply as it struck rocks. Jack raised his head. He caught a whiff of horse and burro scent He was in between Toribio and his animals.

Jack worked his way along the slope hoping to God that the animals wouldn't scent him and give him away to Toribio. Jack stopped short. A naked pinnacle of rock thrust itself up from the steep slope like a warning finger. Close to the side of it, almost as though he was a parasitic growth to it, was Toribio Vasquez with his rifle resting on a protuberance.

Jack cat-footed down the slope. He raised his Colt. "Vasquez!" he said sharply. "Drop that rifle!"

The Winchester clattered to the ground. Toribio began to turn slowly. "Drop the gunbelt, *cabrón,*" ordered Jack. The gunbelt dropped atop the rifle. "You can turn now," said Jack. "With the hands held high, Toribio, my valiant."

"You," said Vasquez as he turned to face Jack. "The Devil gives you luck, *hombre*."

"Where is Lasser?"

"Who knows?"

Jack jerked his head backward. "Two burro loads of supplies and booze. Were you planning to trade with the Yaquis?"

A thin trickle of sweat worked down Vasquez' face from beneath his sombrero. "I didn't know that was you down in the pass," he said.

"You killed my horse and you would have killed me," said Jack. "That was where you made your mistake, Toribio. You should have killed *me* when you had the chance."

"I said that I didn't know it was you."

"Bullshit!" snapped Jack. "Where are Lasser and the others?"

"I do not know."

"*You,* Toribio Vasquez, let them get away with all that loot? Or maybe you already got your split, eh?"

"God, the Lord!" cried the Mexican. "They slipped away from me three days past!"

Jack raised the Colt. "I have been nervous, and not myself since Lasser struck me on the head at Granite Tanks," he explained. "Then the headaches come, striking like a Yaqui arrow! They strike into my skull and at such times, Toribio, my friend, I seem to know nothing of what I do."

More sweat greased the Mexican's broad dark face.

"You should see a doctor, my friend," he said solicitously.

"But then," continued Jack, almost as though he had not heard Vasquez, "my friends tell me of what I have done during those violent seizures."

"What do they tell you, Juano?" asked the Mexican.

Jack smiled sadly. "That I have no control over myself. That I want to kill people, sometimes for no reason at all, even my very good friends. Is it not tragic?"

"These spells," asked Toribio anxiously, "do they come very often?"

"Very often," replied Jack, "and closer and closer to each other."

Toribio shifted a little. "What is it you want to know?"

"You rode with Lasser and the others from Granite Tanks to the Canelo Hills?"

"That is so," agreed Toribio.

"Then you were there at Tolleson's *estancia?*"

Toribio licked his dry lips. He wanted to insist he had not been there, but he knew better than to try that angle.

"I *know* you were there," said Jack quietly.

"Before God! I guarded the horses while the others were in the *casa!* I had nothing to do with the killings!"

"You lie! Why guard half-dead horses when you knew you were going to take Tolleson's fine mounts? You must have been hungry and thirsty. Therefore you were in the house."

Toribio swallowed hard. "Take my word," he pleaded.

"No! Josh Burson told me all about your part in the affair."

Toribio went pale even beneath his dark skin. "He lied! Where is he now? I will throw the lie into his face!"

"The dead cannot hear," said Jack.

"Bacanora," gasped Toribio.

"You want brandy? Time enough for that when we are finished."

Toribio shook his head. "There is a *poblado* southwest of the western side of this pass. Once it was called Bacanora, but that was long ago. It is not the same as the other Bacanora near Durango. This Bacanora is twenty miles southwest of here, Juano. They are there." Toribio smiled a little. "I can go now?" he asked.

Jack studied him. "Confession is good for the soul," he said.

"There is no priest here, Juano."

"I will listen, Toribio," promised Jack. He tilted his head

to one side. "You were in the house at Tolleson's and you were with the girls, eh, *amigo?*"

"Only one!" cried Toribio. "The *older* one!"

"Sixteen years old and a virgin," said Jack.

"It was the liquor! Before God! It was the liquor, Juano! Will you let me go now?"

"You killed my horse. I will need yours."

"No matter! I can ride a burro!" Toribio lowered his hands and turned to pick up his guns.

"Wait," said Jack quietly.

Toribio slowly turned to look at the taut face of Jack Spade. "No," he said.

"Start walking," ordered Jack.

"For the love of God, Juano," breathed Toribio.

"I will count to three," said Jack.

"It is not up to you to judge me," said Toribio.

Jack smiled thinly. "I appoint myself jury, judge, and executioner, Toribio. *One!*"

"It was the liquor I tell you!" shrieked the Mexican.

"Two!"

"I will go back to Arizona and turn myself in, Juano!"

"Three!"

Toribio leaped for his guns. The Colt spat flame behind him. The slug keened from the hard earth. Toribio plunged down the slope. Ten, fifteen, twenty, and thirty feet he made and still Jack did not fire. Toribio legged it, with the cold sweat flying from his face and his slightly bowed legs churning in the air as he leaped rocks and gullies. The safety of the brush was fifty feet away. He had ten feet to go when he looked back. He thrust out his hands to part the brush. The Colt cracked. The soft slug caught Toribio between the shoulder blades, driving him forward into the brush. He was still on his feet when he hit it. The Colt flamed again. The Mexican went down the slope almost as though trying to rise from the ground in flight. He struck far below on the sharp-edged stones and lay still at the very edge of the trail.

Jack mechanically opened the loading gate of the Colt

and ejected the three hot brass shells. They tinkled on the hard ground. Jack fed three fresh rounds into the cylinder and snapped shut the loading gate. He sheathed the Colt and felt for the makings. A burro brayed at the mouth of the pass and was instantly echoed by the two burros up the slope.

"*¡Hola!* Juanito! Where are you?" yelled Augustin from the trail.

Jack lighted his cigarette to show where he was.

Hoofs clattered on the trail. Hunk and Augustin walked toward Toribio leading their animals. Behind them rode Estela, with her shawl over her dark hair. Hunk's horse shied and blew hard at the blood smell of Toribio. "Mother of God!" cried Augustin. "Juano has been at the killing again."

"He sure don't fool around none," said Hunk.

Jack walked down the slope. "It's Vasquez," he said. "He'll be already sweating in Hell."

"Maybe you killed him too fast, eh?" asked Augustin.

Jack shook his head.

"He was at Granite Tanks?" asked Hunk.

Jack nodded.

"That's two of the bunch then," said Hunk. "You aim to kill them all because of what happened at Tolleson's?"

Augustin was already going through Toribio's clothing. He looked sideways with a cunning light in his eyes. "Do we go shares?" he asked.

"Keep it," said Jack.

"Bad luck to take things from a dead man," said Hunk.

"It sure was for Toribio," said Jack.

"Shit!" snapped Augustin as he stood up. "Not even enough for a bottle and a woman."

"His horse and burros are up the slope," said Jack. "I'll need the horse." He walked up to where the animals stood. He checked the *aparejos* on the backs of the burros. They were well stocked with food and liquor. It was a sure sign that Lasser and his *muchachos* were hiding out, for a time at least. "Bacanora," said Jack.

"Burro piss," said Augustin behind him. "I'll take Jerez brandy any day."

Jack turned. The Mexican walked like a cat. "I mean the old *poblado*," he said.

Augustin quickly crossed himself. "It is not a good place, Juano."

"That is where they are," explained Jack. He took the reins of Toribio's blocky dun. "Lead down the burros," he ordered.

Jack switched the saddle from his dead bay to the dun. "The others will be expecting Vasquez," he said over his shoulder. "If one was to ride into Bacanora riding the horse of Toribio Vasquez and leading his burros, dressed in Vasquez's clothing as well, one might get the edge on Lasser and his *muchachos*."

"Leaves me out," said Hunk. He grinned. "I'm too much of a brunette, even for a Mexican."

"I haven't got the shape," added Estela.

They all looked at Augustin. He paled. "Mother of God!" he yelped. "Not *me!*"

"You want into the deal, don't you?" asked Jack.

"Not that bad!" blurted the Mexican.

Jack felt about in the nearest *aparejo* on the back of a burro. He withdrew a bottle of brandy and pulled out the cork with his teeth. He drank deeply, but he never took his eyes off Augustin.

"I am not aching for martyrdom," put in Augustin.

"You're just aching for a profit," said Estela.

"A man got to invest to make a profit," said Hunk wisely.

Augustin took the bottle from Jack's hands. "Bacanora is not a good place, even without those vultures sitting there waiting for me. I do not like to be a target, my friends."

"It's where they are, *chico*," said Jack.

Augustin drank, and drank again. "It will be three to one," he argued.

"Hunk and I will cover you," countered Jack.

"Just like an insurance policy," agreed Hunk.

"Double indemnity," said Jack.

Augustin drank again. His eyes were a little brighter.

"Yuh want in on it," said Hunk, "yuh got to take some of the risk."

Augustin turned mechanically and walked back to the sprawled body of Toribio Vasquez. He stripped the body and dressed himself in Toribio's clothing, and then he mounted his horse. "We will need to trade horses before I enter Bacanora, Juano," he said. He touched his horse with his spurs and rode past the three of them who stood there watching him. He vanished up the trail.

"A hero of Mexico," dryly observed Jack.

"Chacon rides this night," added Estela.

Hunk grinned. "Yeh, but wait until he sobers up, Juano." He walked back toward the body of Toribio. He picked the dead man up as easily as he would have a dummy stuffed with straw and carried him up the slope. In a little while he came back again. "There any of that brandy left?" he asked. Estela silently handed him the bottle. He drank deeply and wiped his mouth with the back of a big hand. "I dumped him into a hole," he said. "I covered him with rocks. It ain't fittin' even a man such as him should be torn apart by the *zopilotes.*"

Jack handed him a cigarette. "You're all heart," he said.

Hunk nodded. "That's what my mother uset'a say." He grinned. "If I wasn't so black I might'a made a good chaplain."

They rode after the Mexican, and in a little while the pass was empty of life. The soft night wind moaned a requiem for Toribio Vasquez. It was a surety that no human being would have done it.

CHAPTER ELEVEN

Bacanora was in a great hollow bounded on the west by a dry watercourse beyond which were fields long untended. The *poblado* itself was composed of a quadrangle of streets established about a square. It had never been a large settlement nor a prosperous one. The roofs that had not collapsed within the interiors of the empty houses were thick with wigs of dried-out grasses that had sprouted in the earth.

Jack Spade focused Hunk's field glasses on the *poblado* which seemed to be dozing in the late-afternoon sun. A shimmering heat haze arose from the sunbaked fields and obscured his vision. There was no sign of life in the empty streets.

"Christ's blood!" moaned Augustin from down the slope behind Jack. "My head is about to explode in this sun! There is water and shade down there, Juano. They are not there. Let us go down there! I am dying!"

"Save his life, Hunk," said Jack over his shoulder. He heard the cork pop out of the bottle and the gurgling as Augustin added fuel to the fire instead of putting it out.

"Tha's enough," said Hunk. He took back the bottle.

"The hammers of Hell are pounding within my poor head," moaned Augustin. "I die!"

"Give him the last sacrament," said Jack to Hunk.

"I left my vestments back in Arizona," replied Hunk.

A faint whorl of dust had arisen from south of the town. A dust devil, thought Jack. He raised his head.

The faint whinnying of a horse came to him. There was a dusty *bosque* of aged cottonwoods and dying willows beside the dry course of the stream south of the town. A horse stepped out into the sunlight and back into the shade again. Jack studied the shadows within the *bosque*. "They're there all right," he reported over his shoulder. "Three horses are picketed in the *bosque*."

There was no sign of men yet. Likely they were holed up in the cool shade of the adobe with the thickest walls. The sun glinted from something near an arcaded adobe that dominated the northwestern corner of the plaza. A sombrero showed just beyond the arcade. The sun was reflecting from its coin silver ornamentation. "Mooney Dade," said Jack, almost to himself.

"The sun is almost gone," reported Hunk.

They waited until the sun died beyond the western mountains. The wind died away and it was very quiet. "Switch your saddle to Toribio's bay, *chico*," said Jack. He looked back at Hunk. "Give me a drink," he said.

"Don't get like Augustin," warned the trooper.

"Not tonight," said Jack.

"You let me in on this one, Juano. Don't you try no solo tonight," said Hunk.

Augustin cinched the saddle. "I don't have a chance," he said.

They waited until the moon rose and cast a faint silver light across the eastern mountains. "It is almost time, *chico*," warned Jack. "Don't wait until the moonlight is too bright."

The bottle gurgled. "It is empty," reported the Mexican. He hurled it bravely into the brush, wiped his mouth with the back of a hand, looked fiercely at Estela, and walked with a swagger to his horse.

"*¡Valiente!*" cried Estela.

Augustin casually waved a hand as he mounted. Hunk

handed him the lead ropes of the two burros. Augustin touched the bay with his spurs and rode to the east around the end of the ridge.

"Stay here," said Jack to the woman. He took his rifle and trotted to the west, followed by Hunk. They cut through an arroyo and reached the dry riverbed. They cat-footed along the sand and gravel of the riverbed and reached the first of the buildings by the time Augustin had reached the road that led through Bacanora.

Hoofs sounded on the hard-packed road. Something moved in the shadows of the arcade at the front of the building behind which Jack and Hunk were waiting. One of Augustin's burros brayed musically.

"It's Toribio!" called out Mooney Dade. "What kept the bastard so long?" A door slammed.

"Likely he got drunk," said Lupo Zamacona.

Jack worked his way along the side of the building with Hunk shadowing him. Jack halted. "That's two of them," he whispered. "Not Lasser. They're both dangerous, but he's the worst of the three. Watch yourself!"

Moonlight was flooding the valley and the town. Augustin rode slowly down the center of the street with his rifle across his thighs. Drunk or sober it took guts to do what he was doing.

"Yuh took your Gawddamned time, Toribio!" bawled Mooney.

Jack eased behind a buttress. Where was Lasser?

"Ain't yuh got a tongue, Toribio?" yelled Mooney.

The difference between the shapes of Toribio and Augustin was quite apparent to Jack. Toribio had been squat and broad-shouldered, while Augustin was tall and slender.

"Wait!" snapped Lupo. "That isn't Toribio!"

Jack ran forward. Mooney stood in the middle of the street staring stupidly at the man on the horse. "Toribio?" he questioned. He dropped his hand to the butt of his pistol.

Augustin lost his nerve. He dropped the lead ropes of the burros and raised his rifle. He fired once. The slug whined from the buttress beside Jack and sprayed his face with shards of plaster and adobe. He leaped aside with tears breaking from his eyes. Augustin had wheeled the dun and was giving it the steel as he raced back the way he had come. The burros galloped between Jack and Mooney.

"It's a trap, Mooney!" yelled Lupo.

Mooney ran toward Jack, but he was looking toward the retreating Augustin. Mooney turned his head and looked right into the muzzle of Jack's rifle. "Stand still and keep quiet, Mooney," warned Jack.

"It's Jack Spade!" yelled the big man. "Lupo! Lupo! For God's sake give me a hand!"

A gun exploded in the street and boots thudded on the hard earth. Mooney grabbed desperately at the barrel of the Winchester and thrust it upward with all his great strength. Jack kneed him and Mooney gasped as he bent forward. He clung to the rifle and jerked at it. Jack's finger accidently pressed the trigger. The rifle bucked back in his hands as it blasted against Mooney's belly. His eyes went wide in his face. "Jesus," he said thickly, and reeled sideways against the building.

Jack ran for the street in time to see a man running for the *bosque*. A gun flamed from a side street. "Hunk!" yelled Jack. There was no answer.

Powder smoke hung in the street, being slowly rifted by the evening breeze. Hoofbeats sounded beyond the southern end of town. Jack ran along the western side of the plaza. "Hunk!" he yelled.

The big trooper sat with his back against a building with blood dripping from his dark face. His pain-filled eyes looked up at Jack. "Creased is all," he gasped.

"Who was it?"

"Lasser," replied Hunk.

"You knew him for sure?"

"I ain't likely to ever forget him," he said.

Jack looked over his shoulder. The two burros were awkwardly galloping toward the *bosque*. "Looks like they'll get their supplies anyway," he said.

"It was my fault," said Hunk. "I jumped the gun."

Jack ripped his scarf from about his neck. "Stop that bleeding," he said. He tossed the scarf to Hunk. "You'll live," he added.

"I'll have a worse hangover than Augustin," said Hunk.

"In a better cause, Hunk," said Jack.

Jack walked back to where he had left Mooney Dade. The big man sat with his back to the scabbing wall and with his big hands resting on his thighs. Jack poked him with the rifle muzzle.

"Yuh done your damnedest with me already," said Mooney.

"That was Lasser and Zamacona that pulled foot?"

"Who else?" asked Mooney thickly.

"Where will they go?"

"Guess." Mooney looked up with a loose grin. "Not to Hell, like me, Jack."

"You'll live," said Jack.

Mooney shook his head. "You tore out my guts with that .44/40, Jack. Funny though, it don't hurt too much now."

"Has Lasser got that payroll money with him?"

"I was gettin' tired of always runnin' anyway," said Mooney.

Jack held the rifle muzzle under Mooney's jaw. He lifted the sagging head. A thin worm of blood ran quickly from the big man's mouth. "Where is he going?" asked Jack.

"Yuh go to Hell, Spade!" said Mooney. "Yuh can't scare me now, man."

"Talk!" snapped Jack.

"He about dead," said Hunk from behind Jack.

"He'll talk! He's *got* to talk!"

Mooney looked up. There was a grin on his rounded face. His head suddenly sagged to one side. A gush of thick, dark blood poured from his slack mouth as he fell onto his side" and lay still.

"Where's Augustin?" asked Jack.

"Likely back in Tres Alamos by now," said Hunk.

"He blew the trap," said Jack bitterly.

"Took guts to do what he done."

"We could have had them all," said Jack. He walked out into the middle of the plaza and looked to the south. A thin wraith of dust was rising from beyond the *bosque*. Sonora was one helluva big place with miles and miles and miles of more miles.

"Three out of five," said Hunk from beneath the shadowed arcade. "Tha's better than nuthin', Juano."

Jack turned and looked at him. "It's the money I'm after," he said.

Hunk nodded. "Yeh," he said.

Jack began to shape a cigarette. Three out of five, but the last two of the five were the most dangerous by far. He heard the sound of hoofs striking the road behind him. Estela reined in her horse and looked down at him. "You're all right?" she asked.

He nodded. "Hunk got creased."

She laughed. "It can't hurt that skull of his."

He looked up at her. "Mooney is dead."

She shrugged. "A great loss."

Jack leaned against the burro that she had led into town. "Lasser and your brother got away. South."

She pushed back her hair from her oval face. "So?"

He studied her. "We don't know where they're going," he said.

Augustin rode slowly into the plaza. He dismounted and wiped the sweat from his face. "I couldn't help it, Juano," he said.

"Bastard!" said Jack. "We might have had them all!"

"You sent a boy to do a man's job," she said.

Augustin's face darkened. "Don't talk like that, woman, or by God. . ." His voice died as he saw the look on her face.

Hunk passed a hand across his eyes. "Ain't no use in gettin' all riled up," he said. "No use in tryin' to chase them *hombres*. Their horses are fresh and ours is about wore out. We got food, watah, and shelter heah. We ought'a stay heah tonight at least, Juano."

"I'm giving the orders!" snapped Jack.

No one spoke. They watched him as he walked to the south end of the plaza. The dust was gone.

Estela dismounted. "Find a fireplace, Hunk," she said. She led the burro behind her as she followed the big trooper.

Jack walked back to the arcaded building. "There's water in the *bosque*," he said to Augustin. "Water the animals."

The smoke arose from the chimney of a big adobe. Jack walked into the patio of the building. The burro was tied to a post beside a door. Hunk walked to Jack. "I got to get watah for her," he said.

"In the *bosque*," said Jack. He waited until the trooper was gone.

She was bent over the hearth of the beehive fireplace. Her split skirt was hiked up in back, revealing her smooth brown legs and her small feet. Her figured boots stood to one side of the fireplace. Jack eyed her rounded hips. She looked back at him. "The black man was right, Juano," she said.

Jack nodded. He leaned against the wall and shaped a cigarette, watching her as she prepared the food. Hunk brought in a water can and placed it beside the fireplace. He looked at Jack. Jack jerked his thumb. "Get rid of Dade," he ordered. Hunk nodded. He glanced at the woman and then at Jack before he left the room.

Estela uncorked a brandy bottle and drank a little of the powerful spirits. She looked at Jack. "Cigarette," she said. He made it for her and placed it between her lips. He lighted it. She tilted her head to one side. "There is only one bed here, Juano," she said. She smiled. "The others can sleep on the floor in here."

Jack took the brandy bottle and drank a little. "You must be tired," he said. He looked at her suggestively.

A swift, knowing look fled across her oval face. "Not *that* tired, Juano!" she cried.

They ate silently. It had been a long, hard ride from Tres Alamos and the pass where Toribio Vasquez had died. They were a long way from the border by now; they had pushed on as fast as they could. It was time to rest a little, and yet Jack knew he could not rest.

Hunk yawned. "Who takes first watch?" he asked.

"Augustin," said Jack.

Augustin silently emptied his coffee cup and then picked up his rifle. He walked from the big room and from the patio to the street. Hunk glanced at Jack and then at Estela. "There is hay in a back room," he said. "A good place for me to sleep."

"Watch out for mice," said Jack.

Hunk picked up his carbine and left the room.

She squatted beside the fireplace with her arms dangling over her knees. A cigarette hung from the corner of her full mouth and she seemed to be lost watching the shaping, dying figures in the thick bed of embers.

"What is it?" he asked her.

She shrugged. "I am tired of this life, Juano."

"Who is not?"

She nodded. "With that money we can buy a hacienda, perhaps, in the Rio Nevome country."

"Not with our split," said Jack.

She slanted her great, dark eyes at him. "Just the two of us?" she asked.

"There is Hunk and Augustin," he said.

"To Hell with them!" she said. She stood up and came to him. "Let them help us catch Burt and Lupo. After that we can get rid of them. The Rurales will gladly take them off our hands. There might even be a reward for Augustin." She laughed. "More profit, eh, Juano?"

"We still have to find them," he said.

Her dark eyes became enigmatical. "We will," she promised.

The fire was dying out. Estela drank again. She wiped her mouth with the back of a hand and looked quickly at him. She handed him the bottle as she walked into the darkness of the next room. In a little while he followed her. She was swiftly undressing near a small window through which came the moonlight to rest on her smooth brown skin. She looked at him wordlessly as she lay down on the big bed that dominated the middle of the room. A faint wraith of dust arose from the old bed.

He sat down at the edge of the bed and idly passed a hand through her hair. "You want to be the wife of a rancher, eh, Estela?" he asked softly.

"Of you," she said.

"There would be children," he went on.

"As many as you would like," she promised.

He kissed her. Her hands worked at his shirt until she pulled it free from his body. She lay back as he peeled off his undershirt. In a little while he lay down beside her. He kissed her and her smooth arms drew <u>him</u> close. "Oh, Juano, Juano!" she cried. It was very quiet. He passed his hands along her body. She came to him, hungry and demanding. He held her back a little.

"First," he said, "where have they gone?"

She pressed her mouth against his. He drew back his head. "Now, Juano," she insisted. *"Now!"* He placed his big hands about the smooth column of her throat. "First," he insisted, "you must tell me where they have gone."

"Later, Juano," she said huskily. She thrashed back and forth on the dusty mattress, thrusting her lower body repeatedly at him.

"Tell me," he said. He tightened his grip.

Her eyes seemed to snap fully open. "Juano," she said. "You're hurting me!"

He leaned closer to her. "No one has to take you from here," he said in a low voice. "Neither Hunk nor Augustin would care whether you went with us from this place, and if you didn't, neither of them would ever talk."

She was really frightened now. Her naked breasts rose and fell, but not from passion. "Please, Juano!" she cried. She gasped as his hands tightened a little more. "Batoato!" she gasped.

He shook her a little. "You are sure?" She nodded and fell back as he released her. He sat at the edge of the bed, feeling for his clothing, and then stood up and began to dress.

"Juano!" she cried.

He buckled on his gunbelt. "What is it, my heart?" he asked.

"Where are you going?" she demanded. She sat up and stared at him in bewilderment.

Jack pulled on his boots. He walked toward the door. "Sleep well," he suggested. "We have a long ride to Batoato."

"You dirty, conniving sonofabitch!" she shrieked.

He slammed the door shut and grinned as he heard her raving in the bedroom. He walked outside into the patio. The moon made the town as bright as daylight. He walked to the center of the plaza and looked south. He knew of Batoato. It was in his own country, the Rio Nevome. It was an old town from back in Spanish Colonial times, when it had been the heart of a *real de minas,* or a group of mines of great wealth. The mines had been worked out over twenty years past and Batoato had declined and almost died, as Bacanora and San Luis Viejo had died. A plague had struck Batoato to add to its burden, and hundreds of people had died in the streets and the houses until the living had fled; the only living things in Batoato had been the *zopilotes* tearing at the putrescent flesh of the dead.

"Where do we go tomorrow?" asked Augustin from behind Jack.

"Batoato," replied Jack.

"It is a nest of thieves and murderers," said Augustin.

"Then you should be at home there, *chico.*"

"Your rich friends are there, Juano?"

Jack nodded.

"There is little law in Batoato," said Augustin. He shaped a cigarette. "Even the Rurales stay away from that place."

"They are there," said Jack simply. "You don't have to go there, *chico.*"

Augustin lighted up his cigarette. "The woman told you?" he asked. "She was not lying?"

"She was not lying," said Jack.

The Mexican looked toward the house where she lay in the bedroom. "It would be interesting to know how you found out," he mused. He slanted his eyes at Jack. "Was it before, or after?"

"I found out," said Jack. He grinned. "She was not satisfied, if that is what you mean."

He widened his eyes. "And you walked out on her?"

"I'm here," replied Jack.

"Mother of God! What a woman!" Augustin took the cigarette from his lips and looked at the house with hungry eyes.

"Go to her," suggested Jack. "She needs a man this night."

Augustin took one step toward the house.

"I'll take your place on guard," added Jack. "Go on, *chico*. It might be the chance of a lifetime."

Augustin sadly shook his head. "She is, perhaps, like the black widow spider who stings her mate to death after the act."

"Are you afraid?" asked Jack.

"Who? Me?" cried Augustin.

Jack flipped away his cigarette. "Either go or let me get some sleep," he said. Augustin did not move. Jack walked to the house next to the one in which Estela might still be waiting for him. He looked back at Augustin. "Batoato," he said.

Augustin shrugged. "It is as good a place as any to die, Juano," he said.

Somewhere in the quiet, moonlighted hills a coyote howled, just once and no more, and then it was very quiet again.

CHAPTER TWELVE

It was almost dusk in the great valley in which Batoato was sheltered. There was a curious liquid quality about the light. Long blue shadows were creeping down the mountain sides and feeling their way into the outskirts of the town. The last light of the sun had lingered for a time over the plaza, etching the lines and irregularities of the ancient masonry and bringing out the soft pastel hues of the buildings, and then it too had faded away into the soft light of the dusk. A wraith of bluish smoke hung over Batoato, hardly disturbed by the faint wind that blew down from the mountains.

From somewhere in the plaza there came the sound of a band that was slightly out of tune. Here and there lamplight began to show as the darkness filled the great valley.

Jack looked at Augustin. "We'll have to keep out of sight as much as possible until we locate them," he said, meaning Hunk and himself. "It's up to you to find out where they are."

"Have no fear," replied Augustin. "There are some ruins not far from the *campo santo*. No one goes there at night. It will be safe enough."

"Why doan anyone go there at night?" asked Hunk.

"It's haunted," replied Augustin.

"Go get the woman," said Jack to Augustin.

Augustin rode back down the slope and through the trees.

The poplars and date palms that thrust their heads up above the narrow, twisting cobbled streets of the old *poblado* seemed to be moving in time to the curiously off-key music of the band.

"Whut he mean by 'haunted'?" asked Hunk.

Jack shrugged. "The place is near the *campo santo*," he said. "There were many dead in the town in the old days. The road from the plaza was strewn with the dead who could not escape from the plague. That is the road near the ruins that Augustin told us about. It's between the ruins and the *campo santo*."

"I ain't sure I'm goin' to like that," said Hunk.

"You afraid of a few haunts?" asked Jack.

"Yes," replied Hunk. "I kin fight a man, but not a haunt, mistah."

Augustin rode up the slope. "She's gone," he said.

Jack turned quickly. "You're sure?"

"Both her horse and the burro are gone."

"She's gone into the town then," said Jack.

"Yes," agreed Augustin, "and you know what that means. She's gone to Lasser!"

"Tha's great!" said Hunk.

Augustin looked nervously down into the town. "Before God," he said softly. "She'll tell them about me."

"That's the chance you take," said Jack. He rode down the slope toward the eastern side of the town.

Jack dismounted in the thick woods just outside the ancient and scabrous wall of the *campo santo*. The tops of the tombs and monuments stuck up beyond the wall, and many of them were at various angles caused by the settling of graves and the heavy masonry of the tombs. Rusted iron-work formed a tracery against the night sky. The place seemed incredibly lonely. Not a soul moved near it. The only sound that could be heard was the dry whispering of the cool evening wind, which brought the faint sound of the band music from the distant plaza to the west.

"Let's get outah heah," urged Hunk.

"They're all dead in there," said Jack.

"Tha's why I want'a get outah heah," said Hunk.

"We're safe enough," said Jack. "Once I hid in such a place for three days."

"And yuh heard nothin'?"

"Nothing living," replied Jack.

Hunk wet his lips. "But yuh heah *somethin',* hey?"

Jack shrugged. "I thought I did."

"Then yuh got outah theah pronto?"

"No. I was more concerned about the living finding me than the dead."

"Yuh got ice watah in them veins, mistah!"

Jack led his horse through the woods beyond the wall of the ancient graveyard. The rutted road was dark and empty. They quickly crossed it and plunged into thicker woods south of the road. The eroded walls of a ruin showed darkly against the night sky. There was no sign nor sound of life about the place. Jack peered into a window. An owl soared right over his head and vanished into the woods.

Jack looked back at Hunk. "Water the horses," he said. "I'll rustle up some grub in here." He took his saddlebags into the ruin and found a room at the rear of the house away from the road side of the ruins. He made a small fire in the beehive fireplace and began to cook the food. It was the woman who now bothered him. She had kept much to herself on the three days' ride to Batoato, and he had seen the hate in her great eyes. He knew she had no use for her brother Lupo, and far less for Burt Lasser, but they had the money she had thought Jack was going to share with her. She knew now he had never intended to share the loot. He wondered if she really knew now why he had come so far south into Sonora. She must know!

Hunk poked his head into a window. "Hosses watahed and picketed," he reported. He stepped into the room. "Sure is quiet around heah," he added.

"Eat," said Jack. He handed Hunk a full plate.

Hunk eyed Jack as he chewed. "How far we from the bordah now?" he asked.

"Maybe two hundred miles," replied Jack.

Hunk shook his head. "A long ways to go back, Juano."

Jack filled his plate. "Who's going back?" he asked.

"Aren't you?"

Jack began to eat. He was never sure whether or not Hunk knew why Jack had come down that far into Sonora. "What about you?" he asked the trooper. "This is as far as I'm riding, Hunk."

Hunk glanced at Jack. "Mebbe I'll git me a job," he said.

"Where?"

Hunk shrugged. "In the mines. Mebbe I can git me a job as a vaquero on one of these ranches."

"Maybe. You ever work in a mine?"

"No."

"As a cowhand?"

"No."

"Sort of lets you out then, doesn't it?"

Hunk emptied his plate and reached for the coffee pot. "What about you?" he asked. "I know you're afteh that money that Lasser got. Supposin' yuh get it. What then?"

Jack shrugged. "Buy a small *estancia,*" he replied.

"You'll need vaqueros," said Hunk.

"You'll have a share of the loot," reminded Jack.

"Yeh! Mebbe we can buy a place together, eh? Or don't Mexicans go partners with a black man?"

Jack spat into the fire. "White, black, brown, yellow, or green, a man is a man to me."

"I hope yuh mean that."

Jack slanted his eyes sideways at Hunk. "Why'd you really cross the border, Hunk?"

"I tole yuh! I bruk an officer's jaw."

Jack nodded. "So you did." He placed his empty plate to one side. "Pass the brandy bottle," he said. He drank deeply and placed the bottle between them. He fashioned a smoke. "Let the fire die out," he said.

They sat there in the darkness lighted only by the fiery tips of their cigarettes. It was very quiet. Now and again, they could hear the music drifting from the plaza.

"Yuh think he'll come back?" asked Hunk after a time.

"He wants his fingers in that loot," replied Jack. "He can't get any of it without me helping him."

"And me," added Hunk.

"You really want in on it then?"

"Why not? We'll need money for that *estancia,* won't we?"

Jack stood up and walked quietly through the empty, echoing house. He stopped within the open doorway that opened onto a pillared veranda. The wind moved the leaves of the trees and brought with it the faint yet persistent music from the town. Jack cocked his head to one side. The music seemed to sound as though it was closer, and it was still off-key.

"They havin' a ball in that town," said Hunk from behind Jack.

"*Fiesta,* most likely," said Jack. He scratched his beard. The hum of voices and the sound of the music seemed ever closer.

"They's someone comin'!" cried Hunk.

There was a faint flickering of light to be seen through the trees from where the road curved along the bank of a stream. The light grew brighter, and the sound of the music grew louder.

"What the hell is it?" demanded Hunk.

"Get back inside!" said Jack. He followed the trooper into the house. "Put out that cigarette!" he said. He walked to a window. The shutters were still hanging on each side of the window, but the top hinges of both shutters had broken off and the shutters hung toward each other. Jack peered between two of the warped slats. He whistled softly. The road seemed to have become a river of fire, as though a silent and fiery lava flow had slid from Batoato out along the rutted road to the *campo santo.* Hundreds of candles were held aloft by silently walking people. The music had stopped, and the only sound was the shuffling of feet on the dusty road and the rustling of the heart-shaped poplar leaves that shook in the cool night wind. The wind brought the hot-waxy scent of the candles to the two hidden men who watched the solemn procession. Here and there along the long line of marchers was held aloft a crudely painted picture of a saint illuminated by the soft, flickering glow of the candles.

"What is it?" whispered Hunk.

The dust from the road lifted above the heads of the marchers and drifted through the smoke of the guttering candles. The head of the procession turned in toward the ornate rusted gates of the *campo santo*. A priest unlocked the gate, and it was pulled open with its hinges stridently protesting.

Something came back to Jack. "What day is this?" he asked over his shoulder.

"Second day in November," replied Hunk. "Why?"

The people walked slowly into the big graveyard and began to scatter down the many winding paths that led to all parts of the *campo santo*.

"It's the Day of the Dead," said Jack quietly.

"What the hell that mean?" demanded Hunk.

"El Dia de los Muertos," repeated Jack, almost as though to himself. "A national holiday, Hunk. It is the day the dead are honored. Look! See the arches of paper flowers being erected over the graves! Look at the children!" The little ones darted here and there on the road and into the cemetery wearing gruesome skull masks. A drum and flute began to sound just within the gateway, and the notes were curiously out of tune.

"Lousy beat," said Hunk.

Jack shook his head. "They play out of tune as an indication of mourning."

A brandy bottle broke in the road. Hunk laughed softly. "Somebody ain't mournin'," he said.

A string of firecrackers rattled and popped in the roadway. A man laughed. The candlelight shone on the rounded side of a bottle being raised to a woman's lips.

"Christ!" said Hunk. "Lookit him!"

A strange figure had appeared in the roadway. It was a man naked to the waist. He wore a flapping black skirt beneath which his dusty bare feet protruded. A black hood concealed his features. Bound across his shoulders and along his extended arms was a heavy bundle of sharply thorned organ cactus and held within the cups of his palms were guttering candles whose hot wax dripped in strings from his seared hands. Blood ran along his arms and down his heaving chest. Once he stumbled and went down on a knee, and then laboriously got to his feet again. No one paid any attention to him as he walked slowly within the gateway of the *campo santo* except to slightly bow the head as he passed by.

"A *penitente*," said Jack quickly. "No one pays any attention to him. He is considered as one dead."

"How long he do that loco stunt?" asked Hunk.

Jack shrugged. "Sometimes hours, sometimes days. Some of them return each year for a number of years to pay for their sins."

"Supposin' they die before they pay off, Juano?"

Jack looked back into the dark face of the Negro. "They come back anyway, Hunk. You see those people bow their heads a little to him?"

"Yes," said Hunk.

"If they don't, the dead person will prevent them from passing."

"Tha's crazy!" said Hunk. "He ain't dead!"

"They don't know that," said Jack. He grinned crookedly. "Do you?" He walked from the dark room into the kitchen and felt about for the brandy bottle. He drank deeply. He heard Hunk pad in behind him. "That's why we heard that music in the plaza," said Jack. "It's like a *fiesta* here in Batoato. That's why there are so many people in this almost ghost town. The *campesinos* come from miles around for the Day of the Dead, to honor the dead, to drink and eat in their honor, to live and make love and dance to the music."

"How long does this go on?"

"All night," replied Jack. He walked to the window and stepped through it to the ground beneath. "I'm going to get closer to the *campo santo*. If Lasser and Zamacona are really here in Batoato they might just be with the crowd there—everyone will come to honor the dead tonight. Stay here and guard the horses. No one will come here. They all think it's haunted. You're lucky, big man."

"Sure am," said Hunk dryly.

Jack walked east and waded through the shallow stream, then followed the eastern bank and crossed the road just this side of the bridge. He again waded the stream when he was opposite the spiked cemetery wall. He walked in a crouch until he found cover on a brush-covered knoll that allowed him to look over the wall of the *campo santo*.

The people moved amid the many graves and mausoleums, erecting their ornate arches of paper flowers and lighting candles, which were stuck in their own grease on the rounded cement tops of the graves. Weeds were being pulled from cracks in the cement. The ceaseless chattering of the many women engaged in the work was in contrast to the solemn silence of the procession. A drunken man danced wildly to the off-key music of the flute and drum until he fell over a grave and lay still. Children darted here and there wearing eerie-looking skull masks.

Jack's head snapped to one side. A tall man had walked as gracefully as a cat between two mausoleums and was lost to view. Jack was sure it was Lupo Zamacona. He would be there that night for sure, for this was the country of the Zamacona family.

Jack waited there as the graves were cleaned. A few people at a time drifted from the cemetery and along the road back toward Batoato. In an hour many of the people had left the *campo santo*. Honor had been done to the dead, and now those who were still alive were hurrying back to Batoato to savor the festive delights of the living.

Jack left the knoll and worked his way through the clinging brush to the wall of the *campo santo*. He peered over a broken part of it. There was no one near the wall. Candles still guttered on the rounded tops of the graves and the melted wax ran down and dripped on the hard earth. There were perhaps twenty people still in the graveyard, and as he watched he saw more of them leave. A man laughed on the other side of a tilted mausoleum. Glass shattered on the ground.

Jack rolled over the wall and landed light-footed in a patch of weeds. His left foot kicked an empty tequila bottle. His feet rustled through drifted leaves as he walked quickly to the rear of a mausoleum. He could hear men talking beyond it. He faded off into the shadows behind a huge mausoleum and peered around the side. Three men stood talking in front of another mausoleum, even larger than the one behind which he stood. One of the men was Lupo Zamacona. As Jack watched, the other two men walked unsteadily toward the gateway.

It was very quiet now in the *campo santo*. Slow footfalls came from behind Jack. The night wind rustled the poplar leaves and flared up the dying flames of the candles. The last of the people had left the graveyard. Lights winked on the tree-bordered road that led back to Batoato. Lupo Zamacona stood in front of the mausoleum shaping a cigarette.

The footfalls sounded closer. Jack stepped in between two buttresses of the mausoleum behind which he was hidden. He looked toward the wide pathway which was central to the *campo santo*. The *penitente* was moving slowly toward the distant gateway. Blood and sweat ran down his naked chest and soaked into the dusty, flapping black skirt he wore. One of the candles, the one which had been burning in his right hand, had gone out, leaving a mass of molten wax risen over the thick blisters of his hand. The smell of blood and sweat came to Jack. He saw the cruel barbs of the organ cactus thrust into the naked flesh of the sinner's back and into the flesh of his arms. Jack quickly bowed his head. The *penitente* made no sound other than the shuffling of his bare, bleeding feet. He passed within spitting distance of Lupo Zamacona, who was now lighting his cigarette. Lupo did not bow his head. He watched the sinner shuffling slowly toward the gateway. The *penitente* passed through and was gone. There was no one left within the *campo santo* except Lupo the Wolf and the man who watched him. Lupo looked about. He nodded and then went into the mausoleum.

Jack cat-footed toward the candlelit mausoleum. He pressed his back against the moldering side of it. Something creaked within the tomb. Jack eased around to the front of it. The heavy iron-barred gate in front of the doorway was half ajar and the heavy bolt-studded door was open. Within the crypt a man stood with his back to the doorway. In front of him stood three heavy caskets, one atop the other to the height of the Mexican's chest, with the lowest casket almost completely sunken into the ground. He was raising the lid of the uppermost casket.

Jack drew out his knife—it would be better if there was no shooting. He moved softly in behind the Mexican. "Lupo," he said quietly. Lupo dropped the lid and whirled like a cat in midair. The knife point was a foot from his belly. "Don't move again, Lupo," warned Jack.

Lupo smiled easily. "You are a long way from Arizona," he said, and then he nodded. "You have come for a share of the loot, eh?"

Jack shook his head. "You were at Tolleson's *estancia*," he said quietly. He did not need to say more.

"So were all the others," said Lupo. "All five of us, and the woman as well. The guilt is wide, Juano."

Jack shook his head. "No longer," he said. "You and Burt are the only two left. Josh Burson is dead, Toribio Vasquez is dead, and Mooney Dade is also dead."

"That was you at Bacanora then?"

Jack nodded.

"I knew it! I warned Lasser, but he laughed at me."

Jack glanced about the moldering crypt. "Why do you stay so late and alone here, Lupo?"

"Perhaps it suits my character. I was about to leave for Batoato. I intended to relieve myself in here, that is all."

"Lift up the lid of that casket," ordered Jack.

"There is nothing in there but dried bones."

"Open it!" barked Jack.

Lupo shrugged. He gripped the heavy lid in his strong hands and began to raise it. He kicked out sideways, supporting himself by holding onto the lid. Jack went back against the wall as the knife was kicked out of his hand. Lupo let go of the casket lid and drew his six-gun. He quickly motioned with his head. "Turn around," he ordered. Jack did so. Lupo drew Jack's Colt from its holster and tossed it through the doorway. "Turn again!" he ordered. Jack whirled, clamping down his left hand on Lupo's gun wrist, while at the same time he jolted home a hard right cross to the jaw. Lupo cursed as he dropped the gun and staggered backward. Jack snatched for the six-gun, but Lupo kicked it into a corner. Jack picked up his knife instead. Lupo kicked the heavy door shut behind him.

They stood there facing each other over the top of the uppermost casket. *"Bueno,"* said Lupo softly. "This is as it should be, eh, Juan Espada?" He drew out his knife and held it high so that the candlelight reflected from the keen-edged steel. "To hell with gringo guns! For men such as us the only true test between us is in the blades of our knives."

Jack felt cold sweat work down his sides. Few men were as skilled with the *cuchillo* as was Lupo Zamacona.

"No one will bother us here, Juano," continued Lupo. "But only one of us will leave here alive."

His gray hairs did not fool Jack. Lupo had not lost the swiftness and stamina of his youth and had coupled them with his years of experience.

"Now the hunt ends for you, Juan Espada," promised Lupo. "You have killed three out of five. A good score! Now it is your turn."

"You talk too much," said Jack dryly.

Lupo cat-footed around the end of the caskets and past the altar bedecked with dusty paper flowers and dead stubs of candles. His face was impassive in the candlelight; only his dark eyes were bright and alert. He flicked out his knife and touched it against Jack's in a quick, crisp slithering of good steel. It was only a test of Jack's reactions and strength of hand and wrist. A low thrust came so swiftly that Jack had barely time to parry the knife and leap back on guard again. The knife of the master came over Jack's and touched his face enough to slit the skin and draw blood, which ran down into the corner of his mouth and began to drip from his chin.

Lupo withdrew a fraction of a second before Jack's sudden attack. He held out his knife with his right hand and balanced himself with his left arm as he swayed back and forth, never taking his eyes from Jack's. Jack bulled in, thrusting hard and unscientifically, and all his blade met was Lupo's blade or thin air. He retreated with warm sweat streaming down his body. The air was getting stifling.

Lupo thrust high and then low and then high again, sweeping the knife across Jack's chest below the throat. Jack retreated again feeling the blood run from the slice across his chest; again the tip had just slit the skin. The fear came to him that Lupo was just playing with him. The knife tip touched his face. "You'll wear that scar in Hell tonight," promised Lupo.

Jack was beginning to feel a little hazy in the mind. Maybe it was the loss of blood. Blood splattered from his face when he made sudden moves. The knife cut Jack's wrist and the blood ran into his hand and greased the handle of his knife.

"Son of a whore!" cried Lupo. "Stand still and die like a man!"

Jack swept out his left hand and knocked the guttering candle to the floor, where it blinked out leaving a strong scent in the darkness. Jack leaped forward and felt Lupo's knife slide over his left arm drawing blood. He raised a knee into Lupo's crotch, and as Lupo bent forward, which Jack could feel although he could not see him, Jack's right arm rose and fell, driving the blade beneath Lupo's left shoulderblade and into his heart. The Mexican fell heavily across Jack's legs and his knife clattered on the hard earth.

Jack felt for the candle with bloody fingers. He lighted it

and placed it on the altar. Jack inspected his wounds with shaking fingers. He touched the slit on his face. Lupo had been half right—Jack would wear another scar, but not in Hell that night.

Jack heaved up the heavy lid of the top casket and held the candle over the opening. Piled beneath a grinning skull were a number of canvas bags. He cut one open, felt within it, and found thick wads of crisp bills. Jack picked up the limp body of the Mexican and dumped it in atop the old bones and the moneybags. "Rest easy, Lupo," said Jack as he dropped the lid.

Jack dropped Lupo's weapons behind the altar and then blew out the candle. He opened the door and walked outside. The graveyard was empty of life. He holstered his Colt. A tequila bottle rested atop a low tomb. There were a few inches of the clear liquid within the bottle. He drained it and hurled the empty bottle high over the mausoleum. It crashed on the hard earth. Jack wiped his mouth and looked at the mausoleum in which Lupo lay stiffening in death. A name had been carved into the ancient stone lintel above the doorway. "Zamacona," read Jack aloud.

CHAPTER THIRTEEN

Jack crossed the road and whistled softly as he neared the ruin. Hunk echoed his soft whistle. Jack stepped into the kitchen. "Give me a light," he said huskily.

Hunk thumb-snapped a match and stared at Jack's face. "God!" he exclaimed. "Yuh been in a cuttin' scrape?"

Jack nodded. He picked up the brandy bottle and wet his scarf with the liquor. He wiped at the cuts, wincing as the brandy stung them. "I found Lupo," he said.

"He's dead," said Hunk. "Otherwise yuh wouldn't be here, Juano. Lemme get some plastah for them cuts." He dug into a saddlebag.

Jack sat down suddenly. The reaction was setting in as it always did after a killing. Hunk ripped off pieces of medicated plaster and sealed the cuts. Then he shaped a cigarette and placed it between Jack's dry lips. He lighted it and searched Jack's face as he did so. "Yuh all right?" he asked.

Jack drank some of the brandy. "Prime," he said quietly. He got up and walked to his saddlebags. He took out a fresh undershirt and shirt and changed into them.

"Where yuh goin'?" asked Hunk.

"To Batoato. Lasser must be there."

"Yuh ain't in no condition to go aftah that killer," protested the trooper.

A soft whistle sounded from the grove that stood between the ruin and the road. A moment later Augustin thrust his head into the window. He eyed Jack. "You look different, *chico*," he observed.

"He's lost about a half pint of blood," explained Hunk. He grinned. "Seems like Lupo the Wolf lost *all* of his blood."

"Lasser is in Batoato," said Augustin as he climbed into the room. He took a drink.

"Did he see you? Did he know who you are?" quickly asked Jack.

"No," replied Augustin. "I stood within five feet of him, and even my mother would not have recognized me then." He reached inside his shirt and quickly pulled a cheesecloth mask over his dark face. He had transformed his head into that of a grinning skull. The effect was so realistic that even Jack felt uneasy. "He was looking for Lupo," said the Mexican.

"He won't find him," dryly said Jack.

"He was drinking," added Augustin.

"So much the better," said Jack.

Augustin reached inside his shirt and withdrew two more masks. "Batoato is in *fiesta*," he said. "No one would even recognize Hunk with one of these on. Very handy, eh, *chico?*"

"You used your head," admitted Jack. He drank again. The brandy steadied him. "Get the saddlebags on the horses," he ordered. "We'll leave them here in the woods. We can walk into Batoato."

They left the grove after they had replaced the saddlebags on the horses. They walked along the rutted road past empty houses whose paneless windows looked out at them like the empty eye sockets of ancient skulls. The music came to them on the night wind, but it was not out of tune this time, for the mourning was over and gladness had taken its place.

Jack looked back over his shoulder at the dark cemetery.

Neither one of his two companions would be with him now if they knew what wealth Lupo the Wolf was guarding in death. Lupo was now a *patron,* a ghostly guardian such as those left by the old Spanish miners, who would kill a slave to leave within a hidden mine shaft so that his ghost would guard their wealth. He laughed softly.

"Tell us the joke, *chico,*" urged Augustin. "I need a good laugh."

"Later, *chico,* later," promised Jack.

They walked into the ancient streets of the *poblado* with their heels echoing from the cobblestones. Jack put on his mask. "We'll split a block before we enter the plaza," he said. "Where did you last see Lasser, Augustin?"

"In front of the cathedral," replied the Mexican, "I did not see the woman."

"She'll be around," said Jack. "Trust her for that!"

Jack looked at the masked Hunk. "You're sure you'll know him, Hunk?"

"I won't ever fo'get *that* face," came the muffled reply.

They separated a block from the plaza. Jack raised his mask and lighted a cigarette. His wounds were drawing tight. He felt a little lightheaded. He finished his cigarette and lowered his mask, and then he walked slowly and leisurely toward the sound of the many voices and gay music.

The swirling life of the plaza swept about him as he walked from the side street toward the cathedral. Cheap perfume and rice powder, human sweat and animal dung, greasy food and strong liquor seemed to hang in an aura over the crowd. The loud music throbbed from a bandstand in the middle of the plaza. A carousel, whirled by a weary, dusty burro, stood in front of the steps that led up to the wide paved area in front of the cathedral. Shrieking children, each wearing a death mask like a uniform, rode the crudely painted wooden horses. All along the sides of the plaza stood lath and canvas booths from which shawled women sold trinkets, food, and liquor; and the most prominent of the articles offered for sale were those commemo-

rating *El Dia de los Muertos.* For days before November 2
death was always in the minds of the *campesinos,* and it was
everywhere present, in many forms, in the plaza that night.
There were displays of the special *panes de muertos,* or bread
of the dead, in animal and human forms, beside candy skulls
with bright, glittering tinsel eyes. There were little toy
coffins from which a skeleton would jump when a string was
pulled, as well as little processions of priests, made of shiny
black paper, carrying paper coffins. There were miniature
altars covered with imitation *ofrendas,* or food offerings, for
the dead. There were dancing skeletons on sticks whose clay
heads leered gruesomely at passersby. There were shining
skeleton necktie pins with weird eyes, dangling ribs, and
fleshless thigh bones that young girls bought to present to
their lovers. Everywhere there were masks, either displayed
in the stalls or on the heads and faces of the merrymakers.
Street hawkers sold sheets of *calaveras* covered with satirical
and mocking verses addressed to well-known people, such as
the policemen, who were referred to as *tecolotes,* or owls; and
even the priests were not spared in the scurrilous verses.

The plaza was thronged with *campesinos* from the valleys
and the hills, as well as the cityfolk of Batoato. Here and
there a horseman would walk with jingling spurs, wearing a
heavy steeple-crowned hat banded thickly with coin silver
ornamentation. The crowd was thick with many women,
from slim young ones to shapeless older ones, and everywhere the *putas* walked, swinging their hips and looking
boldly at all the men, from those who were hardly more
than boys to those whose hair was already white-thatched.

Jack walked up to the broad paved area in front of the
twin-towered cathedral. There were no stalls or hawkers
there, only a few of the black-shawled older women walking
slowly into the candlelit interior of the church. Jack looked
inside toward the great altar, which was ablaze with candles.
There were no benches for the worshippers. They knelt and
prayed on the worn flagging of the broad nave.

He stood at the low wall that edged the paved area,
looking down on the noisy throng for a tall, broad-shoul-

dered man—a gringo who would answer to the description of Burt Lasser. It seemed to Jack that every tall vaquero in Sonora had shown up for the Day of the Dead in Batoato that night.

He walked down the broad stairs and worked his way to the edge of the plaza, ignoring the giggling girls who tried to catch his eye. There was no sight of Hunk or Augustin. He reached the northern side of the plaza opposite the towering cathedral. A tall man passed through the fringe of the crowd and walked toward Jack. His mask was limp with sweat. Jack stepped back into a doorway.

The man stopped and raised his mask. "You American?" he asked.

He was a stranger. Jack shook his head. The man dropped his mask and passed on into a side street.

Jack raised his mask and drank from his flask, and as he did so another tall man looked at him from near the bandstand, and then rapidly walked toward the mouth of a narrow street that led off to the west of the plaza. Jack dropped his mask and walked quickly after the tall man. The man turned and looked back toward the plaza, and his mask was so eerily haunting that it even gave Jack a start. He stepped into a doorway. The man was Lasser! It *had* to be Lasser! He ran down a street at right angles to the one in which the tall man had walked. He cut to his left up a narrow, high-walled lane and ran to the meeting of a narrow street. It was very dark. A woman laughed from within a building.

There was a faint patch of light from a split shutter. The tall man stood there, legs apart, relieving himself against a wall. Jack drew his Colt and closed in on him as silently as a hunting cat. His foot kicked a stone ahead of him. The man quickly turned.

"Lasser!" said Jack.

The man dropped his hand to his pistol. Jack swung his own Colt and the long barrel slapped the man alongside the skull just below his hat brim. The man went down soundlessly into his own puddle. Jack knelt and ripped off the sweat-damp mask. He snapped a match into life and looked down into the face of a total stranger.

Jack faded into the next street when the man groaned. The faint sound of the music from the plaza drifted through the quiet streets. Jack started back toward the plaza. To his left was the front of a great house whose barred windows had been covered with wooden shutters that sealed off any sight into the interior. There was a great *zaguán*, or carriage door, in the middle of the wall. Set within one half of the door was another, smaller door, for those who entered the house on foot.

A woman was singing somewhere within the great house. Jack stopped and raised his head. He pulled off his sweat-soaked mask and walked to the small door. He touched it with his hand and it opened silently. The strong odor of resinous burning wood flowed about him. He stepped within the entry way. The woman was still singing. He knew that voice! It was her— Estela!

He padded through the entry way and looked out on a shadowed patio that had seen better days many years past. The flagging had cracks and great hollows in it from which rank weeds had sprouted. Faint firelight showed within a partly opened door. The woman had stopped singing. Jack drew his Colt. He wet his dry lips. Maybe it wasn't her at all.

He crossed the patio like a ghost and stopped close to the wall beside the partly opened door. He peered into the room. A thick layer of embers lay in a beehive fireplace and the flickering light danced on the peeling walls.

Something hard poked against Jack's back just above the kidneys. A hand reached around him and shoved the door fully open. The draft from the open door swirled over the embers and raised dancing flames.

Jack slowly turned his head to look into a death's head mask not a foot from his own face. The mask was so realistic that for a moment he wasn't too sure he wasn't looking at the real thing. The man silently pointed into the room. Jack raised his hands and walked ahead of him.

"Drop the Colt, Jack," said Burt Lasser.

"It had to be you," said Jack.

"What did you expect?" asked Lasser. "I saw you in the plaza walking around wearing that stupid mask. You didn't fool me, Spade!"

Someone moved in the shadows at the back of the room. "Close the door, Estela," ordered Lasser.

The door slammed shut. She walked to the fire and threw wood on it. As the flames rose and lighted the room she looked triumphantly back at Jack. "He's too handsome to kill, Burt," she said maliciously. "You can't kill the Jack of Spades in this country and get away with it."

"More likely the 'Jackass of Spades'," he said. He laughed softly at his own poor joke. "Where's Lupo?" he asked.

Jack looked back at the man. "How should I know?" he asked. "The last time I saw him was in Bacanora."

"You're lying! He met you when you got here!"

She was intently watching Jack's face. Her eyes flicked toward Burt and then back again to Jack. "Maybe he doesn't know where Lupo is, Burt," she said.

"What did the Wolf do?" asked Jack. "Walk out with his share of the loot, eh, Burt?"

Estela stood up. "He walked out with *all* of it, Juano," she said quietly.

Jack did not move a muscle. It was no time to rib Lasser. The man was humorless and in a killing mood.

The gun muzzle poked into Jack's back. "Where is he, Spade?" asked Lasser.

Jack would have to risk it. It was either that or die with a bullet through his back. One way or another he had to get out of that house even with Lasser holding a gun on him. "At the *campo santo*," said Jack.

"You lie like a real Christian, Spade!" said Lasser.

Jack looked back at him. "You'd better hurry, Lasser. He's got the loot with him. In another hour he'll be so far ahead of you you'll never catch him."

"You hear what he says?" shrilled Estela.

"He's lying, Gawddamn him!"

"Look at his face, you fool! I know him! He's not lying! He can't fool me!" she yelled.

"Go get the horses," he said to her.

"Get them yourself! I'm not letting you get out of my sight with him," she said to Lasser.

"Pick up his gun. Hold him here," ordered Lasser.

She snatched up the Colt and cocked it. Lasser left the room.

Jack studied her. "You're really fooling him, aren't you?" he asked. "Look, Estela," he added, "give me that gun. We can go together to get Lupo and the money." He wasn't lying to her—he meant it, but not quite the way she might expect.

"Why did you really come to Batoato?" she asked.

"For the money," he replied.

She studied him in the growing firelight. She searched his face as though trying to reason out the real truth. "No," she said at last. She narrowed her eyes and her mouth parted a little. A bead of sweat ran down her throat and into the deep cleft between her breasts. "You came here for *him,* not for the money. I should have known! Are you *that* mad, Juano? Does vengeance burn in you as much as all that?"

She knew all right. She *knew* him better than his own mother had known him.

"There isn't much time," he said at last. "Give me the gun, *chiquita!* Together we can get that *estancia.* I know the very place in the Valley of the Rio Nevome."

She came closer to him, but not so close that he could disarm her. Her great eyes searched his face. "You mean that, Juano?"

"You know I do," he said.

She drew back her head and spat full into his scarred face. "There's your answer, Juan Espada!" she cried.

The door swung open. "Let's get out of here," said Lasser. "Lead the horses, woman."

Jack walked ahead of Lasser and behind the two horses to the street. It was empty of life. "Lower your hands," ordered Lasser. "Put on your mask." Jack did as he was told.

Lasser shoved him along the street. "Now you lead the way, mister," said Lasser, "and don't try to outrun a bullet. I won't kill you, Spade, not *yet* anyway, but you'll bleed all the way to the *campo santo* if you make a break."

Jack walked ahead of Lasser and the woman through the narrow, twisting side streets of Batoato with the faint sound of the music and the humming of many voices coming to them on the night wind. The streets were as empty as the pathways in the brooding *campo santo*.

CHAPTER FOURTEEN

Jack halted in the rutted road opposite the gateway of the *campo santo*. The graveyard was empty of life. On the far side of the cemetery one lone candle still guttered and flared making strange and eerie shadow pictures on the scabrous wall of the mausoleum in which Lupo Zamacona lay dead atop the bags of loot.

Estela led up the horses. She looked uneasily at the *campo santo*. "Here?" she asked huskily.

"Here," replied Jack.

"Open the gate," ordered Lasser.

Jack drew back the rusted bar that held the gates together. Minute by minute he was getting closer to a bullet in the back. Either way he would have to risk it, whether or not Lasser and the woman got the loot.

He walked along the dim central pathway toward the great mausoleum of the Zamacona family, which dominated the ancient *campo santo*. His boots crushed broken glass, and the pungent odor of tequila arose about him. He halted in front of the mausoleum.

"Where is he?" asked Lasser.

Jack tilted his head toward the mausoleum. "In there," he quietly replied.

"You loco?" demanded Burt.

"Look and see," suggested Jack.

Lasser looked over his shoulder at the woman. "Go on," he ordered.

Her eyes widened in horror. "In *there?* No, Burt!"

He spat to one side. "It's your own Gawddamned family, isn't it?" He poked Jack in the back with the gun muzzle. "You sure he's in there?"

"Look," said Jack.

"Call him, Estela," ordered Lasser.

"He won't hear you," said Jack.

Lasser looked back at her. "Don't let him move," he said. He walked to the iron gateway and pulled it back. He tested the handle of the heavy wooden door and pushed it back. "Stinks in there," he said. "Lupo?" He snapped a match on his thumbnail and thrust it inside. "Lupo?" he called again.

Jack glanced back at her. His eyes widened as he saw a masked face peer around the side of the next mausoleum. A black hand cautioned him to be quiet. Hunk stepped out onto the pathway and walked softly toward the woman, keeping the two horses between him and her.

Lasser whirled. "Damn you, Spade!" he yelled. "You've tricked me for the last time!" He raised his Colt.

"No! No!" she screamed. She dropped the reins and ran between Jack and Lasser just as the Colt spat flame and smoke. Her body jerked as the heavy slug struck home. Jack jumped back behind the horses. Lasser fired again right over the fallen body of the woman. The roan horse went down with a bullet in its brain. Jack jerked at the scabbarded Winchester hung to the saddle of the other horse. Lasser ran out onto the pathway, trying to get a shot in at Jack. Hunk closed in behind him. At the last second Lasser whirled and fired. Hunk winced. His left fist straightened out Lasser and a rock-hard right smashed against his jaw with almost enough force to rip Lasser's head from his shoulders. He dropped the gun and fell back over the body of the woman.

The powder smoke swirled about them as they stood there with the last gunshot echo dying away in the hills beyond the *campo santo*. Hunk pressed his hand against his side.

"You all right?" asked Jack.

Hunk nodded. "Flesh wound," he replied, "just cut through the skin."

"You came just in time," said Jack.

"I missed yuh in the plaza. I saw Lasser when he got his hosses. I tailed yuh here."

"Where's Augustin?"

Hunk shrugged. "Chasin' a *puta,* maybe."

Jack hooked a boot under Lasser and threw him over on his back. He picked up Lasser's Colt. He knelt beside Estela and raised her head.

She opened her great eyes for a moment. "Juano," she breathed, and then she lay still.

Hunk took off his hat. "She really loved you, Juano," he said.

Jack stood up. "Yes," he said quietly.

Hunk rolled Lasser over on his belly and took his scarf from about his neck. He tightly lashed Lasser's wrists together. "Yuh take him back to Arizona, right?" he asked.

"Yes," replied Jack. He looked at the mausoleum. "The money is in there," he said.

Hunk stood up. "I guess you want your split," he suggested.

Jack studied him. "You damned fool," he said. "You think maybe I didn't know *why* you came here? You deserted only to bring back that money to the Army."

"It was my job to guard it theah at Granite Tanks," said Hunk simply. "I didn' do it."

"You're loco, you know that, don't you?"

Hunk eyed the scarred face of Jack Spade. "And you ain't?" he quietly asked. He touched Lasser with the toe of a boot. "Yuh come over two hundred miles, riskin' your life every mile and every minute to take this pile of shit back to justice. Man, you're locoer more than I am!"

Jack picked up the limp body of the woman. "Open the door," he said. He carried her into the crypt. "Lift the casket lid, Hunk."

"Me?" asked Hunk. "Before God, Juano!"

"Open it!" snapped Jack.

Hunk did as he was told. He looked down into the sightless eyes of Lupo Zamacona.

"Get that carrion out of there," ordered Jack.

Hunk lifted out the stiffening body. His eyes widened when he saw the moneybags. He looked back at Jack. "What do I do with him?" he asked.

"Take him outside," said Jack. "Dump him with the dead horse. Someone will have to bury him."

When Hunk removed the moneybags he took Lupo to the outside of the mausoleum. Jack placed her body in the casket. He looked down at her immobile face, usually so expressive and alive. He bent and kissed her cold lips and then let down the casket lid. He handed the moneybags to Hunk through the doorway and then closed the heavy wooden door. He closed the rusted gate and wedged it tight. He did not look at the sprawled body of Lupo as he led the horse with the unconscious body of Lasser over the saddle from the *campo santo*.

Augustin stood at the gate. He looked past Jack to where Hunk was slinging the moneybags onto his back. "He's got it!" cried Augustin. He drew his Colt. "Get out of the way, Juano!"

Jack gripped Augustin's gun wrist and looked down into the face of the man. "Go get the horses, *chico*," he said quietly. "And don't try anything funny, eh? I have already killed one man this night."

"But he has the money, Juano!"

Jack looked back at Hunk. "That was why he came here," he said.

"But at least we can each get a third of it!"

Jack shook his head. "He's taking it back to Arizona, *chico*."

"You are a fool, Juan Espada!"

Jack looked at Burt Lasser. "I got what I came for," he said simply.

CHAPTER FIFTEEN

They had returned slowly to the north riding by night and hiding by day. From Batoato, now slumbering again as it did all year until each *El Dia de los Muertos,* they had gone to Bacanora, where the cleanly picked bones of Mooney Dade lay in the dust, and beyond Bacanora to the wind-haunted pass where Toribio Vasquez lay buried in an unmarked grave. They had traveled to the sun-blasted waterless plains beyond Tres Alamos and from there to San Juan de la Paz. Due north from San Juan de la Paz they rode, until early one moonrise they topped a ridge and looked down into the valley where San Luis Viejo lay abandoned.

During the long days and nights Burt Lasser had not spoken one word. Augustin had ridden behind Hunk Cabell, who carried the bloodstained moneybags with forty thousand dollars of good United States currency within them. All this time Augustin's mind had repeated over and over again his simple plan—ten cents' worth of ammunition would easily dispatch with Burt Lasser and Hunk Cabell, and, if need be, another five cents would get rid of Juan Espada and thus double Augustin's take. He had not yet got it through his head that Juan Espada did not want the money, but only to take Burt Lasser back to the hangman's rope. Surely the Jack of Spades would throw in with Augustin before they crossed the border into Arizona.

Jack looked sideways at Hunk as he shaped a cigarette. "You all right, *amigo?*" he asked.

Hunk's strained face turned toward Jack almost mechanically. Sweat dewed his dark skin. "It's jes' a fevah, Juano," he said huskily. "We got to have watah."

Jack lighted up. For the past three or four days he had watched a change come over the big trooper. He touched his horse with his spurs and dragged on the lead rope of the horse ridden by Lasser, whose bound hands rested on the saddlehorn. The wind shifted as the eastern sky began to be tinted with a pale milky wash of moonlight.

Jack dismounted in front of the church. He walked into the nave and sniffed the dusty air. There was no stench of decomposition. The trapdoor had well sealed the vault of death beneath the sacristy. Boots thudded on the pavement. "That nigger ain't goin' to make it back to Fort Huachuca, Spade," said Lasser.

"He'll make it," promised Jack. "Besides, what difference does it make to you?"

"Forty thousand dollars," replied Lasser.

"You were dealt out of that hand," said Jack. He kicked together some firewood.

"You're the biggest damned fool in all Sonora," said Lasser. "What difference does it make now if I dance on air in Bisbee? That won't bring back Tolleson and his daughter."

"Shut up!" snapped Jack. He lighted the firewood.

"Besides," persisted Lasser. "How do you know how you'll stand when you get back to Bisbee? They wanted you long before the Granite Tanks thing and the killings at Tolleson's. Can you trust Henderson?"

Jack pushed firewood into the gathering flames. He stood up and looked down at the crackling firewood.

"The old man is dead, I tell you! Yuh can't bring him and the little gal back by having *me* hung! We used to work pretty well together. You take the lion's share of the loot.

Give me a split, say ten thousand. Even five is enough. What do you say?"

Jack swung full-arm and slashed the edge of his hand across Lasser's mouth. He felt the edge of the teeth cut his flesh. Lasser cursed savagely as he fell back against the wall.

"I'll kill you for that!" he snarled. He raised his bound hands and wiped the blood from his mouth, but his cold, unblinking eyes never left Jack's face. Something split in Jack's mind. He plunged stiff-legged through the fire, scattering the burning wood, and smashed at the face of Burt Lasser.

"For Chris' sakes, Jack!" yelled Hunk from behind him. Jack's hands closed on Lasser's windpipe and he put on the squeeze, feeling the power flow from his shoulders and arms into the gathering pressure. He was going to kill Lasser. A hand gripped Jack's shoulder and turned him. A great black fist hit him alongside the jaw and knocked him flat on his back into the scattered firewood. He clawed for his Colt and came up off his feet, thrusting forward the cocked Colt and pressuring the trigger.

Hunk looked at him with pain-glazed eyes. "Yuh didn' want to kill him, Jack," he said quietly.

Jack slowly lowered the Colt. He let down the hammer to half cock. "You hit like an Army mule kicks," he said.

"I *am* an Army mule," said Hunk simply. He kicked the firewood together. Smoke swirled upward and flowed through the nave and out through the windows and the doorway. Hunk stood up from the fire, swaying a little as he did so.

"Take off that shirt," said Jack.

"I'm all right," said Hunk.

"Take off the gawddamned shirt!" snapped Jack. He rolled a cigarette and placed it between Hunk's lips. He lighted it. Hunk began to ease off the shirt. Beads of sweat broke out on his face. The left side of his issue undershirt was black with crusted blood. Jack eased the undershirt up over Hunk's arms and head. A dirty bandage was thickly swathed about the Negro's lean waist.

"What's this?" asked Jack.

"Nuthin'," replied Hunk. He wiped the sweat from his face.

"You're a Gawddamned liar! What is it?" barked Jack.

"I got hit theah in that graveyard," said Hunk.

"You said it was a flesh wound!"

"I lied," confessed Hunk. "We didn' have no time to fool around, Jack. We had to git to the bordah."

"It wasn't that important!"

Hunk looked steadily at him. "Yes, it was," he insisted.

"Sit down," said Jack. He went outside and unsaddled his horse. Augustin was at the water pool with his horse. He watched Jack covertly. "Bring some water, *chico!*" called Jack.

Jack spread out a blanket. He poured the water Augustin had brought into a pan and put it on the fire to boil. He took out his sheath knife. "Lie down, Hunk," he said. As Hunk lay down Jack began to cut away the bandage. The odor that arose from it made him turn his head aside. "Mother of God!" he said. He forced himself to look at Hunk's side. It was swollen and distended and colored a bruised-looking purple, yellow, and greenish hue. Malodorous yellow pus oozed thickly from the bullet hole. "The bullet still in there?" he asked. He knew it was.

Hunk nodded. Jack opened a brandy bottle and gave the Negro a drink. Hunk lay back. His breathing was harsh and heavy, coming erratically like a steam locomotive puffing up a steep grade. "How bad is it?" he asked.

Jack squatted back on his heels and rolled a cigarette. He lighted it. He had seen such a wound before and he knew what had happened to the man who had suffered from it. How could he tell Hunk what he thought, or rather already *knew?*

"Kin yuh dig it out, Jack?" asked Hunk.

"I'm not a surgeon," replied Jack.

"I kin stand it, *amigo.*"

Augustin walked in with saddlebags over his arm. He dumped them near the fire and his dark eyes saw Hunk's side. He looked at Jack. Augustin *knew.* The wound was gangrenous. The still-healthy tissue beyond the dark area of the infection showed red and inflamed. The oozing malodorous pus and blisters around the wound itself were a sure indication of gangrene.

Hunk opened his eyes. "It's gangrene, ain't it? I know. I seen it before. At first I didn' notice nuthin' but the pain 'cause I got such a dark skin, but then I begin gettin' a whiff of myself and I was pretty sure."

"You'll be all right, Hunk," said Jack.

Augustin walked to the door and looked back.

"Cut it out," said Hunk. "I kin take it."

Jack shook his head. "If it was a hand, or an arm, or lower leg, it could be amputated and cauterized maybe."

"Amputation? Is it *that* bad?"

"Worse, *amigo.* You can't have flesh cut right out of your side like a butcher cutting out a roast—not that and live. Don't you see?"

"God have mercy on me," moaned Hunk.

"I'll get you back to Fort Huachuca," promised Jack. "They have surgeons there."

"It's still a long way from heah, Jack."

"We'll move out in a couple of hours. I won't bandage it. Let it drain." Jack stood up and dropped his cigarette into the fire. He could not tell Hunk that it really didn't matter anymore. It wouldn't make any difference if he did reach Fort Huachuca alive. Jack walked outside to the spring.

Augustin blew a smoke ring. "It's gangrene, *chico,*" he said.

"I know."

Augustin looked at his cigarette. "Let Lasser fall asleep," he suggested. "One knife blade across the throat and you'll save yourself the trouble of getting him back to Bisbee. The big black man is a living dead man. He won't even make it to the border. We can split the forty thousand, *chico.*"

"No," said Jack.

"What the hell do I get out of this? I've risked my life a hundred times to get that money back! What's in this for me?"

Jack smiled a little. "The reward money for Lasser. You can have it, *chico*. Only you'll have to collect it in Bisbee."

Augustin spat into the pool. "I can stand much from you, Juano, but not nobility."

"The money is not ours," said Jack. He looked toward the rising moon. "I'll cook some grub. Take guard now. We'll leave after moonset." He walked toward the church.

"I can't go back over the border!" yelled Augustin. "I ask you again! What the hell do I get out of this?"

Jack turned and grinned crookedly. "Your life, you cheap bastard, and the satisfaction of a job well done, for once in your stinking life!" He walked on to the church.

Augustin's eyes never left the back of Jack Spade until he was out of sight.

"Do not move suddenly, *chico*," said Augustin. Something poked into Jack's chest. He opened his eyes and raised his head. He looked along the dull barrel of a rifle and into the dark eyes of Augustin. "Get up," said the Mexican.

Jack sat up. The nave of the church was in shadows except where the moonlight streamed in through the open windows and the cracks in the walls and the roof. The fire was a thick bed of ashes with here and there a red eye of fire peeping through. Jack looked toward Hunk. The big trooper was asleep and the sound of his breathing was harsh and heavy. Lasser was gone. Jack looked up at Augustin. "You've found a real partner, *chico*," he said. "He'll get rid of you the first chance he gets."

"He is a good man! He'll make a good *segundo* in the *corrida* I plan to organize here in Sonora."

"There's one born every minute," dryly observed Jack.

A spur chimed faintly in the doorway. Lasser came in, trailing a Winchester. "The horses are ready, *amigo*," he said to Augustin. He slewed his eyes sideways toward the money-bags lying between Hunk and the wall. "Hey, nigger!" he called out. "Get up!"

Hunk slowly raised his head. Lasser dropped some firewood atop the ashes. "Get up!" repeated Lasser. Hunk placed a hand against the wall and the other against his side.

He slowly got to his feet. "Get away from them moneybags," ordered Lasser. Hunk walked a little way, swaying as he did so.

"He's almost gone," said Augustin. "Should I spare him a bullet, Burt?"

Lasser spat into the fire. "Maybe we ought to bury 'em in the same grave," he suggested. "They think so much of each other."

"Brothers under the skin," murmured Augustin.

Lasser picked up the moneybags and hefted them. "Forty thousand," he said. He grinned.

The fire flared up. Lasser shaped a cigarette and walked around the fire with the moneybags slung over his shoulder. He bent to pick up a branch to light his cigarette. Hunk moved quickly. A big, wide foot shoveled into the thick ashes and burning branches and threw them high toward Augustin's face. Hunk leaped over the fire and rammed a shoulder against Lasser, driving him back against the wall. The moneybags fell into the fire. Augustin dropped his rifle and grabbed at his seared face. He jumped back and yanked his Colt from its holster. He fired blindly toward Hunk. Hunk hit Lasser again and dropped him unconscious to the floor. He whirled and closed in on Augustin. His great arms encircled the screaming Mexican.

Jack snatched the moneybags from the fire. Lasser opened his eyes and raised his head, at the same time reaching for his Colt. Jack came off the floor in a leap, extending his right leg. The bootheel connected solidly with Lasser's chin and put him out again.

A cracking sound came faintly to Jack. He turned. Hunk dropped the Mexican and stepped back. He went down on one knee and then the other. He held out his hands toward Jack. The front of his undershirt was fast turning red with blood. "It's better this way, Jack," he said. He fell sideways and lay still.

Jack stepped over Hunk. Augustin lay with his back at a strange angle. His dark eyes stared unseeingly up at Jack.

Jack lashed Lasser's wrists behind him. He found a

rusted spade and in the moonlight he dug a grave in the soft earth not far from the spring. He lifted Hunk and, staggering with the weight of the body, carried him to the grave. After wrapping the trooper in a blanket and placing the body in the grave, he filled in the earth, tramped down on it to compact it, and mounded the grave with rocks from behind the spring. He found a piece of bleached-out board and cut an inscription in it by the light of the waning moon. "Corporal Henry Cabell, C Company, Tenth U.S. Cavalry," he read aloud. He cut another line. "Died in line of duty." He walked down the slope and then looked back. *"Adios, amigo,"* he said quietly. *"Vaya con Dios."*

CHAPTER SIXTEEN

The winter moon was rising above the eastern range beyond the great Valley of the San Pedro. The dark silhouette of a mounted man appeared on a naked ridge to the south of the *bosquecillo* that followed the water-course at the bottom of the ridge. The horseman sat his horse and looked almost as though he was a black painted tin cutout etched against the moonlighted sky. He touched his horse with his spurs and rode down the ridge followed by another horseman, whose bound hands rested on his saddlehorn.

"You stopping *here?*" asked Burt Lasser halfway down the slope.

"We need water," said Jack Spade.

The hoofs clattered on the loose rock at the bottom of the ridge. Thin dust arose and drifted off before the wind.

"What about Apaches?" asked Lasser. "We're making enough noise to raise the dead."

"You'd like that, eh, Lasser? Jim Tolleson and little Lucy are buried down there, you bastard!"

"Yuh got no proof I killed 'em!"

Jack rode slowly along the line of willows and dusty cottonwoods. There would be no fear of Apaches at the *estancia*. They would know of the killings there, and they'd want no part of the restless dead who spoke in the voice of Bu, the Owl. Lasser wouldn't know that of course. Let him sweat!

The wind whirled the dried windrows of leaves and rattled the vanes of the locked windmill. The moonlight shone on the dull pewter surface of the water in the stock tank. Someone, not long past, had let the windmill run to fill the tank.

"They'll hang you next to me!" threatened Lasser.

"I hope not," said Jack dry. "I'd rather hang alone."

Jack dismounted and looked toward the darkened house. An eerie feeling came over him. "Get down," he said to Lasser.

Lasser cursed softly as he slid awkwardly from the saddle. "These lashings are cutting off my blood supply," he complained.

"They should be around your neck," said Jack.

"Cut me loose and talk to me like that!" threatened Lasser.

Jack yawned. "I owe you to Cochise County," he said. "Go get a drink, you bastard."

Lasser was looking beyond Jack. His eyes widened. "No," he said in a low voice.

Jack stared at him. "What is it now?" he asked.

"It's her! She's there waitin' for me!" cried Lasser.

Jack whirled. There was something white and indefinite in the shadows beneath the back *ramada* of the house. He narrowed his eyes.

"It's her, I tell you!" cried Lasser.

Jack bent his head forward. The vague figure moved and came out into the pale moonlight. Jack's flesh crawled. He stepped back a little. It was a haunting sight as the young girl came soundlessly toward the two men. "Jesus God!" husked Jack. "It's little Lucy!"

"We done it!" cried Lasser. "We killed 'em! God have mercy on me!" He turned and ran awkwardly toward the *bosquecillo*.

She came closer and held out a hand. "Jack?" she questioned. "Is it you? Jack Spade? It's Sue Tolleson, Jack. Why do you look so strangely at me?"

He held out his arms to her and she came to him and pressed her face close against his chest. "I'm all right now, Jack," she said. "They told me what I had done to you."

Matt Henderson stepped from the porch with Amy Tolleson at his side. "Spade?" asked the sheriff.

"I just lost my prisoner, Sheriff," said Jack.

"What about the others?" asked Henderson.

"Judged, condemned, and executed," replied Jack.

"By an authority greater than that of Cochise County," added the sheriff. He walked to Jack's horse. "I'll go get Lasser," he said.

Amy came to Jack. "I never expected to see you again," she said quietly.

"You almost didn't," he said. He searched her face. There was something different about her.

"We brought Sue here on the chance she might regain her senses," said Amy. "She's all right now."

Jack held the younger girl close. "Thank God for that," he said.

"You'll get your pardon, Jack," added Amy.

He nodded.

"You must be hungry and tired," she said. "We'll dress and get you something to eat." She led Sue toward the house.

Jack watched the older girl. Something came back to him; something he had long forgotten in the months he had been away. It was something she had said just before he had left the house on Clawson Street. "Jack," she had said suddenly. "Even if you don't return there will always be part of you with me." He knew now what that something was.

Henderson came back through the *bosquecillo*, driving Lasser ahead of him on foot. "You've got fat saddlebags, Jack," said the sheriff.

"Forty thousand dollars' worth," said Jack. "It's the payroll money from Granite Tanks."

"How'd you get it?" asked the sheriff.

"I'll tell you the story over a bottle of brandy and a good cigar," replied Jack. "But not now, Henderson."

Henderson lighted a cigar and fanned out the match. "What now for you, Jack?" he asked.

Jack shrugged. "*¿Quien sabe?*" he asked.

"Is it Juan Espada or Jack Spade?"

"It depends on where I'm welcome," replied Jack. "I can't go back to Sonora now, Sheriff."

Henderson looked about the neat little *estancia*. "Nice place here," he observed. "You'll get your pardon, Jack. You'll get a nice piece of reward money as well. She's a fine young woman, Jack."

"I know," said Jack.

The lights went on in the darkened house. Sue laughed musically.

"Maybe you wouldn't want to live here where Jim and Lucy died," suggested Henderson.

"They were my friends," said Jack.

They walked together toward the house.

Sometimes in the following years Jack Spade would ride up on a great ridge that overlooked the moonlighted border country to the south of his *estancia*. He always went alone and he never told his wife where he was going and why. He would sit there in the saddle, smoking and listening to the voices in the dry night wind. Sometimes he almost thought he heard the throaty chuckle of Hunk Cabell and the musical laughter of Estela Zamacona, but he was never sure. It was a good many years before Amy Spade realized that her husband rode out there alone every November 2nd, but she never knew why.

AMBUSH ON THE MESA

CHAPTER ONE

Call to quarters blew across the wide parade ground of Fort Craig and died away across the Rio Grande. The New Mexico night was as soft as velvet. Hugh Kinzie led his tired dun across the parade ground toward post headquarters. The dry wind swept the low mesa and flapped the canvas of the long rows of Sibley tents. Yellow lamplight dappled the barren ground from the windows of the post buildings. Hugh tethered his dun, slapped the dust from his clothing and entered headquarters.

An orderly looked up from his desk as Hugh entered. "Kinzie," he said, "the Old Man has been expecting you."

"I'm here," Hugh said shortly.

The orderly hurried into an inner office and then returned. "Major Roberts will see you, Kinzie. How was it down South?"

"Rough."

Hugh walked into Roberts' office. Major Roberts stood up and held out his hand. He peered at Hugh from under bushy eyebrows. "What's the news from the South?" he asked in his twanging Vermont speech.

Hugh gripped the major's hand and then sat down. "There are Confederates at Fort Thorn. Just a patrol. Baylor has his Second Regiment of Texas Mounted Rifles at Mesilla. General Sibley is en route from San Antonio to join Baylor. He is said to have Riley's, Green's and Steele's regiments of mounted rifles; Steele's and Riley's field batteries. Baylor has a few mountain howitzers."

Roberts drummed stubby fingers on his desk. "Then all this talk of the Texans having a big buffalo hunt is strictly nonsense."

Hugh grinned. "They'll be hunting Yankees, sir."

Roberts looked up quickly. "We'll be ready for them. You've done outstanding work, Hugh. Are you going to stay on as civilian scout?"

"No."

"We need every loyal man for the defense of New Mexico. Why don't you re-enlist? I can get you a sergeant-major's stripes in the Mounted Rifles."

"You know how I feel about that, sir."

Roberts nodded. "Yes. I recommended you for a commission again. The courier brought back the answer from Santa Fe yesterday."

"And?"

Roberts looked away. "There is some question about your loyalty."

Hugh smashed a fist down on his thigh. "Why? Because I was born in Virginia? For God's sake, sir! I left there when I was seven years old to come west to Missouri with my father and mother. I fought for my country in the Mexican War when I was only sixteen. I served honorably in the Mounted Rifles until just last year. I've been scouting for the Federals since this war started. What more do they want?"

Roberts raised his head. "I wouldn't have recommended you for a commission unless I believed you were loyal."

"How can Colonel Canby turn me down then?"

Roberts shoved a box of cigars toward Hugh. "Take it easy. It just so happens that many of the old regulars have joined the Confederacy."

Hugh took a cigar and angrily bit the end from it. He lit up and drew the smoke gratefully into his lungs.

"Officers . . . every one of them. Claiborne, Crittenden, Loring, Lee and Johnston."

Roberts lit a cigar and eyed Hugh through the smoke.

"Have you heard from your elder brother Ronald lately?"

Hugh looked up quickly. "No. The last thing I heard he was a captain in the infantry at Fort Buchanan. Why do you ask?"

Roberts leaned forward. "The officer in charge of Fort Buchanan destroyed a large quantity of supplies there when the forts in Arizona were abandoned. The garrison marched to New Mexico."

"Then Ron is here?" asked Hugh eagerly.

"Your brother resigned his commission in the United States Army and went down into Mexico. It is said that he went to Texas and took service with the Confederacy."

Hugh stared at Roberts. "He always believed in state's rights. But he was Virginian to the core. I consider myself as a Missourian."

Roberts waved a hand. "I know. But Ronald Kinzie was disbursing officer at Buchanan. Twenty thousand dollars in negotiable government drafts disappeared at the same time he left for Mexico. Do you understand?"

"That's a damned lie! Ron might have joined the Confederacy—it would be like him—but he'd never steal from the Government!"

Roberts shrugged. "Times and men have changed."

"Do you believe the story?"

"No. Your brother forwarded a letter from Mexico in which he stated he had turned the money over to a certain Lieutenant Winston who was leaving for Fort Ayres. Winston has since vanished."

"Then he has it!"

"Perhaps. You've been to Fort McLane?"

"Near Santa Rita del Cobre? Yes. Major Linde had a battalion of the Second Infantry there up until last June."

"Fort McLane has since been abandoned. But Linde was to have received those drafts from Winston, who was supposed to arrive at Fort McLane with some people from Fort Ayres. Winston never showed up."

"It's rather poor evidence against Ron."

"There is a way you can clear Ron and prove your loyalty, but I hesitate to ask you."

"Shoot!"

"Canby wants those drafts. That's the first part of the problem. The second part is this: Captain Maurice Nettleton commanded Fort Ayres. He was supposed to have left the post some weeks ago, traveling to Fort McLane with his command. Nettleton and his command have vanished. Canby wants a search made for them. I can't send a force to do the job. I need every man I have to defend the Rio Grande Valley should Baylor and Sibley attack us."

"Why is Nettleton so important?"

Roberts leaned forward. "It isn't Nettleton we're interested in as much as it is his wife. Marion Nettleton was Marion Bennett before her marriage. The only child of Shelton Bennett of Missouri."

Hugh whistled softly. "Boss Bennett."

"The very same. Bennett has been raising hell. Orders have been sent to Canby to find her. I don't have to remind you that Shelton Bennett is an important factor in the political picture of Missouri. President Lincoln is anxious to have Missouri held for the Union. If anything happens to Marion Nettleton, Bennett, in his narrow-mindedness, might just throw his influence to the side of the Confederacy."

Hugh grinned wryly. "And you want me to go into Apache country to find twenty thousand dollars and the daughter of a boss politician to prove my loyalty?"

"Not *me*, Hugh. I just thought it might be your chance. Canby is raising unadulterated hell with me for not locating her."

"One man instead of a regiment? Who do you think I am?"

"I don't know of any other man in this department who might possibly do it."

Hugh relit his cigar. "For a posthumous commission? It

comes high, particularly when every two-bit politician in New Mexico, not to mention the whole damned United States, is raising a command of his constituents so that they'll vote him in as commanding officer."

"You're a bitter man, Hugh Kinzie."

Hugh studied the officer. "Would you do it?"

"I've been a regular for more years than I care to admit. Then too, I'm a Vermonter. It makes a difference."

Hugh slapped a hand against his thigh. "If a man is loyal to his country, does it matter *where* he comes from? Winfield Scott is Virginia born."

"So is Robert E. Lee," said Roberts dryly.

Hugh stood up and paced back and forth. "I know in my heart that Ron didn't take those drafts with him. It isn't so much the chance of a commission that drives me on now. It's clearing him."

"Then you'll go?"

"Yes. Tonight. I'll get a fresh horse. I can be in the Black Range foothills by dawn."

Roberts stood up. "I knew you'd go. I'll need good officers before this war is over. If you succeed, I'll see to it that you get commissioned in my squadron."

Hugh looked down at the faded green stripes along the seams of his trousers. "I'd like that," he said quietly.

"You were one of the best sergeants in the mounted rifles. Draw anything you need for your trip."

"Can I draw courage?"

"You've a full supply, Hugh."

Hugh gripped Roberts' hand and then left the building. He stood for a time on the parade ground listening to the dry whispering of the desert wind. He looked toward the west, where Dasoda-hae, He That Is Just Sitting There, the giant chief of the Mimbreno Apaches, was king. He was almost in his seventies now, but was still physical and spiritual leader of his tough warriors. The whites knew him by another name . . . Mangus Colorado . . . Red Sleeves.

CHAPTER TWO

Hugh Kinziee lay in the rustling mesquite looking down at the dim quadrangle of Fort McLane. Someone had played hell there. Roofs had been caved in and the corrals had been torn down. From a busy frontier post it had degenerated into just another ghostly ruin.

Hugh rested on his elbows and studied the terrain. He had reached the hills just before dawn the day before and had stayed hidden all day. At dusk he had gone on, paralleling the old rutted Spanish road which wound through the low hills. A strange feeling had come over him as he traveled. Before the war there had been posts all the way to the Colorado River. Now they had all been abandoned, and the Apaches once again held full sway over their big country. Between Fort Craig on the Rio Grande and Fort Yuma on the Colorado there was nothing to show that the vast lands were still part of the United States. For all he knew he was the only loyal man west of Fort Craig and east of Fort Yuma.

Hugh half cocked and then capped his Sharps. He eased his Navy Colt from its holster and checked it. Only seven shots between him and hell. But he was at his destination now. He might as well go ahead with his dubious mission.

He passed the post cemetery with its mounded graves

and tilted headboards. He stopped beside a tumbledown abode and eyed the littered quadrangle. He padded forward. His boots grated on broken glass and crunched rusting tin cans. Mattresses had been ripped and their contents scattered everywhere. The shattered wood of crates and boxes was mingled with other debris. A pile of Sibley tents and good blankets had been slashed and then set afire.

Hugh walked softly to the old post headquarters. The roof had collapsed. He eyed the mounds of roof beams and dried adobe which filled the interior. It would take him days to dig down into that mess to look for the lost drafts. The wind moaned through the ruins as he completed his inspection. He had known all along that he'd never find them. That left Marion Nettleton to be found in a country where Apaches prowled like tigers of the desert looking for white men . . . and women.

Fort Ayres, as he recalled it, had been a one-company post on a fork of the Gila, about eighty miles to the west. Eighty miles of danger. South of Fort McLane there was nothing except the old Butterfield Trail, now abandoned. Beyond that was almost waterless country clear down to and over the Chihuahua border. North of the abandoned fort was the roughest country he had ever seen. The brooding Black Range, without roads, and with but few known trails. He had heard there were ruins in there built hundreds of years ago by the Hohokam: the Old Ones. They had lived and prospered there, tending their patches of maize, and building their cliff dwellings, only to vanish many years before the all-conquering whites had invaded the Southwest.

Hugh padded back into the brush. The abandoned fort depressed him. He had to find Marion Nettleton and he had to keep his hide whole. Neither task would be easy, and he knew which of the two was most important to him.

His horse nickered as he approached. He led the buckskin to the north. He missed the speed of his big dun but the buckskin had a stamina in him that the dun lacked.

There was a waterhole in the Pinos Altos some miles north of the abandoned fort. He followed the rutted track through the darkness until the buckskin whinnied. He had smelled the water. Hugh picketed the horse and went ahead on foot. He halted a hundred yards from the waterhole and tested the night with his senses. There seemed to be nothing but the night wind rustling the brush, but still he waited. It was a sixth sense he had developed in his years on the frontier. He circled the waterhole and dropped flat on a knoll which overlooked the low ground around the waterhole. Apaches would always avoid camping near waterholes. They camped on high ground, water or no water.

He eyed the brush about the waterhole. Something moved. Then a burro brayed softly. Hugh moved downwind and crept through the brush until he could see the dull sheen of the water. A man was sitting up in his blankets. Hugh could see the dim silhouette of his steeple-crowned hat. Probably a Mex.

The man stood up and raised a rifle. "Who is there?" he called out in Spanish.

"A friend."

The rifle hammer clicked back. "Who are you?" called out the man.

Hugh took a chance. "An army scout."

"There are no American troops this far west of the Rio Grande."

"I am."

"Come forward then with your hands high."

Hugh snapped his carbine ring to the swivel on his sling, then swung the Sharps behind his back. He eased his Colt in its holster, then walked forward out of the brush.

The Mexican was a little man. He eyed Hugh. "What do you do here?"

"I am looking for a party of Americans."

"I am alone here."

Hugh looked about. The burro was picketed in the brush. There was no one else in sight. "I want water," he said.

"There is enough for you."

"Then I'll get my horse."

The Mexican hesitated. He scanned the swaying brush.

"Why are you afraid? Do I look like an Apache?"

"There are none within miles. I made sure of that, senor."

"Then let me get my horse."

"I will be right behind you."

Hugh shrugged. He walked back toward the buckskin with the little Mexican a safe distance behind him. Hugh led the horse to the water and let him drink. He turned to the little man. "I am Hugh Kinzie," he said.

"Jorge Dura, at your service."

"What do you do here, Jorge?"

Dura lowered his rifle. "When the soldiers left the fort they did not take some of their horses. They are in these hills. I am looking for them."

Hugh knelt and drank. The edge of the waterhole was dotted with hoof marks into which the water had seeped. There had been many horses there, and not too long before. "You have seen Americans hereabouts?" he asked over his shoulder.

Dura nodded. "Some Americans were west of here. They were soldiers."

"Any women?"

"Yes . . . two of them."

Hugh stood up and held out his tobacco pouch. Dura cradled his rifle on his left arm and took the pouch. He swiftly rolled a cigarette. "This is dangerous country for Americans." he said.

"I know."

Dura lit up. His eyes were hard in his small brown face. "Why do you look for them?"

"I have been ordered to do so."

Dura sucked at his cigarette. "They had good horses and weapons. Pack mules, laden with supplies."

"Which way did they go?"

Dura jerked a thumb over his shoulder. "Into the Pinos Altos. Toward the headwaters of the Gila."

Hugh looked at the dark heights. "Why?" he asked, almost to himself.

Dura rested his rifle butt on the ground and leaned on the long barrel. "I do not know. There is no way out of those mountains. Perhaps they went there to avoid the Mimbrenos."

Hugh nodded. Whoever was in charge of the party didn't know that country. Few white men had been in there. It was an unmapped wilderness. Beyond the mountains were the Plains of San Augustin. If they got through they could turn east toward the Rio Grande. *"If* they got through," he said aloud.

Dura shrugged. "It is madness."

Hugh led the buckskin from the water. Dura bothered him. No man who knew Apaches and feared them would camp near a waterhole at night.

"Where do you go?" asked Dura.

"Back to the Rio Grande."

Dura glanced down at his rifle. "That is a fine horse you have."

Hugh nodded. He rested his hand on his pistol butt. "I intend to keep him."

Dura smiled. He knew these big Americanos and the skill they had with the revolving pistols. "Yes," he said quietly. "Go with God, friend."

"Go with God, Jorge Dura."

Hugh led the buckskin around the waterhole. Dura watched him. Then he saddled his burro and packed his blankets. He mounted and rode swiftly to the south. Mangus Colorado would welcome news of a party of rich Americans wandering around in the rough hills. Perhaps Jorge Dura could get his hands on some of their riches, through the graciousness of Mangus Colorado. It was well worth the risk.

CHAPTER THREE

The false dawn was graying the eastern sky when Hugh found the first traces of the party ahead of him. A spur lay in the rough trail. A mile beyond that he found many tracks on a soft patch of earth. They were damned careless about covering their route. An Apache kid could have trailed them without half trying.

The sun was up when he found another trace of them. A horse had fallen on a rough patch of the trail. Boot tracks showed where they had stood around the fallen horse and got him up on his hoofs. It was as plain as a page of print.

The hills crowded in on Hugh as he went on. There was no chance of losing the trail, for there was no other route for them to follow. From the tracks he deduced that there were at least a dozen people in the party.

He looked back to the south as he climbed a ridge. A thread of smoke showed against the sky like coarse hair lying on pale blue cloth. He rubbed his bristly jaw. Farther to the west another scarf of smoke hung against the sky. Now he knew there was no chance of going back to the south.

He crossed a shallow rushing stream, probably a fork of the Gila. They had watered their horses here. The tracks showed plainly on the far side of the stream. He followed the great valley, constantly looking back over his shoulder. The smoke had drifted away.

Cholla, agave and some mescal stippled the valley floor, while above him the slopes were clothed with juniper, pinon and scrub oaks. He looked up ahead. The mountains were high, rough and seemingly endless. It looked like a one-way trip into uncharted country.

Higher and higher he went. Douglas firs, ponderosa pines and spruces began to appear. A deer surveyed him from a slope, then disappeared into the trees. Long-crested jays chattered at the lone rider who disturbed their secluded haunts. A black bear shambled off in the distance. But there was no sign of human life other than the imprint of hoofs, always going north.

He was almost certain that he was on the trail of the Nettleton party, for he couldn't figure out who else it could be. If they had been Confederate sympathizers they would have trended southward. They were making a trail through that wilderness as though they were traveling on a highway back in civilized country. Hugh was almost tempted to turn back and make for the Rio Grande, but there was always the memory of those smoke signals against the vast sky behind him.

A massive peak towered at least eight thousand feet high to his left. Far to the north he could see another giant of the mountains. It was a country he could have enjoyed if the tigers of the human species weren't somewhere behind him. No matter how careful he was about his own trail, the trail of the party he was following was too plain to erase. Still, one man might get into the mountains and get away front any pursuers. The temptation was strong.

The stream was wider now. He reached a place where it forked. Beyond the fork he could see land which had once been cultivated. Nature had almost erased the signs.

Darkness mantled the mountains, and he was just about to seek a hiding place for the night when he caught the odor of burning wood borne to him on the gentle wind.

Hugh dismounted and took his carbine. He led the

buckskin into a thicket and tethered it. Then he went forward through the trees toward the smell of the smoke.

He could see the flickering of flames as he topped a rise. He squatted low and eyed the fire. The murmuring of voices came to him. Americans. The odor of cooking meat mingled with the smell of the smoke. Beyond the fire he could see horses. A soldier stood guard on a knoll, leaning on his rifle, but he was watching the people at the fire rather than the darkness behind him. Having a guard there really didn't make any difference, for the Mimbrenos could have ringed that camp as silently as ghosts, waiting for their chance to move in.

Hugh stood up and walked forward. "Hello, the camp!" he called. Then he prudently stepped behind a tree. The guard whirled and raised his rifle. The rest of the people stood about the fire, staring into the darkness. A woman walked into the shadows. A tall officer swiftly drew out his pistol.

"Who is it?" called out the guard.

"Hugh Kinzie. Scout from Fort Craig."

"Come forward into the light!"

"Put out that damned fire, you fools! Are you trying to make sitting ducks out of yourselves?"

"Who does he think he is?" snapped an officer.

Hugh came forward, holding his carbine above his head. A slightly plump officer with captain's bars on his shoulder straps stepped forward. "Captain Maurice Nettleton," he said. "We're from Fort Ayres. Who sent you?"

Hugh grounded his carbine and rested his hands on it. "Major Benjamin Roberts, commanding Fort Craig."

Nettleton tugged at his dark side whiskers. "How did you find us?"

Hugh looked at the blazing fire. "It wasn't hard," he said dryly. "You've left a trail plain enough for an *ish-ke-ne* to follow."

The tall officer came forward. He was only a few inches taller than Hugh but was half as wide. His shoulders filled out his blouse, threatening to break through the seams. *"Ish-ke-ne?* Say, who the hell are you?"

Hugh ignored the big man. "Tell your men to douse that fire," he said to Nettleton.

"But we haven't eaten yet," said Nettleton.

Hugh walked forward. He kicked dirt over the fire. "You'll be eating in hell by dawn if you don't put it out."

The tall officer placed his hand on the butt of his pistol and swaggered forward. "I'd like proof of who you are," he said threateningly.

Hugh looked info the face of the officer. His eyes were the coldest gray-green he had ever seen. "I told you who I was," he said quietly.

"I know that. What proof do we have you're Hugh Kinzie from Fort Craig?"

A woman came out of the darkness, "It's Hugh Kinzie, all right," she said quietly. "Hello, Hugh."

Hugh turned. "Katy Corse," he said.

Katy Corse brushed back her dark hair. "It's like you to show up in the wilderness," she said quietly. "And like you to vanish just as quickly."

Hugh flushed. "What are you doing here, Katy?"

The big officer gripped Hugh by the shoulder. "I was talking to you," he said. "Don't you know an officer when you see one?"

Hugh looked the big man up and down. "Yes. Why?"

Nettleton came forward. "Now, Mr. Clymer," he said quickly, "I want no trouble."

Hugh looked about the camp. There were eight other men watching him. One of them was an officer. The others were enlisted men, with the exception of a gaunt man who was dressed in somber black. "Where were you planning to go, Captain Nettleton?" he asked.

Nettleton wet his lips. "We tried for the Rio Grande and heard the Mimbrenos were between us and the river. We didn't want to go too far south because of the Confederates. So we decided to come north through the mountains, then turn east toward the Rio Grande near Soccorro."

"Just like that," said Hugh dryly. "Who knows the way through that?" He waved a hand toward the black bulk of the mountains.

Nettleton flushed. "There was nothing else we could do."

Hugh kicked more dirt on the fire. He looked at the closest enlisted man. "Get some water," he said.

The enlisted man got a big canteen and emptied it on the burning wood.

Hugh stood there in the dimness. The pungent odor of the wet wood floated about him. "There's no more time to talk," he said. "Let's get moving."

Clymer raised his head. "You're just an enlisted man," he said. "You've got all-fired guts taking charge."

Hugh shook his head. "I'm a civilian scout, Clymer. It's obvious there isn't a man here who knows the Apaches and this country. If you want to get out of these damned mountains with a whole skin you'll do as I say."

Clymer raised a thick hand. Nettleton drew himself up. "See to it that the horses are ready, Mr. Clymer," he said.

Clymer eyed the captain for a moment, then spat deliberately into the smoking embers. "Phillips!" he roared.

The third officer came forward through the drifting smoke. Clymer thrust out a thick arm. "Get the horses ready," he said.

Hugh rubbed his jaw. "Is your wife here, sir?" he asked Nettleton.

Clymer whirled. "What's it to you?" he snapped.

"Is she here, sir?" asked Hugh quietly.

Nettleton nodded. "Of course she is. She's resting in her tent. Why do you ask?"

"Her father has been riding hell out of the War Department to find her. That's all."

Nettleton plucked at his lower lip. "I was worried about that."

Clymer waved a hand. "I could have got her through safely," he said loudly.

Nettleton watched the big officer walk away. "What do you want us to do, Kinzie?" he asked.

"Move north to find a place where we can defend ourselves."

"You fear an Apache attack?"

"Yes."

Nettleton swallowed. He looked off into the darkness. "I'll get my wife." he said. He hurried off.

Katy Corse looked at Hugh. "It's been quite a while, Hugh," she said.

Hugh nodded. "Where's your husband?" he asked.

"I didn't get married." she said quietly.

"So?"

"Herbert died a month after you left Fort Buchanan."

The enlisted men were saddling the horses. A mule brayed. "Damn you, jughead," said a trooper. "You got the biggest mouth."

Katy Corse looked at Hugh and then turned on a heel. She walked toward the tent amongst the trees.

A man wearing corporal's stripes looked after Katy. "A nice girl," he said.

"Yes," said Hugh softly. "I never expected to see her again."

"She came through the Gila country a week or so before we left Fort Ayres. Said she was heading for the Rio Grande. There was no way for her to go on. Captain Nettleton made her wait until we were ready to leave. I'm Harry Roswell. I've heard of you, Kinzie. You used to be a sergeant in A Company of the Mounted Rifles."

"Yes." Hugh impatiently looked at the men working amongst the horses and mules. "They act like they've got all thumbs."

Roswell nodded. "We're a mixed-up lot here, Kinzie."

"Three officers and a handful of enlisted men. Where are the rest of the men from Fort Ayres?"

"We had a beef herd at the post. Nettleton was scared to death he'd get blamed if we lost them. He started the herd out under charge of Mr. Winston and most of the men."

"So?"

"Chiricahuas stampeded the herd right through their

first night's bivouac. We found what was left of some of them the next day. It wasn't pretty. Nettleton lost his nerve and headed into the hills. Short of supplies and low on ammunition. That's us."

"What's on those pack mules?"

Roswell laughed dryly. "Mrs. Nettleton's clothes. Nettleton's silver service and dress uniforms. Records from Fort Ayres."

"That all?"

"Yes. Wait . . . I forgot . . . There are some cases of liqueurs and brandy."

"Nettleton's?"

"Nettleton's."

"For God's sake!"

"Do not take the name of the Lord thy God in vain," a sepulchral voice said just behind Hugh.

"Who are you?" asked Hugh as he turned.

"Do not blaspheme. I am Isaiah Morton."

Morton was the gaunt-looking civilian Hugh had seen in the background. Even in the dimness he could feel the burning eyes of the man studying him.

Roswell spat. "Morton joined us on the trail west of Fort McLane. Said he was going to convert Mangus Colorado."

"They are God's children, even as you and I, Brother Roswell."

Roswell snorted. "That's open to argument."

"Roswell! Where the hell are you?" The harsh voice sounded like a stick being dragged along a picket fence.

Roswell grinned. "That's the first soldier," he said. "I'd better get busy."

A thick-bodied man came up in the darkness. The stripes and diamond of a first sergeant showed on his sleeves.

"Hello, Matt," said Hugh easily.

Matt Hastings thrust his head close to Hugh. "Kinzie! I thought you had taken a discharge."

"I did."

Hastings raised his head. "You're a scout now?"

"Yes."

"The army must be hard up for good scouts."

Hugh tilted his head to one side. *"And* first sergeants. So you finally got your diamond, Matt. You bucked hard enough for it."

Hastings looked back over his shoulder. "I know more about soldiering than any man jack in this J Company outfit."

Hugh nodded. Matt Hastings hadn't changed. Hugh had known him at Fort Stanton and later in Arizona. He was a ring-tailed roarer, self-educated, with the biggest bump of self-esteem on any horse soldier Hugh had ever met in his years of service.

"Well, don't I?" snapped Hastings.

"You sure as hell have forgotten anything you learned about Apaches. Camping in front of a fire."

"There aren't any Apaches within fifty miles."

"Too bad you didn't look back over your shoulder some time this afternoon. You would have seen their signal smokes."

"Boots and saddles!" roared Clymer through the darkness.

Hugh went back for his buckskin and stood there for a time listening to the night sounds. It was no use. There was enough uproar from the darkened camp to drown out anything else he might have heard.

There was a slender woman standing beside Maurice Nettleton when Hugh came back to the camp. She wore a scarf over her dark hair. Nettleton helped her up on a horse. Hugh looked curiously at her as he mounted. Her face was in shadow, but he could see that she was pretty. He wondered if Boss Bennett would ever see her again.

The noisy cavalcade rode up the trail. Hugh dropped back to cover the rear. Isaiah Morton jogged along on his sway-backed nag. The jackleg preacher looked up at the dark heights looming ahead of them. "A land of darkness, as darkness itself; and of the shadow of death, without any order, and where the light is as darkness," he said dolefully.

Hugh glanced at him. "Have you got a gun?" he asked.

"No."

Hugh leaned over and slashed his reins across the rump of the preacher's nag. "Then get up there and do your prophesying!"

A trooper was sitting his horse at the side of the trail. He grinned at Hugh. "I can't prophesy, scout," he said. "But I can shoot."

"Good!"

"The name is Chandler Willis."

"Hugh Kinzie."

Willis swung his carbine across his thighs. He shifted his chew and spat. "Looks like a long night," he said laconically.

"Yes. What kind of officers do you have here?"

"Nettleton lives by the book. Never goes far without looking for some regulation to cover what he's doing. Ain't never quite sure of himself for my money."

"And Clymer?"

Willis grinned. "Fancies himself a real stud with the ladies. Got the morals of an alley cat. Let Nettleton think he's runnin' the shebang. Darrell Phillips ain't a bad hombre. Got breedin', he has. Might make a good soldier if he didn't have to serve under those other two."

"What kind of an officer was Lieutenant Winston?"

"One of the best. A real man. Wasn't with us long. Come from Fort Buchanan on special duty, or so I heard tell."

"What kind of special duty?"

Willis eyed Hugh. "How should I know?" All I know is that Nettleton wouldn't send Phillips out with them steers, and Clymer wouldn't go. So Nettleton orders Winston. He *had* to go."

Hugh nodded. "Did they find Winston's body?"

"Yep. Only way we could tell him was by his uniform."

Hugh looked west. Maybe the drafts had been trampled into the dirt along with the bodies of the troopers. Maybe the Apaches had found them and thrown them away, not knowing their value. There wasn't a chance now of clearing Ron. He shrugged, then looked up the column. He could see Katy Corse riding beside Marion Nettleton. Now and then she steadied the captain's wife in the saddle when they hit rough spots on the trail. Hugh wondered if he could finish the second part of his task. Chances looked slim on that too.

Hugh looked back down the dim trail. Below them he could see an eye of fire winking in the darkness. The wind had fanned an ember into life. These greenhorns had left a trail as easy to follow as the Oregon Trail across the plains of Kansas.

Willis looked back. "You think them 'Paches are back there somewheres?"

"I know it, Willis."

They went on through the darkness with fear riding close behind them.

CHAPTER FOUR

Captain Nettleton called a halt just when the false dawn showed over the eastern heights. Hugh spurred forward, leaving Chandler Willis as rear guard. Nettleton was close beside his wife, holding her in her saddle. "We'll stop here and make a fire," he said to Hugh.

"No fires," said Hugh shortly.

Able Clymer stood up in his stirrups. "Captain Nettleton is in command, Kinzie."

Hugh looked at the belligerent bull moose of a man. "We'll have cold tack," he said quietly.

Darrell Phillips rode forward and then turned his horse. "There's some kind of an old wall here," he said. "It might serve as a defensive position."

Clymer spat. "Listen to the soldier," he said.

Hugh kneed his buckskin past Clymer. He rode up to Phillips. Someone, long ago, had built a wall in front of a steep slope of rock. "It'll do," said Hugh.

Clymer was arguing with Nettleton about something. His voice was too low for Hugh to hear what he was saying.

Nettleton straightened himself in his saddle. "We'll do as the scout says, Mr. Clymer. We must trust him."

Darrell Phillips's handsome face darkened. "Clymer is a bully," he said.

Hugh nodded. "He's still obeying orders though."

Phillips nodded. "Yes, but for how long? If he had his way we'd all be under his filthy thumb." He looked at Marion Nettleton. "She's exhausted," he said.

"Katy is holding up."

"There's a difference. Marion is gentle bred."

"Out in this country a woman is judged for what she can do rather than from how she was bred."

Phillips's dark eyes studied Hugh. "You knew her before?"

"Yes. Last year when I was at Fort Buchanan."

"Good friends, I take it?"

Hugh looked quickly at the officer. "Yes. She was engaged to Herbert Oglesby, a corporal in the dragoons."

"I see. She'd make a good wife for an enlisted man."

Hugh leaned forward. "She'd make a good wife for *any* man, Mr. Phillips." He spurred his buckskin back toward the party.

Phillips shrugged. He looked at Katy Corse. She was riding astride, like a man. Her shapely legs were exposed from the knees down, and she seemed to be perfectly at home in the saddle. For the first time since he had seen her at Fort Ayres he realized that she was a damned attractive woman.

Hugh sat his buckskin as the enlisted men carried food and weapons behind the low wall. Marion Nettleton was seated on a rock. Her husband bustled about her, pulling her shawl about her shapely shoulders. Hugh eyed her. Her oval face had evidently been protected against the hot suns of the Southwest, for it still had a cameo quality to it. Her eyes were large, almost too large for her face. There was a petulant look about her full lips.

"Are you all right, my dear?" asked Nettleton.

"Maurice, do stop annoying me," she said. "I'll have my coffee here."

Nettleton looked up at Hugh and then bit his lip. "We're not to have a fire," he said.

"Why? I want hot coffee. It's such a little thing to ask."

Nettleton looked at Hugh. Hugh shook his head. He kneed his horse down the trail. Behind him he heard her petulant voice. "I'd like to know who is in command here, Maurice."

Willis was squatted on a rock above the trail. "No signs yet," he said.

"There will be."

Willis looked up the canyon. "What's up there?"

"Damned if I know."

The trooper shifted his chew. "Jesus! What a mess!"

"I'll go along with you on that."

"A man or two could get through, traveling at night, lying low by day."

Hugh studied the enlisted man. "I think so. But we have two women to take care of."

"Who? Me? I didn't enlist to take care of no women."

"You're still under orders, Willis."

"Yeah. But for how long? Clymer hates Nettleton's guts. Phillips hates Clymer's guts. Sergeant Hastings hates everybody's guts."

"And you?"

The cold pale eyes held Hugh's. "I'm thinking about my guts."

Hugh looked down at his Sharps. "You'll stick," he said.

Willis shifted a little. "Mebbe. Mebbe not. Don't threaten me, Kinzie. I don't scare easy. Besides, there's others in this outfit as ain't too happy about herding these officers and women through this hellhole of a country. You'll find out in time."

Hugh rode back down the trail. He was a good two miles from the temporary camp when he saw the smoke drifting from a peak. It was closer than it had been yesterday. He rolled a smoke and hooked his left leg about his saddlehorn. He lit up and eyed the distant smoke. The horses were worn thin. They needed at least a day's rest. There was a hell of a trail ahead of them.

Hugh rode back to the camp just as the sun showed up over the eastern heights. The women were resting on blankets. Isaiah Morton was reading a battered Bible. Corporal Roswell was up the slope with his carbine resting across his thighs. A burly private stepped in front of Hugh. "I'm Dan Pearce," he said in a New York accent. "What's the odds of us getting through, scout?"

Hugh slid from his saddle. "Fair."

Pearce had a hard face with small green eyes. There was a furtive look about him. "You talk with Willis?" he asked.

"About what?"

"Breaking loose to try for the Rio Grande."

"Yes."

"So?"

"If he goes, he goes alone. If I see him taking off, I'll kill him."

Pearce raised his head. "Hardcase, eh?"

"No. But I've got a job to do and I aim to do it."

Hugh turned his back on Pearce. Pearce stared at Hugh's broad back for a moment, then he walked down the trail toward Willis. The two of them sat on the rock ledge, talking quietly.

A trooper was busy picketing the horses. Hugh walked over to him. "Put them on separate picket lines," he said.

The trooper turned a good-humored face toward Hugh. "Can I ask why?"

"If they're stampeded we can save most of them. On one picket line the whole kit and caboodle would go."

The trooper nodded. "By God, I'da never thought of that. The name is Jonas Stevens."

Hugh nodded. "You're not getting much help," he said. He uncoiled a picket line and drove the picket deep into the soft soil. He picketed Phillips's fine chestnut.

Stevens looked back at the camp. "Don't seem to be any of them who want to work together. When I enlisted at Jefferson Barracks in fifty-nine we got lectures on how the army always works as a team. Looks like I'm the only one around here that remembers it."

Hugh picketed another horse. "I do," he said quietly.

They worked together picketing the horses near a patch of grass. Hugh walked over to the pack mules. They were dead beat, for no one had thought of removing their packs. Stevens helped him remove the packs. "Poor jugheads," he said.

Abel Clymer came toward them. "Take it easy with those packs," he said.

Hugh turned and shoved one of them at the big officer.

Clymer staggered back until he got his balance. "Damn you!" he said.

Hugh grinned. "Pitch in," he said.

Clymer threw the pack on the ground at Hugh's feet. For a moment he eyed him angrily, then he turned on a heel and strode toward his own horse. He took the saddlebags from it and placed them over his arm. He looked back at Hugh and then strode to the camp.

"Nice fella," said Stevens dryly.

"Bull moose."

"Yeah, but he ain't no pushover, Kinzie. Watch yourself."

"Were you there when Winston and his men were found?"

Stevens shuddered. "Yes. What a mess!"

"Any of Winston's personal baggage found?"

"None. Everything was stamped into the ground. Men, blankets, food . . . everything. Why do you ask?"

"I thought someone might have brought his effects along. For his family, you know."

"Nope. Nothing. Besides, we got enough of a load with Nettleton's personal property. Silver, liquor, clothing and such like. Practically no food, but all of Nettleton's stuff. Hell of a note, ain't it?"

Hugh nodded. He picketed a mule. Stevens studied him as he worked. He rubbed his bristly jaw and then shrugged. *Personal* effects," he said dryly. "Jesus Christ!"

Hugh walked back to the camp.

A neat little soldier holding a tin plate came toward Hugh. He held it out. "Embalmed beef and hardtack," he said quietly. "It isn't much, I'll allow, but just about all we have."

Hugh waved a hand. "Keep it. I've got my own supplies."

The little man nodded. "Thanks. I'm Myron Greer, orderly for the officers."

"Nice job," said Hugh.

Greer shrugged. "I was company clerk at Ayres. Mr. Clymer told me to take over as orderly to relieve Willis. He said Willis was a man, not a frightened worm."

Greer spoke in cultured tones. The man had been educated. He didn't look like the type who would make a hard-riding, hell-for-leather dragoon.

Hugh rolled a smoke. "How is it an educated man like yourself ended up as a company clerk in the dragoons, Greer?"

Greer smiled sadly. "Liquor."

"I've heard that one before. My old squadron commander used to say that when he got a clerk worth anything the man was a drunkard."

Greer looked up. "Kinzie, if it weren't for whisky there wouldn't *be* any clerks in the army. You wouldn't happen to have a drink, would you?"

Hugh shook his head. There was a bottle of mezcal in one of his saddlebags, but he knew damned well Greer wouldn't settle for one drink. He'd need the whole bottle.

Nettleton came over to them. "Greer!" he said pettishly. "Mrs. Nettleton wants some cold clear water."

Greer held out his free hand. "The canteens are full, sir."

"Find a spring."

"Yes, sir."

Hugh shook his head. "He'll have to stay here."

"Afraid he'll run off?" snapped Nettleton. "Greer? He's scared to death right now."

Hugh looked south. There was still a wisp of smoke against the sky. "So am I," he said.

Greer shambled off toward the camp. Nettleton took

out a silver cigar case, selected a cigar, clipped the end with a silver clipper which depended from a silver chain. He put the cigar into his mouth and lit it. "What do you suggest we do?" he asked.

"Rest here. I doubt if they can get past us to attack from the west, east or north. Willis is on guard. I'm going to scout up the canyon."

"There are no Apaches there."

"We don't know the country. From now on we'll have to find a trail. It'd be too damned easy to end up in a box canyon and have to backtrack. We'd lose hours, if not days."

"I see. What do you think our chances are?"

Hugh took out his tobacco pouch. "You're the third or fourth person who has asked me that today."

Nettleton jerked his cigar from his mouth. "I don't want you talking too much to these enlisted men. Keep your counsel for the officers."

Hugh rolled a smoke. "The enlisted men are in this too," he said quietly.

Nettleton's face tightened. He looked down at the green-striped trousers Hugh wore tucked into his boots. "You were an enlisted man yourself?"

"Yes."

"Mounted Rifles?"

Hugh nodded as he lit up.

"They never did have much respect for an officer."

Hugh looked at the angry officer. "I didn't find it so. I do recall one of our surgeons saying that the officers of the Mounted Rifles were all gentlemen, brave and generous to a fault—but the most cantankerous lot he had ever met. There wasn't much chance for an enlisted man to be disrespectful to an officer in *my* regiment, Captain Nettleton."

Nettleton looked away. "Well, get on with your job." He strode back toward the camp.

Hugh walked to his horse and got his canteen and Sharps. Katy Corse came up and placed her hand on the buckskin's nose. "You're not taking him, are you?" she asked.

"No."

"I didn't think you would. He's tired."

"He's got more bottom in him than any other mount here."

"I believe it."

Katy brushed back her dark hair. "You've never forgiven me, have you, Hugh?"

"You made your choice."

"You never gave me much hope."

"I didn't fall all over you like Herbert Oglesby did."

"Herbert was a fine man."

Hugh hooked his canteen to his belt. "You would have ended up being a corporal's wife, perhaps a sergeant's wife, Katy."

"So? You were just a sergeant."

"I'll get my commission."

She leaned against the horse. "If we get out of here."

"We've got to."

She studied him. "I used to think you were different from your brother, but now I think differently."

"How so?"

"He was all business. Is it true he joined the Confederates?"

"That's what they're saying."

"And you?"

He looked up quickly. "You know I'll stay with the Union."

"This war will split a lot of families."

"Ron and I were never very close."

"Maybe that's why you want a commission, to prove to yourself you're as good a man as he is."

"Katy, sometimes you talk too much."

She smiled. "You haven't changed."

"I'm too old to change, Katy." He unsaddled the buckskin and dropped the saddle on the ground. "Did you know Lieutenant Winston?"

"Yes. I rode with him from Fort Buchanan to Fort Ayres. He practically ordered me to."

"I can't imagine anyone giving *you* orders," he said dryly.

"Why do you ask about him?"

"Just curious."

She shook her head. "There's more to it than that. It's about those government drafts, isn't it?"

"Yes."

She looked toward the camp. "I think he had them with him. They were part of your brother's responsibility, weren't they?"

Hugh nodded.

"I stayed at Fort Ayres when he went on with the beef cattle. He was sent to his death. The cattle weren't worth the loss of all those men and especially of a man like him."

"What about the drafts?"

"I'm not sure he had them, Hugh, but he was always so careful to sleep with his head on his saddlebags. He protested against having to take charge of the beef herd but Nettleton insisted. Nettleton really wanted Abel Clymer to lead the herd—just to get rid of him—but Clymer has Nettleton under his control. At least he did until you got here."

"So?"

"When we reached the place where the cattle had been stampeded, Mrs. Nettleton and I were ordered to stay back so that we wouldn't see what had happened. From what the men tell me, it was awful. But no drafts were brought back to the camp. I'm almost sure of that."

"Who led the men to the place where Winston was killed?"

"All three of the officers went."

"Anyone else?"

"Corporal Roswell, Privates Pearce, Willis and Stevens." She gazed at him closely. "What are you thinking about, Hugh?"

"About going on a scout."

"Is that all?"

"That's all," he said shortly. He walked away from her.

As Hugh passed the camp he heard Mrs. Nettleton call

out. "Katy! Do get some water and bathe my temples, like a good girl."

Hugh looked back as he reached the trees. Mrs. Nettleton acted as though everyone in the camp were enlisted in her personal service. There was one person who wasn't—Hugh Kinzie.

CHAPTER FIVE

The trail didn't improve as Hugh walked north from the camp. It was tough going afoot, even for a man in top physical condition. Deer eyed him from afar, seemingly unafraid of him, and he knew by that sign that they were unaccustomed to seeing humans in their country. As he went on, he occasionally saw ancient fields which had been cultivated by the Hohokam.

It was about noon when he found the trail. It was plainly marked on the earth, trending to the northwest into a rough-walled canyon. There were no indication of wheel ruts nor hoof marks. It had been made by foot travelers, and had been well used.

Hugh shoved back his hat and wiped the sweat from his forehead. He eyed the trail, following it until it was lost to sight in thickets and rock formations, beyond which he could see a humped shape rising high into the sky—a rocky mesa stippled with scrub trees and big pines. He wondered who had made that trail and where it went. He looked to the northeast. There the country was a jumbled mass of mountains, seemingly impassable. Maybe the trail led to the San Francisco, for its headwaters were to the northwest. To follow the trail would entail hard marches, forcing the party to go miles out of their way. But possibly there was a way to trend east again toward the Rio Grande. Yet he did not want to chance breaking a way through the range to the east.

Hugh sipped water from his canteen and then began to follow the trail. There were places where rock slides covered it. There were other places where floods had swept away all traces of the trail, like a giant broom. But he found it again after he had lost it for a time. The walls of the canyon came close together and he walked along looking high above him to see brush and graying driftwood wedged in cracks and crannies. A flash flood would fill the narrow canyon with water many feet deep, sweeping everything before it.

Long shadows were slanting down the slopes when he climbed over a jumbled mass of rock thickly grown with thorny brush. Beyond him he could see where the canyon widened; its walls slanted back on the left below the great mesa he had seen. To the right the walls were almost sheer, seemingly awaiting a gunshot to make them crumble in an avalanche. He looked up the canyon, but the shadows were thick up there and a great shoulder of rock protruded into the canyon to block his vision. There was no way of knowing whether or not the trail continued around the rock shoulder or petered out in a chaos of rock.

He sat on a rock and studied the canyon. There was a curious, even line of rock, high on the left wall. It rose in several tiers and seemed to be of a different color than the rest of the rock. Dark patches, curiously even, showed at regular intervals along the rock line. He felt for his field glasses and then remembered he had left them at the camp.

He stood up and picked up his carbine, still looking at the curious rock formation. He shrugged and turned away. He wasn't in that lonely country to study geology.

Once he left the mouth of the canyon, he headed swiftly back toward the camp. The sun was gone behind the western heights and a cool wind blew against his back, chilling him through his sweat-soaked shirt.

A shot flatted off as he neared the camp. The echo slammed back and forth between the heights on either side. Hugh trotted forward, cocking and capping his Sharps. Then he saw the people of the party behind the low wall where they had made their camp. Greer, the orderly, was running toward the wall with his carbine in his hands.

Hugh came up behind the camp. Stevens turned swiftly and raised his carbine, then lowered it as he saw Hugh. Greer stumbled wearily to the wall and grounded his carbine. "Apaches," he said in his high-pitched voice.

Carbines were thrust over the wall. Abel Clymer took out his Colt and cocked it. He strode back and forth as though he were on the quarterdeck of a frigate going into battle.

Hugh dropped over the wall. "Get in here, Greer," he said.

Greer was helped over the wall by Stevens. His face was white with fear.

"Did you actually see an Apache?" asked Hugh.

"Yes."

Hastings spat. "He's liable to see anything."

Greer wiped the cold sweat from his narrow face. "I was on guard, Kinzie," he said nervously. "The wind was rustling the brush. Then I saw the brush move a hundred yards from me. There was something dark in amongst the brush. I shot at it."

Hugh gripped him by the shirt front. "But did you see a warrior?"

Greer looked at the people surrounding him. Then he looked away. "Well, now I'm not so sure."

Clymer raised a big hand. "I ought to buck and gag you," he said.

"Saddle the horses," said Hugh. "Get the pack mules ready."

"Why?" asked Nettleton. He wet his lips. "If there are no Apaches out there we can spend the night here."

"You've had a full day's rest. The horses and mules are all right now. We couldn't hold this position if the Apaches got above us. First thing you'd know, they'd stampede the animals, then sit up on those heights and shoot at us. We'd be like fish in a barrel."

Phillips rubbed his jaw. "He's right."

Clymer shot a look of scorn at Phillips. "You're both as panicky as Greer."

Nettleton looked down the canyon. "What did you find, Kinzie?"

"There is a trail north of here."

Nettleton looked at his wife and then sighed deeply. "Good! Then we can make for the Rio Grande."

"No. There's no way through there that I could find. This trail leads northwest, possibly to the San Francisco."

"We're not going that way," said Clymer.

Hugh looked at him. "Then stay here. I'm going north. If all of you want to take a chance on that trail you'd better go with me."

Nettleton nodded. "Then we must chance it."

Clymer twirled his Colt by its trigger guard, then deftly slid it into his holster. "Phillips! See to the horses."

Phillips flushed. Clymer treated him like a corporal instructing a raw recruit. Then without a word he beckoned to Willis, Pearce and Stevens, and led them to the animals.

Hugh walked south down the canyon. He stopped at the place where the guard had been. The canyon was deep in shadow. A hawk floated high overhead on a leisurely hunt for food. Suddenly he flew swiftly off to the west. There was no other sign of life down there, but there was a brooding air about the place.

Hugh scanned the brush. It moved in the wind. A more stable man than Greer would have thought something was moving about in the brush.

Hugh walked back to the camp. Roswell was saddling Hugh's buckskin. "See anything?" he asked.

Hugh shook his head.

"Greer scares easy."

"Nerves have a way of failing in this country. Maybe it's what you don't see that frightens you."

Roswell nodded. "I know what you mean."

Hugh led the buckskin to the wall. Mrs. Nettleton stood there with her shawl over her shoulders. "You'll ride all night after that hard scout up the canyon?" she asked.

Hugh took off his hat. "It's my job, Mrs. Nettleton."

She took in his broad shoulders and slim waist. Hugh was suddenly conscious of his whiskers and sweaty clothing.

"You feel better now?" he asked.

"Yes, thank you. Will it be a hard ride?"

He smiled. "Anywhere within fifty square miles around here is a hard ride."

"Will we ever reach the Rio Grande?"

He looked away. "Certainly."

She came closer. "Don't lie to me."

He looked down at her. "All right, then. It's a fifty-fifty chance. Maybe less."

She looked at her husband. He was checking the lashing on a mule pack. "Maurice is worried about me. But I'm tougher than he thinks I am."

Hugh grinned. "You should be. You're Boss Bennett's daughter, aren't you?"

She smiled. "You know of him then?"

"I'm from Missouri too."

She placed a hand on his arm. "Now I feel better. Stay close to me on the trail, Mr. Kinzie."

"I will."

He watched her walk gracefully toward her horse. Abel Clymer held its reins. He looked over her head at Hugh, and there was cold hate on his broad face.

Hugh swung up on his horse. Katy Corse rode up to him. "I see you have the same old fascination," she said.

"What's bothering you, Katy?"

She looked at Marion Nettleton. Clymer was standing there talking to her, with a smile on his face. "Her." she said.

"Meaning?"

Katy tilted her head to one side and studied Hugh. "There are some women who like all men. They think men have been put on earth for one purpose . . . to take care of them, and them alone."

"Katy, set your mind at rest. I want to get this party to safety, then go about fighting a war. Right now I haven't got time to worry about Marion Nettleton beyond getting her to the Rio Grande." He spurred forward and left her.

"I wonder," Katy Corse said softly.

Darrell Phillips posted Willis and Stevens at the rear of the party, then rode over to Katy. "You're ready?" he asked.

She glanced at him. "As ready as I'll ever be, Mr. Phillips."

He leaned close to her. "My friends call me Darrell."

"Darrell, then."

"Thanks," he said.

They rode together at the rear of the party.

CHAPTER SIX

Any Apache within a mile would know where the struggling party was. The thought was Hugh Kinzie's as he sat his horse by the side of the trail listening to the noisy progress up the dark canyon. Hoofs clashed against rock. A mule bawled now and then. Metal clashed against metal. Men cursed. The cacophony rose up into the night and echoed loudly from the canyon walls, magnifying the din manyfold.

There would be a new moon that night, of that Hugh was sure. It would help to show the trail, but it would also show the travelers to keen Mimbreno eyes. But if they had been traveling in ink, the noises they made would reveal them to anyone.

Hugh cut a chew and stowed it into his mouth. He wanted a smoke, but knew better than to make a light. As the noise of the party was dimmed by the distance, he became aware of the natural night sounds. The moaning of the wind through the canyon. The rustling of brush. The occasional cry of a night bird.

He looked down the canyon. He was sure that sonofabitch Jorge Dura had split the wind to alert the Mimbrenos. He should have killed him with no more compunction than a mountain lion has when killing a deer.

Hugh slid a hand along his cold carbine barrel. If he saw Dura with the Mimbrenos he'd break his own neck to get a bead on him.

Hugh wondered which of the men in the party he could rely on in a tight fight. He discarded Greer and Nettleton. Greer would run; Nettleton would be worried about his wife. Hastings would fight. He had guts, for all his big mouth. Stevens and Roswell would be steady. Pearce and Willis would look out for their own rumps. Isaiah Morton would be down on his knees. Phillips had a high sort of courage, in Hugh's opinion. Clymer might be the type of big bully who turns yellow when a little man stands up to him. It was all in the deck and the Apaches had marked cards.

He listened again to the night sounds. Greer might have seen an Apache. If he had, there would be more of them, probably nosing around like questing hounds at the deserted camping place.

Hugh touched the buckskin with his spurs. There was nothing but darkness behind him as he rode up the canyon, but his imagination peopled it with Mimbrenos, moving silently and swiftly on the trail.

———

THE MOON WAS CASTING A SICKLY pale light into the canyon when the party reached the place where the ancient trail trended northwest. Hugh called a halt. The light was good enough for them to continue on into the big canyon he had seen beyond the rock wall.

The men dismounted. Clymer helped Marion Nettleton to the ground. Katy Corse slid from her saddle and glanced at them. Nettleton bustled over to his wife, glanced angrily at Clymer and then looked at her. "Are you all right, Marion?" he asked.

"She's fine, Captain." said Clymer.

"I didn't ask you, Abel."

Clymer shrugged and then went to his horse. He took

his canteen and drank from it, watching Nettleton and his wife.

"The big stud is working overtime, as usual," said a dry voice behind Hugh.

Hugh turned. It was Chandler Willis.

"Got a chew, scout?" asked Willis.

Hugh silently handed him his plug. Willis cut off a chew and stowed it in his wide mouth. He worked it into pliability and then spat. *"Bueno!"* he said.

"Where's Pearce?"

Willis shrugged. "Somewheres. Taking care of nature's call, most likely."

"Get him. Go back down the trail. Watch and listen. For God's sake keep quiet."

Willis hitched up his gunbelt. "Shore. I been around red-sticks before."

"Where?"

"Apaches. Comanches. Lipans. Kiowas. Tonks."

"You're from Texas?"

Willis shifted his chew and spat forcefully. "Now I didn't say that, did I?" He wandered off into the shadows. "Hey, Dan!" he called out. "Get your carbeen. We got guard."

"Again? Ain't there no other soldiers around here?"

Willis laughed. "Just you and me, sonny. *Vamos!*"

The two troopers tramped down the canyon. Hugh could hear Pearce cursing luridly as he stumbled along.

Hugh walked up to the party. "We'll follow this trail for a way yet. It's tough going, but we can get through. We'll walk from here on."

"What's up ahead?" asked Phillips.

"More canyon. It gets bigger as you go along."

"Can we get out of it?"

"I don't know."

Clymer raised his big head. "What do you mean?"

Hugh leaned against a boulder. "Just what I said."

"I don't like your lip, scout. And I don't like the idea of stumbling through these mountains on an unknown trail."

"You can always go back."

Clymer balled big hands and planted them on his hips. "Trusting one man. I don't like it. How do we know who and what you are?"

"Look in the social register," said Hugh dryly.

"Kinzie? Kinzie? You have a relative at Fort Buchanan some weeks "back?"

"My brother was there for a time. Captain Ronald Kinzie."

Clymer came closer to Hugh. "That turncoat? He went over to the Rebels, didn't he?"

"I don't know."

"You don't know or you won't say? Which?"

Hugh straightened up. "I said I didn't know."

Clymer raised his head. "There's something about you that doesn't ring true, Kinzie."

"So?" said Hugh quietly.

Clymer came closer. He glanced down at Hugh's holstered Colt. "You lead us into hell's half acre without knowing where you're going."

"I'm with you."

"Yeah," sneered Clymer. "For what reason?"

Isaiah Morton came between them. "Let us have peace," he said.

Clymer hurled him aside with one huge hand. The man hit the ground, hard. Roswell pulled him to his feet. Nettleton hurried forward. "Clymer," he said. "Stop this madness. Kinzie is doing his best."

"His best isn't good enough."

"Then I *order* you to stop!"

Clymer didn't take his eyes from Hugh. "Go back to your wife, Nettleton," he said quietly.

Nettleton flushed.

"We're all on our own here," Clymer said.

Hugh looked down at Clymer's Colt. "If you're on your own, Clymer, you'd better make your play now."

Boots clashed on the loose rock. Chandler Willis came up to the party. "We'd better get movin'," he. said. "I think there are 'Paches down the gulch."

Hastings took his eyes from Clymer and Hugh. "You seeing things, too, Willis?"

Willis spat. "I didn't see nothing. But I heard a horse whinny down the canyon, and we ain't left any behind, have we, Sergeant?"

Hugh looked at Nettleton. "We'd better move on," he said. "I'll have to lead the way."

Nettleton nodded nervously. "Sergeant Hastings, stay as rear guard with Pearce and Willis."

"Yes, sir."

Clymer still stood there like a bull waiting to smash a china shop. Hugh picked up his carbine. He looked at Clymer. Clymer turned and walked to his horse.

Isaiah Morton raised his voice. "Let us be kind, one to another," he intoned. "For are we not all brothers?"

"Shut up!" said Clymer. He checked his plump saddle-bags and then led his horse up the canyon.

"Tough cob," said Jonas Stevens to Hugh. "You didn't have to worry. I had my carbine aimed at his back all the time he was chousing you."

"Thanks," said Hugh dryly.

Hugh led the buckskin past the little column. The big mesa loomed to the west, silvered by moonlight, lonely and cold-looking. He led the way over the rock slides, listening to the din behind him as hoofs clashed against rock.

The trail darkened as he entered the narrow canyon. Every instinct in Hugh Kinzie, honed by years of dangerous living, seemed to scream against going up that narrow hall of rock. It was different when an enemy could be seen and shot at; here there was nothing but the silent menace behind them. That was the worst part of it. Hugh could pull out. He'd make it somehow, afoot or on horseback. But somehow he seemed to see the calm face of Katy Corse in front of him, taking the rough trail as well as any of the men.

Hugh canted his head, listening to the sounds. High above him he could see where the moon silvered the rocks. They seemed to move and sway as the shadows of the wind-agitated brush played across them. An awful responsibility seemed to come and settle on Hugh Kinzie's shoulders, like the Old Man of the Sea who had plagued Sinbad. Hugh tried to shake off the feeling. Sinbad had been a wanderer like himself. They had a lot in common, but Sinbad had always played a lone game, looking out for his own tough rump.

It was a helluva country. It looked smooth and peaceful at a distance, like a sleeping cat. But rile the cat and the sharp claws came out from beneath the silken fur to rip and tear. Get deep into the country and feel the godawful loneliness drape itself about your shoulders. Feel the eerie qualities of the mountain night, engendered by the softly moaning wind and the shifting shadows.

The trail he was following, for instance. Who had made it? Where had they come from and where had they vanished to? They were long dead now. Hugh shook his head to drive away these thoughts. An old scout had once told him the best man for scouting in that country was a man who used his imagination to think only of liquor and women, and cut it off short when gruesome thoughts tried to worm their way into his head.

The great rock wall loomed ahead of him. He led the buckskin up the rough way. At the top he stopped and looked down. Clymer was helping Marion Nettleton up the first slope. Katy Corse was just behind them. Hugh could hear the men cursing as they tried to get the animals started up the slippery rocks.

It took them half an hour to get all the animals to the top. Hastings and his two men appeared as the last mule scrambled clumsily up to the top.

Nettleton shoved back his hat and looked into the great canyon, bathed in ghostly moonlight. "Is there water here?" he asked.

"I don't know. We'll have to ration ourselves."

"Great!" grunted Clymer.

Hastings, Pearce and Willis reached the top. All eyes surveyed the canyon. There was a quality of deep loneliness about it. When anyone spoke, he unconsciously did so in a whisper, as though standing in the nave of a great cathedral.

Hugh led the buckskin down the steep slope. There was no use in telling the others to follow. They were on a one-way road.

Hugh reached the bottom when one of the mules stumbled into a hole, fell sideways, then rolled down toward Hugh. The mule bawled once, then landed heavily ten feet from Hugh.

"Damn you, Pearce!" yelled Clymer. "You did it!"

Pearce turned to look up at the officer, his face contorted. "What the hell did you want me to do, sir? Hold him back by his damned halter?"

"Damn you! I'll have you bucked and gagged! I'll string you up by your thumbs! I'll have you court-martialed! You'll be drummed out of the service to the Rogue's March!"

"You'll have crap, Clymer! That's all you'll have!"

Hastings raised his carbine. He slammed the butt between Pearce's shoulders. "That's enough out of you!"

Pearce went down head first, cracking his head against a rock. He shook his head and then felt the blood flowing down his face. He opened his mouth as he looked at Hastings. Then he shut it. But there was pure hell in his cold green eyes.

Hugh walked to the mule. It was dead. He cut the pack lashings and pulled the packs free with the help of Roswell. "Lost a good mule for this junk," said the corporal.

Nettleton stopped behind them. "Place those packs on another mule, Roswell."

Roswell turned, a strange look on his face. "Sir? Those other two mules are overloaded as it is."

"Then put them on a horse!"

"Whose?"

They were all down at the bottom of the slope now. Nettleton looked from one to the other of them and then down at the packs. "That's our silver," he said pettishly. "Our wedding gift from my father-in-law. What would he say if we left it here?"

Willis laughed softly in the background.

Hugh took his bridle reins. "Is there any food in those packs?"

Nettleton shook his head. "Just the big silver set and some of my extra uniforms packed about them. Perhaps a few dishes and some household goods."

"Good! Let it lie."

Nettleton looked at his wife. She nodded and Nettleton went to his horse . . .

Clymer was grumbling again as Hugh led the way across the canyon floor. It was still rough going because of scattered rocks and thick brush. "No water. No trail," he said. "Led by the brother of a rebel. What next?"

Stevens was beside Hugh. He looked back. "Why don't you shut him up, Kinzie? I know you're not afraid of him. Why do you let him ride you like this? He's been doing it ever since you joined us."

Hugh looked at the trooper. "I've got a job to do, Jonas. To get this party to the Rio Grande."

"And then?" Stevens looked closely at Hugh's taut face. Hugh didn't have to tell him anything. It was written on the scout's face like a page of print.

"God help Clymer," he said softly.

CHAPTER SEVEN

H ugh looked back as he reached the end of the tumbled rock piles. He could see the rock wall which almost blocked the canyon. It looked like the great rock walls of the ancients. There was no sign of life on it. He had half expected to see a row of warriors standing there watching the party below them.

The wall behind him stuck in his mind as he led the buckskin through a thicket of brush. It brought back the curious even line of rock he had seen on the left wall of the canyon earlier that day. He turned and looked toward it. His jaw dropped. He stopped short.

"What is it?" asked Stevens.

Hugh swallowed dryly. "Look," he said hoarsely.

"For God's sake!"

Phillips came up behind them. "What is it? Apaches?" Then he stopped and looked with wonder in his dark eyes.

The arched roof of an enormous cave extended for many yards along the face of the mesa side. Filling it was a silent city of stone built in terraces reaching back into the great cave. The moonlight bathed the mortared walls in soft light. Windows and doors stood out in the stark relief of their shadows. Here and there a round or a square tower stood up, breaking the irregular line of the tops of the main structures. It looked like a brooding medieval castle transported by some magical means to the mountains of New Mexico.

The rest of the party crowded up behind them. "What's holding us up?" snapped Nettleton.

Phillips silently extended an arm to point toward the mesa wall.

"What a curious rock formation," said Marion Nettleton.

"It ain't real, is it?" asked Dan Pearce.

"I've heard of these places," said Darrell Phillips slowly. "It's a cliff dwelling."

"There anyone there?" asked Willis. He hefted his carbine.

Hastings spat. "I saw a place like that in Arizona once. Only it wasn't near as big."

Harry Roswell walked forward. "It's real enough. There's one something like it out near the Santa Cruz. The greasers call it Casa Grande."

"Who built it?" asked Katy Corse.

"The Hohokam . . . the Old Ones," said Hugh quietly. "I noticed it late this afternoon, but it was hard to see. I should have known what it was . . . those old fields we saw along the way . . . a trail where no trail should be."

They stood there in the moonlight looking up at the cliff dwelling. One of the mules suddenly brayed loudly. The echo rang from the cliff wall. Hugh turned quickly and raised his carbine.

"Shut up!" yelled Clymer at the mule.

"One jackass telling the other to shut up," said Willis.

Hugh padded back and looked toward the rock wall behind them. Mules were the best sentries there could be in Indian country. They could smell a warrior a mile away.

Something moved at the bottom of the rock wall. Hugh raised his carbine and then lowered it. He was getting as jittery as Greer. He studied the darkness at the bottom of the slope. Something had moved near the mule. Maybe a prowling coyote. There was one thing he knew for sure: Apaches loved sweet mule meat.

He backed toward the party. "Get around those rocks," he said over his shoulder.

"What is it?" asked Nettleton.

"I don't know. There's something at the bottom of the rock wall near the mule."

"My silver!"

"Damn your silver! Get moving!"

Hugh watched the place where he thought he could see the body of the mule. Hoofs clattered behind him as the horses and mules were led off the trail.

Roswell came up beside Hugh. He wet his lips. "You see 'em?"

"No."

"They there?"

"I think so."

"We can't fight out here."

"They won't attack at night."

"Yeah. But what about dawn?"

"That's it. Start the rest of them toward that cliff dwelling. Pronto!"

Hugh could hear Nettleton's peevish voice. "Why does he want us to go up there?"

"We can't hold off an attack out here in the open, sir," said Roswell.

"He's right," said Phillips.

"Supposing there are Indians up there?"

Clymer laughed. "If there are, they've been dead a couple of hundred years. No fear, Captain, unless you're afraid of ghosts."

"You try my patience, Mr. Clymer!"

"Jesus God," said Hugh to himself.

Hugh backed around the rock formation and trotted after the rest of them. They made enough noise to start every sleeping echo in that great canyon into wide-awake action.

Close up under the dwellings there was a great talus slope of broken stone stippled with thorny brush. The horses shied at the slope but the two mules slogged on.

Nettleton started up the slope, dragging Marion by her arm. Katy Corse looked back at Hugh. "Are you all right?"

Hugh wiped the sweat from his face. "Yes."

Dan Pearce stood to one side staring up at the silvery dwellings. "By Jesus, Chand," he said to Willis, "maybe there's treasure up in there. Gold, maybe."

Willis looked quickly at the others. "Shut up, you damned fool," he said.

They made clashing progress up the slope. Hugh came up last. The east end of the canyon seemed devoid of life. Maybe he had imagined seeing something move near the dead mule.

A crude low wall of unmortared stones ran the length of the first terrace. There was a place where it had crumbled, and through this place they led the animals onto a long flat terrace of irregularly shaped flat stones. The interstices had been filled with packed earth. Here and there along the terrace were rounded areas in the center of which was a sort of trap door. The shafts of crude ladders projected from some of them.

The walls of the closely joined buildings were pierced with small rectangular windows and curiously shaped doors. They looked like the capital letter T, with an exceptionally wide cross bar. Here and there crude ladders still rested against the sills of upper-story doors. Sagging wooden walkways rested on beams which projected from the walls, forming a means of entry into second-story dwellings.

The structures, close up, now showed signs of ruin. Roofs had tumbled in, filling the interiors of the small rooms. Walls had crumbled, littering the terraces and passageways between structures. Clumps of brush had sprung up in patches of earth, and an occasional stubborn tree had rooted itself where its seed had been carried by the wind.

No one spoke. They studied the ancient structures with questioning eyes. The silence was broken only by the stamping of one of the animals and the sighing of the wind through openings in the buildings.

Hugh at last broke away from his trance. He walked to the far end of the terrace and looked down into the moonlit canyon. A coyote howled from the heights across from the ruins. A moment later another coyote answered the first one, this time from the east end of the canyon. Hugh nodded. The Apaches were experts at animal calls, but the trained ear could detect a difference. How many of them were out there? If they were already on the far side of the canyon they could now block the way to the San Francisco. It was time to make a decision. Stay at the ruins, where they could defend themselves, or try for the only exit from the canyon. If the Apaches caught them on the canyon floor they would be wiped out. If they stayed at the ruins they would be hemmed in until hunger and thirst drove them into the open. They were damned if they did and damned if they didn't.

Darrell Phillips came along the terrace, still looking up at the ancient structures. "Amazing," he said as he reached Hugh.

"Yeah."

"How long do you think they been here?"

"Quien sabe?"

A coyote howled from far to the west. Hugh nodded. Darrell Phillips looked curiously at Hugh. "What's wrong?"

"Listen."

The wind moaned through the canyon. Minutes passed. Then from the west, on the ruins side of the canyon came a coyote howl. The net was completely around them now. The catch was in the net.

"Just a coyote," said Phillips. He laughed.

"No. Mimbrenos."

"You're sure?"

Hugh merely looked at the young officer. Phillips nodded. "I should have known better than to question you."

Phillips waved an arm at the cliff dwellings behind them. "This is a strange tiling. These people were an agricultural people, probably simple and peaceful. Why would they build their city up here in a place difficult to reach when they could have built equally as well out on the flats?"

"You tell me."

"Because something drove them up here, forcing them to build a fortress to live in, as our ancestors did in the Dark Ages when bands of robbers roamed the country."

"So?"

"The Apaches are nomadic as are the Navajos. Do you suppose their ancestors forced these people to live like this?"

"It's possible."

Phillips picked up a stone and dropped it over the wall. It hit far below and then rattled down the slope. "There is a curious parallel here, Kinzie."

"Yes?"

Phillips looked across the moonlit canyon. "We've been driven up here because we too are forced to protect ourselves against nomadic brigands."

"I see what you mean."

"One other thing bothers me."

"Yes?"

Phillips looked at Hugh. "What happened to the people who lived here?"

Hugh shoved back his hat. "I see what you mean. I'll tell you this: I'm not licked yet. No damned Mimbreno is going to sit out there like a spider in his web waiting for Hugh Kinzie to blunder into it. Let's go! We've got work to do."

They walked back along the terrace. Phillips glanced at Hugh. "You knew Katy Corse pretty well before the war, didn't you?"

"You asked me that once before."

"Yes."

"Why do you ask me again?"

Phillips flushed. "I suppose I forgot."

"Don't josh me, Mr. Phillips. I have no claim on her."

Phillips smiled. "Thanks."

Hugh stopped and gripped the young officer by the arm, swinging him around easily so that he faced Hugh. "You said that time that she'd make a good wife for an enlisted man. I said she'd make a good wife for *any* man. Do I make myself clear?"

Phillips tried to pull away but the strong fingers dug into his left bicep like steel wires. "Don't threaten me, Kinzie," he said in a low voice.

Hugh released him. "I wasn't threatening you. I was just reminding you that Katy Corse is a lady, as good as any lady you've ever met, and a helluva lot more of a real woman than Marion Nettleton." Hugh strode toward the others.

Nettleton looked down into the deserted valley. "Are they out there?"

Hugh nodded. "We'll stay here until we are sure they're gone."

"How long will that be?"

"*Quien sabe?*"

"I don't like it, Kinzie. We have very little food and water."

Hugh glanced at the two pack mules. "There might be some water. As for food . . . well, those three mules you started out with could have carried enough cold tack for a platoon."

"Sure, sure," said Clymer. "But we can't do anything about that now."

"We can do this," said Hugh quietly. "Place all food under guard and ration it. We might knock down a deer or a bear, if we're lucky. Until that time we're under short rations."

Nettleton wet his lips. "Sergeant Hastings," he said "take charge of all the food; gather the canteens. Place them in one of these small rooms and put a guard over them."

Hastings saluted. "Stevens and Greer! Come with me. Check all saddlebags, cantle and pommel packs for food."

Willis leaned against the wall. He glanced at the two packmules. "I hope that includes Nettleton's liquor," he said. "I could do with a slug or two."

Abel Clymer walked toward his horse. He took the saddlebags. "Greer!" he said. "Check these for food."

Greer shambled over. He was scared to death of the Apaches, but he looked like he'd rather face them than Abel Clymer. "I'm sure there isn't any food in there, sir," he said.

"Check them!" said Hugh.

Clymer flushed. He thought he had picked his man in Greer, and he had been right, but he hadn't figured on Hugh Kinzie.

Greer unbuckled one of the bags and thrust in his hands. He felt around, then drew out his hands and opened the other bag. He felt around in it. Then suddenly he looked up at Clymer with an odd expression on his face. Clymer eyed the little clerk steadily. Greer withdrew his hands and buckled the straps. "All right, sir," he said. "You're clean."

Clymer spat over the wall and hooked his saddlebags over his left arm. "Willis!" he said. "You clean out one of the rooms for Mrs. Nettleton."

"Yes, sir." Willis walked toward the row of structures. He glanced at the pack mules as he did so. A man could use a drink about now.

Hastings had the food piled up against a wall. There were about a dozen cans of embalmed beef, some slabs of dry-looking bacon, several containers of hardtack. The small amount Hugh had brought with him had been added to the pile.

"Ain't a helluva lot, is it?" asked Stevens of Hugh.

"About enough for two days if it's stretched thin."

"The Lord will provide," said Morton solemnly.

"He'd better start issuing," Pearce said.

Clymer strode over to one of the openings in the terrace floor. He tested the ladder with his hand. "Too fragile for me. Who's lightest here? You . . . Greer!"

Greer rubbed a dirty hand across his mouth. "Me . . . sir?"

Clymer nodded impatiently. "Take a look down there."

Greer walked over to the ladder and looked down into the hole. "I haven't got a light."

Clymer handed him a block of Strike Anywhere matches. Greer took them and broke one off. He drew the match across his belt buckle and held it down into the hole. It flared up in the draft. He dropped it down into the hole and stared after it. "Can't see a thing," he said.

Clymer shoved Greer toward the hole. "Go on," he said.

Hugh took a picket line from a horse and walked over to Greer. He made a loop in the line and passed it over Greer's head and then under his arms. He drew the loop tight about Greer's chest "Go on," he said.

There was naked fear on Greer's thin face. "What's down there, Kinzie?"

Hugh grinned. "A floor. It can't be a mine shaft."

"You're sure?"

"I'm not sure of anything except that I won't let go of this picket line." Hugh fastened his end of the line to his saddle, then coiled up the slack.

Clymer spat. "Get going, Greer."

The little man looked at Hugh and then at Clymer. Then he gingerly placed his feet on the ladder and began to go down. He took his time. Hugh could hear him breathing harshly as he tested each shaky rung.

Clymer shoved back his hat. "Yellowbelly," he said.

"I didn't see you racing to get down there, Clymer," said Hugh.

There was no sound from below. Then suddenly something snapped. A high-pitched scream seemed to shoot out of the hole like a rocket. Wood splintered, and there was the thump of a falling body. From the sound of it Greer hadn't fallen far. Hugh drew in on the line. The little clerk screamed again. "Give me a hand!" snapped Hugh at Clymer. They hauled Greer up, easing him through the hole. Hugh stared at Greer's face. It was a mask of blood.

Marion Nettleton screamed, "What's down there?"

Greer sank to the ground, pawing at his bloody face. Incoherent cries seemed to be pistoned out of his mouth at intervals. "It was awful!" he finally managed to gasp.

Hugh gripped Greer by the collar. "What, you fool!" he said. "What was it you saw?"

Greer's eyes were wide in his face. "Nothing! I saw nothing! It was the feeling I had down there."

Hugh unfastened the picket line from Greer. He passed the end under his arms and lashed it. "Stevens," he said, "feed out the slack as I go down."

Hugh went down into the darkness, feeling out with his legs as he went down. It was only a short distance. He hit hard earth with his feet and drew down a little slack from the line. He lit a match and looked about. The flickering light of the big match revealed a circular room, perhaps twenty feet across. A low shelf completely encircled the wall, and from it rose a number of low pilasters which held up the roof. The shelf was supported by an ingenious framework of cribbed logs covered with the hard earth of the terrace.

Hugh lit another match. The packed floor had been sprayed by the blood from Greer's nose. An eerie feeling came over Hugh as he stood there. He pulled at the picket line, then raised himself hand over hand until he pulled himself out onto the terrace. He looked at the others. "Nothing down there," he said.

Greer was wiping his face. "No? Maybe something you can't see, but there's something down there, Kinzie, and you know it. I can see it in your eyes!"

Some of the onlookers were nervous. Others stood there with drawn faces. There was something about the whole occurrence which had triggered strange thoughts in their minds. The whole place had an eerie, haunting quality about it, as though unseen eyes were always watching them.

Willis crawled out of a room. "Got it fairly well cleaned out," he said. "Lotsa trash in there. Mrs. Nettleton, you'll be all right in there."

Nettleton looked at Greer. "Get Mrs. Nettleton settled in there. For God's sake, get the rest of that blood off of your face." Nettleton turned toward Clymer. "Form a guard, Mr. Clymer."

Clymer looked at Phillips. "Take over, Mr. Phillips," he said shortly.

Later, as Hugh carried his blankets into one of the shelters which still boasted a roof, he looked out along the terrace. Stevens was pacing back and forth at the far end. Pearce leaned against a wall at the other end. The horses had been unsaddled and the mules unloaded. From somewhere in one of the small rooms he could hear a strident snoring. There was no sign of life in the canyon.

Hugh straightened out his blankets. Harry Roswell raised his head from where he was lying. "You think they'll bother us?" he asked.

Hugh pulled off his boots. "Not likely. Unless we try to leave. They don't like these places. Places of the Dead, they call them. They'll bide their time until we're ready to pull out."

"Then we'll get it."

"Maybe . . . maybe not."

Hugh dropped on his blanket and looked up at the dim ceiling of the little dwelling. He wondered how many years had passed since the builders of the room had slept there.

Roswell rolled over and looked again at Hugh. "What happened to Greer down there?" he asked quietly.

"Nerves."

"You feel anything down there?"

"No."

Roswell rubbed his jaw. "You looked a little pale when you came up."

Hugh rose up on an elbow. "Look, Harry. I don't like this place. I don't like the deal we're in. But I'm not going to lie awake talking about ghosts, if that's what you mean."

Roswell lay back and covered his eyes with his right arm. "Sorry, Hugh," he said.

The wind moaned through the little window and small doorway. It sighed along under the great arch of the cave high above the cliff-dwelling ruins. From somewhere down the canyon a coyote howled softly.

CHAPTER EIGHT

Hugh was up at dawn. He shivered in the cold wind as he stepped out onto the terrace. Roswell was on guard with Greer. Hugh rolled a smoke and handed the makings to Roswell. "How did it go, Harry?"

Roswell looked out over the dim canyon. He shrugged. "As quiet as the grave."

Hugh grinned. "A neat comparison."

Roswell lit his smoke. "Greer is acting peculiar."

"What's wrong?"

"Something has cracked inside of him."

Hugh nodded. "I've been expecting it. I'm going to look around."

Hugh glanced at Greer as he walked behind the little clerk. Greer was standing at the edge of the terrace, looking off into the dimness of the canyon, mumbling softly to himself.

Hugh worked his way over a pile of debris in a passageway between two dwellings. High above him the arched roof of the great cave showed darker streaks of deep red. They blended into black splotches where the cave roof ended. The streaks were at almost regular intervals and Hugh finally deduced that the smoke from the fires had discolored the reddish-brown rock.

There was a triangular space behind the back walls of the last row of dwellings, forming a long passageway between the walls and the slanting roof of the cave. It was littered with trash. Hugh picked up a finely shaped pottery bowl decorated with a black-on-white design.

Hugh walked east the length of the passageway. It ended against the blank wall, stained by the smoke of ancient fires. He walked back the other way, feeling the utter loneliness of the place. He picked up a square of yucca matting, pieces of pottery and a flint arrowhead.

Then he was at the western end of the passageway. Here there was a semicircular area, littered with ears of dried corn. There was a great fault in the cave wall, forming a narrow V-shaped crack in the rock. It had been carefully filled with mortared rock. Hugh skirted the crumbling wall at the end of the passageway, and eased his way through a narrow door into the bottom floor of a square, three-storied tower. A notched chicken ladder rose up to the next floor. Hugh climbed up to the second story. There was no ladder leading up to the third story, but he was able to stand on a pile of debris, grasp the edges of the trap door, and pull himself up into the top story. The roof had fallen in at one side. The light of early morning came in through a window, and flooded in through the gap in the roof.

Hugh walked over to the window, and standing well back from it, he looked out over the canyon. The tower afforded a fine place to watch the whole area in front of the ruins. There wasn't a sign of life on the brushy floor of the canyon. Hugh looked across to the far wall. He could have sworn the brush at one point moved a little against the wind.

Hugh rolled a smoke and studied the canyon. A good rifleman in the tower could sweep the slopes in front of the ruins. He knew they could hold the ruins against fifty Mimbrenos. But would the Mimbrenos attack? It was a place of the dead, and their superstitious fears would work on them enough to keep them at a distance. But they could let the lack of food and water drive the White-eyes from the ruins. It shouldn't take long.

Hugh looked along the terrace below him. Willis was kindling a fire from shattered roof poles. Stevens was filling a large coffeepot with water from a canteen. Greer was squatted against the front of a dwelling, his thin hands hanging down in front of his knees. Morton was on the terrace just below the tower with his battered Bible in his hands.

Katy Corse came out of one of the dwellings. She swept back her long hair with her hands, and thrust a comb into one side of the deep black tresses. She walked to the edge of the terrace and stood there, breathing deeply of the fresh morning air. Hugh thought that Katy Corse would be at home anywhere.

Darrell Phillips walked toward Katy. She laughed as he said something. They stood there together looking out toward the canyon, almost as though they were safe in some park back in the East.

Dan Pearce came out between two buildings, looked up and down the terrace, then furtively ducked back into a passageway again. First Sergeant Hastings was checking over the small stock of food, shaking his head as he did so. Harry Roswell was inspecting the horses picketed along the terrace.

Captain Nettleton came out of the room in which he had spent the night. "Is that coffee ready, Stevens?" he called out.

"No, sir."

"Hurry it up."

"The fire isn't hot enough, sir."

Nettleton threw his hands up in petty anger. He looked into the room he had just left. "It won't take long, dear," he said.

Hugh thought of the lack of water. Maybe he should stop Stevens from making the coffee. But he had stuck his neck into enough bickering already, without going so far as to deprive them of their morning coffee.

Hugh dropped down to the second floor of the tower. There was a startled exclamation from the first floor, then the crush of boots against the debris-littered floor. Hugh looked down through the opening. The first floor was empty. He turned on a heel and jumped to a side window, looking down into the narrow passageway between the wall and the end wall of the great cave. It was empty. But he did see something. Across from him was a rock shelf, slanting down and away from him. There was a thin trickle of moisture glistening against the wall.

Hugh pulled up the chicken ladder and thrust it across the gap between the tower and the rock shelf. He teetered across. There was a shallow pan of water there, hardly enough to wet the rock. There was a slow dripping from the trickle against the wall. Hardly enough water to keep one person alive for long, much less thirteen. "Thirteen!" he said aloud.

He walked back across the ladder and replaced it where he had found it. He'd keep the knowledge of the water to himself for a time, until he figured out what to do. He passed back into the triangular passageway. It was empty of life.

Hugh walked out on the terrace. Abel Clymer appeared at the far end and glanced at Hugh, then he came toward the fire. Hastings was doling out the meat and hardtack. "Willis," he said, "you and Pearce take morning guard."

Willis stopped with his meat halfway to his wide mouth. "Hell, Sarge! I was on four hours last night."

"We're not running this outfit from a duty roster."

Willis glanced at Phillips, at Clymer and then at Hugh. "There's some here had a full night's sleep," he said.

Hugh leaned against a wall. "We can get by with one guard during the day," he said. "Send him to that tower at the west end. He can see the whole terrace, the slope, and a good part of the canyon from up there. Good field of fire."

Clymer's eyes held Hugh's for a moment, then the big officer turned away. "Captain Nettleton," he said loudly, "how long are we going to stay here?"

Nettleton put down his coffee cup. "Until we're sure there are no Apaches out there," he said.

Clymer laughed. "We haven't seen any yet. Maybe there aren't any out there."

"Walk down the slope," said Hugh. "Take a little stroll up or down the valley. If you don't come back then you'll know they're out there."

"I don't like this," said Clymer. He looked at Hastings. "Send out a man to look around."

Hastings stood up. He wiped big hands on his thighs. "One man, sir?"

"Did you expect to send a squad?" asked Clymer sarcastically.

Hugh rolled a smoke. He eyed Clymer. "Ask for a volunteer, Hastings," he suggested.

The men looked away. Hastings wet his cracked lips. "Any volunteers?" he asked uncertainly. No one spoke up.

Hugh shifted a little. "You've got two good junior officers here, Captain Nettleton. A good officer wouldn't send a man on a detail he wouldn't take on himself."

Clymer scowled. Phillips went pale beneath his tan. Nettleton stood up and placed his coffee cup on a rock. "Why, yes," he said brightly. "That's it! Mr. Clymer, you and Mr. Phillips decide between yourselves who is to go."

Clymer looked at Phillips. "You go," he said.

Phillips felt about in his trousers pocket. "We'll flip for it," he said quietly.

Clymer spat. "Forget it. Forget the whole thing!" He stamped off down the terrace.

Willis softly laughed as he picked up his carbine and walked toward the tower to stand guard.

The heat of the afternoon seemed to hang in the silent canyon like a thick issue blanket. There wasn't a breath of wind. Nothing stirred. The sky was a pitiless blue, without even a cloud to suggest shelter against the blazing sun.

Hugh was in the tower, studying the far wall of the canyon with his field glasses, feeling the sticky sweat rolling down his sides. He lowered the glasses and wiped the misted eyepieces with his bandanna. Now and then one of the horses whinnied pitifully, to be answered by the dry braying of a mule. Something scraped below Hugh. He turned and looked at the opening in the floor.

There was a rattling noise from the first story. Hugh cased his glasses and walked softly to the opening. He looked down through both openings. Harsh breathing came up to him. Hugh moved. A piece of stone rolled over the edge of the opening and dropped on the chicken ladder which was between the first and second stories. Boots crushed against debris.

Hugh leaped over to the side window of the tower. He thrust his head through the window. Dan Pearce looked up at him. "What's on your mind, Dan?" asked Hugh.

Pearce flushed. "Water," he said.

"You'll have to wait."

"Willis says there's water around here somewhere."

"There is. But it isn't in that first-floor room."

Pearce looked down. "Hell," he said. "I thought there might be something a man could pick up and take along with him."

"Such as?"

"Gold, maybe."

Hugh grinned. "These people were farmers, Pearce."

Pearce squinted his eyes as he looked up. "You find anything?"

"Pottery. Arrowheads. Matting. That's all."

"They must have had something of value."

Abel Clymer entered the passageway. He stared at Pearce. "What are you doing in here?"

Pearce straightened up. "I'm next on guard, sir."

"Then get up in that tower!"

Pearce glanced sideways at the big officer. He entered the tower and came up beside Hugh. "Sonofabitch," he said. "He's been poking around these ruins himself. Always was looking for something to lay his hands on back at Fort Ayres."

"Such as?"

"Money. Women. Liquor. What else is there?"

Hugh handed Pearce the glasses. "Keep away from the water," he said.

Pearce glanced out of the side window. "Ain't enough there to wet a blotter," he growled.

"Just the same . .leave it alone."

Pearce spat dryly as Hugh went down through the opening.

Clymer was still in the passageway. He eyed Hugh. "You've got influence with the captain," he said. "Get him to give us orders to move on."

"We've been through this before."

Clymer flushed. "Mrs. Nettleton isn't standing this heat too well."

"Who is?"

Clymer gripped Hugh by the shirt front and drew him close. "Damn you! Don't get me riled, Kinzie!"

Hugh dropped his carbine butt on one of Clymer's feet. Clymer grunted in pain and stepped back. The carbine muzzle prodded the big officer in the belly. "Get out of my way," said Hugh softly.

Clymer limped backwards. His eyes were filled with feral hate as he watched Hugh walk out onto the terrace. A soft laugh came from high above Clymer. He looked up to see the grinning face of Dan Pearce. "Damn you, Pearce!" said Clymer. "I won't take anything from *you!*"

Pearce shoved a stone over the edge of the window. It hit Clymer on the head. Clymer clawed for his Colt but Pearce leisurely rested his carbine barrel on the bottom of the window. He cocked the hammer. His eyes met Clymer's. Clymer released his hold on his pistol and limped back into the passageway. Pearce touched the partially healed scar on his head, then spat dryly down into the passageway.

CHAPTER NINE

Myron Greer sat in a narrow space between two buildings. It was shadowy in there, but it was still hot. He could feel the sweat running down his thin body. He ran his tongue about inside his dry mouth. But it wasn't water he wanted; he needed something far stronger than that.

Strange thoughts went through Myron Greer's mind. He felt as though he should get up and walk to the edge of the terrace, climb over the wall, then slide down the slope to the vast canyon floor. Somewhere out there he might find a drink.

Maybe the scout, Hugh Kinzie, had a bottle. Those men usually had one, although they didn't drink when they worked. Too dangerous. But it was handy for cleansing wounds and easing their pain.

Above him a lizard scuttled about, dropping bits of mortar down on Greer's bare head. He didn't move.

Maybe the people who had built these crazy cliff dwellings had learned how to ferment corn. But these people had been gone for generations. Anything they had left would have been long dried up by now. Still, if it had been well sealed and buried in the ruins, there might be a little bit of it left, and it would have a wallop like a dose of canister.

Greer raised his head. A hammer started thudding inside his skull while an iron band seemed to tighten around the outside of it. He looked out across the canyon. He didn't see the far wall shimmering and waving in the heat, but rather he saw a whirling, grayish mass, which seemed to form itself into a cone, like the inside of a whirlpool. It seemed as though he could run to the edge of the terrace and dive into the whirlpool to be swept away into its cool depths.

Abel Clymer walked up and down the triangular passageway behind the ruins. It was a little cooler in there, or so it seemed. His right instep throbbed where that sono-fabitch Kinzie had dropped the steel-shod butt of his Sharps. Kinzie's time would come, but Clymer wasn't ready to get rid of him yet. Clymer wanted to get out of this hell hole and take Marion Nettleton with him. He wet his thick lips as he thought of Marion Nettleton. "Jesus," he said softly.

If he could get her back to the Rio Grande and show up at Santa Fe with her, he'd be the biggest damned hero in the Southwest. With rapid promotions the order of the day, he, Abel Johnston Clymer, first lieutenant, United States Cavalry, could ask for anything. With Bennett behind him he might eventually get a brigade. General Clymer! That was the ticket!

Clymer stopped at the far end of the passage and wiped the sweat of heat and ambition from his broad face. Maurice Nettleton was in his way. Nettleton had money. That was why Clymer had stayed his little game until he had found a stake for himself. Well, he had it now. The next thing to do was to get Nettleton to move out of there, one way or another. With Kinzie to guide him, Clymer could break through. It might not be easy to get rid of Kinzie, but that job had to be done too. Then it would be Santa Fe, and the plaudits of the department commander. Then on to St. Louis and the firm, friendly handclasps of Boss Bennett. Despite the clinging heat, Clymer shivered a little in his ecstasy. "Captain Clymer. Major Clymer. Colonel Clymer. *General Clymer!*" he said aloud.

Dan Pearce peered through Hugh Kinzie's field glasses. He studied the east end of the canyon. Somewhere in the haze was that damned dead mule with Nettleton's silver still in the packs. Dan had seen the silver service back at Fort Ayres. It wouldn't take a man long to get back to that stinking mule and cut those packs loose. He could cache the silver and come back for it some day. Maybe he and Chandler Willis could make a break for the river, but there wasn't enough value in the silver for two to share it. The thing to do was get the silver, hide it, then talk Willis into going out of the canyon with him. Two would have a better chance than one. Three could make it without too much trouble— if the third man was Hugh Kinzie.

Darrell Phillips looked down at his Wellington boots. Made by Bascomb of London. The best boots in the whole department, and he had to wear them into this country. The boots were scuffed, and one of them had a slit clear through the fine leather. No amount of polishing and buffing would ever make these boots look like anything worthwhile again.

Phillips closed his eyes and leaned back against the warm wall of the little room he shared with Clymer. He wrinkled his nose a little. Abel Clymer carried an animal-like odor about with him even when he was freshly scrubbed. Clymer had given him nothing but hell from the first day he had showed up at Fort Ayres. According to regulations both Abel Clymer and Darrell Phillips were officers and gentlemen. Their commissions had made them both officers. The difference between the two of them was that Abel Clymer had reached the miraculous estate of being a gentlemen by the act of becoming an officer, while Darrell Phillips had been born a gentleman and would die as one.

Phillips thought of Katy Corse. She would have been as much out of place in his mother's drawing room as Abel Clymer would have been, but there was something refreshing about her, despite her easy frontier manners. Somehow she had been able to ease the pain of his bitter loneliness. She was attractive and well formed . . . He shuddered a little as he thought of bringing her home to his mother.

He stood up and picked up his hat. Katy was outside somewhere. He had to see her, to talk with her.

Chandler Willis slitted his eyes as he looked out over the canyon. Damned if he had seen any Apaches, but he knew as well as the big scout did, that they were there. Lying in the brush on the heights across the canyon; maybe even up on the mesa which rose above the cliff dwellings. Willis had almost made his break back there when they had found the smashed remains of Winston's cattle-herding detail. He could have maybe made his way to the Rio Grande alone, then south to join Baylor's Second Texas Rifles at La Mesilla. But two men had been watching him: Lieutenant Clymer and First Sergeant Hastings. Either one of them would have shot him if they had figured he was going to desert to the Confederacy.

Chandler Willis cursed his luck. He had killed a man back on the South Llano in the fall of '59, and had made it across the Rio Grande the range of a rifleshot ahead of the dead man's relatives. From there he had drifted to Fort Bliss, where he had enlisted for a winter's feed and shelter. Hastings had tagged him with the nickname Snowbird because of that.

Willis shifted and spat again. That damned Yankee Pearce was up to something crooked. He needed Chandler Willis for something. Something for Pearce's profit, not Willis's. Yankees were all alike.

He wondered how loyal Hugh Kinzie was. He was tough enough to be a real Tejano. Maybe he was thinking of joining the Confederacy. The two of them together could clean out this bunch of Yankees, and ride like kings into La Mesilla with a mess of rifles and equipment, plus some damned good horse and mule flesh.

Maurice Nettleton looked down at his sleeping wife. Sweat dewed her oval face. Her soft lips were parted, showing her even white teeth. Her breasts swelled against the material of her traveling dress. Nettleton swallowed hard. A cold greenish wave of fear flowed through him as he thought of losing her.

She had made him. He had been an obscure second Lieutenant of dragoons at Jefferson Barracks when he had met her and had instantly fallen in love. He had come from a fairly well-to-do family, which made it possible for him to court her. Shelton Bennett had always said he wanted a son-in-law as tough in the rump as he was, but it wasn't really the truth, for Shelton Bennett ruled everybody who would allow him to. And his daughter, too, for all her soft looks, was as hard as nails. She had married young Maurice Nettleton because she had thought he was the kind of a man she could mold to fit her needs. Her judgment had been faulty.

Their first years of married life had been like a dream. Living in the fine big house in St. Louis; having his promotion come through years ahead of time; getting assigned to department headquarters as a staff officer. Then Shelton Bennett had quarreled with somebody in the War Department. It had been enough to have Maurice transferred to godforsaken Arizona. The pain had been assuaged a little by his promotion to captain. Marion had looked on the affair as a gay adventure. But Maurice had been badly shaken. The country was too big and dangerous. He'd had no experience with these hard-bitten frontier soldiers. Abel Clymer, who had run Fort Ayres before, listened to Maurice with some respect, but he still ran the post. Then the slow realization had come over Maurice that Clymer was making a strong play for Marion. He was solicitous with her, and used every opportunity to show up Maurice.

Maurice Nettleton began to fan his wife. He could hear Abel Clymer's bull voice in the next room, where he was riding Darrell Phillips. Nettleton looked at the fine engraved Colt pistol in his holster, one of a pair presented to him by Shelton Bennett. Nettleton felt his hands tremble; He hated violence and bloodshed. All he wanted to do was get his wife to safety, then get himself assigned to a staff job where he could be beside his wife when she needed him. But if Abel Clymer stood in the way, he would see that Maurice Nettleton would fight for his own.

Matt Hastings pulled his soggy shirt up over his head and swabbed his armpits with it. He had a fresh shirt in his pommel pack, but he had been saving that for his entry into Santa Fe. In twenty years' service he had bucked his way up through the ranks by his ability to follow orders, and always look like a soldier. There had been a time when the diamond of a top soldier was all he desired, but the rumors of war changed Matt Hasting's ambitions. For the first time in his army career he began to think of wearing shoulder straps instead of chevrons. Instead of obeying his officers' orders implicitly he had begun to think that perhaps he knew more than they did. He had begun to burn the midnight oil reading every military book he could lay his hands on. Matt knew them all by heart, which was a hell of a lot more than that bumbling Captain Nettleton could say, or Abel Clymer with his big mouth, or Darrell Phillips with his sensitive face and fine manners.

Matt wiped off his carbine and pistol. He'd hold this J Company outfit together if it was the last thing he ever did.

The sun had died in the west, weltering in rose and gold. Purple and black shadows mantled the mountains. A cooling wind crept out of the hills and rustled the brush.

Jonas Stevens walked along the line of thirsty horses. They had been jerking at their picket lines. Jonas touched his cracked lips with his tongue. He had saved his ration of water for that day, but there wasn't enough for one of the animals. The lack of water was one of the many things he had never figured on when he had asked for duty in the Southwest. Not for himself, but for the animals. It was different back East. Plenty of good water and fine grazing for cavalry mounts. Jonas patted the nose of one of the horses. He looked down into the dim canyon. Maybe there was water down there somewhere. Kinzie hadn't said so, but Kinzie was a secretive sort. But if there *was* water down there, Jonas Stevens would see to it that the horses and mules got to it.

Harry Roswell was standing his guard shift in the tower. He looked down at his two stripes. He wore them because he always obeyed orders without question, even those of a corporal who was senior to him. Matt Hastings had once said that seniority amongst corporals and second lieutenants was like virtue amongst whores, but Matt Hastings was a capable first sergeant worth half a dozen green officers.

Roswell touched his two stripes and then straightened his hat. He gripped his carbine and threw back his shoulders. His seniors could rely on him to carry out their orders. He dropped through the opening in the floor and felt about for the chicken ladder.

It was pitch dark in the canyon. A coyote howled. The wind moaned through the chasm, rustling the brush, and haunting the cliff-dwelling ruins with ghostly whisperings. Something moved furtively at the wall that edged the front of the terrace. A man rolled over the wall and landed softly on the slope. He lay there a while, listening to the night. Then he eased his way down the slope until he reached the brush at the bottom. Then he was gone through the brush, heading for the east end of the canyon.

Isaiah Morton sat in the darkness of a tumbledown room, with his back and head pressed against the warm wall. His Bible lay open on his lap, and one of Isaiah's spatulate fingers rested on the page. It was too dark to read, but it really didn't matter, for he knew the book by heart. He was sure that God had placed him in his present company for some obscure but righteous reason of His own. They were an ungodly lot. Their passions and desires were close to the surface. There was no inner peace in any of them. Some of them laughed at Isaiah Morton, but he had taken it as part of his martyrdom, part of the task which had been given to him in a vision. For Isaiah Morton had been picked to bring Christianity to Mangus Colorado. It had been said that an old priest had tried to do so many years before. But he had failed. Some said that Father Font had been a good man, and had failed not because of anything he had done, or had not done, but rather because his own people had betrayed Mangus Colorado.

The scout, Hugh Kinzie, a hard and violent man, had said the Mimbrenos were waiting for their chance out in the darkness. When that chance came they would strike and kill. Isaiah tried to conjure up a picture of Mangus Colorado. "He sitteth in the lurking places of the villages: in the secret places doth he murder the innocent: his eyes are privily set against the poor." Isaiah Morton stood up and paced back and forth. "He lieth in wait secretly as a lion in his den: he lieth in wait to catch the poor: he doth catch the poor, when he draweth him into his net." Isaiah's harsh voice rang out, echoing from the walls. "He croucheth, and humbleth himself, that the poor may fall by his strong ones!"

Someone called out along the terrace. Isaiah's voice died away. A faint murmuring echo came from the arched rock wall high above the cliff dwellings. Cold sweat bathed Isaiah's gaunt body.

From somewhere in the darkness a dry voice spoke up. "If them Apaches didn't hear that, they're deaf. He's a shoutin' minister, that man is."

Isaiah bowed his head in prayer.

Marion Nettleton was still tired. She had had more rest than anyone else in the party, and had been exposed to the least amount of hardships. She lay awake in the darkness, trying to imagine she was in her big bed in the cozy room in her father's castellated monstrosity of a house back in Missouri. She had a strong will, and a fine imagination, but she could not fight back the eerie darkness of the ruins, always pressing in for every advantage.

Maurice was outside somewhere, bumbling about, trying to play the part of the frontier soldier. Maurice had always been good to her. She had fallen in love with him, or thought she had, because he had had all the outward manifestations of the kind of man she wanted, but time and closer acquaintance had showed her how wrong she had been. He was on the defensive with her now, catering to her every wish, pampering and petting her, when she had hoped for a man like her father, who ruled women, and everyone else for that matter, with a will of iron.

Marion had come west with Maurice, hoping that he would assert himself and build up a reputation, but unfortunately he had been too long under the hard thumb and the strong will of Shelton Bennett. They hadn't been at Fort Ayres more than a month when it was obvious his men were laughing at him. Mother Nettleton was his nickname behind his back. Marion often had wondered what they called her behind her back until one day she had overheard two noncoms talking together about her. She had not been mentioned by name. "The Little Corporal," one of them had said.

Marion hadn't been too nervous when they had left Fort Ayres. Now doubt had a firm hold on Marion Nettleton. She had depended on these people for her comforts; now she was dependent on them for her very life. Maurice had bungled as usual. If he had abandoned the beef herd he would not have lost the largest part of his company, as well as the services of a skilled Indian fighter. If he had moved swiftly toward the Rio Grande, instead of traveling almost leisurely for the comfort of his wife, he might have escaped the net cast about him by Mangus Colorado. Now he was more concerned about his wife's little desires than about the dangers surrounding them. Hot coffee, a soft place to sleep, warm blankets in the cool nights, and cold water during the hot days: none of those things would matter if a screaming horde of bloodthirsty Apaches came down on them and ripped Marion's clothes from her, and ripped the ivory citadel of her shapely body with greasy hands.

Marion sat up and slowly fixed her hair. She had once thought Abel Clymer was the man to save her. At first she had hated the scout, Hugh Kinzie, with his sharp orders and bitter eyes. But Hugh Kinzie could save her if anyone could. Marion stood up and brushed her clothing. There would be a moon that night. He had once promised to stay close to her on the trail. This night she would give him his chance. Not too much, just enough to set the hook in tightly.

There was a faint suggestion of the moon in the eastern sky. Dan Pearce looked back over his shoulder. He could just make out the cliff dwellings up on the slope behind him. No one had followed him. It would be quite some time before that three-striped bastard Sergeant Hastings missed him. By that time Dan would have the silver service and any other loot from the mule packs cached away.

Dan padded through the brush. It was almost like the old days back at Five Points when he had prowled the streets looking for drunks to smash and pluck. He looked up at the high walls of the canyon. It was almost like walking through a narrow street in New York, between rows of sagging tenements. Dan Pearce would make it all right. He had the luck and the guts.

Katy Corse slowly hooked up the front of her dress. The heat of the day was long gone and a cool wind whispered up the canyon. She wanted a bath and clean clothing, but she cast the thought from her mind. There was hardly enough water for drinking purposes, and the only women's clothing available belonged to Marion Nettleton. She hadn't offered Katy the use of any of it.

Katy walked out onto the dim terrace. There was a brooding quiet about the canyon. She could feel, rather than see, the men of the little party, staring out into the dimness and listening to every night sound. She had been through experiences like this before. At Tubac she had lived through an attack when she had been fifteen years old. Her mother had been killed in that one. In 1858 her father had been the sutler at Fort Buchanan, and Katy had helped him. Two years later he had been killed by Apaches while bringing in supplies. Katy had turned over the sutler's store to Cass Wilkerson. Cass had kept her on as his clerk. It was then she had met Hugh Kinzie.

Katy felt the breeze cool her warm flesh. She had fallen hard for Hugh Kinzie, probably because he hadn't paid much attention to her on a post where every trooper, one way or another, honestly or dishonestly, had tried to gain her favor. Hugh Kinzie was a great deal like his brother Ronald. Strangely enough, Katy had been interested in Captain Kinzie, but he had paid no more attention to her than he had to his horse or dog. Hugh seemed to have been a little more human, but still had that Kinzie aloofness about him.

Herbert Oglesby had played up his suit vigorously to Katy about the same time Hugh had seemed to be a little interested. Katy liked Herbert and had used him to place a little jealousy in Hugh Kinzie, to see what he'd do. Katy had overplayed her hand, for Hugh had shied away like a badly broken horse. In common with most of the men on the post, he had assumed she was Herbert's woman. Nothing she could do, within reason, had changed Hugh's coldness toward her. Herbert had proposed. She had accepted, hoping Hugh at last would do something. He hadn't. One day he was there; the next day he was gone into the hazy mountains. A month later Herbert Oglesby had died with a flint arrowhead buried in his chest.

Katy walked to the edge of the terrace. Somehow, every time she tried to be nice to Hugh, she put her foot into it. Hugh was feisty, and had to be handled with a fine touch, and Katy Corse seemed to lack that touch.

A man came up behind Katy. She turned quickly, hoping it was Hugh. She looked up into the dim face of Darrell Phillips. There wasn't any hesitation in him. He swept her close and pressed his lips against hers. She was so surprised, there was no fight in her.

"If you're going to dally," a dry voice said behind them, "you'd better get off the skyline. The moon is coming up."

Phillips released her and turned quickly to look into the amused face of Hugh Kinzie. "You've no right to come up on us like this!" snapped Phillips.

Hugh looked out into the canyon. "You're close enough to that slope for a Mimbreno to come up on you and have a knife into your back before you'll even smell his stink."

Phillips raised a hand. He stepped forward.

Hugh smiled. "Don't do anything you'll be sorry for, Mr. Phillips."

Phillips lowered his hand. In front of Katy Corse, he wanted desperately to prove he was a man but not at the expense of fighting Hugh Kinzie.

Hugh raised his head. "You'll be on guard tonight. We'll all take turns. The enlisted men are getting tired of doing all the work. We're all in this. We'll have to forget about rank for a while."

"All right, Kinzie."

Hugh looked at Katy. "Don't get too far from any of the men, Katy." He turned and walked away into the darkness like a great lean cat.

Darrell Phillips looked at Katy. "What did he mean by that?"

She looked away. Her hands closed into tight little fists. "Damn you," she said hotly. "Get away from me!"

Phillips reached out a hand toward her, hesitated, then turned on a heel and walked away.

A blanket of silence seemed to have settled over the great canyon. Even the wind had died away. It was almost as though the canyon was waiting for something to happen.

CHAPTER TEN

Captain Nettleton had called a council of war. Pressures were working within him. Clymer was bullying him. Phillips certainly wasn't looking up to him. But most of the pressure came from Marion. She had a way of letting a man know how she felt about him without even opening her mouth.

Maurice paced back and forth in front of the watchtower. Hugh Kinzie leaned against the tower wall. Abel Clymer squatted beside the terrace wall with his huge hands dangling between the frayed knees of his trousers. Darrell Phillips alone stood straight up, with squared shoulders, his hands folded together in front of him.

Nettleton plucked at his lower lip. "Gentlemen," he said hesitantly. "We must decide on a plan. Our food is almost gone. There's hardly enough water for us, and the animals are in bad shape for lack of it. Another day of this heat and they'll all be dead."

"Apaches don't attack at night," said Abel Clymer. "What's to prevent us from stripping away all excess equipment and making a try to get out of here?"

Then Darrell Phillips spoke up. "Perhaps we could make a sortie against the Mimbrenos. Say half a dozen good men could leave here when the moon is gone and climb up the canyon wall to strike the Mimbrenos in their camp."

Nettleton looked at Hugh pleadingly. Hugh shifted his chew and spat leisurely.

Nettleton paced back and forth. "Both suggestions are good. Perhaps, by combining them, we can work out an effective means of escape."

"Such as?" asked Hugh quietly.

Nettleton turned. "We can lighten the loads of the horses and mules. Some of us can remain here with the women. Others, capably led, can attack the Mimbrenos, thus diverting them from those of us who are down here. While the Mimbrenos are being diverted, the women can be started for safety. Then, when the women have a good start, those who have been holding the Mimbrenos can follow the main party, covering their retreat until we're out of the canyon."

Chandler Willis was on guard up in the watchtower. Hugh heard the trooper shuffle his feet, then spit hard against the cave wall a few feet from the side window of the tower. Hugh didn't have to see Willis's face to know how it looked.

Nettleton was now fully taken up with his masterful plan, carried away by the way the pieces of the plan fell together neatly and surely. "We will divide into two parties. The attacking party will, of course, be led by one of us. One of us must take charge of the main party here. A man of judgment, who can gauge the precise time to move out."

"That leaves two of us," said Hugh dryly.

Nettleton hesitated. This was the crucial time. His plans always appeared well on paper, but getting men, those creatures of varied impulses and emotions, to follow his cleanly outlined plans had always been the problem of Maurice Nettleton. He straightened up. After all, he *was* the commanding officer. "I will take personal command of the main party, with Mr. Phillips as my aide. The main party will, of course, include the ladies, Sergeant Hastings, Corporal Roswell, Private Stevens and Mr. Isaiah Morton."

Abel Clymer raised his big head and stared at Nettleton.

Nettleton looked away. "Mr. Clymer will lead the attacking party, with Mr. Kinzie as scout. The party will consist of Privates Willis, Pearce and Greer."

There was a soft whistle from up in the tower. "Jesus Christ," said Chandler Willis.

Abel Clymer got to his feet and cracked the knuckles of his left hand. "As senior officer, Captain Nettleton, I, rather than Mr. Phillips, should be with the main party."

Phillips raised his head. "The captain has given his orders," he said.

Clymer whirled. "So? Maybe you talked him into it? I've got a good mind to break your damned jaw, Phillips!"

Phillips dropped his hand to his holstered Colt. Clymer moved in close and gripped the younger officer by the shirt front. "You haven't got the guts to pull that gun on me," he snarled. "Admit it! You talked Nettleton into taking you instead of me!"

Nettleton bustled forward. "Clymer! I'm in command here!"

Hugh stood up straight and spat his wad of chewing tobacco over the terrace wall.

"You're the big man around here," said Phillips softly. "Show Marion Nettleton what a *real* big man you are by protecting the rest of us. Clymer."

Clymer slashed a big hand across Phillips's face. Phillips jerked back his head. Clymer swung him about and rammed his back up against the tower wall. "Damn you! I'll protect her, all right! While you're out there holding back those Apaches!"

Hugh pushed Nettleton aside. He drew out his Colt and cocked it. He rammed the muzzle into Clymer's back. "Come on, stud," he said. "Lay off the heroics. The whole damned plan stinks in the first place. We're not going through with it."

Clymer released Phillips. He turned his head to look into Hugh's shadowy face. "You haven't got the guts to shoot, Kinzie," he said with a sneer.

Hugh stepped back. The big man had some guts. Hugh holstered his Colt.

Nettleton came forward. "What do you mean about not going through with the plan?" he demanded.

Hugh looked out into the quiet canyon. "Those horses and mules wouldn't get ten miles. We don't even know if there is a trail beyond this canyon. If you left here right now it would be daylight long before you got out of this canyon. The damned thing may go on for miles, every inch of it overlooked by the Mimbrenos. As for your so-called sortie, if you took every man you have here you'd all be dead long before you reached the 'camp' of the Mimbrenos, as Phillips called it. They haven't any camp with rows of tents and bivouac fires going. They're lying out in the brush in the darkness, listening to every night sound. You could walk right through the middle of the camp and never know it was there until knives came up from the very ground itself to gut you. If five of us went looking for those bastards in the dark, as was suggested here, none of us would come back, and if we did get a crack at them before they got us, we'd hardly make a dent in their forces. Then they'd be after the main party. They could outrun our horses afoot"

Clymer spat. "So? What do *you* suggest?"

Hugh shrugged. "It seems I'm the only one here without an idea."

Phillips wiped the blood from the corner of his mouth. "Perhaps one man might get through to the Rio Grande and bring back help."

Nettleton bobbed his head. "A capital thought, Mr. Phillips."

Clymer glanced at Hugh. "*Him,* I suppose?"

"You can volunteer," said Hugh dryly.

"Will you go?" asked Nettleton. He gripped Hugh by the arm.

"I could go. I *might* get through. But as for bringing back help, that's out of the question. There aren't enough men in the Department of New Mexico right now to defend the

Rio Grande Valley. Canby certainly won't send troops into these mountains to get wiped out."

Clymer wet his thick lips. He glanced back at the dwelling where Marion Nettleton was. "Perhaps I could get through with one of the women."

Phillips touched the corner of his mouth. "I can do the same," he said.

Maurice Nettleton hesitated, as he always did. He looked at Hugh. "My wife," he said quietly. "I know she wouldn't go without me, but perhaps I can force her to." He looked hopefully at Hugh. "What do you think, Kinzie?"

"Go ahead," said Hugh. "Mr. Clymer is willing."

Nettleton tugged at his side whiskers. "I didn't have him in mind. You're the most skilled of us in this type of business. We can cover you until you're in the clear. Marion is not strong, but she has courage. Will you take her?"

"You mean you're sacrificing yourself to save your wife?" asked Hugh dryly.

"Yes."

"You seem to have forgotten something, Nettleton."

"So?"

"Katy Corse."

The sudden quiet that followed Hugh's words was suddenly broken by the splitting crash of a gun at the east end of the canyon. The report slammed back and forth between the canyon walls.

"An attack!" cried Nettleton. "Turn out the guard!"

Booted feet slammed on the terrace. Shadowy figures formed along the terrace wall. Matt Hastings buckled on his gunbelt. "Check your carbines! Check the caps on your revolving pistols!" he said. "Corporal Roswell!"

"Here!"

"Greer!"

"Here!"

"Pearce!"

There was no answer. Hastings looked up and down the shadowed terrace. "Pearce!" he called out angrily.

Willis appeared on the terrace.

"Stevens!" said Hastings.

"Yo!"

"Willis!"

"Here!"

Hastings shoved back his hat. "Where's Pearce?"

"Damned if I know, Sergeant." said Willis. He glanced up the canyon.

"Anyone see him?" asked Hastings.

There was no answer.

"That sonofabitch go over the hill?" asked Hastings.

"Couldn't blame him," said Willis.

"Shut up!"

The canyon was quiet again. Hugh padded behind the enlisted men and stopped at the far end of the terrace. He looked toward the great rock wall. The shot had come from somewhere near it.

Hastings came up behind Hugh. "What do you think?" he asked.

Hugh shrugged. "You find Pearce?"

"No."

They waited. Now and then one of the waiting men moved. One of them coughed. A carbine butt thudded against the terrace.

Hastings looked at Hugh. "You think it was him, Kinzie?"

Hugh rubbed his jaw. "The shot came from near that dead mule. There was silver on the mule. You think Pearce would want that silver enough to go up there?"

"He had larceny in his soul."

Hugh looked up at the sky, then down at the ground. "Wherever he is, his damned larceny took him there then."

"Maybe he's lying out there wounded."

Hugh looked along the mesa wall. There was a faint trail there, with a sheer wall rising up beside it to the mesa top. "I can take a look-see along that," he said quietly. "I might be able to see down into the canyon from there."

"He ain't worth it," a dry voice said behind them.

"Shut up, Willis," said Hastings.

Willis grinned. "I'll go along with the scout," he said.

Hugh vaulted over the low wall and handed his carbine to Hastings. "You can see us from here. I'm not worried about them getting at us from the mesa side. But they can get up through that brush to below the trail. If they come at us, keep firing between us and them."

Willis leaned his carbine against the wall and loosened his Colt in its holster. "Shoot at anything what don't wear a hat, Sarge," he said.

Willis followed Hugh along the steep slope until they reached the trail. There was no sign of life. Silence ruled the canyon.

A hundred yards from the ruins, Hugh looked back over his shoulder. The face of the trooper was plain to see in the moonlight. There was something about Chandler Willis that didn't quite fit right with Hugh. He was a hard worker and usually willing. He did his duty, no more, no less. Yet he always seemed to be waiting for something.

Hugh paused at a place where a rock shoulder cast deep shadows against the mesa wall. The moon shone on the areas of sand and rock with a silvery light. The rocks and brush drew etched shadows behind them. There was no movement.

Willis scratched his corded throat. "Now what?"

Hugh studied the canyon floor. It looked as empty as a crater on the moon. Something warned him to go back. He had no particular liking for Dan Pearce.

"Let's go back," suggested Willis quietly.

"I thought you wanted to make a break from the party," Hugh said.

Willis half closed his eyes. "Now, scout," he said quietly, "you got no idea of making a break now."

Hugh looked down into the canyon, trying to locate the place where the mule had died.

"You haven't, have you?" persisted Willis.

"No. But why did you come along with me?"

"I don't want nothing to happen to you, scout."

Hugh glanced at the secretive man beside him. "Stay here," he said. "Cover me until I'm out of sight in that brush clump near the big rock fall."

Willis nodded. He shifted his chew and spat. "Be careful, scout. I don't want nothin' to happen to you."

"Your concern touches my heart," said Hugh dryly.

He slipped along the trail, using every patch of concealment, until he was even with a thicket of brush which rested at one end of the great rock fall. He loosened his knife in its sheath and swiftly touched his Colt butt. Then he eased down the slope and into the brush, moving like a hunting panther.

He reached the first slope of the rock fall, which had angled out from the canyon entrance. Sometime in the past, there had been another great rock fall, which had cascaded down the first slopes, leaving a transverse ridge of loose rock down the older slope. The mule had died just beyond the ridge.

Hugh's every nerve seemed to be sensitized. He could smell the pungent odor of the brush, still warm from the heat of the day, mingled with the sour smell of his sweat-soaked clothing. He stood absolutely still except for his eyes, which scanned the moonlit terrain ahead. Now and then his nostrils quivered as he drew in a sharp breath, trying to get a scent. Something puzzled him. The mule had been out there long enough to develop gasses. Sense of smell and hearing should have been warned by now, for dead things can whisper restlessly when cool night air contracts warm flesh.

Hugh got down on his knees and crawled forward slowly, feeling his way with his hands, settling loose rock and placing each knee carefully. Sweat worked down his body and he mentally cursed the scouring his hands and knees were taking from the sharp edges of rock.

He lay flat just before he reached the crest of the ridge. He listened, then crawled forward, easing into the shadow of a tilted slab of rock. He looked down the far slope. Then he knew why he hadn't got wind of the mule. He could see the moonlight on the big white bones. The carcass had been stripped for meat and guts, as cleanly as though buzzards had been at work. Apaches had a preference for sweet mule meat.

The moonlight shone dully on something else, beyond the ravaged carcass of the mule. Something like pools of water dappling the sandy earth. Hugh was puzzled until he remembered the silver service.

Where in the hell was Pearce? Maybe the burly New Yorker hadn't come out here at all. Maybe the gun had been shot at something else. Maybe . . . The thought trailed off in Hugh's mind. He slowly turned his head to look along the rock ridge, then down into the canyon, then up the steep northern wall, to follow along the rock which almost blocked the entrance. A Mescalero had once told him something he should have remembered: "White-Eyes hear shot. Run like hell to see what happen. Tinneh hear shot. No run to see. Stay tight in hiding place. Wait. Wait Wait, until sure no one in ambush."

Hugh bellied down the slope in the shelter of the brush. He lay flat beside a large boulder. There was something ahead of him, dimly seen through the tangled brush. Something white. He inched forward on the warm earth until he could see what it was.

The body lay on its back, the thick mats of curly black hair in deep contrast to the whiteness of the skin. The skin looked unusually white compared to the mahogany brown of the big hands. The contorted face was yet another hue. Hugh looked away for a moment. The skull had been crushed and blood had coated the broad face in a dark mask. The bloody eyes stared unseeingly up at the moonlit sky.

Hugh inched back. Something else caught his eye. Dan Pearce clutched a beautifully formed silver creamer in his right hand.

Hugh did not hurry on his return trip, although the hounds of fear ran silently at his heels. He made his way carefully up the slope until he reached the place where

Chandler Willis waited for him. There was no need to say anything to Willis. He knew.

They walked slowly back toward the cliff dwellings. They were almost to the crumbling wall when Willis spoke softly. "One down," he said. "Twelve to go. Who's next, scout?"

CHAPTER ELEVEN

Matt Hastings marked it down in his little notebook. "Pearce, D. A., Pvt—from duty to deceased," he said. He wrote down the time and date.

"What's the A stand for?" asked Willis.

"Aloysius."

"Jesus," said Willis. "No wonder he'd never tell me."

Isaiah Morton stood at the edge of the terrace with his lean hands clasped together. "Therefore thus saith the Lord of hosts, the God of Israel; Behold, I will feed them, even this people, with wormwood, and give them water of gall to drink."

"There he goes again," said Willis.

Isaiah Morton raised his voice. "I will scatter them also among the heathen, whom neither they nor their fathers have known: and I will send a sword after them, till I have consumed them."

The men looked at each other with wide eyes. Hastings closed his notebook. "Morton," he said quietly, "this J Company wasn't issued a chaplain, and if it had been, I'd tell him to say something cheerful from the Good Book. Any more of that stuff out of you and I'll heave you over the wall so you can go amongst those heathen, whom neither us nor our fathers have known. *Comprende?*"

Morton's eyes seemed to shine through the darkness. He stalked off down the terrace. "They shall have eyes and they shall see not," he intoned. "They shall have ears and they shall hear not."

"Makes my skin crawl," said Hastings. "The man is a Jonah."

They could hear the horses and mules plainly. Stevens looked toward them. "By God, Sarge," he said hoarsely, "they're really suffering. I can't listen to 'em much longer."

Hastings opened his mouth to curse Stevens, and then he shut it. They were all horsemen. None of them liked the idea of letting the horses suffer. Hastings looked at Hugh. Hugh raised his head and drew a forefinger across his lean throat.

Hastings nodded. "I'll tell the captain," he said.

"Tell him what, Sarge?" demanded Stevens.

"None of your damned business."

Stevens stepped forward and dropped his carbine across his left forearm. "You mean you're going to kill off those horses?"

Hastings lowered his right hand to his Colt butt. "Not all of them. We've got three extras now. Pearce's mount and the two pack mules. God knows there isn't enough water for those that will be left, but we'll have to sweat out a day or two more before we figure out what to do with them."

Stevens cocked his carbine. "You're not going to kill any of them," he said quietly. "Let them go. They'll take care of themselves."

Hastings eyed the trooper. "Look, jaybird," he said, "we're out of food. I don't like horse or mule meat but I'll be damned if I'm going to starve as long as I can get some of it. Now you let down the hammer of that carbine and get to your post before I show you the hard way who's first soldier around here."

Stevens stood there for half a minute, then he eased

down his carbine hammer and walked slowly toward the west end of the terrace.

"The sonofabitch actually thinks more of them damned animals being kept alive than he does of us eating," said Matt Hastings.

"Who'll slaughter them?" asked Hugh.

Hastings whirled. "Not me!"

"Then who?"

"You!"

Hugh shook his head. "I killed my best horse two years ago when Comanches had me cut off from the column. Dropped him with a shot between the eyes to use him so I could fort up in a buffalo wallow. I can still remember how he looked just before he got the bullet."

Hastings pulled at his lip. "Yeah, yeah."

The five of them stood there in the dimness: Hugh, Hastings, Roswell, Willis and Greer. Hastings cleared his throat. "We can draw straws," he said.

"No need," said Harry Roswell. "I'll do it."

The other four looked quickly at Roswell. Greer wet his thin lips, then turned and walked away. Willis shoved back his hat, shrugged, and then sauntered toward the east end of the terrace.

"Both mules and one of the horses," said Roswell. "Which horse?"

Hastings shrugged. "Pick out the worst of the lot." He grinned as he looked toward the shadowy line of animals tethered at the west end of the terrace. "Stevens's," he said.

Roswell leaned his carbine against the wall and reached for his Colt. Hugh placed a hand on Roswell's wrist. "Use the knife." he said. "We can't spare ammunition. Besides . . . we don't want to arouse the Apaches."

Roswell nodded. He wet his lips. Hugh drew out his heavy sheath knife and handed it to the noncom. Roswell hefted it, then walked toward the animals.

"Lead them away one at a time from the others!" called out Hugh. "If the rest of them smell the blood they'll get excited."

Roswell nodded without turning.

"I couldn't do it," said Greer from the shadows.

"You can't do anything," said Hastings.

"Maybe the officers won't like it," said Greer.

Hastings spat. "There'll be a helluva lot more they won't like before we get out of this hellhole."

Roswell was holding the first horse by the bridle reins now. Somebody spoke to him.

"Whose horse is that?" asked Hugh suddenly.

Hastings stared. "Stevens's," he said.

Hugh started forward. "The damned fool should have known better."

Roswell was dragging at the bridle reins of Stevens's bay. Suddenly there was a sharp cry from Stevens. He hit Roswell with the butt of his carbine. The noncom staggered toward the terrace wall, dropping the knife. Stevens was up on his bay. He shrieked like a Comanche and drove the excited bay against the horse next in line. The horses and mules jerked at their tethers. One by one they broke loose, neighing sharply and clashing their hoofs against the floor of the terrace.

Stevens whooped. He slapped at the nearest rumps with his hat. A horse leaped the terrace wall and crashed down the slope. Roswell screamed as the frenzied animals surged toward him. He was driven against the wall. Then the horses and mules smashed against the wall. Rocks crumbled as the hoofs struck sparks from them. Then the whole mass of them were over the wall and floundering down the slope in an uproar that echoed and re-echoed through the canyon. Dust rose in a pall and swept back toward the cliff dwellings.

Hugh raced toward Roswell. He could see Stevens behind the stampeding animals, waving his hat and screaming wildly. The group of horses and mules reached the bottom of the slope and crashed through a dense thicket. Then they were in the clear, racing toward the east end of the canyon with a steady drumming of hoofs.

Nettleton ran alongside Hugh. "What happened?"

Hugh didn't answer. He crouched beside Roswell. The

noncom was unconscious. Blood stained his face and ran from the corner of his mouth. One arm hung at an awkward angle. A bubbling sound came from his throat as he breathed.

The bitter smell of dust hung in the night air. The drumming of the hoofs was dying away when the flat crack of a rifle carried to those who stood on the terrace.

"I wonder what he thought he was doing?" asked Katy

"He's loco," said Chandler Willis.

Hugh wiped the blood from Roswell's face. "He's in a bad way. Help me set him into one of the rooms."

Willis and Hastings helped Hugh with the injured man. Katy Corse came into the room after they lowered Roswell onto his blanket. "Get some cloth for bandages," said Hugh over his shoulder.

Katy bent forward and pulled up her skirt. She looked at the torn and dirty petticoat she wore. "It won't help him any to put cloth like this against his wounds."

Hugh wiped the blood from Roswell's chin and neck. "Ask Mrs. Nettleton for some of her things. She's got a packful of them."

Katy nodded. She left the room. Hastings looked down at Roswell. "What do you think, Kinzie?" he asked softly.

Hugh stood up. "He's all smashed up inside."

Hastings shook his head. "I never thought he'd take me serious when I told him to kill Stevens's horse."

Willis leaned against the wall. "You knew damned well he always did what he was told, Sarge."

Hastings looked up. "Yeah. Yeah."

Abel Clymer burst into the room. "Hastings!" he snapped. "We've got to get those horses back at once."

Far down the canyon another shot cracked faintly, like a faggot snapping in the fireplace.

"If the lieutenant will tell me how," he said coolly, "I'd be glad to try."

Clymer looked from one to the other of the three men standing in front of him. "Who's responsible for that stampede?"

"If we told you, what would you do, Clymer?" asked Hugh. "Court-martial him?"

"We're trapped for sure now!" snapped Clymer.

Hugh studied the blustering officer. "You've been trapped ever since you left the Fort McLane trail and came up into these mountains."

There was doubt in Clymer's eyes now. He looked down at Roswell. "How badly is he hurt?"

"He's all smashed up inside, Mr. Clymer," said Hastings. "You think he'll live?"

Hastings stared at the big officer. "I hope so, sir!"

Clymer looked about the dim room. "Where's Greer?"

"Somewhere outside."

Clymer turned and left the room.

Hastings eased Roswell's head back onto a fold of the blanket. "Clymer sounded almost like he wanted Roswell to die . . . I wonder why?"

"I suppose he figures Roswell will be nothing but a burden now," Hugh said.

Katy Corse came in, carrying a petticoat over her arm. "Get some water, Willis," she said.

Willis looked at Hugh. Hugh nodded. Willis left the room. Hastings took a stub of candle from his pocket and lit it, placing it in a wall niche. The flickering yellow light seemed to accentuate the ghastly pallor of Roswell's face. Katy handed the petticoat to Hastings. "Rip it up," she said.

Hastings whistled as he felt the fine material. "My God, but our cat had a fine long tail, Katy. What'd she say when you asked her for it? "

Katy brushed back her hair. "I didn't ask her. If I had, and she'd refused me, I would have taken it anyway."

Hugh walked outside. Abel Clymer was partway down the slope, staring off to the west as though he could penetrate the gigantic shoulder of rock which blocked off the mysteries of the western part of the canyon.

Darrell Phillips came up behind Hugh. "I wish he'd take a walk up that canyon," he said softly.

Hugh looked quickly at the officer. "We're getting short-handed," he said. "First Pearce. Then Stevens and Roswell. Morton is useless and Greer isn't much better."

Phillips waved a hand. "All the same, I wish to God he'd walk into an Apache trap."

"Who's on guard?"

"I don't know."

"Damn it!" Hugh turned on a heel and walked toward the watchtower. He turned quickly into the narrow passageway. There was a sudden movement in the darkness. Boots grated against rock. Then something smashed and tinkled against the rock wall. The pungent odor of strong liquor flowed toward Hugh. He darted forward but whoever had dropped the bottle was gone in the darkness of the passageway which led behind the cliff dwellings.

Hugh returned to the terrace. Hastings and Willis were with Roswell and Katy. Nettleton was with his wife. Phillips was standing at the far end of the terrace looking down into the canyon. Abel Clymer was partway down the slope, looking in the direction the horses and mules had gone. Hugh nodded. He walked to the passageway which led back to the triangular passageway behind the dwellings. There was a furtive movement in the darkness. Hugh reached out with a big hand and clamped it on Greer's shirt collar. He drew the squirming little man toward him.

Greer struck at Hugh. Hugh shook him a little. Greer bared his yellowish teeth. "You've got no right to treat me like this!"

Hugh thrust his face close to Greer's. "You drunken little bastard! Where did you get the stuff?"

Greer drew back. "Down in one of those round rooms below the terrace."

Hugh shoved the little orderly back against the wall. "There was a time when nothing short of a jab in the rump from Satan's pitchfork would have made you go down there."

Greer shakily held out a hand. "Don't tell the captain," he pleaded.

"Have you got another bottle?"

"No!"

Hugh swiftly passed his hands over the little man's body. Greer was clean. Hugh thrust a big finger under Greer's nose as though he was admonishing a little child. "I get one whiff of liquor from you, Greer, and I'll break your goddamned neck like a match stick. *Comprende?*"

Greer straightened up. He stroked his skinny neck. "A man has to have something around here to keep up his courage."

"You never had any in the first place."

"Go to hell, Kinzie!"

Hugh stepped back. "Get your carbine. Get out on that terrace and keep your eyes peeled."

Greer watched Hugh walk back toward the terrace. The little orderly scurried back into the triangular passageway. He reached up into a cleft and gripped a bottle. Swiftly, with shaking hands, he drew out the cork. He tipped up the bottle and let the flaming liquor flow down his open throat. He gulped as though he were tasting mother's milk, then took down the bottle, corked it and cached it. He wiped his mouth with the back of his dirty hand and grinned in the darkness. "Go to hell, Kinzie," he said softly.

Hugh walked to the ladder which protruded from one of the openings in the terrace floor. He eased his way down it until his feet hit the floor. He took out a candle stub and lit it, placing it on one of the low shelves which encircled the room. Part of the contents of the mule packs had been stored in the room. Hugh lifted some of the articles with a boot toe, shaking his head as he did so. Boxes of clothing, hat boxes, bags of odds and ends and several tablecloths. There was no liquor amongst the things.

Something moved up on the terrace. Hugh blew out the candle and climbed the ladder. Greer was at the west end of the terrace, looking down into the canyon. There was no one else on the terrace. Hugh heard Harry Roswell groan in deep-seated agony. He walked to the next underground opening and went down the rickety ladder. He relit the candle and looked about the room. There were some rawhide panniers lying to one side. Hugh knelt beside them and opened the first of them. The necks of bottles showed through the straw packing.

The ladder creaked. Hugh turned. A pair of heavy legs showed coming down through the opening. Hugh squatted on his heels. Abel Crymer's broad shoulders came down through the opening. He eyed Hugh suspiciously. "What are you doing down here?" he demanded.

Hugh looked down at the liquor pannier. "Rosewell might need some of this before he's through," he said.

Clymer stood on the ladder, breathing heavily. His eyes were slitted. "That's Nettleton's property," he said.

Hugh stood up. "All the same, Roswell is in bad shape. If it helps to ease his pain he can drink the whole damned load."

Clymer stepped onto the gritty floor and raised his head. "I said it was Nettleton's property."

Hugh leaned back against one of the low pilasters which held up the cribbed log roof. "How is it you're suddenly so concerned about Nettleton's property?" he asked softly.

Clymer flushed. "What do you mean?"

Hugh looked up at the ceiling. "Nothing."

Clymer didn't quite know what to do. Kinzie did not respect his bars and he certainly wasn't afraid. "You mean Mrs. Nettleton?" he blurted out at last.

Hugh looked surprised. "Why, *Abel!*"

Clymer spat to one side. "She's a lady," he said. "As an officer and a gentleman, it's part of my duty to see that she's safely escorted to Santa Fe."

"Bravo!" said Hugh dryly.

Clymer thrust out a big hand, stabbing the forefinger toward Hugh's face. "You're nothing but a God-damned civilian scout. I don't like your attitude and I don't like you. Now get up there and take care of your job."

Hugh reached down and took a bottle from the pannier. He read the label. "This will do for a starter," he said. He walked past the big man and stopped at the bottom of the ladder. He looked back over his shoulder. "You're nothing but a God-damned army officer. I don't like your attitude and I don't like you. I'll take care of my job, Clymer, and I'm wondering if you can take care of yours before we get out of this mess."

Hugh climbed the ladder. He walked over to the room where Harry Roswell lay in agony. He handed the bottle to Katy. Matt Hastings eyed it. Chandler Willis wet his thin lips. Katy looked at the bottle. "Do you think he can take it?" she asked.

Hugh shoved back his hat. Sweat dewed Roswell's ghostly face in great clear beads. "There isn't anything else," he said.

"How long will he last?"

"*Quien sabe?*"

Roswell opened his eyes. "I was only doing my duty," he said clearly.

"Sure. Sure," said Hastings. He wiped the sweat from Roswell's face.

Roswell stared up at the ceiling. "I always did my duty," he said. "Jonas had no right to do that. He should be court-martialed for what he did."

"Sure," said Hastings. He glanced at the bottle. "How does it feel, Harry?"

Roswell closed his eyes. "Bad. I'm all busted up inside, Sergeant."

Katy handed Hastings the bottle. The first sergeant worked the wire and wrapping from the cork and pulled it out. He poured some of the liquor into a tin cup and gently lifted Roswell's head and shoulders. The injured man sipped at the liquor. Then he gulped at it.

Hugh tapped Chandler Willis's shoulder. "Get outside," he said. "Greer is on guard and I don't trust him."

Willis grinned. "And you trust *me*, Kinzie? How nice!" He picked up his carbine and walked outside.

Hastings looked up at Hugh. "What's bothering him?"

"Who knows?"

"He thinking of pulling foot out of here?"

"Who isn't?"

Hastings stood up. "I'll break his God-damned back if he tries."

"If you catch him, Matt. Besides, he won't try it alone."

"Meaning?"

"He might have tried it with Pearce. He wants me to make a break with him."

Hastings came close to Hugh. "Don't try, Kinzie," he said. "I've seen J Company outfits, but this is the worst yet. We've lost three men now. The only way any of us will get out of here alive is by all of us sticking together. I think you could make it alone . . . but you won't."

"How so?"

"You've got a certain sense of honor."

"That all?"

The hard eyes bored into Hugh's. "I'll kill any man, officer, enlisted man or civilian who tries to make the break alone."

Hugh shrugged. He walked to the door. "Katy," he said, "I'll have Mrs. Nettleton come in after a while to relieve you."

Katy brushed back her dark hair. Then she laughed. "Hugh, there are times when you reveal an unconscious sense of ridiculous humor."

"She'll be here," said Hugh. He walked out on the terrace.

Matt Hastings squatted beside Katy. "*That*, I'll have to see," he said.

CHAPTER TWELVE

Marion Nettleton smiled as Hugh came into the room she shared with her husband. Maurice Nettleton looked up. "How is Roswell?" he asked.

"Not good."

Nettleton bit his lip. He tugged at his sideburns. "We can't afford to lose another man, Kinzie."

"I took the liberty of appropriating one of your bottles of liquor for him. To ease the pain."

"Quite all right. Poor fellow. Is there anything else we can do for him?"

"Yes. Miss Corse is taking care of him now. I'd like Mrs. Nettleton to relieve her off and on during the night."

Nettleton stood up. "Absolutely not! Mrs. Nettleton is far too delicate of constitution for such work."

Marion Nettleton looked at her husband. "Why, Maurice!" she said quickly. "I'll be more than glad to help. I'm a soldier's wife. I must learn to do this type of work."

Maurice Nettleton stared at his wife. There were times when he wondered about her. She had once said she'd never have children because of the pain and mess involved. It had struck sharply home to him and he had never forgotten it. Now here she was volunteering to attend a badly smashed sick man who hadn't had a bath in several weeks. It was beyond Maurice Nettleton to figure her out.

Marion looked at Hugh. "What time do you want me there?"

"In about an hour. Katy will spend most of the night with him, but she must have some sleep. You can work it out with her."

She smiled. "I'm sure we will."

Hugh left the room. He glanced back at it. He had expected something quite different from Marion Nettleton. No wonder she had that poor bastard of a husband under her pretty thumb.

Myron Greer looked out of the tower window. The moon bathed the canyon in pure silver light. The liquor was bubbling gently inside him. He grinned as he leaned on the sill of the window. That God-damned Hugh Kinzie wasn't all he seemed to be.

Greer looked up the terrace. Kinzie was at the far end with Darrell Phillips. Greer slid down to the next floor of the tower and then down into the first floor. He stood there in the darkness, listening like a prowling coyote. He was too damned clever for Kinzie to outmaneuver. Greer leaned his carbine against the wall and eased his way into the passage.

From up above him he could hear the occasional dripping of water. Myron Greer didn't need food nor water when he had a bottle cached away.

He worked his way down the cluttered passageway at the rear of the dwellings, fumbled in the niche for his treasure, then drew the bottle down to his lips. He drank sparingly and replaced the bottle. He walked partway back to his post, feeling the liquor flame within him. Maybe he'd better have another snort. He might not be able to leave his post again. He hurried back to the niche. He got the bottle and uncorked it, then stopped short. Something had moved down the passageway toward the east end of the dwellings. He corked the bottle and raised it toward the niche. He could see the man fairly well now. It was Abel Clymer. No one else would fill the passageway as the big officer did.

Abel Clymer was fumbling about in a pile of fallen rocks and debris. He did not look toward Myron Greer. Greer took the cork from the bottle and drank deeply. Craftily, he hid the bottle in another place. Then he eased his way back toward his post, stopping at the corner of the tower to watch Clymer.

Clymer was concentrating on something. Then he replaced whatever he had in his hands in the hole and covered it with rocks and debris. Greer faded around the corner and climbed up to his post. His head was swimming a little with the exertion, and his feet stumbled on the notches of the chicken ladder. He drew himself up into the top room of the tower and leaned for a time against the wall. The room seemed to sway and lift a little as though it were floating on water.

The moon was at its highest. Jonas Stevens lay on his face, clawed fingers buried to the second joints in the bloody sand. He looked curiously flattened. He had seen the Apache before he had fired. Jonas had spurred his bay to get ahead of the stampeding horses and mules and had succeeded just in time to be slammed from his saddle by the impact of a heavy rifle ball. The horses and mules had done the rest. The horses and mules Jonas Stevens had been trying to save.

Harry Roswell opened his eyes and looked up into the oval face of Marion Nettleton. "Is it time for First Call?" he asked.

"No," she said quietly.

He closed his eyes. "I thought I heard the trumpet." He coughed harshly.

She raised his shoulders and head. The sour smell of the man sickened her. She wondered how Katy Corse had been able to spend the last two hours sitting here beside the dying man. She lowered the trooper and wiped his face with a damp cloth. His breath was sour and thick with liquor fumes. Drying blood caked his lips. His breathing seemed to bubble deep in his chest. Sweat broke out on his pallid forehead.

Marion reached over and pinched out the candle. The moonlight streamed in through the small windows. A cold finger of fear seemed to trace the length of her spine, almost as though Death had entered the room the instant she had put out the candle, and had touched her to let her know he was there waiting the end too.

Darrell Phillips was standing his guard at the east end of the terrace. Death had struck hard three times within the past few hours. Dan Pearce had died out on the sands. Jonas Stevens had died somewhere down the canyon. Harry Roswell was fencing with Death in a losing battle. There was a cold loneliness in Darrell Phillips. There was a finality about the way things were happening. The course of events was shaping toward an ending which would, in all probability, find Darrell Phillips cold in death. He couldn't face it alone. He had to have Katy Corse beside him, so that her feminine strength would fill in the gap in his own strength, and the two of them together could face the end.

Abel Clymer leaned against a wall watching Hugh Kinzie. That damned scout had his nose into everything. Abel wondered if Kinzie had gone down into the underground room solely to find liquor for Roswell. Kinzie was always prowling around like a damned lean cat.

Kinzie knew how Abel felt about Marion Nettleton. Kinzie was always so damned sure of himself. That was one reason Abel had to take it easy. There was no one in the party who could serve Abel Clymer as Hugh Kinzie could. The two of them might get out of this death trap and could take Marion Nettleton along to boot. Kinzie could be gotten rid of later when safety was in sight. Sweat broke out on Clymer's body. His hands shook in expectation. With Marion Nettleton and the stake he had cached away he'd be the biggest hero west of the Mississippi.

Clymer wet his lips. There were four men who had been with him when he had found Winston's body. Corporal Roswell, Privates Pearce, Willis and Stevens. Roswell was dying. Pearce was dead, and Stevens probably was, too. That left that slit-eyed bastard Willis to be reckoned with. He was secretive and sly. How much did he know?

Abel Clymer faded into the darkness as Hugh Kinzie walked slowly along the terrace, looking out into the mysterious moonlit canyon. A coyote howled softly from the top of the far wall.

Isaiah Morton pressed his thin hands against his burning eyes. There was a fire deep in his soul which seemed to gain in intensity as the days went on. There was no hunger in him and very little thirst, but his desire to carry the word of God to the heathens who held the party trapped, gained in intensity even as the insatiable flame which raged within him.

"Oh, my God, why dost thou persecute me?" he whispered. He laced his thin fingers together and pushed his hands downward as he raised his head and eyes upward. He shivered a little in his ecstasy of desire. "I will bring them truth, and the truth shall set them free. I shall make them walk as children of the light."

Hugh Kinzie padded along the terrace carrying the liquor panniers. He did not see the eyes that watched him from the tower. Hugh bent his head to enter the low doorway of the room where Harry Roswell was dying. "How is he?" he asked Marion.

She wearily brushed back a wisp of damp hair. "Asleep," she said.

"Bueno!" Hugh placed the panniers in a corner.

She eyed the panniers. "You don't think he'll need all that?"

"No. But it's safer here."

"Why?"

Hugh squatted beside her and felt for his tobacco pouch. "The food is almost gone. We've lost two men and will lose another before long. Nerves are getting frayed. At times like this men will turn to liquor for Dutch courage."

"A courage that quickly lets them down."

"Yes. May I smoke?"

She nodded. "If I may have one too."

She studied him as he rolled her a cigarette. "You're not surprised?"

He shook his head. "I've spent too much time along the border to think twice about women smoking." He placed the cigarette between her full lips and lit it with a lucifer. The spurt of flame lit up her oval face. He blew out the match without taking his eyes from her.

She looked away. "You didn't make one of them for yourself," she said.

He jerked his head. "Oh!"

She watched his big fingers as they deftly rolled the cylinder of tobacco. "You seem to do everything well."

He placed the cigarette in his mouth and lit it. "Everything?"

"Everything I've seen you do, that is."

"That's better."

They smoked without speaking. Hugh looked at Harry Roswell. His face had undergone a subtle change; it seemed longer and sunken. It was as though the skull was trying to come through the flesh.

"Do you think there is a chance?" she asked.

"No."

"I didn't think you'd give up easily."

He glanced quickly at her. "Me? I'm not giving up. I thought you were talking about Harry."

"Well?"

He sat down with his back against the wall. "Some of us might make it to the Rio Grande."

She shivered a little despite herself. There was a fatalism in him she had not expected. But this was a man who could be depended upon.

Hugh inspected his cigarette. "My job is to get you to safety, Mrs. Nettleton."

She was startled. It was almost as though he had read her mind.

Hugh stood up. "I'll admit things look black, but it could be worse. We haven't been attacked in here. We have a little water."

She ground out her cigarette. "No horses. A handful of men, half of whom are useless encumbrances."

He shrugged. "I said *some* of us wouldn't make it."

"But you will?"

"Yes."

She stood up suddenly, standing so close to him her full breasts touched his shirt. "You once told me it was a fifty-fifty chance. Maybe less. You also promised me that you would stay close to me on the trail. Is that promise still good?" She placed her slim hands on his shoulders and looked up into his eyes. Her own promise was in her eyes. She knew how to use her weapons.

Hugh slid an arm about her waist and crushed her to him, feeling her breath on his face. She shivered a little as he bent his face close to hers. "Don't you think this is a hell of a place for dallying?" he asked softly. "With a dying man at our feet and your husband not fifty feet away?"

Her face flushed and then went taut. She bit her lip as she realized he was making a fool out of her. She struggled to break free. Suddenly he released her. She raised her hands to rake his face to bloody ribbons, but he was too fast for her. He kissed her so hard he bruised her lips and his whiskers scored her delicate skin. Then he shoved her back and walked to the door. He looked back at her.

"Take good care of Harry," he said quietly.

"Damn you!"

He grinned. "Remember you're a lady," he said with a strong hint of laughter in his voice.

She hurled a cup at the wall as he vanished from her sight.

Abel Clymer pressed his big body flat against the wall as Hugh Kinzie padded past. Clymer's thick lips drew back as he looked at the broad back of the scout. Clymer rested a hand on the butt of his revolving pistol. He had overheard them talking in the dwelling. He withdrew his hand. Let them talk. Both of them were part of his plan, and he wasn't part of theirs. Abel Clymer could play a waiting game. His time would come . . .

A coyote howled softly up the canyon. A night bird chirped from the brush. Harry Roswell opened his eyes and looked up at Marion Nettleton. "I wish . . ." he said thickly. "I wish . . ." His voice faded away. His breathing stopped but his eyes were wide in his head.

Marion Nettleton stared down at the dead man. Then her control broke. She screamed, and screamed again, awakening the canyon echoes.

CHAPTER THIRTEEN

They buried Harry Roswell behind a crumbling wall in the debris from a fallen roof. There was no marker on the grace. No one would ever come here to find his grave, Hugh thought as he watched Chandler Willis and Matt Hastings finish the burial.

Hastings looked up at Hugh. "Where's Greer?"

"He was on guard."

"He isn't there now."

"Sleeping somewhere, then."

Hastings nodded. He took out his little notebook and marked it down. "Roswell, H. L., Corp.—from duty to de—"

"What's the 'L' stand for?" asked Willis as he wiped the sweat from his lean face.

"Lemuel."

"Jesus."

Isaiah Morton clasped his thin hands together and looked down at the unmarked grave. "Gone from this earth to his reward in Heaven," he said. "Our loss is Heaven's gain."

"That sonofabitch Stevens is responsible for this," said Matt Hastings.

"You mark Stevens down in your little book, Matt?" asked Hugh.

"Yes."

"How did you mark it?"

Hastings looked up. "Absent without leave. How else?"

"My God," said Hugh. "Always the first soldier."

"Our band of lost sheep gets smaller every day," said Morton. He bowed his head. "The Lord is my shepherd."

"Gives me the creeps," said Willis.

The midmorning sun was beating down into the quiet canyon. The heat was soaking into the cliff dwellings. There wasn't a breath of wind to bring relief.

"You'd think them officers would have come," said Willis.

Hugh nodded. The signs were plain. Everyone was thinking of himself now, and that included Marion Nettleton.

Willis opened up his shirt and scratched his lean belly. "Any mess?" he asked Hastings.

"Nothing."

"This ain't the army anymore. A man could leave right now if he had a mind to."

Hastings closed his book and stowed it away in his pocket. "Yeah," he said quietly. "Except for two things."

Willis spat leisurely. "What's to stop a man?"

Hastings held up two dirty fingers. "One," he said softly, "the Apaches. Two, me."

Willis yawned. He straightened up and then he walked down the pile of debris and into the triangular passageway.

"He's right," said Hugh.

Hastings turned quickly. "What do you mean?"

"It isn't the army anymore, Matt. Each to his own from now on."

Hastings wiped the sweat from his face. "Go ahead, Kinzie. I won't try to stop you."

Hugh slid down the crumbling pile of debris. "I'll try to get some game," he said over his shoulder.

Morton was praying. Hastings eyed the cadaverous preacher. "Any way you can get some of that manna from Heaven?" he asked.

Morton did not answer.

"How about the miracle of the loaves and fishes?" asked Hastings.

Morton did not move. Hastings shrugged and left the room.

The strays came drifting down the canyon about noon. Five of them. All horses. It was Darrell Phillips who saw them first. "Look!" he called out in a cracked voice.

The others, with the exception of Myron Greer, ran out of the rooms where they had been trying to avoid the heat. They crouched behind the low terrace wall and looked at the horses.

"They've had water," said Hastings.

"They've had grass," said Willis.

The men looked at each other. Abel Clymer rested big paws on the top of the wall. "I'll give any man fifty dollars who'll bring in one of those horses."

There was a moment's silence and then Chandler Willis laughed dryly.

Hugh Kinzie eyed the far wall of the canyon. There was no sign of life. Whoever was directing the cruel game was a genius. He had timed it just right. Morale and unity were beginning to show great cracks throughout the little besieged party of White-eyes.

"A hundred dollars," said Abel Clymer.

"Shut up," said Hugh.

The strays drifted slowly into the shade of a great shoulder of rock. So near and yet so far. But it was worth far more than a hundred dollars to cross that stretch of baking rock and sand. It was worth a man's life.

By midafternoon the heat was intense. There was no trace yet of wind in the lifeless air. Nothing moved, not even the strays, who stood with bent heads in the hot shadow of the rock shoulder.

Matt Hastings ran his tongue over his cracked lips. He looked at Hugh. "What do you think?" he asked.

"Don't try it, Matt."

"Maybe after dark?"

"They have ears like dogs."

"Yeah."

Minutes ticked past. Hastings slid his carbine forward and checked the cap. He placed his hand on his pistol butt. He looked at Hugh from out of slitted eyes.

Hugh held up a thumb and looked up from beneath the brim of his hat. A buzzard floated high overhead in the windless air like a scrap of charred paper. The shadow flitted across the yellowish floor of the canyon.

Matt Hastings rested his head on his forearms. "Bad luck," he said.

The steady pounding of Hugh's heart seemed to be like the swinging pendulum of a clock marking the slow passage of time. Sweat trickled greasily down his body and he realized it had been quite some time since he had bathed. He touched his face. The bristles were thick upon his jaws.

Hastings suddenly laughed. It sounded so strange to Hugh that he raised his head to stare at the big first sergeant. Maybe he was cracking up. Hastings' sunburned face was set in a grin, but there was no mirth in his eyes.

"What's the joke?" asked Hugh.

Hastings tenderly touched his cracked lips, aggravated bythe strain of his wide grin. "I was thinking of old Dobe-gusndi-he. He was a subchief of the White Mountain Apaches. Never could catch the wily old bastard. Finally one of his warriors sold him out for a sack of bullets, a butcher knife and a bottle of red-eye. We closed in on him near Escudilla Mountain. Run him to earth in a box canyon just like this. He had no water. No food. Damned little powder and ball." Hastings rested his head wearily on his forearms.

"So?"

Hastings looked up. He wiped the sweat from his eyes. "We had him . . . lock, stock and barrel. But he wouldn't surrender. Not that old devil. But we got him."

"How?"

"Wasn't no sense in charging in on him. He was like a cornered rat. Mr. Ballard was our CO—a good soldier and a mathematician. He studies the lay of the land. The Apaches was holed up under a big cave just like this one we're under. Open ground in front—no cover at all. No way to get at them from either side or from the top. But we got 'em. All of 'em."

"Keep talking. It kills the monotony."

"Yeah. Well, as I said, Ballard was a mathematician. He looks at the slope of the cave roof, does some figuring. Says something about the angle of rebound being the same as the angle of incidence. Whatever that meant at the time I didn't know, but I learned damned soon. Ballard tells us to aim at the cave ceiling. We fired volleys until the barrels were misty with heat. At first we heard screams. Then groans. Then nothing. Ballard stands up like he was on parade and walks right into that God-damned cave like there was nobody there."

"So?"

Hastings looked steadily at Hugh. "Those slugs had bounced down from the roof right into those Apaches behind the boulders. Jesus but it was awful! The slugs had key-holed into them. There was pieces of skull with hair still on them scattered all over. Not one of them poor bastards was alive. It looked like we had given them a dose of canister or grape at pointblank range from a mountain howitzer. But we didn't lose a man."

Hugh felt a little sick.

Hastings closed his eyes. "Ballard got a promotion. Later he was ordered to West Point to teach mathematics."

"It figures."

Hastings looked up at the reddish rock which formed the roof of the cave over the dwellings. "That place was just like this."

Hugh leaned back against the terrace wall. "I've been trying to figure out what Dobe-gusndi-he means."

Hastings laughed dryly. "That's the joke. It means invulnerable."

"Stop," said Hugh. "You're killing me."

Hastings stared at Hugh for a minute, then burst into cackling laughter. "That's one thing I've always liked about you, Kinzie," he said. "You've got the dryest God-damned sense of humor."

Hugh stood up and looked back at the heat-soaked dwellings. "Speaking of dryness," he said quietly. "I'm going to take a look-see for Greer."

"I hope that sonofabitch is dead. He never was a soldier and never will be."

"We might need him before we get out of here."

"Him?" Hastings spat dryly. "He's nothing but a burden. Like that psalm-singing bastard Morton."

Hugh shrugged. "We'll have to do something before long, Matt."

Hastings rubbed his jaw. "Yeah. But what?"

"Na-tse-kes."

"What in the hell is that?"

Hugh looked out at the canyon, silent and foreboding under the brilliant sun. "One thought at a time, over and over again in the mind, exclusive of all others."

"Sometimes I think you're part Injun."

"One thought at a time: how to get out of here . . . *alive.*" Hugh walked toward the dwellings.

Hastings rubbed the stock of his gun and looked across at the far wall of the canyon. "Yeah," he said softly. "Yeah. I know what you mean, hombre."

Hugh looked along the line of crumbling dwellings. Thirteen people had come there for sanctuary. Three of them were dead. The sanctuary had become a prison and the sentence for each of the remaining ten people there was death.

CHAPTER FOURTEEN

Myron Greer lay in the hiding place he had found. There he was safe from the prying eyes of the others in the party. His liquor supply had run out and he had been looking for more when he had found his hiding place. A roof had collapsed at one side, forming a triangular-shaped pocket between the floor and the wall. Greer had crawled inside and had carefully arranged rocks to conceal the entrance. It was stifling hot. His clothing was soggy with sweat and irritated his itching skin. Now and then the white worms seemed to moil and heave in his gut. A mallet thudded steadily at the base of his skull, and opening his eyes, even in the semidarkness, seemed to send a lance of burning pain deep into his skull.

There was a searing thirst in Myron Greer's throat and a more terrible thirst in his soul. He rested his head against the gritty earthen floor of the dwelling. It had always been the same with him. He had never quite fitted anywhere. As a child he had been unwanted, even by his playmates, because of his ungainliness and lack of skill even in the simplest sports and games. His father had been a big, powerful man with a huge bump of self-ego and a determination to push himself to the top. Myron's mother had protected and defended him, encouraging him with his books and studies. He had been better than average in that, in any case.

In college he had found out that the bottle is a good prop for a man who is never sure of himself. It had carried him through four years. By the end of that time he had a degree and a perpetual thirst which kept him from holding a job for more than a month or two. He was all right until he got his wages, then the glass spurs—whisky glasses—would take over, and Myron Greer would get on a two- or three-day drunk, lose his job, and suffer for a week with the after-effects of the rotgut. Gradually he had managed to stay drunk most of the time to escape a hangover and the more feared sieges of remorse.

He had drifted West and while drunk he had enlisted, to fill out a recruiting sergeant's quota for the month and to prove to a derisive group of fellow drunks and giggling hurdy-gurdy girls that Myron Greer really *was* a man.

Greer gently beat his throbbing head on the floor. He was sicker than he had ever been on coming out of a bout with John Barleycorn. The only thing that would help was more of the same. Hugh Kinzie had taken the liquor from the rooms below the terrace and had been keeping an eye on that marvelous store of liquid joy.

Suddenly he remembered seeing that big sonofabitch Clymer pawing around in a pile of debris the night before. Greer sat up suddenly and smashed his head against one of the ancient roof beams. He winced. Then he licked his dry cracked lips. Maybe Clymer had cached a bottle there. It was worth the try. But only after dark.

Boots grated behind the hiding place. Greer lay down quietly. They were looking for him. It was just like the days when he was a child and he would hear the thud of his father's feet coming up the stairs to make sure Myron wasn't reading in bed. Then Myron would shrink under the covers and draw his legs up toward his belly. He would wrap his arms about himself and lie perfectly still until his father was gone. Slowly he drew up his legs and then wrapped his thin arms about himself. He closed his eyes. Maybe blessed sleep would come this way.

The sun had died in the western skies in a phantasmagoria of pink, rose and gold. The canyon was deep in thickening shadows. Heat still filled the canyon, waiting to be dispersed by the night winds. The five stray horses drifted from in front of the cliff dwellings in search of the *tinaja* further down the canyon. There was plenty of water for them there.

Bats flitted through the darkness, emerging from their daylight hiding places. Jack rabbits pattered through the brush and bounded toward the waterhole. Small gray foxes moved about in their ceaseless search for rodents. Kit foxes hunted for mice and lizards along the rock ledges. It was the nocturnal merry-go-round: small animals killed and ate smaller animals only to fall victim to larger predators. The night was the time for the hunter.

Hugh Kinzie wiped the sweat from his face. Chandler Willis shifted his chew and spat. "I ain't seen the little sonofabitch since he relieved me on tower guard so's I could help bury Harry Roswell."

"You don't suppose he's left the dwellings?"

Willis grinned crookedly. "Him?" He's got a bottle stashed somewheres. Little bastard wouldn't give me a drink. He'll stay around until he drinks up all the liquor. But even all that rotgut wouldn't make Myron Greer go out into that damned canyon."

Matt Hastings appeared from the darkness and looked at them. "You find him?" he asked.

"No," said Hugh.

Hastings smashed a fist into his other palm. "I'll kick his skinny ass up between his shoulderblades!" he said.

They began probing into the many empty rooms. Hugh used sotol stalks he had found lying in a pile in one of the rooms, to light his way. He peered into one room after another. Some of them were filled with collapsed roofs, while others were as empty as last night's whisky bottle. He could hear the others looking for the frightened little man.

Hugh passed down the triangular passageway. A man came out of the darkness. "What are you doing here?" asked Clymer.

"What the hell do you think I'm doing? Looking for four-leaf clovers?"

Clymer raised his big head. "Someday," he said thickly, "I'll . . ."

"Get out of my way," Hugh said.

"You find Greer?"

"If I had I wouldn't be looking for him."

"I'll break his God-damned neck when I get my hands on him."

Hugh shook his head as he walked further up the passageway. Everyone was worried about the missing little man, and yet each of them was threatening death to him if they found him. Hugh almost wished the little man had gone down into the canyon and had died quickly.

Abel Clymer placed a hand on a crumbling wall and swung up onto a pile of roof debris.

His big booted feet sank a little into the loose debris. "Greer!" he roared through cupped hands. "Come out! Damn you, I'll flay you alive!"

Five feet below Abel Clymer, Myron Greer raised his head as he heard the muffled voice. Fear settled on Greer like a musty shroud.

Clymer stamped his big feet. "I'll kill him!" he said.

The debris suddenly settled beneath Clymer. Ancient cedar roof beams snapped within the settling debris. One of them sheared off diagonally and slid downward. Its tip penetrated under Greer's left shoulderblade. The relentless weight of the sinking dried mud and rock drove the sharp tip into Myron Greer's heart.

Maurice Nettleton listened impatiently as Matt Hastings told him of Greer's mysterious disappearance. "Damn it," he snapped. "The man couldn't have left the ruins! He hasn't the guts of a mouse."

"All the same, sir, he can't be found."

Nettleton waved a hand. "Mark him in the book," he

said. "Sergeant, someone must make an attempt to break through and bring in help."

Hastings nodded.

Nettleton looked at Hastings' face. "The man who volunteers and succeeds will receive a fitting reward, not to mention the gratitude of my wife and myself."

"I understand, sir."

They eyed each other in the darkness. Nettleton placed a hand on Hastings' shoulder. "I need not tell you that we're in a highly perilous position here, Hastings."

Hastings nodded again. He stepped back and saluted. Then he smartly about-faced and walked away. "The sono-fabitch," he said under his breath.

Hastings bent his head to enter the low doorway of the room where Hugh Kinzie and Chandler Willis were waiting for him. Hastings pulled off his shirt and swabbed his armpits with it. "Who's on guard?"

"Morton," said Willis.

"Him? Jesus! You out of your mind?"

Hugh waved a hand. "He can see and hear even if he is half cracked. What did Nettleton say?"

"Mark him in the book."

Willis scraped at his dirty fingernails with his knife, eying Hastings now and then as the first soldier wrote down the entry in his book by the light of a candle stub.

Hastings touched his cracked lips with his tongue. "Greer, M. M., Pvt.—from duty to absent without leave."

Willis leaned forward. "What's the second 'M' stand for, Sarge?"

"Matthias."

"Jesus."

Hastings closed the book and looked up at Hugh. "The Old Man wants someone to make a break for help."

"We talked about that before."

Hastings leaned back against the wall, wincing as the hot surface touched his naked back. "I need not tell you that we're in a highly perilous position here, Kinzie."

Hugh looked queerly at the first sergeant.

Hastings grinned. "Those were his last words to me," he said.

"What were your last words to him?" asked Willis.

"The sonofabitch. Only he didn't hear me."

"I wish he had."

Hugh reached behind him and took a bottle out of the pannier. He pried out the wire-wrapped cork. "We'll have a drink on the Old Man," he said.

They drank silently. The bottle went around three times. Suddenly Willis laughed. The other two looked at him. "Tell us the joke, Willis," said Hastings. "I'd like to laugh too."

Willis grinned. "Captain Nettleton," he said. "First Lieutenant Clymer. Second Lieutenant Phillips. First Sergeant Hastings. Private Willis! You get it?"

The other two looked at each other. Then they began to laugh. "By Jesus," said Hastings. "Just like a God-damned Mex *revolutionario* army. All officers and noncoms . . . no privates."

Hugh passed the bottle around again. Then he corked it and placed it in a niche. A moment after he did so Darrell Phillips thrust his handsome face into the doorway. "What's going on here?" he asked.

Three innocent faces eyed Darrell Phillips. "Why, sir," said Hastings, "nothing. Nothing at all. We were just having a bit of a joke, as you might say."

Phillips stared at them. "Joking? Here?" He shook his head and vanished into the darkness.

"Maybe we shoulda offered him a drink of the captain's booze," said Hastings.

"To hell with him," said Willis. "He's got something else on his mind."

"Such as?"

"Katy Corse."

Hugh looked quickly at the trooper. "What do you mean?"

Willis grinned. "I seen her switching that little rump of hers at him. She's too good for us. She's working on him.

Probably waiting for him somewheres out there in the darkness for a little ride on the two-headed beast."

Hugh moved like a cat. His left hand gripped Willis's shirt front. He dragged the trooper up to his feet. His right hand slashed back and forth from one side to the other until Willis sagged in the grip of Hugh's big hand. Hugh dropped the semiconscious trooper to the floor and looked down at the bloody ruin he had created. Then he flicked the blood from his hand.

"Jesus," said Hastings. He looked down at Willis and then at Hugh. "You had no call to do that."

The blood mist cleared from Hugh's mind. He snatched up his carbine and walked outside. The liquor was boiling in his mind. He had been a damned fool to drink on an empty stomach. He strode to the tower and climbed up beside Isaiah Morton.

Morton looked at him. "Are we doomed, Mr. Kinzie?" he asked quietly.

"You may be. I'm not."

The first faint light of the moon showed in the sky. Morton looked out at the canyon. "The hand of the Lord was upon me, and carried me out in the spirit of the Lord, and set me down in the midst of the valley which was full of bones.

"And caused me to pass by them round about: and, behold, there were very many in the open valley; and, lo, they were very dry.

"And he said unto me, Son of man, can these bones live? And I answered, O Lord God, thou knowest.

"Again he said unto me, Prophesy upon these bones, and say unto them, O ye dry bones, hear the word of the Lord.

"Thus saith the Lord God unto these bones; Behold, I will cause breath to enter into you, and ye shall live."

Hugh looked down toward the terrace. Katy Corse was with Darrell Phillips. Isaiah Morton raised an admonishing finger. "She doted upon the Assyrians her neighbors, captains and rulers clothed most gorgeously, horsemen riding upon horses, all of them desirable young men.

"Then I saw that she was defiled, that they both took one way."

Hugh turned. "Get to hell out of here," he said thinly. "Gather the canteens and fill them from that water basin."

Morton stepped back.

Hugh drew the fanatical man close to him. "And keep your prophesying to yourself." He shoved the man toward the ladder.

Morton rearranged the front of his coat. He opened his mouth to speak.

"Git!" said Hugh.

Morton climbed clumsily down the chicken ladder.

Hugh looked at Katy and Phillips. The officer was close to her, speaking swiftly and quietly. Hugh gripped the edge of the crumbling window and felt his strength pour out of him as he watched them.

The moon began to silver the sands and etch the shadows of the brush upon them. But there was a different light this night upon the high ground north of the silent canyon—a reddish glow pulsated irregularly against the night. Then the wind began to creep up the canyon, sweeping an odor across the mesas. Not the odor of mesquite and juniper, but the rich odor of roasting meat.

The tempting odor was borne on the wind. It seemed to search with invisible tendrils until it permeated the air throughout the cliff dwellings. Nine people raised their heads and inhaled the titillating scent.

Chandler Willis wiped the blood from his battered face. Matt Hastings had left. Willis felt for the cached bottle. He drained it and raised his arm to hurl the bottle angrily at the wall. Then he lowered it. A thought that had been in his mind for some time began to take on more important proportions. He stood up and snuffed out the candle. He picked up his carbine and walked out on the terrace. All of them were standing there looking across the canyon to where the glow of the fires illuminated the night sky. The odor of the roasting meat clung tempting and inviting over the ruins.

Willis padded to the back of the tower and looked up at it. He had noticed that Hugh Kinzie was missing. Willis slipped into the lower room and stood there in the darkness listening. He worked his way up to the second floor and waited again. He could hear the gritting of boots on the top floor and the dripping of water in the natural catch basin on the cave wall.

Willis eased up the chicken ladder until he could thrust his head into the floor opening. He could see the broad shoulders of Hugh Kinzie outlined against the window. Willis wet his cracked lips. He rose a little higher.

Hugh Kenzie spoke over his shoulder. "Come on up," he said. "I'm sorry I lost my temper."

Willis climbed up into the room. He leaned his carbine against the wall. Cold sweat soaked through his stinking shirt. The scout must have eyes in the back of his head and ears like a dog.

Willis walked up beside the scout. "I didn't have no call to insult the lady," he said apologetically.

"Forget it."

"Seems like a man talks sometimes without thinking."

"We all do."

"Yeah. Smell the meat?"

"How can you miss it?"

They stood there like two small boys looking into a candy shop window.

Willis looked at Hugh. "You speak Apache?"

"A little."

"You ever been friendly with 'em?"

Hugh looked quickly at Willis. "I've known a few. Why?"

"Nothing. Just wonderin'." Willis cleared his throat. "They all speak the same tongue?"

"There are some dialectal differences, but one of them can usually make his thoughts known to one of another tribal division."

"Supposin' you met one and wanted to be friendly. What would you say?"

Hugh shrugged. *"Nejeunee.* Means good friend, or you

could say *schicho,* which means friend. Or *schichobe,* which means, old friend, you behold me!"

"Anything else?" persisted Willis.

"*Sikisn.* Brother."

"Well. Well. You do know something about it. *Gracias, amigo.*"

Hugh leaned against the wall and eyed the trooper. "I might add that anyone but an Apache is an enemy. They take no chances."

Willis looked surprised. "I was just curious."

They could hear Morton down in the passageway. The canteens clattered together hollowly. Willis slapped Hugh on the shoulder. "No hard feelin's?"

"None."

"*Gracias.*" Willis went down through the hole in the floor.

Hugh scratched his lean jaw. Willis was beginning to act odd, like some of the others.

Isaiah Morton began to fill the first canteen. "And the people thirsted there for water; and the people murmured against Moses, and said, Wherefore is this that thou hast brought us up out of Egypt, to kill us and our children and our cattle with thirst?

"And Moses cried unto the Lord, saying, What shall I do unto this people? they be almost ready to stone me.

"And the Lord said unto Moses, Go on before the people, and take with thee of the elders of Israel; and thy rod, wherewith thou smotest the river, take in thine hand, and go.

"Behold, I will stand before thee there upon the rock in Horeb; and thou shalt smite the rock, and there shall come water out of it, that the people may drink. And Moses did so in the sight of the elders of Israel.

"And he called the name of the place Massah, and Meribah, because of the chiding of the children of Israel, and because they tempted the Lord, saying, Is the Lord among us, or not?"

Chandler Willis stood for a long time in the shadows. His mind was digesting a daring plan. There was no doubt in him that he must get away from the trap they had all fallen into. There was no organization left; each must look out for himself from now on and to hell with the hindmost. Besides, he was the only flunky left of the group which had entered that damned canyon of waiting death.

Those Apaches were smart. They hadn't lost a warrior in the whole process. All they had to do was sit where they were and wait for the White-eyes to die of starvation, then move in and gather up the spoils. They already had the horses and mules. It was a cinch.

Willis touched his bruised face. He hadn't expected the attack from Hugh Kinzie but he should have known better.

Willis had never really expected Kinzie to throw in with him, and now he was sure about it.

Hunger pains gnawed at his belly. It was time to pull foot. He'd try to work his way out of the canyon. If he was seen he'd talk to the Mimbrenos in the words taught him by Hugh Kinzie. He'd offer them liquor he'd steal from Nettleton's cache. He'd make it all right.

Willis slipped into the little room where Harry Roswell

had died because he had obeyed his orders. Willis slid two bottles inside his filthy shirt. He hooked his canteen to his belt and walked outside. Katy Corse and Darrell Phillips were still talking. Hell of a place for dallying. There was no one else in sight. The wind carried the inviting odor of roast meat to him.

Willis walked to the west end of the terrace. Hugh Kinzie was talking with Isaiah Morton. Willis eased over the crumbling wall and stood in a shadow, listening. Hugh Kinzie moved around in the tower room. Willis dropped to his belly, cradling his carbine in the crooks of his elbows, then worked his way under cover down the slope until he reached a place where a jungle of rocks and brush allowed him to stand up without being seen. He looked back at the dwellings, then thumbed his nose at them. Then he was gone through the thick brush, padding his way silently toward the huge rock shoulder which hid so many secrets from the people in the cliff dwellings.

Katy Corse stood at the edge of the terrace feeling the warm wind move her sweat-damp hair. It was the heat more than the hunger which bothered Katy; Darrell Phillips bothered her more than both of them together.

Darrell Phillips stood with bowed head, hands gripping the crumbling top of the wall. There was a sickness in him at being trapped in this alien place, with bloodthirsty primitives waiting out there in the shadows to kill, torture and rape.

The two of them had been standing there for three-quarters of an hour at least, and Darrell Phillips had been doing most of the talking.

Katy placed a hand on his shoulder. "You're really frightened, aren't you, Darrell?"

He raised his head. "In a way. Aren't you?"

She shrugged. "Yes. But it seems deeper in you."

He came closer to her. "You do understand me then! You want to understand me."

She smiled a little. "You mean no one understands you?"

He flushed. "Not like that. It just seems that you do more than the others."

She nodded and looked out across the canyon. It was always so. Officers came and went, and more than half of them she had met had told her, or intimated the same thing. But once they had left for duty in other parts, she had been completely forgotten. It had happened a number of times before. If she survived from this experience, it would happen again.

Phillips turned his back on the brooding moonlit canyon. "I keep trying to people the canyon," he said quietly.

"Yes. It seems as though the shadows and the moving brush are like figures from a Walpurgis Night."

He shivered a little. "With the Beltane fires glowing on the heights."

"You mustn't let your imagination run riot"

"How can I prevent it?"

She tilted her head to one side. "You should never have become a soldier."

He jerked his head and looked at her. "I've always wanted to be a soldier, Katy."

"Why? To prove to everyone that you're not afraid?"

It was as though she had driven a needle bayonet into him. He gripped her by the arms. "No! Katy, it's one thing to face white men in civilized warfare and quite another to fight against these human tigers. I've heard stories of what they do to captives. It makes me sick inside. So sick that I can't think clearly. Believe me when I say that I'm not a coward. You must believe me!"

She looked up into this face. "Yes," she said softly.

"I can lead a charge against breastworks and never falter. I can stand artillery fire and the volley of musketry. I'm not afraid of hand-to-hand combat with sword and pistol. But this is breaking me down. The eternal waiting. The silence. The deaths of Pearce, Stevens and Roswell, and the disappearance of Greer. Almost as though death is standing in the shadows, reaching out now and then with a bony finger to tap each one of us on the shoulder. It might be you next. It might be me."

She touched his flushed face. "Control yourself."

He placed his hand over hers and pressed it close to his cheek. "Katy," he said tensely, "it isn't the thought of dying that frightens me. It's the *way* of dying."

His body began to shake. Tears filled his eyes. She took him by the hand and led him to one of the rooms. She sat down on the floor and drew him down to her. He placed his head on her lap. His sobs came at regular intervals.

Hugh Kinzie watched Katy and Darrell Phillips enter the dwelling. It seemed as though a vial of acid had been broken inside of him. For a moment he thought of going down there and killing Darrell Phillips, but then he got control of himself.

It was quiet; it was too damned quiet.

Hugh Kinzie raised his head. He couldn't see or hear anything, but he could sense something about to happen.

———

CHANDLER WILLIS PADDED across the canyon seeking the shelter of the great shoulder of rock which projected into the canyon. There was no sign of life other than the occasional scuttering of a small nocturnal animal.

Cold sweat worked down his sides and greased his carbine stock beneath the grip of his hands. His head turned constantly from side to side as he advanced. Something seemed to warn him to go back, but he could not force himself to do so once he had made his decision to desert. He wasn't really deserting, he assured himself. He was just looking out for Number One.

———

MARION NETTLETON STIRRED RESTLESSLY in her sleep. Maurice Nettleton raised himself on an elbow and looked down at her. She was getting thin. There were dark circles beneath her lovely eyes. The sands of time were running out on the trapped party. Maurice Nettleton placed his hand on his Colt. There would be one shot for her, and he hoped to God he would have time to kill her before they got hold of her. Then he hoped he would have time to kill himself so that he wouldn't have time to think of the horrible thing he had been forced to do.

Abel Clymer was eating. He crouched in the triangular passageway, feeling the sweat run down his face as he spooned greasy tough meat into his mouth from a can of embalmed beef. He had cached three cans of the repulsive stuff so that he would be able to keep strength in his body for the time when he would make his break with Marion Nettleton. He glanced at the debris pile to his left. Under it was something else he had to take along.

———

Isaiah Morton placed the canteens in one of the rooms. He felt no hunger. He was used to fasting and self-torture in his effort to eliminate the thoughts of bodily comfort from his mind, leaving it free for the work of the Lord. He squatted in the dimness and began to pray.

———

Matt Hastings was cleaning his weapons. He jerked the pull-through out of his carbine barrel and held the weapon up to the light of the moon to check the barrel. Two Colts, loaded and capped, lay on his blanket, freshly cleaned and oiled. He loaded his carbine and capped it. Then he took out his sheath knife and began to sharpen it. The steady *wheet-wheet-wheet* of steel against stone kept time to his thoughts. No damned greasy Mimbreno was going to get Matt Hastings without a hell of a fracas. He'd take enough of them along with him to act as his pallbearers to hell.

———

CHANDLER WILLIS WAS ALMOST around the rock shoulder, holding his breath, hoping to God that the canyon wasn't a box.

The warrior materialized from the brush almost as though raised from a prone position by the strings of a master puppeteer. He was fifty feet from Chandler Willis. He did not move, but watched the white man with great liquid eyes.

Willis stopped with one foot planted forward. His carbine was in the crook of his left arm. He slowly extended his right hand, palm toward the silent buck. *"Nejeunee,"* he said clearly.

The warrior stood there as though carved from the very rocks behind him.

Chandler Willis swallowed dryly. *"Schicho!"* he said.

The wind moaned about the rock shoulder. The warrior stood like a statue.

Willis raised his head. *"Schichobe!"* he mouthed.

The musket roared inches from the back of the deserter's head, smashing in the back of his skull. The blood sprayed out and stained the clean sands. Candler Willis was dead before he knew what had hit him.

The crashing discharge of the big musket slammed back and forth between the canyon walls and then slowly died away down the canyon. The warrior lowered his smoking weapon and hooked a toe under the dead man's body. He rolled him over. Willis's arms flung outward. The killer spat and looked at his mate. *"Nejeunee! Schicho! Schichobe!"* he said.

The two Mimbrenos laughed.

The killer lifted his buckskin kilt and slapped his naked haunch. He spat on the body. *"Yah-tats-an!"* he said.

Hugh Kinzie ran to the terrace wall and looked in the direction from which the gun shot had come. Matt Hastings stopped beside him. "What is it?" he asked.

"Quien sabe?"

Nettleton came to them. "Who was it?"

Hugh looked along the terrace. Marion Nettleton was leaning against a dwelling wall. Isaiah Morton was beside her. Katy Corse stood beside Darrell Phillips. He had his arm around her waist. Abel Clymer walked out of a passageway and stopped behind Hugh. Hugh caught the odor of food on the big officer's breath.

"Where's Willis?" asked Hastings suddenly.

They all looked at each other, then looked down the quiet canyon. "Mark it in the book, Matt," said Hugh.

"You're sure?"

Hugh nodded. "He wanted to know how to say a friendly greeting to them," he said.

"He got his answer the hard way," said Hastings, wetting his cracked lips. "I'll mark it down." He looked at Hugh. "He didn't have any middle initial," he said. He walked to his quarters.

Maurice Nettleton walked slowly back to his wife. His shoulders were rounded. He silently took her by the arm and led her into their quarters.

Darrell Phillips turned suddenly and walked to the far end of the terrace.

Katy Corse looked at Phillips, then walked toward Hugh.

Katy stopped beside Hugh. "Was it Willis?"

"I haven't any doubt about it," he said coldly.

She placed a hand on his arm. "What's wrong, Hugh?"

"Go back to him," he said, jerking a thumb at Phillips.

"What do you mean?"

There was a sneer on his face as he looked down at her.

"You didn't have much time to get anything done with him in that room," he said.

Her right hand lashed his face. She turned on a heel and ran to her quarters.

Far down the canyon a coyote gave voice and was answered by one of his mates.

CHAPTER SIXTEEN

The moon was on the wane. The cliff dwellings seemed as deserted as they had been before the arrival of the party. Hugh padded back into the triangular passageway. He walked softly along it until he found a place where something lay on the ground. He knelt and looked at it. It was a piece of ragged tin. He fingered it, rubbing grease from it. He sniffed at his fingers. Embalmed beef. Hugh stood up and looked about. Clymer had been eating recently. No one else had a scrap of food.

Hugh looked at a debris pile. It looked as though it had been disturbed. He began to remove rocks. Something grated on the ground behind him. He whirled in time to have a big fist driven hard against his jaw. He went down hard and hit his head against a rock. He tried to get up but Clymer drove a boot against his side. Hugh grunted in pain. He rolled away from the big man and got to his feet in time to meet a smashing attack. Clymer drove in piston-like blows, battering alternately at Hugh's face and belly, until Hugh was driven back into a corner where the rock wall of the cave met the end of the row of dwellings. Hugh's head bounced from the wall. He covered up and worked his way around the officer.

Clymer danced about on his big feet. "You sonofabitch," he said thickly. "You nosy bastard!"

Clymer drove in hard again. Hugh parried the blows with elbows and forearms. The very weight and speed of Clymer's attack began to work against him. Hugh drove in a hard left jab, snapping Clymer's head back. He followed through with a smash low to the belly. Clymer grunted. He staggered back with his arms outflung, allowing Hugh time to close in hard and fast, driving blows to the belly.

Clymer hit the wall. He got in one good punch but paid a high price for it. Hugh swung from the waist, uppercutting the big man. Teeth and lips smashed together. Hugh planted a right over Clymer's heart. The big man bent forward in time to catch a neat uppercut. He sagged and slid down to the floor.

Hugh stepped back. "You loco bastard," he said thickly.

Clymer ran a hand across his battered mouth and flicked the blood against the rock wall. He shook his head and got up on his feet. Then he hunched forward, dropping his right hand to his pistol. Hugh clamped his left hand on Clymer's right wrist. He sank his right fist deep into Clymer's belly. The officer's sour breath exploded into Hugh's face. He grunted in pain. Hugh dropped his hand to his own Colt and freed it from its holster. He rammed the muzzle into Clymer's belly and looked into the wide, frightened eyes. "You sonofabitch," he said quietly, "I'd like to cut you down to size."

Hastings and Nettleton came up behind Hugh. "What is this, sir?" snapped Nettleton.

Hugh stepped to one side but kept his revolver in his hand. The big man had shaken him badly, and Hugh began to feel weak from the lack of food.

Clymer looked at Nettleton. "This man attacked me in here for no reason that I know of, sir. The man is demented."

Nettleton looked steadily at Hugh. "What have you to say for yourself, sir?"

Hugh shrugged. "I was looking around back here. Clymer jumped me for no reason at all."

"Is this true, Mr. Clymer?" asked Nettleton.

"No."

"He knows why I was looking around back here," said Hugh.

"Well?" demanded Nettleton of Clymer.

Clymer wet his thick lips. He looked away from his commanding officer. "I had a little food cached back here," he said.

Nettleton raised his head. "Food? All supplies were to be turned in to Sergeant Hastings. You deliberately disobeyed my orders, sir!"

Clymer swelled up his chest. "I'm a big man, sir. The biggest of all of you. I wanted to keep strength in my body for our escape, knowing it would depend on me to get Mrs. Nettleton to safety."

"Jesus," said Hastings softly.

Nettleton raised a shaking hand. "You will consider yourself under arrest, Mr. Clymer."

Clymer stared at him. Then he laughed. "Under arrest? Where will you put me, sir?" He laughed again and swung out a thick arm to indicate the canyon. "We're all prisoners, you pompous idiot! With dozens of jailors thirsting for our blood! Damn you, Nettleton! You got us into this. Now let a better man get you out of this unholy mess!" Clymer stalked off.

Hugh rubbed his battered jaw. Suspicion began to form in his mind. Clymer wasn't gutty enough to kill a man for a can of embalmed beef. There was something else he was hiding.

Nettleton looked as though he had been kicked in the belly. He looked at Hugh and then at Hastings. "We'll say no more about this," he said.

Hugh nodded.

Nettleton hesitated. "Did you find any food? Not for myself, you understand," he said hastily, "but for Mrs. Nettleton."

Hugh shook his head. "Nor any for Miss Corse, either," he said.

Nettleton jerked his head as though he had been slapped. "Yes. Yes. Of course." He placed a hand on Hugh's arm. "Tell me, Kinzie: is there a chance of escape?"

Hugh looked down at him. "I don't know."

"Will you try to get a message through?"

"If I can get out of this canyon, sir, it would be days before I could bring back help. If I did bring back help, what would we find when we got here?"

Nettleton nodded. "Yes," he said quietly. "Of course." He turned away and walked out toward the terrace.

Hastings eyed Hugh. "Now how about the truth, Hugh?"

"Damned if I know. I knew Clymer had been eating. I came in here and found a piece of tin from a beef can. I was poking around to find his cache when he got me from behind."

"I wish you'd killed the big stud."

Hugh felt his jaw. "He damned near killed me."

Hastings looked down the passageway and spoke in a low voice. "Watch your back, Hugh."

Hugh nodded. "What are we going to do now, Matt?"

Hastings spat. "I'm not going to sit here to be caught like a rat."

"So?"

Hastings raised his head. "No gut-eating Apache is going to crack my skull to keep my spirit from haunting him."

Hugh looked closely at the veteran. "I'll need you when the time comes to make the break. You're the only one I can trust now, Matt."

Hastings stepped back. "Yeah." He walked away.

Hugh stared at the first soldier. A subtle change had come over Hastings.

Hugh walked toward the tower. He stopped in the semi-circular area at the west end of the passageway. His boots crunched ancient maize cobs. He looked up at the rock fault which had been carefully sealed with rocks and mortar. Then he looked up at the cave ceiling. It must be many yards thick between the ceiling and the mesa top. He looked at the sealed fault again. He passed a hand over the smooth surface of the mortared rocks. They had taken great pains to seal it off. What was behind it?

Hugh climbed up into the tower and walked across the beam they had placed to reach the water pan. He placed a hand in the thin sheet of water and pressed its coolness against his aching face. He squatted there in the dimness, wishing for a smoke. His head throbbed. It was hard to think. He eyed the glistening trickle of water. It seemed to come from the very pores of the rock itself. He crawled over to it and pressed a hand against it, trying to fathom from whence it came. He looked up at the rock roof again. How many yards to the mesa floor?

Hugh closed his eyes. A faintness seemed to come over him. He tried to shake it off. The fight had taken a hell of a lot of strength out of him.

He walked across the narrow bridge they had made to reach the water. He stepped down from the window ledge and full into a soft body. Marion Nettleton slid her arms about his neck. "Are you all right, Hugh? I couldn't rest when Maurice told me what had happened."

He looked down at her. The faint odor of rich perfume came from her.

"Hugh, is there any chance for us at all?" she whispered.

"All I have to have happen now is to have the captain walk in on us."

She shook her head. "He's lying down. He broods a lot. Hugh, he can't get me out of here."

"And you think I can?"

She moved closer and the faintly sour odor of her sweat came to him mingled with the rich perfume. Hugh almost grinned. Marion Nettleton wasn't going to stink like the rest of the common folk. But the combination of odors was typical of her. There was a stink behind her looks and polish. He took her arms from around his neck.

"When the time comes, Marion, we'll all know who is going to be saved. Like Resurrection Day."

She replaced her arms about his neck and pressed her lower body hard against his. "Don't send me away," she said softly.

Hugh was tempted. The sands of time were trickling away fast and it had been a long time since he had had a woman, and the last one he had had wasn't in a class with Marion Nettleton, except that she had had some sense of honor despite her moral code. "You'd better get back to your husband," he said.

For a moment she hesitated. Hugh almost took her then and there, but she turned away and left the room. He shrugged and followed her. Katy Corse came out of the shadows and looked up at him. "You didn't have much time to get anything done with her in that tower," she said.

Hugh scratched his jaw. Then he smiled. He broke into a wide grin and then laughed aloud. He swept her to him and kissed her hard. Then he pushed her away. "Can *he* kiss you like that, Katy? Tell the truth."

She bit her lip. "Damn you, Hugh Kinzie," she said. She walked to her quarters.

Darrell Phillips stepped out in front of Hugh as he followed Katy. "Where are you going?" he asked quietly.

"None of your damned business, Phillips."

"I can't fight you as Clymer did, but I can ask you out as a gentleman!"

Hugh grinned again. "Jesus Christ but everybody is touchy tonight. She's all yours, Phillips."

Phillips watched Hugh walk to the far end of the terrace. Abel Clymer came out of his room and stopped beside Phillips. "Someday I'll break his God-damned back," he said.

Phillips glanced at the big man. "If he doesn't break yours first, Clymer. I almost wish to God he had."

Clymer turned quickly. "I'll smash in your pretty face," he snarled.

Phillips stepped back. "I'll put a bullet into your belly first. Clymer."

Clymer glanced down at Phillips's gun. Then he looked into the taut, cold face. "There'll be a showdown before long," he said. "Then all these little problems will be settled. By God, Phillips, I'd like to see those Apache squaws working over you with knife and fire."

Phillips went pale. He bit his lip and turned away. A sour flood seemed to rise in his throat. Behind him Abel Clymer laughed aloud.

CHAPTER SEVENTEEN

Darrell Phillips had the guard just before dawn. A cold wind swept through the canyon just as the first traces of the false dawn tinged the eastern skies. He shivered a little and drew his blanket about his shoulders. There was a dull gnawing ache in the pit of his stomach, and his head throbbed a little. He had amused himself during his watch by thinking of the fine restaurants he had dined in back east. A poor way for a half-starved man to spend his time.

He felt better with the coming of light, for the darkness was peopled with phantoms who seemed to leer and gibber at him from behind every rock and clump of brush.

He hunched his shoulders beneath the blanket and thought of Katy Corse. It was she who had brought him the blanket as he had gone on watch. She was trying to understand him in the goodness of her heart. It was his damned imagination that caused him so much trouble. It had always been so. The actuality had always been less fearful than the expectancy. She had placed a probing finger on his secret. She knew why he had become a soldier. To prove to the world that he had courage. He knew he wasn't really a coward. Not as much as some men, in any case. Somehow he had thought that wearing blue and brass would prove to everyone that he was as brave as any man. He had seen little action at Fort Ayres, but what he had seen after several slashing Apache raids on stage stations and lonely ranches had been branded on his mind with letters of fire. There seemed to be a thick green mucous of fear clogging his soul.

The light was better now. He looked down the slope. There was a strange growth there. Something alien. He stared at it, and then opened his mouth. A shriek that did not seem to emanate from his mouth awoke the canyon echoes. It was almost as though someone else had done it.

Hugh Kinzie burst from his room holding his Sharps carbine at hip level. He stared at Phillips's ghastly white face. The officer dropped his carbine, pointed down the slope, then turned away to retch violently.

Hugh looked down the slope. A white man lay there, stripped to the buff. His head was curiously misshapen. It was Chandler Willis—or what had been Chandler Willis.

Hugh gripped Phillips by the shoulder. "Make sure the women don't see this." He shoved Phillips toward the dwellings. The officer walked as though in a dream, dropping the blanket from his shoulders.

Matt Hastings came up at a trot and looked down at Willis. "I knew it," he said.

Hugh nodded. "At least he wasn't tortured," he said.

Hastings spat dryly. "For God's sake, Hugh, if they get at me and wound me, make damned sure you save a slug for me. You'll remember that?"

"Yes."

"I'll do the same for you."

"*Gracias*" said Hugh dryly.

"I'll go down and noose a picket line on his body. We can draw him up here and bury him."

Maurice Nettleton looked down at the body. "When did they put him there?"

"*Quien sabe?*" said Hugh. "The point is that they dragged that body clear across the canyon and placed him not thirty feet from the man standing on guard."

Nettleton touched his throat. There was a sickness

apparent on his face. "If I had only tried with all speed for the Rio Grande." he said.

"You didn't."

"We might have been safely at Santa Fe by now."

Hugh spat over the wall. "It's a little late to think about it now."

Hastings passed them carrying a coiled picket line in his hand. He vaulted the wall and slid down the slope. He worked quickly, glancing now and then over his shoulder. Hugh knelt behind the wall with his cocked carbine in his hands, watching the opposite canyon wall.

Hastings finished. He came up the slope, uncoiling the line. They pulled the battered corpse up to the wall and lifted it over. Hugh looked away from the smashed head.

They buried Chandler Willis in a hole behind one of the buildings. Abel Clymer leaned against the wall watching them as they finished the burial. Hastings marked it in the book. "I had a feeling he'd make a break," said Matt Hastings.

Hugh nodded. "Five down; eight to go, as *he* would have said."

"At least he's out of this mess."

Hugh scratched the bristles on his face. "The chips are all down now, Matt."

Hastings leaned back against a wall. There were dark circles under his eyes, and his uniform was beginning to hang loosely on his thick body. "If we didn't have the women," he said quietly, "we could all make a break for it. We're all handy with sidearms. Except Morton. I'd rather die fighting than like a rat in a trap."

"We can't leave the women, Matt."

"There's one way out."

They looked at each other.

"It isn't time yet," said Hugh. "Besides . . . who would do it? Roswell might have; he always obeyed orders. I'll not do it until the last possible moment."

Hastings touched his cracked lips. "We can draw straws."

"I said I wouldn't do it now!"

"We can make it easy on them. A bullet in the back of the head when they don't expect it."

"No!"

"Look, Hugh! We won't all get out of this mess. Six men might make it after dark. Sure, some of us will get it. But I'm enough of a gambler to take my chance. One man might break free. I'll take those odds against sitting there waiting for the end. Another day of this and we'll all be too weak to make a mile on foot."

Hugh watched Clymer walking toward the watchtower. "Clymer could."

Hastings figured the butt of his Colt. "I once thought I'd plug him in the back in the first action we got into."

"Our loss would be Heaven's gain, as Isaiah would say. Let's go and talk with the others."

They gathered in front of the watchtower as the sun began to flood the canyon. Nettleton's hands shook as he buttoned up his blouse despite the heat. Clymer squatted with his back against the tower. There was a set look on his broad face. Phillips seemed pale beneath his tanned face. Now and again he wet his lips and looked across the empty canyon. Hastings stood up with his big hands folded atop his carbine muzzle. Isaiah Morton was there in body only.

Nettleton looked about. "We must do something," he said nervously. "My wife is not well. There is no food left."

"No horses either," said Clymer.

"Yes. Yes."

"If you had listened to me, we would have made a break out of here some days ago," said Clymer.

"Let us look forward, Mr. Clymer."

Clymer laughed. "To what?"

"I wanted to make a sortie then," said Darrell Phillips.

"Yeah," said Clymer. "You were going with the captain here as *aide*. Who was detailed to lead the attack? Me! Well, I'm not leading any attack now, sonny."

"We haven't enough strength in numbers for that now," said Nettleton.

They looked at each other. None of them had an idea.

The realization that death was a surety instead of an even chance weighed on them.

Isaiah Morton opened his eyes. "Perhaps we could reason with our red brethren. Surely there is some pity in them. Are they not the Lord's children as well as we?"

"You talk with them," said Clymer.

"Yes! I am willing."

"He don't talk their lingo," said Hastings.

"Kinzie does," said Clymer slyly.

They all looked at Hugh. He shook his head. "They're out for our blood."

Phillips walked to the edge of the terrace. "Perhaps, after dark, before the moon rises, we could scale this side of the canyon and pull the ladies up by means of the picket ropes."

Nettleton rubbed his jaw. "Perhaps. What do the rest of you think?"

"Sounds all right, sir," said Hastings, "but maybe they're up there too."

"Yes," said Nettleton. He paced back and forth. "But we can try. Yes! We'll do it!"

Hugh shrugged. "It's our last chance," he said. He studied the others.

Clymer stood up. "I'll go," he said.

Hastings nodded. "Count me in, sir."

Isaiah Morton wandered off. He looked out across the canyon. Voices seemed to speak into his ears. Hunger and thirst were forgotten as he walked back and forth, trying to clearly understand the words which he heard. He stopped and stood at the edge of the terrace for a long time staring at the motionless brush which rimmed the edge of the far canyon wall.

CHAPTER EIGHTEEN

They worked swiftly in the gathering dusk. There was no dissension amongst them now. Picket lines were tied together and coiled. Picket pins were bundled together so that they could be carried easily to where they would be wedged into rock crevices as improvised pitons. Clymer carried the bundle of pins. Phillips carried the coiled picket lines. Hastings was the only one who carried a carbine, and he had added another Colt to his armament. Nettleton was to stay with the women. Hugh was to scale the canyon side. Morton had vanished into the ruins to commune with his Lord and himself.

Hugh had stripped off his shirt and had removed his boots. He expected to cut the very devil out of his feet, but they would be surer than his heavy boots. He led the way to the west end of the terrace and eased over the wall, followed by the others. Hugh padded along the slope and topped fifty yards from the end of the ruins. He looked up at the canyon wall. One place was as good as another. Phillips and Clymer came softly up to Hugh in the darkness. Hastings faded down the slope and took up a position where he could cover the approaches to the ruins and the scaling party.

Hugh worked his way up a tip-tilted slab of rock. He stopped at the top and strained his eyes upwards, studying the rock formations above him. The wall was solid looking, but there were places where frost and rain had hastened the work of decomposition. Hugh reached back and took the ends of the coiled lines from Phillips. The young officer was breathing harshly. Clymer handed Hugh one of the picket pins. He fastened the bundle to a spare picket line and fastened the free end to Hugh's belt.

Hugh felt the cliff face. It was solid enough. He began to work his way upward, sweating coldly at the thought of having one of the picket pins clash against the cliff.

He cursed as he placed his hand in a clump of catclaw growing in a thin pocket of soil on a ledge. His hand smarted like fire as he climbed up. He was up fifty feet before he had to wedge a picket pin into a crevice for a foothold. He worked slowly, breathing quickly as he worked the tip of the pin into a solid position. He pulled himself up a little and tested his weight on the pin. It gave a little, and then held. He pulled himself up higher by a handhold and rested a foot on the pin. He felt the bundle of picket pins drag a little at the end of the line fastened to his belt.

A faint wind carried down the canyon, bearing the sweetish odor of decomposition with it. Hugh wiped the sweat from his stinging face. It must be Dan Pearce making himself known as the cooling night air contracted his gas-swollen belly.

Hugh worked up onto a narrow transverse ledge and felt for another handhold. The dull buzzing warned him and he jerked back his hand as something struck just where it had been. The rank odor of the rattler tainted his nostrils. He pulled back his head, trying to spot the scaly body. There was a rustling movement and then a dull scraping noise. Sweat began to drip into his eyes.

Some damned fool down below tugged at the line fastened to Hugh's belt. His foot slipped and he was forced to grab for the ledge again. His fingers closed on something scaly, and he felt the hard rattle buttons beneath his fingers. There was no time to think or jump. He gripped hard just above the rattles and jerked the thick heavy body from the ledge. As it reached full length he snapped hard. The rattler hung lifeless in his hand. Pebbles and dirt pattered down far below him. He heard a muffled curse.

Hugh hung there by one hand, feeling his foot slip on the lower ledge. He wanted to drop the heavy rattler but he knew damned well if that cold body struck one of those nerve-taut men below, unadulterated hell would break loose for sure. Juggling the rattler with one hand, he gripped tight with the other and then swung the limp body up onto the ledge where it struck heavily. Then he followed it, dropping flat on top of it, feeling the cold scales beneath his naked chest and belly.

A greenish sickness came over him. He wondered how much worse things could get before he escaped or earned the blessed oblivion of death.

He figured he was up at least sixty feet. Mentally he calculated that the ceiling of the great cave which housed the ruins was at least eighty to one hundred feet above the tallest structure. Then the top of the mesa was at least thirty to forty feet higher than that. He shook his head, then wiped his bleeding palms against the rough material of his trousers. He felt weak and lightheaded, and he rested his head against the warm rock, fighting off vertigo which came and went spasmodically.

He felt for the line which hung from his belt and began to pull up the heavy bundle of picket pins, easing it when the bundle began to swing too much, trying to get a straight vertical pull. The picket line cut into his raw palms and the salt of his sweat made them feel as though he were dipping them into acid.

He felt the bundle bump the edge of the ledge and he pulled it up beside him. A small rock was brushed over the edge. It bounded from a projection and then struck sharply far below. He lay still, listening with all his power.

ISAIAH MORTON STOOD by the terrace wall. The darkness was so thick that it could almost be felt. He thrust out a gaunt hand encrusted with dirt and pawed at the darkness as though he could rift it sufficiently to see the far side of the canyon. "My heart is sore pained within me: and the terrors of death are fallen upon me.

"Tearfulness and trembling are come upon me, and horror hath overwhelmed me.

"And I said, Oh that I had wings like a dove! for then would I fly away, and be at rest.

"Lo, then would I wander far off, and remain in the wilderness. Selah!"

———

KATY CORSE SAT with her elbows resting on her knees and her hands cupping her oval face. She looked straight ahead, almost unaware of Marion Nettleton, who sat across from her. Now and then Marion's dry sobbing drifted to Katy through the haze which seemed to envelop her. The sobbing grew louder. "Be quiet!" hissed Katy.

"I'm afraid."

"Who isn't?"

"But it affects me worse than it does you, Katy."

"Maybe. I'm thinking of those men out there, risking their lives for us."

"It's their duty."

Katy dropped her hands. "You *would* think so. Don't you ever think of anyone but yourself?"

Marion bit her lip. "You're talking to a lady, Katy Corse."

Katy stared at her, then threw back her head and began to laugh.

Marion closed her hand on a stone; it would be so easy to close her mouth. "If it weren't for you," she said quietly, "the men might have been able to get me out of here. Hugh Kinzie can do it."

"And have himself killed? I'd rather have him leave me and save himself."

"Why don't you get Darrell Phillips to save you? You certainly threw yourself at him! I'd laugh if it weren't so tragic. You . . . a frontier doxie, thinking Darrell Phillips is really interested in you."

Katy stood up. She clenched her hands. For a moment she almost reached down to grip Marion by the hair and drag her to her feet. "I often wondered how deep your breeding went," she said quietly. "I can see now that it's a pitifully thin veneer."

"Ladies!" hissed Maurice Nettleton from the doorway. "You must be quiet!"

Marion glanced sideways at her husband and then up at Katy. "We'll take this up some other time," she promised.

Katy laughed. "Any time."

Maurice Nettleton shook his head. He walked to the edge of the terrace. He could hear Isaiah Morton mumbling another of his eternal prayers. "Be quiet!" said Maurice Nettleton out of the darkness. "Those men are trying to save our lives!"

Isaiah held up his thin arms. "Cast thy burden upon the Lord, and he shall sustain thee: he shall never suffer the righteous to be moved!"

Nettleton drew out his pistol and cocked it. "Damn you! You and your prating and praying! You should be on guard here while I should be out there helping them! Now keep your mouth shut at least!" Nettleton turned and hastened to the west end of the terrace to see if there was any sign of progress.

Morton thrust an accusing finger toward Nettleton. "But thou, O God, shalt bring them down into the pit of destruction: bloody and deceitful men shall not live out half their days: but I will trust in thee."

———

HUGH KINZIE STOOD up on the ledge and felt above him. He was sick with horror that he might touch another diamondback and run out of what little luck he had left. His hands scrabbled in vain. He felt for a picket pin and inserted it into three different crevices until it seemed to hold firm. He looked back over his shoulder. There was a faint grayish-yellow tinge in the eastern sky. The moon was slowly rising. He worked slowly, forcing himself to remain calm as he worked up the cliff.

He was a good forty feet from the top when he suddenly became aware that he could see better. He looked back. The canyon was still in deep shadow. But the eastern sky was lighting.

He clung to a picket pin. He looked up. He was sure he could make it by himself and still not be seen by the prying eyes of the Mimbrenos. The temptation was strong. The odds of getting the rest of them out were hopelessly high. He closed his eyes and rested flat against the cliff face.

It would take him another half-hour to reach the top. By that time he could be seen against the cliff face. But he could go over the top and make tracks during the night until he was free at last from their almost unseen captors.

Hugh Kinzie slowly wiped the sweat from his face with his free hand. It was no use. He couldn't do it. He'd have to go down now and they'd have to wait until the moon was gone to finish building their perilous ladder to freedom.

Hugh felt for the pin under him and eased himself down until he reached the upper ledge. He picked up the body of the snake and tied it behind him. Then he felt for a foothold. The moon was beginning to light the canyon. Already he could distinguish the slope below the terrace. There was something moving there.

The clear voice came up to him and echoed through the canyon. "Hear my cry, O God; attend unto my prayer.

"From the end of the earth will I cry unto thee, when my heart is overwhelmed: lead me to the rock that is higher than I.

"For thou hast been a shelter for me, and a strong tower from the enemy.

"I will abide in thy tabernacle forever: I will trust in the cover of thy wings. Selah!"

There was a muffled exclamation below Hugh. Then boots smashed against the earth. Rocks began to roll down the slope.

Hugh looked back. Isaiah Morton was walking down the slope with his arms held high above his head.

There was a flare of light from the far side of the canyon. Then a faggot curved gracefully through the darkness, trailing a stream of sparks. It struck in the thick dry brush and scattered bits of burning wood. In a moment the brush caught the flame and began to burn swiftly. The light showed Isaiah Morton walking confidently toward the west end of the great canyon.

Phillips and Clymer were running for the cliff dwellings. Then rifles began to crash from the northern rim of the canyon, kicking up spurts of dust close to the two officers.

Hastings stood up. "Hugh! I'll cover you! Come on! Shake the dust!"

Isaiah Morton walked through the flaming brush, seemingly in a trance. The Mimbrenos did not fire at him. Instead they poured their fire toward the two officers who were scrambling over the wall. Slugs whispered through the smoke and slapped against the dwellings. Nettleton fired wildly, at an impossible range for his six-gun.

Hastings looked up at Hugh with wild eyes. "Damn it! Come on!"

Morton walked on through the crashing hell of the rifles and the crackling of the flames. "The Lord is my shepherd; I shall not want.

"He maketh me to lie down in green pastures: he leadeth me beside the still waters.

"He restoreth my soul: he leadeth me in the paths of righteousness for his name's sake."

Hugh jumped from the last ledge and slid down the tip-tilted slab of rock. Slugs slapped against the canyon wall. Hastings fired his carbine and swiftly reloaded. Then he stood up and looked back at Hugh. "Run, you bastard! Run!"

Morton stumbled and fell. He got up and walked on.

"Yea, though I walk through the valley of the shadow of

death, I will fear no evil: for thou art with me; thy rod and thy staff they comfort me."

Hugh snatched up the coiled line and the remainder of the picket pins. He plunged into the brush. The flames were roaring and dancing, casting weird shadows and spurts of reflected light from the canyon walls. It was as bright as day.

Hastings fired his carbine. Slugs smashed into him. He walked forward with a Colt in either hand, staggering a little as more slugs smashed into him. His body jerked. "You red bastards!" he yelled. "I'm coming! I'm coming!"

Hugh tripped and fell behind a rock ledge. He lay still as rifles crackled in harmony with the blazing brush. Someone yelled from the cliff dwellings. Carbines began to rattle from the terrace wall.

Hastings was reeling across the bright canyon floor, pumping alternate shots from both Colts. Halfway across the canyon he pitched forward on his face and lay still. His body jerked as slugs pounded into it.

Isaiah Morton was almost to the granite shoulder. He turned and looked back. "Surely goodness and mercy shall follow me all the days of my life: and I will dwell in the house of the Lord forever."

Then he was gone into the shadow beneath the rock shoulder.

———

HUGH RAISED HIS HEAD. The flames had died away leaving red ember eyes winking on the canyon floor. It was quiet again. The odor of burnt cloth, brush and flesh mingled with the acrid gunpowder smoke.

He hunched himself along behind the ledge, stopping and listening now and then. The silence had descended again after the savage outburst of musketry.

Hugh worked his way up the slope. There was a scuffling of feet behind the terrace wall. A head appeared. Hugh rolled over behind a bush and waited. A carbine cracked flatly, awakening the echoes again. The report seemed to bounce back and forth between the canyon walls, then died away in the distance.

"Hold your fire!" called out Hugh. "It's Kinzie!"

Hugh waited a moment or two and then crawled up to the wall. He crawled quickly over it and dropped on the terrace floor. His breath came hot and thick in his throat. He rested his head on the paved terrace. Then he looked up into the dim face of Abel Clymer. The big officer was holding a carbine in his hands.

"Well, that was a fiasco," said Clymer.

Hugh sat up and nodded.

Someone moaned in the shadows. "Who's that?" asked Hugh.

Clymer spat over the wall. "Phillips. He caught a slug in his left thigh."

"Bad?"

"Thigh bone is broken."

Hugh wiped the sweat from his face.

Nettleton came to them. "You're all right, Kinzie?"

"Yes."

"Who would have thought that mad preacher would have done that?"

Hugh shrugged. "At that, maybe he's smarter than the rest of us."

"How so?"

"He trusted in a miracle. He got one."

"But they'll torture and kill him."

Hugh shook his head. "Mind-gone-far," he said.

"Meaning?" asked Clymer.

"They'll know he isn't right in his mind. . or is he? No matter. It's a profanation to kill such a one."

"But he'll die out in the mountains!" said Nettleton.

"Does it matter?"

Clymer looked toward the dwellings. Phillips groaned. "Now we've got another burden," he said sourly.

Nettleton touched his throat. "Why did Hastings attack them?" He shook his head. "It was madness."

Hugh nodded. "Matt never could stand this type of stuff."

"But he was so strong."

"The type that cracks suddenly. The *heshke* came over him—the wild killing craze. He's better off, like Morton."

Hugh got up. He walked to the tower and threw the snake into the lower room. Then he climbed to the water pan and bathed his face and raw hands. He went down to the small dusty room where Darrell Phillips now lay. Katy Corse had cut away the trousers and under drawers from his left leg. Great beads of sweat dewed Phillips's white face. Now and then he gritted his teeth to keep from moaning.

Hugh knelt beside the wounded officer.

"The femur is broken," said Katy quietly.

Hugh glanced at her. There was little hope on her face. Hugh examined the leg. The slug was still embedded in it. "We'll have to get that slug out."

She nodded. "We have alcohol, knives, and I think there are some surgical implements in Nettleton's baggage."

"Get them. We'll need a fire in here to heat the water."

"Yes, Hugh."

He looked quickly at her. She smiled. "I knew you'd take charge," she said.

Hugh bathed Phillips's face after Katy had left. Phillips opened his eyes. "Where's Katy?" he asked.

"She'll be back."

Phillips closed his eyes. "I'm sorry I panicked," he said. "It must have been hell up there on that cliff."

"It was."

He opened his eyes again. "How bad is it?"

"Bad enough. The bone is smashed, I think."

He beat a fist against the blanket. "Helpless," he said softly. "It was bad enough before; now it's sheer hell."

"They won't get you, Darrell."

The officer eyed Hugh. "You won't let them, will you, Kinzie?"

Hugh shook his head.

CHAPTER NINETEEN

Sweat soaked Hugh's clothing as he finished with
Phillips. They had tried to soak him into insensibility
with alcohol, but even so the young officer had
groaned and writhed under the knife. Then he had fainted.

Hugh sat back against the wall watching Katy bandage
the thigh. The fresh blood quickly stained through the fine
cloth. Hugh fingered a ruffle which Katy had ripped from
the last of Mrs. Nettleton's petticoats. Katy glanced at him.
Hugh flushed and then stood up. "I'll get some food," he
said.

"Where?"

"Never mind. I'll get it."

————

THERE WERE ONLY six mouths to feed now. Hugh walked
along the terrace. Clymer stood in the shadows with his
carbine across his left arm. "How is he?"

"Are you really interested?"

"We're in bad enough shape without a cripple holding us
back."

"There's a way out, Clymer."

"There is?"

Hugh nodded. "Put a slug into his head."

Hugh walked away. Clymer gripped his carbine and raised it. Then he lowered it. "Not time yet," he murmured.

———

HUGH WIPED the sweat from his face and began to cut the cooked meat into equal portions. He placed it on a tin plate and then kicked dirt and debris over the fire. He looked up at the mysterious walled-in fault above the fire. He wiped his knife on his filthy trousers, resisted the temptation to gnaw at a portion of meat, and then walked out onto the terrace.

Clymer eyed the plate. "Meat! By Jesus, Kinzie! I can't wait."

"We'll eat together."

They gathered in the room where Phillips lay. Hugh silently passed out the succulent meat.

"You're a miracle worker!" said Nettleton. "By Heaven, Kinzie, this is delicious!"

They ate quickly. Clymer wiped his mouth with the back of his hand. "Any more?"

"No," said Hugh. He finished his meat.

Marion Nettleton picked at her portion, eying Hugh whenever she was sure her husband wasn't watching her. Katy judiciously fed Phillips the best parts of her portion and his. The sick man ate a little and then lay back covering his pale face with his right arm.

"What is it?" asked Nettleton. "By Heaven, the father-in-law would love this. I must get some for him."

Hugh stood up. "There's plenty available," he said. "I should have thought of it before."

Marion Nettleton stopped with her fork halfway to her mouth. "Hugh! What is it?"

"Never mind. Eat."

Clymer stood up. "Answer the lady," he said.

Hugh started for the door. Clymer gripped Hugh's shoulder and whirled him about. "Answer the lady," he said.

Hugh spat. "Listen, you big tub of guts: she's eating, isn't she? It's food, isn't it? Take it and be thankful."

Katy stood up and looked from one to the other of them. "I know what it is."

"Well?" demanded Marion.

"Rattlesnake," said Katy.

Marion Nettleton threw her plate across the room. She turned pale and suddenly jumped up and ran to the door, holding her hand over her mouth.

Clymer set his jaw. "Damn you, Kinzie!"

Hugh grinned. "The Lord will provide," he said. "Best damned diamondback steaks I ever ate."

Hugh walked outside. Marion Nettleton was bending over the terrace wall. Always the lady, thought Hugh. He walked to the tower and picked up the coiled picket lines. Then he walked around to the place where the fault had been walled in. His carbine leaned against it. He thumped the mortared rocks with his Sharps butt. It was as solid as Gibraltar, or so it seemed. He climbed up into the second floor of the tower and tried it again. He was rewarded with a hollow sound.

Hugh eyed the wall. A pick might break through, if he had one. A sledge might crack through, if he had one. He squatted at the window, studying the wall. Somewhere, in his past, he had once read a book on medieval siege operations. "Why not a battering ram?" he said aloud.

Hugh began to gather his materials. A heavy roof beam would do for the ram, but he needed a means of suspension. He went out on the terrace. Nettleton and Clymer were talking in low voices. They stopped as Hugh approached. Hugh explained his plan to them.

Nettleton rubbed his dirty face. "Do you think we can break through?"

Hugh shrugged. "We can try."

"If the Mimbrenos hear the noise they'll be suspicious."

"Do you have any other ideas about a way of escape?" Nettleton shook his head. "Let's try it," he said.

———

It had taken them all of two hours to rig the device. Beams had been braced in the upper floor of the tower, and they had been extended through the window to rest against the wall. Hugh rigged plaited picket lines from the beams and from them they depended on a solid beam, even with the second-floor window. There was hardly enough room to swing the beam in the little room, but they had no other choice.

Nettleton passed around a bottle after they finished. "Now what?" he asked.

Hugh took a good slug. "We'll have to figure out the best time to begin smashing the wall."

"We won't have much time once the Mimbrenos hear us," said Nettleton thoughtfully.

"Supposing we *don't* smash the wall?" asked Clymer.

"That's a damned silly question," said Hugh.

Nettleton took another drink. "I'll have the ladies ready," he said.

"What about Phillips?" asked Clymer.

Hugh stood up. "We'll worry about that when the time comes."

"I'm worried about it now," said Clymer.

"You mean you're worried about getting out of here yourself and to hell with everybody else."

Clymer reached for the bottle. "Someday . . ."

———

Darrell Phillips opened his eyes as Katy wiped his forehead with a damp cloth. "How are they doing?" he rasped.

"They've been up there for a couple of hours."

"We should have thought of that before . . . before this happened."

"We won't leave you, Darrell."

"I know you won't. But what about them?"

She patted his bristly cheek. "I'll stay with you," she said.

MARION NETTLETON GATHERED her things together. Her stomach still rebelled at the thought of the horrible food she had partially eaten. She tied a scarf around her head and tucked in a loose strand of hair. Still, it had been Hugh Kinzie who had held them together thus far. Phillips would die. Maurice would bumble and fumble as he always had. Clymer, instead of paying his usual attention to Marion, had become preoccupied with something else. That left Hugh Kinzie. He would get her out. He'd get her back to civilization. She sipped a little water to get rid of the taste of the meat. "And if he dies on the way," she said aloud, "so much the better!"

MAURICE NETTLETON, in his meticulous way, went about making sure everything was ready. Not that there was much to get ready, but it salved Nettleton's conscience. He knew he had lost command of the party even before they had been trapped in the canyon. Man after man had died or disappeared. It wouldn't be easy to explain, now that First Sergeant Hastings lay dead out in the canyon, for he had kept all the records. Nettleton shook his head. There would be a great deal of explaining to do. Still, they might look upon him as somewhat of a hero for getting the remainder of his party to safety. If only that loudmouth Abel Clymer had gone the way of the others.

Nettleton padded about. He gathered up the extra weapons and carried them to the tower. He filled the canteens and placed them with the weapons. He looked up at the ram and nodded in satisfaction. This would make a good story to tell in the officers' clubs when he got back to duty in the east.

He came out of the tower and heard a scrabbling noise further up the triangular passageway. He walked east toward the noise. A big figure bulked in the darkness. It was Abel

Clymer, down on his hands and knees, digging in debris. Nettleton opened his mouth and then closed it. Kinzie had accused Clymer of caching food for his own use. Nettleton stepped in between two buildings and raised the flap of his holster.

Clymer pulled something from the hole and dusted it off. He looked up the passageway and then felt in his pockets. He opened the saddlebag he had unearthed and lit a match. Swiftly he began to take something from the bag and stow it inside his shirt.

Nettleton walked forward. He drew and cocked his Colt "Mr. Clymer," he said.

Clymer turned quickly. He held a fold of papers in his big hand. The match flickered out.

"What is that, Mr. Clymer?"

"Personal papers."

"You're sure?"

"Certainly!"

"Let me see."

"You have no right to see them."

Clymer extended the papers.

"Light a match, Mr. Clymer."

Abel Clymer produced and lit a match. Nettleton looked at the papers. Then he looked up coldly at Clymer. "The government drafts from Fort Buchanan. How came you by them, sir?"

"I was protecting them, Captain."

"So? *I* am in command here. Give me the rest of them, sir!"

Clymer looked past Nettleton. There was no one else in sight. He slid a hand inside his shirt. Then he moved swiftly. He knocked Nettleton's hand up into the air. His right fist smashed fully against Nettleton's jaw. Nettleton staggered against the wall. Clymer snatched the Colt from Nettleton's weakened hand. Nettleton swayed toward Clymer. Clymer thrust out his big right hand and closed the massive fingers about Nettleton's soft throat. Nettleton struggled. Clymer forced the smaller man to his knees. Carefully he placed the cocked Colt on the debris. Then he closed his other hand about Nettleton's throat. There was no sound but the frenzied scraping of Nettleton's feet on the gritty earth and Clymer's harsh breathing.

Clymer lowered the lifeless man to the ground. He stowed away the drafts. Then he picked up the captain and carried him into a dwelling. He piled debris over the body. Then he stepped back and spat on the rude grave.

———

Hugh Kinzie looked at Marion Nettleton. "I just can't find him," he said.

"He must be somewhere around here."

"He isn't. I've looked high and low."

"Perhaps he went out into the canyon?"

"If he did, he'll stay there."

"Yes." She came close to Hugh. "There is a chance for us, isn't there?"

"Who knows? We can try. He looked down at her. "I'll look for him again."

"Do so," she said coldly.

Hugh walked outside. Clymer stood by the crumbling wall. "He isn't to be found," said Clymer. "Last I saw of him he was poking about on the slope at the west end."

Hugh eyed the big man. There was something wrong somewhere. "We'd best get ready," he said.

———

Katy Corse was binding a splint about Darrell Phillips's smashed leg. The man was in agony, she knew, but she would see to it that he went along.

Darrell Phillips placed a hand on Katy's soft dark hair, vaguely wondering what it would be like freshly washed and combed and with a ribbon in it. "A red ribbon," he said.

She looked down at him. "What was that?"

"Nothing." He raised his head. "Is there any hope, Katy?"

"We'll get you out."

"I mean, any hope for us together?"

She pressed him back on his blanket. "I'm sorry, Darrell."

He nodded his head. "I thought so."

She stood up. "I'll see how the others are," she said.

He waited until she left and then drew his Colt out from under the blanket. It was freshly loaded and capped. He cocked it and slid it under the blanket again . . .

It took time to get Darrell Phillips out of the room and onto the terrace. He stifled his groans, and mercifully fainted when Clymer bumped hard against his smashed thigh.

They placed him in the passageway below the water seep. Hugh wiped the sweat from his face. "We'll block the other passageways," he said, "so they can't break through."

Clymer nodded.

They piled debris in the triangular passageway to the east of the tower, piling it high and forming a rude abatis with shattered beams, six feet higher than a man's head.

Hugh checked everything. The two women stood in the passageway. Katy Corse held a carbine in her left hand. A gunbelt circled her slim waist. She tied the canteen straps together and placed the canteens inside the lowest room.

Marion Nettleton shook her head as Katy extended a pistol to her. "I've never learned to use one," she said.

"It's simple. Cock the hammer so . . . point the muzzle and pull the trigger."

"I'm afraid."

Katy shrugged. She slid the extra pistol under her gunbelt.

Hugh looked at the three of them. "We'll wait until just before dawn."

"Why ?" demanded Clymer.

"Two reasons. One, we'll have light to see. Second, we've got to give Nettleton every chance to get back."

"If he does."

Hugh looked at Marion Nettleton. She seemed

unconcerned.

Hugh had gathered together a pile of sotol stalks. "We can use these for light in there," he said.

They all eyed each other. There was one thought uppermost in their minds: was it a dead end?

———

THE HOURS DRAGGED PAST. There was no sign of life from the Mimbrenos. They could afford to wait another day and then move in without trouble.

Hugh paced the terrace with his carbine in the crook of his arm. Now and again he looked up at the darkened roof of the huge cave, wondering about that mysterious walled fault. There was no sign of Maurice Nettleton . . .

The sky was lighter now. Hugh looked down into the canyon once more. He could see Matt Hastings' body lying there. "So long, amigo," he said quietly . . .

Hugh stopped beside Phillips. "We're about ready," he said. "I'll carry you into the lower room so that you won't get hit by debris . . . if there is any."

Phillips moved quickly, drawing his revolver out from under his shirt. "I'll stay here," he said.

"You're loco!"

Phillips shook his head. "No, I can't burden you. Get on with your work. Good luck."

Hugh moved a little.

Phillips raised the Colt. "No. Don't try. You've got Katy to think of."

Hugh stepped back. He passed the wounded man. *"Muy hombre,"* he said.

Darrell Phillips smiled for the first time in many days.

———

CLYMER EASED his big shoulders through the opening into the second floor. He waited for Hugh. They placed their hands on the beam and tested it. "Ready?" asked Hugh.

Clymer nodded.

They swung together. The beam end thudded against the rocks and bounced heavily back. They swung again and again. "No good!" said Clymer.

"Keep trying, you big bastard!"

Sweat streamed from their bodies. The beam began a steady thud-thud-thud against the stubborn wall. The Hohokam had built well . . .

High on the northern wall of the canyon the Mimbrenos threw back their blankets as they heard the thudding noise coming from the Place Of The Dead. They stood up and got their weapons . . .

A rock cracked and then fell from the wall. Another shifted and then fell. The end of the beam was fraying and splintering. Again and again the tattoo went on. Sweat streamed from the bodies of the two big men and a foul miasma rose from their stinking clothing to mingle with the bitter smell of dust . . .

Silently the Mimbrenos came down the canyon wall, testing the dawn air with all their senses. They stopped on the canyon floor and faded into the unburned brush . . .

The beam smashed through. Clymer went off balance and hit the wall. Hugh hung onto the beam and grinned. "Made it," he said.

They smashed with renewed fury. Rocks and ancient mortar crumbled beneath the savage onslaught.

————

Darrell Phillips wet his lips and then began to crawl toward the terrace wall, inching his way along until he could pull himself up on his good leg. There was a movement on the slope just below him. A bushy head rose from the brush. The Colt roared. The big slug smashed the buck back down the slope.

Phillips set his jaw. The agony in his leg made him feel faint. He braced his elbow on the wall and fired at a darting Mimbreno. The warrior fell and rolled down the slope.

"*Zastee! Zastee! Zastee!* Kill! Kill! Kill!" chanted the aroused warriors.

Rifles flashed in the light of dawn. Bullets pattered against the dwelling walls and sang eerily off into space. Phillips fired twice more, adding another notch to his tally. Then he stood there and laughed.

The Mimbrenos had scuttled for cover, shrieking in dismay . . .

There was now a hole in the wall big enough for a man to get through. Clymer and Hugh worked swiftly, cursing in their mad haste. They shoved beams across into the hole. Marion was helped up the ladder by Katy.

They could hear the smash of rifle and pistol fire near the terrace. Clymer leaned out of the west window and snapped out a few shots from his Colt.

Hugh tightened his belt, thrust some sotol stalks into his shirt, then teetered across to the hole, carrying his carbine. He turned and looked back. Katy was standing there, helping Marion up onto the shaky makeshift bridge.

Hugh looked down into the hole. It was pitch black down there. He hastily lit a sotol stalk and waved it to make sure it would burn. He looked down again. The floor of the fault sloped steeply upward and was littered with something brownish. But he felt a blessed draft of cold air on his heated face. There was a way through!

He dropped the stalk. It was about ten feet down to the floor. Katy passed canteens and weapons across to Hugh. Hugh reached across for Marion. Her face was set as she came across. "Put your legs through and drop," said Hugh.

She shook her head.

"Go on, Hugh!" called Katy.

Rifle fire broke out again. Clymer fired steadily. Hugh hung for a moment and then dropped, hitting hard on something which crackled below his feet, loosing a curious musty smell. He looked up, vaguely seeing Marion. "Drop!" he yelled. "Damn it, woman! Drop!"

Then she landed heavily beside him and clung to him. Above them they could hear the muffled roaring of guns.

Katy landed beyond them. Then the big body of Clymer came through the hole. They clambered up the steep slope toward the fresher air, floundering through material which cracked and snapped beneath them. Hugh fell heavily. His free hand touched something smooth and round.

Clymer cursed. "Move on!" he yelled.

Darrell Phillips jerked as a slug smashed into his right shoulder. He shifted his Colt to his left hand and steadied the heavy weapon. Somehow he felt calm and cool. A bushy head appeared beyond the wall. Phillips fired, driving the buck from sight.

He raised his head. "Come on, you bastards," he said.

A knife flew through the air and struck him in the left side of the neck. He fired his last shot. Then a bullet struck him full in the forehead and he went down for eternity.

The firing had died away. Hugh struggled to his feet, still clutching the rounded object in his free hand.

"Light!" roared Clymer. He lit a match and held it out. They looked about them. Marion Nettleton looked at the rounded thing in Hugh's hand. Then she looked down at her legs, buried up to the knees in loose material. Then she screamed again and again as the match flared out in the draft.

Hugh dropped the brown skull he held in his hands. He moved, feeling the dry bones crackle beneath his feet. Katy Corse drew in a sharp breath.

Marion Nettleton screamed again and then became silent.

"Jesus!" said Clymer. "It's their catacombs!"

Hugh gripped Katy by the arm and pulled her up the slope. They could hear the others floundering around below them.

"You think they'll come through the hole?" called Clymer.

Hugh grunted. "Into here? You wouldn't get them within half a mile of this place if they knew it was here."

He cracked his head against a rock wall. He felt for a sotol stalk and lit it. The passageway was narrow, hardly wide enough for them to get through. He worked his way upward until he felt the coolness of the dawn wind pouring about him. Then suddenly his head emerged even with the mesa floor. "Wait!" he cautioned Katy.

He crawled out on the ground and lay still, listening and peering about. The brush swayed in the wind. There was no sign of life. He pulled Katy up beside him. She shivered in the coolness. "Thank God!" she said.

Clymer pushed Marion up ahead of him. Her face was pale and drawn. She dropped on the ground and lay still.

Hugh picked up his carbine. "I'll scout," he said.

He padded through the rustling brush. There wasn't a warrior in sight. He worked his way to the edge of the mesa and cautiously peered down into the canyon. There were no warriors down there either.

He returned to the others. "Keep your eyes peeled," he said to Clymer.

"Where are you going?"

"Down below."

"You loco?"

"You'll see."

Hugh slid down the slope, wrinkling his nose at the musty odor. He looked up at the hole. He could hear slurring voices faintly through the hole. He grinned as he thought of those superstitious bucks dropping down into the charnel house. He gathered up half a dozen skulls and threaded a picket line through the eye holes. Then he hauled them up to the mesa top.

"You damned fool!" said Clymer. He clamped a dirty hand over Marion's mouth to stifle the scream that trembled on her lips.

Hugh cut mesquite branches and bundled them together. He thrust one into a cranny and placed a skull atop it, facing the hole. "Just in case," he said. "Let's go!"

They walked toward the west, keeping to the lower ground. Hugh planted another skull at a place where they could make their way down the western slopes.

CHAPTER TWENTY

The sun was high when they rested in a cleft which cracked through a great pillar of rock. There had been no sign of pursuit. Hugh let them rest for an hour, then drove them on. They descended the side of the huge brooding mesa and stopped again in the middle of the afternoon.

It was dusk when they reached a small stream. They filled canteens and then went on until the faint moon tinged the eastern sky.

Hugh looked back at the mesa. "Starvation Mesa," he said.

THEY REACHED the San Francisco in four days of hellish travel. In all that time Marion Nettleton spoke hardly a word. Katy took care of her as though she were a child, binding cloth about her small feet, and feeding her with the meat of a deer Hugh had killed. Abel Clymer didn't speak much either.

They rested at the river for two days, then trended north along its course, keeping away from the faint trails they saw. It was murderous going, but Hugh drove them like cattle.

They found a good spring after three more days of travel. Here they made camp and rested. Hugh killed another deer and fashioned rude moccasins for the women. It was as though they had wandered off the earth and were traveling on some unknown, uninhabited planet.

―――――

HUGH COULD FEEL the pebbles through the thin soles of his boots as he waded across the stream. He had caught a reflection of himself in a clear pool and hadn't recognized himself. His beard was matted and filthy and his clothing wasn't fit for a self-respecting scarecrow. He dropped on the far bank of the stream and drank the cold water. Then he left the stream and headed steadily through the rough mountains, heading for the Rio Grande. The others were three days' travel behind him, holed up in a cave near a good spring.

Suddenly he passed a huge outcropping of rock and looked out on a distant plain, mottled with the drifting shadows of clouds. There was a thread of dust rising not more than a mile away from him. The sun sparkled on something. He took out his field glasses with shaking hands and looked at the dust. "Troopers!" he said. "By God, Troopers!"

―――――

HE LED the two horses and mules up the rocky trail. "Hello the cave!" he called.

Abel Clymer appeared carrying his carbine. "Kinzie!"

Katy Corse came out of the cave and brushed back her hair with a tired hand. She smiled when she saw Hugh.

Hugh tethered the mounts and took a pack from one of them. "It isn't much as to quality," he said, "but there's plenty of it. I met a patrol from Fort Craig. They were looking for Apache raiders."

"Why didn't they come for us?" demanded Clymer.

Hugh looked at the big man. "I was lucky enough to get

horses and mules from them. As it was, some of them had to ride double."

"How far are we from the Rio?"

"About sixty-five miles."

Clymer was busy opening the pack. "We'll leave tomorrow."

"Yes."

Clymer ripped open the pack and reached for a chunk of jerky. Hugh clamped a hand on the officer's wrist. "Remember the ladies," he said quietly.

Hugh carried the pack into the cave. Marion Nettleton was lying down. She sat up at Katy's urging and obediently ate what was handed to her.

They ate silently, looking at each other. "I never thought we'd make it," said Katy.

"We're not out of here yet," said Hugh.

Marion Nettleton carefully brushed hardtack crumbs from her filthy dress. "I'd like some cherries for dessert," she said.

Clymer stopped his sandwich halfway to his mouth. "What the hell!"

Marion smiled. "With fresh cream over them."

Katy stared at her.

Marion looked at Hugh. "I always have cherries when they're in season," she said. There was a peculiar look on her face. She touched her hair and then leaned back against the side of the cave. "After dinner I'll have them bring my pony cart around and we'll all go for a ride. I have two matched Shetland ponies."

"Jesus," said Clymer. "She's gone looney!"

Katy looked at the two men. "Get out of here!"

They walked outside. Hugh reached inside his shirt and brought out a packet. He undid it and handed Clymer three cigars. He kept two for himself. "Lieutenant Espinosa sent these with his compliments."

Clymer bit off the end of one of the dry cigars and lit up. He eyed Hugh through the smoke. "You tell him what happened?"

"All I said was that we'd been attacked by Apaches and there were only four of us left. I didn't feel like going into details."

"Good."

Hugh looked quickly at the big man.

Clymer waved his cigar. "I mean, being as I'm in command now, I'll have to make out a report to the department commander, and I'll be blasted if I want to go through all the details."

"Yes." Hugh lit a cigar. "Funny damned thing about Nettleton vanishing at the last minute. You don't suppose he broke free by himself?"

"Hell no!" Clymer scratched himself. "You say we're about sixty-five miles from the Rio, eh?"

"Roughly."

"Hard trail?"

"Not too bad."

"How does it go?"

Hugh sucked at his cigar. "Past that big peak just to the north and east. Follow the San Augustin Plains north for a time, then head east again between the Gallinas Mountains and the San Mateos."

"That's all?"

"That's all."

"Seems damned easy."

"It is."

Clymer stood up. "Well, I'll clean up a little."

"There's soap in the pack."

Clymer nodded and walked away.

"I wonder if that sonofabitch ever thanks anybody for anything," said Hugh to an inquisitive jaybird.

The jay twitched his head and flew off. Hugh laughed.

Katy Corse came out of the cave. She looked down at Hugh. "Thanks," she said.

"It's all right, Katy. It's my job."

"We owe you our lives."

"Forget it."

She sat down beside him. "She's going back to her childhood, Hugh. She just told me she had more party dresses than any girl in town, and that she'd rule the White House better than Dolly Madison when her father became president."

Hugh shook his head. "She'll be all right after a rest."

"I suppose the loss of Maurice did it."

He eyed her. "Marion? Don't be silly. She never thought of anyone but herself."

"She seemed to like you, Hugh."

He grinned. *"Everybody* likes me, Katy!"

She stood up and eyed the ruins of her dress. "I wish you could have brought us some clothes," she said.

"I'll go right back!" Hugh stood up. "I'm sure those cavalrymen will have at least four or five ladies' dresses in their saddlebags."

"You're a fool, Hugh Kinzie."

Suddenly he drew her close and kissed her hard. "I know," he said. "You'll forgive me, Katy? I did a lot of thinking when I was alone on the trail."

She returned his kiss. "There's nothing to forgive, Hugh."

They walked toward the cave. "Watch Clymer," she said quietly. "He's been acting peculiar."

"He always did."

"He's been asking me if I was sure she'll live long enough to reach the Rio Grande."

"Very solicitous."

"He worries me."

Hugh shrugged. "You'll soon be rid of him," he said.

———

HUGH LAY on his blanket listening to the voices of Marion and Katy coming from the cave. Katy sounded like a mother talking to a ten-year-old girl. The wind soughed through the trees. Clymer had rolled up in his blanket long ago and was asleep twenty feet from Hugh. Hugh lay there for a long time listening to the night sounds. Something was missing.

Then he realized what it was. Clymer was a heavy breather and his deep breathing while he slept had always annoyed Hugh.

Hugh got up on an elbow and looked through the shadowy dimness toward Clymer. Not a sound came from the big man.

One of the mules brayed suddenly from down in the hollow. Hugh stood up and picked up his Colt. He padded toward the hollow. Suddenly he stopped and looked toward Clymer. Best to wake him up if Apaches were prowling about.

Hugh stopped beside the big man and bent down to place a hand on his forehead in order to wake him up without startling him. He stared down at the sleeping man and then stood up. Quickly he stepped behind a tree. He eyed the darkness, listening for every sound. The soughing of the wind; the rustling of small rodents; the splashing of the creek.

Hugh circled around through the trees to his own blanket. Swiftly he gathered dry grass and placed it in a heap. He threw the blanket over it and patted it here and there to make it look as though a body were beneath it. Then he placed his hat at the head end. He pulled off his boots and placed them beside the dummy. Then he eased into the brush and squatted there, ten feet from his bed.

Abel Clymer walked softly for a man his size. He had heard that damned mule bray but he had heard nothing from the camp. He eased through the scrub trees until he could see Kinzie's body beneath a bush.

Clymer drew his knife and tested the edge on a broad thumb. He wet his thick lips and felt inside his shirt for the government drafts. The game was all but won. First get Kinzie and then Katy Corse. Marion Nettleton was out of her mind. The whole thing fit together neatly.

He'd be the biggest damned hero in the Southwest. All he had to do was say Kinzie and the girl had been ambushed on the last leg of the journey to the Rio Grande. Kinzie had done his job. Katy was not to be reached by money or threats. Marion was mind-gone-far, as Kinzie had said of Isaiah Morton. No one would listen to her ramblings, and even if she did regain her sanity, Clymer could always say she had imagined many of the things which had actually transpired.

Hugh heard Clymer before he saw him. He squatted lower to get the big man against the sky. Clymer stopped behind a tree. Then Hugh saw the upraised arm and the knife. "Clymer," he said harshly.

Clymer moved with instantaneous reaction. He whirled and lunged toward the sound of Hugh's voice. Hugh foolishly rose to meet the attack. He was driven aside as though by a charging grizzly. His Colt flew from his hand.

Clymer whirled and struck savagely at Hugh with the knife. The tip raked across Hugh's chest. Hugh grunted in pain. Clymer laughed. Hugh jumped behind a tree, feeling for the knife in the sheath at his back. It was gone. Bark flew from the tree as Clymer slashed viciously at Hugh.

Hugh jumped back. Clymer charged again. This time Hugh gripped Clymer's knife wrist with his right hand. He stepped aside, thrusting his right leg in front of Clymer. Clymer fell heavily over the leg.

Hugh felt about for a rock or a branch. Then he was forced to retreat as Clymer rolled to his feet, roared like a bear, and came on again. Hugh's foot slipped and he went down before the mad rush. His wind was nearly knocked out of him. Clymer slashed at Hugh's face. The blade sank into the dirt inches from his head.

Hugh kneed the big man in the groin. They rolled over and over down the slope. Clymer's head hit a tree. He shook it. Then he got up to meet a straight left which drove him back. Hugh followed through with a right hook. Clymer was staggered, but there was a tremendous vitality in his body.

Hugh stepped back. His foot hit something. It was his Colt. Clymer hurdled a log and came at Hugh, weaving a pattern of cuts and slashes at the air. He mumbled to himself.

Hugh fired from the hip. Clymer staggered as the slug

hit home. He shook his big head and came on again. Hugh fired two more times. The shots awoke the echoes. Birds scattered from the trees.

Clymer swayed in a cloud of powder smoke. He stared at Hugh with bulging eyes. "Damn it!" he said. "I'm not supposed to die like this. Not General Clymer!"

Hugh stared at the big man. Then Abel Clymer pitched forward on his face and lay still with the powder smoke rifting where he had fallen.

Hugh thrust his Colt under his belt. He walked to Clymer and rolled him over. The cold green eyes were already clouding.

Katy ran to Hugh. "What happened?"

"He tried to kill me."

Hugh felt for the big man's oxlike heart. Something crackled beneath the filthy shirt. Hugh unbuttoned it and felt inside. His fingers moved in an unpleasant stickiness. He drew out a thick fold of papers.

Hugh stood up. He lit a match and handed it to Katy. He looked at the papers. "Government drafts," he said. He wiped the blood from his fingers. "I've done my job," he said quietly.

"He would have been quite the hero to come into Santa Fe with two women, one of them Boss Bennett's daughter, and with twenty thousands dollars' worth of government drafts in his hands."

"*Two* women? You didn't think he'd take you there to talk, did you, Katy?"

She shivered. "Come stay with me in the cave, Hugh."

"With *her* there?" He shook his head. "You stay with me instead, Katy."

She looked up at him. "All right, Hugh."

Hugh helped her up the slope. They did not look back . .

———

THEY DREW rein on a rise and looked to the east. There was a darker green line against the light green and gray of the brush flats. Hugh turned to Katy. "The Rio Bravo," he said. "The Rio Grande!"

She leaned over and rested a hand on his.

"I have more party dresses than any other little girl in town," a calm voice said behind them.

"Yes, Marion," said Katy.

"You must call me Miss Bennett."

"Miss Bennett."

"That's better."

Hugh turned north rather than south. "There are garrisons all the way up the Rio," he said. "We can travel in style to Santa Fe."

"It's all over, isn't it, Hugh?"

He shrugged. "I've cleared my brother and brought back Marion Bennett."

"*Miss* Bennett," insisted the calm voice behind them.

"Miss Bennett," said Hugh.

"You'll get your commission now," said Katy.

"Probably."

"I'll wait for you, Hugh."

He smiled. "I know you will. But it will be a long wait."

She glanced at him. "As sweetheart or wife, Hugh?"

"Both," he said.

Hugh looked back at the distant mountains, hazy purple and mysterious. They had taken heavy toll from the thirteen souls who had dared to enter them.

Hugh looked at the calm, peaceful face of Marion Nettleton. She had paid the greatest price, and yet the most merciful one. He looked at capable Katy Corse and knew he had a fit mate for himself. He had a woman to love and a war to fight. That was enough for any man.

TAKE A LOOK AT FORT VENGEANCE AND SHADOW VALLEY

Two Full Length Western Novels

THE ODDS ARE AGAINST SURVIVAL IN THIS CLASSIC WESTERN DOUBLE.

Major dan Fayes was sent on a mission to Fort Costain in Arizona to end the apache reign of terror. It was then that the Apaches struck swiftly, armed with new henry rifles.

The Texas Ranger is beset by many unexpected and dangerous obstacles to overcome before reaching the final showdown...

Fort Vengeance and Shadow Valley: Two Full Length Western Novels includes *Fort Vengeance and Shadow Valley*.

AVAILABLE NOW

ABOUT THE AUTHOR

Gordon D. Shirreffs published more than 80 western novels, 20 of them juvenile books, and John Wayne bought his book title, Rio Bravo, during the 1950s for a motion picture, which Shirreffs said constituted *"the most money I ever earned for two words."* Four of his novels were adapted to motion pictures, and he wrote a Playhouse 90 and the Boots and Saddles TV series pilot in 1957.

A former pulp magazine writer, he survived the transition to western novels without undue trauma, earning the admiration of his peers along the way. The novelist saw life a bit cynically from the edge of his funny bone and described himself as looking like a slightly parboiled owl. Despite his multifarious quips, he was dead serious about the writing profession.

Gordon D. Shirreffs was the 1995 recipient of the Owen Wister Award, given by the Western Writers of America for "a living individual who has made an outstanding contribution to the American West."

He passed in 1996.

www.ingramcontent.com/pod-product-compliance
Lightning Source LLC
Chambersburg PA
CBHW010824250626
47169CB00010B/2941